TUCK

"What is it to me?" repeated Bran, his tone half-mocking. "In truth, it is *everything* to me. I came h   ask your king to raise his war band and return with me to help le   m in the fight. Unless, of course, *you* would care to take the thro   in his absence . . . ?" He regarded Hywel pointedly and then turned   ze to the others around the board. No one volunteered to usurp   authority, prisoner though he was.

"I thought not," co   an. "It is true that I came here to ask your king to aid m   g the Ffreinc from our homeland and freeing Elfael from   tyranny of their rule. But now that I know that my best hope   otting in a Ffreinc prison—for all he is my kinsman, too—I wi   until I have freed him."

Bran's kinsmen stare   m in silence that was finally broken by Trahaern's sudden bark of laughter.

"You dream big," th dark Welshman laughed, slapping the table with the flat of his han "I like you."

The tension eased   ce, and Tuck realized he had been holding his breath—nor was he the only one. The two younger Cymry, silent but watchful, sighed with relief and relaxed in their elders' pleasure.

"It will take more than a priest's robe to fetch Gruffydd from Wolf Hugh's prison," Meurig observed. "God knows, if that was all it took he'd be a free man long since."

The others nodded knowingly, and looked to Bran for his response.

"You have no idea," replied Bran, that slow, dangerous smile sliding across his scarred lips, "how much more there is to me than that."

BY STEPHEN R. LAWHEAD

King Raven Trilogy
Hood
Scarlet
Tuck

STEPHEN R.
LAWHEAD

TUCK

King Raven: Book Three

www.atombooks.co.uk

ATOM

First published in the United States in 2009 by Thomas Nelson, Inc.
First published in Great Britain in 2009 by Atom
This paperback edition published in 2010 by Atom

A CIP catalogue record for this book
is available from the British Library.

ISBN 978-1-904233-75-6

Printed and bound in Great Britain by
Clays Ltd, St Ives plc

Papers used by Atom are natural, renewable and
recyclable products sourced from well-managed forests and certified
in accordance with the rules of the Forest Stewardship Council.

Mixed Sources
Product group from well-managed
forests and other controlled sources
www.fsc.org Cert no. SGS-COC-004081
© 1996 Forest Stewardship Council
FSC

Atom
An imprint of
Little, Brown Book Group
100 Victoria Embankment
London EC4Y 0DY

An Hachette UK Company
www.hachette.co.uk

www.atombooks.co.uk

Dedicated to
The Outlaw Tony Wales

PRONUNCIATION GUIDE

Many of the old Celtic words and names are strange to modern eyes, but they are not as difficult to pronounce as they might seem at first glance. A little effort—and the following rough guide—will help you enjoy the sound of these ancient words.

Consonants – As in English, but with the following exceptions:

c: hard – as in *c*at (never soft, as in *cent*)

ch: hard – as in Ba*ch* (never soft, as in *church*)

dd: a hard *th* sound, as in *th*en

f: a hard *v* sound, as in o*f*

ff: a soft *f* sound, as in o*ff*

g: hard – as in *g*irl (never soft, as in *George*)

ll: a Gaelic distinctive, sounded as *tl* or *hl* on the sides of the tongue

r: rolled or slightly trilled, especially at the beginning of a word

rh: breathed out as if *h-r* and heavy on the *h* sound

s: soft – as in *s*in (never hard, as in *his*); when followed by a vowel it takes on the *sh* sound

th: soft – as in *th*istle (never hard, as in *then*)

Vowels – As in English, but generally with the lightness of short vowel sounds:

a: short, as in c*a*n
á: slightly softer than above, as in *a*we
e: usually short, as in m*e*t
é: long *a* sound, as in h*ey*
i: usually short, as in p*i*n
í: long *e* sound, as in s*ee*
o: usually short, as in h*o*t
ó: long *o* sound, as in w*o*e
ô: long *o* sound, as in g*o*
u: usually sounded as a short *i*, as in p*i*n
ú: long *u* sound, as in s*ue*
ù: short *u* sound, as in m*u*ck
w: sounded as a long *u*, as in h*ue*; before vowels often becomes a soft consonant as in the name G*w*en
y: usually short, as in p*i*n; sometimes *u* as in p*u*n; when long, sounded *e* as in s*ee*; rarely, *y* as in wh*y*

The careful reader will have noted that there is very little difference between *i*, *u*, and *y*—they are almost identical to non-Celts and modern readers.

Most Celtic words are stressed on the next to the last syllable. For example, the personal name Gofannon is stressed go-FAN-non, and the place name Penderwydd is pronounced pen-DER-width, and so on.

TUCK

PROLOGUE

Wintan Cestre
Saint Swithun's Day

King William stood scratching the back of his hand and watched as another bag of gold was emptied into the ironclad chest: one hundred solid gold byzants that, added to fifty pounds in silver and another fifty in letters of promise to be paid upon collection of his tribute from Normandie, brought the total to five hundred marks. "More money than God," muttered William under his breath. "What do they do with it all?"

"Sire?" asked one of the clerks of the justiciar's office, glancing up from the wax tablet on which he kept a running tally.

"Nothing," grumbled the king. Parting with money always made him itch, and this time there was no relief. In vain, he scratched the other hand. "Are we finished here?"

Having counted the money, the clerks began locking and sealing the strongbox. The king shook his head at the sight of all that gold and silver disappearing from sight. *These blasted monks will bleed me dry,* he thought. A kingdom was a voracious beast that devoured money and was never, ever satisfied. It took money for soldiers, money for horses and weapons, money for fortresses, money for supplies to feed the troops, and as now, even more money to wipe away the sins of war. The gold and silver in the chest was for the abbey at Wintan Cestre to pay the monks so that his father would not have to spend eternity in purgatory or, worse, frying in hell.

"All is in order, Majesty," said the clerk. "Shall we proceed?"

William gave a curt nod.

Two knights of the king's bodyguard stepped forward, took up the box, and carried it from the room and out into the yard where the monks of Saint Swithun's were already gathered and waiting for the ceremony to begin. The king, a most reluctant participant, followed.

In the yard of the Red Palace—the name given to the king's sprawling lodge outside the city walls—a silken canopy on silver poles had been erected. Beneath the canopy stood Bishop Walkelin with his hands pressed together in an attitude of patient prayer. Behind the bishop stood a monk bearing the gilded cross of their namesake saint, while all around them knelt monks and acolytes chanting psalms and hymns. The king and his attendants—his two favourite earls, a canon, and a bevy of assorted clerks, scribes, courtiers, and officials both sacred and secular—marched out to meet the bishop. The company paused while the king's chair was brought and set up beneath the canopy where Bishop Walkelin knelt.

"In the Holy Name," intoned the bishop when William Rufus had taken his place in the chair, "all blessing and honour be upon you and upon your house and upon your descendants and upon the people of your realm."

"Yes, yes, of course," said William irritably. "Get on with it."

"God save you, Sire," replied Walkelin. "On this Holy Day we have come to receive the *Beneficium Ecclesiasticus Sanctus Swithinius* as is our right under the Grant of Privilege created and bestowed by your father King William, for the establishment and maintenance of an office of penitence, perpetual prayer, and the pardon of sins."

"So you say," remarked the king.

Bishop Walkelin bowed again, and summoned two of his monks to receive the heavy strongbox from the king's men in what had become an annual event of increasing ceremony in honour of Saint Swithun, on whose day the monks determined to suck the lifeblood from the crown, and William Rufus resented it. But what could he do? The payment was for the prayers of the monks for the remission of sins on the part of William Conqueror, prayers which brought about the much-needed cleansing of his besmirched soul. For each and every man that William had killed in battle, the king could expect to spend a specified amount of time in purgatory: eleven years for a lord or knight, seven years for a man-at-arms, five for a commoner, and one for a serf. By means of some obscure and complicated formula William had never understood, the monks determined a monetary amount which somehow accorded to the number of days a monk spent on his knees praying. As William had been a very great war leader, his purgatorial obligation amounted to well over a thousand years—and that was only counting the fatalities of the landed nobility. No one knew the number of commoners and serfs he had killed, either directly or indirectly, in his lifetime—but the number was thought to be quite high. Still, a wealthy king with dutiful heirs need not actually spend so much time in purgatory—so long as there were monks willing to ease the burden of his debt through prayer. All it took was money.

Thus, the Benefice of Saint Swithun, necessary though it might be, was a burden the Conqueror's son had grown to loathe with a passion. That he himself would have need of this selfsame service was a fact that he could neither deny nor escape. And while he told himself that paying monks to pray souls from hell was a luxury he could ill afford, deep in his heart of hearts he knew only too well that—owing to the debauched life he led—it was also a necessity he could ill afford to neglect much longer.

Even so, paying over good silver for the ongoing service of a passel of mumbling clerics rubbed Rufus raw—especially as that silver became each year more difficult to find. His taxes already crushed the poor and had caused at least two riots and a rebellion by his noblemen. Little wonder, then, that the forever needy king dreaded the annual approach of Saint Swithun's day and the parting with so much of his precious treasury.

The ceremony rumbled on to its conclusion and, following an especially long-winded prayer, adjourned to a feast in honour of the worthy saint. The feast was the sole redeeming feature of the entire day. That it must be spent in the company of churchmen dampened William's enthusiasm somewhat, but did not destroy it altogether. The Red King had surrounded himself with enough of his willing courtiers and sycophants to ensure a rousing good time no matter how many disapproving monks he fed at his table.

This year, the revel reached such a height of dissipation that Bishop Walkelin quailed and excused himself, claiming that he had pressing business that required his attention back at the cathedral. William, forcing himself to be gracious, wished the churchmen well and offered to send a company of soldiers to accompany the monks back to the abbey with their money lest they fall among thieves.

Walkelin agreed to the proposal and, as he bestowed his blessing, leaned close to the king and said, "We must talk one day soon about establishing a benefice of your own, Your Majesty." He paused and then, like the flick of a knife, warned, "Death comes for us all, and none of us knows the day or time. I would be remiss if I did not offer to draw up a grant for you."

"We will discuss that," said William, "when the price is seen to fall rather than forever rise."

"You will have heard it said," replied Walkelin, "that where great sin abounds, great mercy must intercede. The continual observance and maintenance of that intercession is very expensive, my lord king."

"So is the keeping of a bishop," answered William tartly. "And bishops have been known to lose their bishoprics." He paused, regarding the cleric over the rim of his cup. "Heaven forbid that should happen. I know I would be heartily sorry to see you go, Walkelin."

"If my lord is displeased with his servant," began the bishop, "he has only to—"

"Something to consider, eh?"

Bishop Walkelin tried to adopt a philosophical air. "I am reminded that your father always—"

"No need to speak of it any more just now," said William smoothly. "Only think about what I have said."

"You may be sure," answered Walkelin. He bowed stiffly and took a slow step backwards. "Your servant, my lord."

The clerics departed, leaving the king and his courtiers to their revel. But the feast was ruined for William. Try as he might, he could not work himself into a festive humour because the bishop's rat of a thought had begun to gnaw at the back of his mind: his time was running out. To die without arranging for the necessary prayers would doom his soul to the lake of everlasting fire. However loudly he might rail against the expense—and condemn the greedy clerics who held his future for ransom—was he really prepared to test the alternative at the forfeit of his soul?

PART ONE

Come listen a while, you gentlefolk alle,
    That stand this bower within,
A tale of noble Rhiban the Hud,
    I purpose now to begin.

Young Rhiban was a princeling fayre,
    And a gladsome heart had he.
Delight took he in games and tricks,
    And guiling his fair ladye.

A bonny fine maide of noble degree,
    Mérian calléd by name,
This beauty soote was praised of alle men
    For she was a gallant dame.

Rhiban stole through the greenwoode one night
    To kiss his dear Mérian late.
But she boxed his head till his nose turn'd red
    And order'd him home full straight.

Though Rhiban indeed speeded home fayrlie rathe,
    That night he did not see his bed.
For in flames of fire from the rooftops' eaves,
    He saw all his kinsmen lay dead.

Ay, the sheriff's low men had visited there,
    When the household was slumbering deepe.
And from room to room they had quietly crept
    And murtheréd them all in their sleepe.

Rhiban cried out "wey-la-wey!"
    But those fiends still lingered close by.
So into the greenwoode he quickly slipt,
    For they had heard his cry.

Rhiban gave the hunters goode sport,
    Full lange, a swift chase he led.
But a spearman threw his shot full well
    And he fell as one that is dead.

CHAPTER I

Tuck shook the dust of Caer Wintan off his feet and prepared for the long walk back to the forest. It was a fine, warm day, and all too soon the friar was sweltering in his heavy robe. He paused now and then to wipe the sweat from his face, falling farther and farther behind his travelling companions. "These legs of mine are sturdy stumps," he sighed to himself, "but fast they en't."

He had just stopped to catch his breath a little when, on sudden impulse, he spun around quickly and caught a glimpse of movement on the road behind—a blur in the shimmering distance, and then gone. So quick he might have imagined it. Only it was not the first time since leaving the Royal Lodge that Tuck had entertained the queer feeling that someone or something was following them. He had it again now, and decided to alert the others and let them make of it what they would.

Squinting into the distance, he saw Bran far ahead of the Grellon, striding steadily, shoulders hunched against the sun and the gross injustice so lately suffered at the hands of the king in whom he had trusted. The main body of travellers, unable to keep up with their lord, was becoming an ever-lengthening line as heat and distance mounted. They trudged along in small clumps of two or three, heads down, talking in low, sombre voices. *How like sheep*, thought Tuck, *following their impetuous and headstrong shepherd.*

A more melancholy man might himself have succumbed to the oppressive gloom hanging low over the Cymry, dragging at their feet, pressing their spirits low. Though summer still blazed in meadow, field, and flower, it seemed to Tuck that they all walked in winter's drear and dismal shadows. Rhi Bran and his Grellon had marched into Caer Wintan full of hope—they had come singing, had they not?—eager to stand before King William to receive the judgement and reward that had been promised in Rouen all those months ago. Now, here they were, slinking back to the greenwood in doleful silence, mourning the bright hope that had been crushed and lost.

No, not lost. They would never let it out of their grasp, not for an instant. It had been stolen—snatched away by the same hand that had offered it in the first place: the grasping, deceitful hand of a most perfidious king.

Tuck felt no less wounded than the next man, but when he considered how Bran and the others had risked their lives to bring Red William word of the conspiracy against him, it fair made his priestly blood boil. The king had promised justice. The Grellon had every right to expect that Elfael's lawful king would be restored. Instead, William had merely banished Baron de Braose and his milksop nephew Count Falkes, sending them back to France to live in luxury on the baron's extensive estates. Elfael, that small bone of contention, had instead become property of the crown and placed under the protection of Abbot Hugo and Sheriff de Glanville. Well, *that* was putting wolves in charge of the fold, was it not?

Where was the justice? A throne for a throne, Bran had declared that day in Rouen. William's had been saved—at considerable cost and risk to the Cymry—but where was Bran's throne?

S'truth, thought Tuck, *wait upon a Norman to do the right thing and you'll be waiting until your hair grows white and your teeth fall out.*

"How long, O Lord? How long must your servants suffer?" he muttered. "And, Lord, does it have to be so blasted hot?"

He paused to wipe the sweat from his face. Running a hand over his round Saxon head, he felt the sun's fiery heat on the bare spot of his tonsure; sweat ran in rivulets down the sides of his neck and dripped from his jowls. Drawing a deep breath, he tightened his belt, hitched up the skirts of his robe, and started off again with quickened steps. Soon his shoes were slapping up the dust around his ankles, and he began to overtake the rearmost members of the group: thirty souls in all, women and children included, for Bran had determined that his entire forest clan—save for those left behind to guard the settlement and a few others for whom the long journey on foot would have been far too arduous—should be seen by the king to share in the glad day.

The friar picked up his pace and soon drew even with Siarles: slim as a willow wand, but hard and knotty as an old hickory root. The forester walked with his eyes downcast, chin outthrust, his mouth a tight, grim line. Every line of him bristled with fury like a riled porcupine. Tuck knew to leave well enough alone and hurried on without speaking.

Next, he passed Will Scatlocke—or Scarlet, as he preferred. The craggy forester limped along slightly as he carried his newly acquired daughter, Nia. Against every expectation, Will had endured a spear wound, the abbot's prison, and the threat of the sheriff's rope . . . and survived. His pretty dark-eyed wife, Noín, walked resolutely beside him. The pair had made a good match, and it tore at his heart that the newly married couple should have to endure a dark hovel in the forest when the entire realm begged for just such a family to settle and sink solid roots deep into the land—another small outrage to be added to the ever-growing mountain of injustices weighing on Elfael.

A few more steps brought him up even with Odo, the Norman monk who had befriended Will Scarlet in prison. At Scarlet's bidding, the young scribe had abandoned Abbot Hugo to join them. Odo walked with his head down, his whole body drooping—whether with heat or the awful realization of what he had done, Tuck could not tell.

A few steps more and he came up even with Iwan—the great, hulking warrior would crawl on hands and knees through fire for his lord. It was from Iwan that the friar had received his current christening when the effort of wrapping his untrained tongue around the simple Saxon name Aethelfrith proved beyond him. "Fat little bag of vittles that he is, I will call him Tuck," the champion had said. "Friar Tuck to you, boyo," the priest had responded, and the name had stuck. *God bless you, Little John,* thought Tuck, *and keep your arm strong, and your heart stronger.*

Next to Iwan strode Mérian, just as fierce in her devotion to Bran as the champion beside her. Oh, but shrewd with it; she was smarter than the others and more cunning—which always came as something of a shock to anyone who did not know better, because one rarely expected it from a lady so fair of face and form. But the impression of innocence beguiled. In the time Tuck had come to know her, she had shown herself to be every inch as canny and capable as any monarch who ever claimed an English crown.

Mérian held lightly to the bridle strap of the horse that carried their wise hudolion, who was, so far as Tuck could tell, surely the last Banfáith of Britain: Angharad, ancient and ageless. There was no telling how old she was, yet despite her age, whatever it might be, she sat her saddle smartly and with the ease of a practiced rider. Her quick dark eyes were trained on the road ahead, but Tuck could tell that her sight was turned inward, her mind wrapped in a veil of deepest thought. Her wrinkled face might have been carved of dark Welsh slate for all it revealed of her contemplations.

Mérian glanced around as the priest passed, and called out, but the friar had Bran in his eye, and he hurried on until he was within hailing distance. "My lord, wait!" he shouted. "I must speak to you!"

Bran gave no sign that he had heard. He strode on, eyes fixed on the road and distance ahead.

"For the love of Jesu, Bran. Wait for me!"

Bran took two more steps and then halted abruptly. He straightened and turned, his face a smouldering scowl, dark eyes darker still under lowered brows. His shock of black hair seemed to rise in feathered spikes.

"Thank the Good Lord," gasped the friar, scrambling up the dry, rutted track. "I thought I'd never catch you. We . . . there is something . . ." He gulped down air, wiped his face, and shook the sweat from his hand into the dust of the road.

"Well?" demanded Bran impatiently.

"I think we must get off this road," Tuck said, dabbing at his face with the sleeve of his robe. "Truly, as I think on it now, I like not the look that Abbot Hugo gave me when we left the king's yard. I fear he may try something nasty."

Bran lifted his chin. The jagged scar on his cheek, livid now, twisted his lip into a sneer. "Within sight of the king's house?" he scoffed, his voice tight. "He wouldn't dare."

"Would he not?"

"Dare what?" said Iwan, striding up. Siarles came toiling along in the big man's wake.

"Our friar here," replied Bran, "thinks we should abandon the road. He thinks Abbot Hugo is bent on making trouble."

Iwan glanced back the way they had come. "Oh, aye," agreed Iwan, "that would be his way." To Tuck, he said, "Have you seen anything?"

"What's this then?" inquired Siarles as he joined the group. "Why have you stopped?"

"Tuck thinks the abbot is on our tail," Iwan explained.

"I maybe saw something back there, and not for the first time," Tuck explained. "I don't say it for a certainty, but I think someone is following us."

"It makes sense." Siarles looked to the frowning Bran. "What do you reckon?"

"I reckon I am surrounded by a covey of quail frightened of their own shadows," Bran replied. "We move on."

He turned to go, but Iwan spoke up. "My lord, look around you. There is little enough cover hereabouts. If we were to be taken by surprise, the slaughter would be over before we could put shaft to string."

Mérian joined them then, having heard a little of what had passed. "The little ones are growing weary," she pointed out. "They

14

cannot continue on this way much longer without rest and water. We will have to stop soon in any event. Why not do as Tuck suggests and leave the road now—just to be safe?"

"So be it," Bran said, relenting at last. He glanced around and then pointed to a grove of oak and beech rising atop the next hill up the road. "We will make for that wood. Iwan—you and Siarles pass the word along, then take up the rear guard." He turned to Tuck and said, "You and Mérian stay here and keep everyone moving. Tell them they can rest as soon as they reach the grove, but not before."

He turned on his heel and started off again. Iwan stood looking after his lord and friend. "It's the vile king's treachery," he observed. "That's put the black dog on his back, no mistake."

Siarles, as always, took a different tone. "That's as may be, but there's no need to bite off *our* heads. We en't the ones who cheated him out of his throne." He paused and spat. "Stupid bloody king."

"And stupid bloody cardinal, all high and mighty," continued Iwan. "Priest of the church, my arse. Give me a good sharp blade and I'd soon have him saying prayers he never said before." He cast a hasty glance at Tuck. "Sorry, Friar."

"I'd do the same," Tuck said. "Now, off you go. If I am right, we must get these people to safety, and that fast."

The two ran back down the line, urging everyone to make haste for the wood on the next hill. "Follow Bran!" they shouted. "Pick up your feet. We are in danger here. Hurry!"

"There is safety in the wood," Mérian assured them as they passed, and Tuck did likewise. "Follow Bran. He'll lead you to shelter."

It took a little time for the urgency of their cries to sink in, but soon the forest-dwellers were moving at a quicker pace up to the wood at the top of the next rise. The first to arrive found Bran waiting at the edge of the grove beneath a large oak tree, his strung bow across his shoulder.

"Keep moving," he told them. "You'll find a hollow just beyond that fallen tree." He pointed through the wood. "Hide yourselves and wait for the others there."

The first travellers had reached the shelter of the trees, and Tuck was urging another group to speed and showing them where to go when he heard someone shouting up from the valley. He could not make out the words, but as he gazed around the sound came again and he saw Iwan furiously gesturing towards the far hilltop. He looked where the big man was pointing and saw two mounted knights poised on the crest of the hill.

The soldiers were watching the fleeing procession and, for the moment, seemed content to observe. Then one of the knights wheeled his mount and disappeared back down the far side of the hill.

Bran had seen it too, and began shouting. "Run!" he cried, racing down the road. "To the grove!" he told Mérian and Tuck. "The Ffreinc are going to attack!"

He flew to meet Iwan and Siarles at the bottom of the hill.

"I'd best go see if I can help," Tuck said, and leaving Mérian to hurry the people along, he fell into step behind Bran.

"Just the two of them?" Bran asked as he came running to meet Siarles and Iwan.

"So far," replied the champion. "No doubt the one's gone to alert the rest. Siarles and I will take a stand here," he said, bending the long ashwood bow to string it. "That will give you and Tuck time to get the rest of the folk safely hidden in the woods."

Bran shook his head. "It may come to that one day, but not today." His tone allowed no dissent. "We have a little time yet. Get

everyone into the wood—carry them if you have to. We'll dig ourselves into the grove and make Gysburne and his hounds come in
after us."

"I make it six bows against thirty knights," Siarles pointed out.
"Good odds, that."

Bran gave a quick jerk of his chin. "Good as any," he agreed.
"Fetch along the stragglers and follow me."

Iwan and Siarles darted away and were soon rushing the last of
the lagging Grellon up the hill to the grove. "What do you want *me*
to do?" Tuck shouted.

"Pray," answered Bran, pulling an arrow from the sheaf at his belt
and fitting it to the string. "Pray God our aim is true and each arrow
finds its mark."

Bran moved off, calling for the straggling Grellon to find shelter
in the wood. Tuck watched him go. *Pray?* he thought. *Aye, to be sure—
the Good Lord will hear from me. But I will do more, will I not?* Then he scuttled up the hill and into the wood in search of a good stout stick to
break some heads.

CHAPTER 2

S wift and furtive as wild things, the women and children disappeared into the deep-shadowed grove. Bran called all the men
together at the edge of the wood. "We have six bows," he said.
"Iwan, Siarles, Tomas, Rhoddi . . ." He paused, eyeing the men gathered around him, assessing their abilities. His gaze lit on one of the
eager young men who had joined the Grellon following the loss of
his family's home to the Ffreinc. "You, Owain, will join me. I want a
guard with each bowman to watch his back and retrieve any arrows
that fall within easy reach. So now, archers and guards come with
me. The rest of you go with Tuck and help protect the others."

"We want to fight too," said one of the men, speaking up.

"If any of the Ffreinc get in behind us," Bran told him, "you'll
have your hands full right enough. Tuck will tell you what to do."

As Bran turned to lead his small group of archers to their places
at the edge of the grove, a hand reached out and halted him. "Lend
me a bow. I can draw."

Bran turned and shook his head. "I know, Will—when you're healed and practiced."

"Even crippled as I am I'd wager I can still draw better than anyone here—saving only yourself, my lord."

"No doubt," Bran allowed, placing a hand on the man's shoulder. "But let be today, Will." Bran's eyes slid past Will to Noín and Nia, and the young, round-shouldered, whey-faced Ffreinc monk hovering a few steps away. "Look after your family and your friend here—and take care of Angharad. See that none of them come to harm. That will be help enough."

Bran hurried away to join the archers, and Will turned to the worried young monk behind him. "Come along, Odo," he said. "Follow Noín and help her see to the old woman and her horse, and look sharp, unless you want Abbot Hugo to get his hands on you again."

They hurried to join the others in the hollow, and Tuck gathered the rest. "This way!" he called, and led his crew of seven unarmed warriors to a small glade midway between the archers and the hollow where the rest of the Grellon had found their hiding places. "We will stand here," he told them. Then, raising his stubby oak branch lengthwise, he held it high, saying, "Get one of these to hand quick as you can, and hurry back. We'll make ourselves scarce behind the trees there, and there"—he pointed out the nearby boles of massive oaks—"and over there. If any Ffreinc get past Bran and the others we'll do for 'em."

The last words were still hanging in the air when there came a cry from the edge of the wood where Bran and the bowmen were waiting. As the shout echoed through the grove, they heard the fizzing whir of an arrow as it sped from the string. Almost instantly, there followed a short, sharp scream and a crash. A heartbeat later, a riderless horse careered into the wood.

"Bless me," remarked Tuck. Turning to his company, he said, "Get some wood in your hands, lads, and make a good account of yourselves. Go!"

As the forest-dwellers scattered, two knights burst into the grove in full gallop. One of them had an arrow sticking out of his shield, and the other had a shaft buried deep in his thigh. Both turned their horses and prepared to attack the archers from behind. But even as the great steeds slowed and came around, the soldiers seemed to crumple upon themselves; their weapons fell from slack hands, and both plunged from the saddle with arrows jutting from their backs like feathered quills.

Tuck heard a call from beyond the grove, and suddenly the attack was finished. They waited a few moments, and when no other riders appeared, the Grellon darted out to retrieve the arrows, pulling them from the dead knights.

"Here," said Tuck, gathering the shafts, "I'll take those. The rest of you get back out of sight."

The friar quickly made his way to the edge of the grove, where the archers were hidden amongst the trees. He hurried to the first one he saw.

"Siarles," he called softly. "What's happened? Have we turned them away?"

"No, Brother," replied the forester. "They're down the valley." He pointed down the slope, where a body of knights was milling about on horseback. "They're just regrouping. They'll charge again when they get their courage banked up." He cast a glance behind him into the grove. "The two that broke through—what of them?"

"Dead, I think. Or as good as." He handed over the retrieved arrows.

"That makes three, then," said Siarles, sticking the shafts in the soft earth at his feet.

"God with you," Tuck said, "and with your bow." He made a hasty sign of the cross and hurried back to his place behind the tree to await the next attack. In a little while he heard the hard drumming of horses' hooves. The sound grew, and when it seemed the riders must be on top of them, he heard the thin, singing whine of arrows streaking to their marks—followed by the awful clatter of horses and heavily armoured men crashing to earth.

The second attack faltered and broke off as quickly as the first, and for a moment all was quiet in the grove again, save for the agonized whinny of a dying horse. Again, Tuck waited a little space, and when nothing else seemed about to happen, out he crept and ran to speak to Siarles.

"Is that the last of them?"

"Maybe." Siarles gestured with his bow toward the valley. "They've gone away again, but I can't see what they're up to this time."

"Pray they've had enough and decided to go home and lick their wounds." Tuck peered around the trunk of the tree to the near hillside, taking in the corpses of four more horses and men lying in the grass. But for the arrows sticking out of their bodies, they might have been napping in the sun. The guards of the archers were already at work pulling arrows from the bodies. "Looks like they've gone," the friar concluded.

"Just to be sure, you and yours best stay hid until Bran says it's safe to come out."

The friar returned to his crew of defenders to find that they had stripped the weapons from the fallen knights. One of the Grellon offered him a sword. "Thanks, but no," he replied. "You keep it. I'm at my best with a staff in my hand. I wouldn't know what to do with an awkward long blade like that. Now get back to your places and stay alert."

The third attack was long in coming, but when it came the Ffreinc struck as before, charging straight for the grove—and as before, the arrows sang and horses screamed. But this time three knights succeeded in getting past the archers. Arrows sprouting from shield and hauberk, they pounded into the grove swivelling this way and that, looking for something to slash with their swords.

The Ffreinc charge carried them past the tree where Tuck was hiding. Gripping his branch, he lunged out as the nearest horse passed, thrusting the sturdy length of oak in amongst its churning hooves. The resulting jolt nearly yanked his arm from his shoulder. The makeshift staff was torn from his grip and went spinning across the ground. But his aim succeeded, for the horse stumbled to its knees, pitching its rider over its broad neck as it went down.

The knight landed with a grunt on the soft earth, arms flailing, weapons scattering. Tuck ran for his staff and snatched it up. The unhorsed knight made to rise, but the stalwart priest gave him a sharp rap on the back of the skull which sent his pot-shaped metal hat rolling. A second tap put him to sleep.

Two of the Grellon were on the unconscious knight instantly. They rolled him over; one relieved the soldier of his sword and belt, and the other took his dagger and shield. They pulled his mail shirt up over his head and tied it there, then quick-footed it back to the shelter of the trees.

"God have mercy," breathed Tuck, and looked around to see what had become of the other two knights. One had quit his saddle owing to the wounds he had received and was lying on his side on the ground wheezing like a broken bellows; the other was in the grip of three Cymry who were taking turns bashing him with their clubs while he slashed wildly with his sword. The nimble Welshmen dodged the strokes and succeeded in hauling the knight from the saddle. While one of the Cymry seized the reins of the horse, the other two pounded the enemy into dazed submission. One of them wrested his sword from an unresisting hand and, with a swift downward stroke, dispatched the Ffreinc with it.

Three more knights appeared—charging in hard from the wood to the right. Their sudden appearance so surprised the Grellon that they were thrown into a momentary confusion. But as the foremost knight passed beneath the low-hanging branch of an oak one of the Grellon dropped onto the rear of the horse as it passed beneath him. Throwing his arms around the soldier's neck, the forest-dweller hurled himself from the horse, dragging his enemy with him. The horse careened on, and as the knight squirmed in the grasp of the Welshman, two more of the Grellon rushed to help subdue the armoured soldier.

Before the two remaining knights could rally to the aid of their fallen comrade, they too were under assault by screaming, sword-wielding Cymry. More horses were crashing through the wood— they had circled around and were attacking through the grove. Tuck, cursing the duplicity of the Norman race, ran to find Bran.

"Rhi Bran!" he shouted, making for the edge of the grove. "Rhi Bran!"

"Here, Tuck!" came the reply, and Bran appeared from behind a tree a few hundred paces away. "Over here!"

The priest scrambled to him fast as he could, his short legs stumbling over the uneven ground. "We're attacked!" he shouted, pointing with his staff. "They've come round to take us from behind."

"The devils!" shouted Bran, already running to head off the assault. "Iwan! Siarles! To me! The rest of you stay where you are and keep them busy. Make every arrow count!"

The three archers reached the glade to find five mounted knights in a deadly clash with four Grellon. The knights were stabbing with spears and slashing with swords, and the Cymry danced just out of reach, darting in quickly to deliver clout after clout with their makeshift staffs.

"Iwan—the two on the left," ordered Bran, nocking an arrow to the string. "Siarles—the one on the right. I'll take the two in the centre." He grasped the string in his two-fingered grip, pressing the belly of the longbow forward until it bent full and round. "Now!"

The word was hardly spoken when it was overtaken by a buzzing whine as Bran's arrow streaked across the shadow-dappled distance. Before it had reached its mark, two more arrows were sizzling through the air. There was a sound like cloth ripping in the wind, and the knight in the centre of the swarm was thrown back over the cantle of his saddle and off the rear of his mount. Two more knights followed the first to the ground, and as the two remaining Ffreinc soldiers swerved to meet this new threat, they were set upon by the Cymry, who pulled them down from their horses and slew them with their own weapons.

More knights were pounding into the glade now, charging in force. They came crashing through the underbrush in twos and threes. Tuck held his breath and tightened his grip on his staff. It seemed that Bran and the others must surely be overwhelmed. But the three bows sang as one, sending flight after flight of arrows streaking through the glade. Horses screamed and reared, throwing their riders, who were then set upon by the Grellon. Other soldiers, pierced by multiple shafts, simply dropped from the saddle, dead before they reached the ground.

Four knights just coming into the grove were met by three others fleeing the slaughter. The four newcomers glimpsed the carnage, then wheeled their mounts and joined their comrades in quick retreat.

"Get the weapons!" shouted Bran, already racing back to rejoin those at the front line. "Iwan, stay here and give a shout if any come back."

But the Ffreinc did not return to the attack.

One long moment passed, and then another. No more knights entered the glade from behind, and none dared challenge the archers on the front line again. The lowering sun deepened the shadows in the grove and began to fill up the valleys, and still the attack did not come. The Grellon watched and waited, and asked themselves if they had beaten the enemy back. Finally, when it appeared the assault had foundered, Tuck joined Iwan and the two ran to find Bran at the edge of the grove.

"What do you reckon, my lord?" asked Iwan. "Have we turned them aside?"

"So it would appear," Bran concluded.

"I dearly hope so," sighed Tuck. "All this rushing about is hard on an old fat man like me."

"But they may be waiting for us to show ourselves," Bran suggested.

"Or for nightfall," Iwan said, "so they can take us under cover of darkness."

"Either way," said Bran, making up his mind, "they will not find us here. Get everyone up and ready to move on."

The Grellon assembled once more and, like ghosts drifting away on the vapours of night, faded silently into the depths of the wood.

The men had stripped the weapons from the enemy soldiers—swords and lances mostly, but also daggers, helmets, belts, and shields. Arrows were retrieved, and three uninjured horses led away, leaving the heavy saddles and tack behind.

By the time the setting sun had turned the sky the colour of burnished bronze, the grove was abandoned to the dead, who lay still and quiet in the soft green grass.

"May God have mercy on their vile and wretched souls," Tuck whispered, hastening away, "and grant them the peace they have denied to others." Thinking better of this crabbed prayer, he added, "Welcome them into Your eternal kingdom—but not for my sake, Good Lord, no—but for the sake of Your own dear Son who always remembered to forgive His enemies. Amen."

CHAPTER 3

Hereford

Baron Bernard Neufmarché unexpectedly found himself in complete agreement with Lady Agnes, who was determined to make the wedding of her daughter Sybil splendid in every way possible. Much to his amazement and delight—for the baron had long ago resigned himself to a wife he considered little more than a frail ghost of a woman—the baroness was now a creature transformed. Gone were the headaches, vapours, and peculiar lingering maladies she had endured since coming to Britain. She was energetic and enthusiastic, tireless in her work at organizing the wedding. Major military campaigns received less attention, in his experience. What is more, the too-slender Agnes had gained weight; her previously skeletal figure had begun filling out to a more robust shape, and a wholesome glow of ruddy good health had replaced her customary sickly pallor.

This change in the woman he had known fully half his life was as surprising as it was welcome. He had never before seen anyone altered so utterly, and he revelled in it. Indeed, the renewal of his wife affected him far more deeply than he could have imagined. His own outlook had altered as well. Something like gratitude had come over him; he looked at the world around him with a warm and pleasant feeling of contentment. For the first time in a very long time he was happy.

For all this, and more, he had his Welsh minions to thank.

On reflection, the baron thought he knew almost to the precise moment when the change—no, the *transformation*—of Agnes began. It was in the churchyard of the little Welsh church where they had laid to rest the body of his vassal, King Cadwgan of Eiwas. Something had touched his wife at the funeral, and when the three days of observance drew to a close, the rebirth had begun.

Perhaps nowhere was the change more evident than in her view of the Welsh themselves. Where before Lady Agnes had considered them subhuman savages, a nation of brutish barbarians at best, now she viewed them more as unfortunates, as children who had survived an infancy of deprivation and neglect—which she was now intent on redressing.

Sybil's wedding was just the beginning; once she and Prince Garran—no, the young man was king now, it must be remembered—once the two young people were married, Lady Agnes planned nothing less than the rehabilitation of the entire realm and all its people. "They only want a town or two and markets," Agnes had informed him a few weeks ago, "some proper churches—good stone, mind—and a monastery, of course. Yes, and a better road. Then farms would flourish. I do believe it would be one of the finest cantrefs in the land."

"They are cattle herders, mostly," the baron had pointed out as he skimmed through a list of provisions he was amassing for the wedding.

"That, I suspect, is because they know little else," she concluded. "We shall show them how to husband the land."

"Teach them to farm?"

"*Bien sûr*," she replied lightly. "Why not? Then they will have things to trade in the markets. With the money that brings, they can begin making something of themselves."

In Agnes's view, the pitiful Welsh holdings were to be built up and made productive, the wasteland tilled and the wildwood managed—as in her father's prosperous estates in Normandie. With the considerable aid and support of the Neufmarché nobility, Eiwas would become a dazzling jewel, a bright and shining star leading all of Wales into a glorious new day of abundance and prosperity.

This was in the future, thank heaven—just thinking about the work involved made the baron tired. Nevertheless, he had to admit that he liked this new, industrious, spirited, far-thinking wife much better than the frail, sharp-tongued, sickly old one. And, truth be told, her plans for the cantref were not so very different from his own. Now that she was of similar mind, accomplishing his will in Eiwas and establishing himself more firmly in Wales would be that much easier. Yes, forging a lasting alliance through the marriage of his daughter to a Welsh king was a match that made good sense in more ways than one.

For his part, Bernard had assembled all the necessary supplies for a feast the like of which he was sure no one beyond the March had ever seen. It was his intention that the occasion should be spoken of in awed tones by his Welsh vassals for years to come. He wanted to cow them with a spectacle of such stunning opulence that they would fight one another to be next in line to receive such largess from his hand.

There was also the matter of a house. After all, as the doting father of the bride, he could not allow his precious daughter to live in the tumbledown wooden fortress that was Caer Rhodl. She would have a proper house of stone, with solid stone walls to keep her and his grandchildren—when they came along—safe from the buffeting winds of war and strife. Not that he expected trouble; since his defeat of King Rhys ap Tewdwr in the lightning conquest of Deheubarth things were much more peaceful in the region. He was, he felt, succeeding in winning over the inhabitants of that southern cantref just as he had won over the people of Eiwas.

Still, in Wales, one never knew what to expect. It was better to be ready for whatever martial crisis might arise—not to mention the fact that it would eventually become a convenient base from which to extend his power deeper into Wales. To that end, he had his master builder draw up plans for a castle with stout ramparts, a high donjon, garrison, stables, flagstone yard, and, surrounding all, a steep-sided moat. The house and its castle would be his wedding gift to the couple.

King Garran, proud Welshman that he was, would no doubt have rejected outright the suggestion that his stronghold was inadequate in any aspect. But if the fortress came as a wedding gift for himself and his new bride—well, the young king could hardly refuse it. Baron Neufmarché would have his way in the end.

Thus, as the days drew down toward the celebration, the baron put the finishing touches on his elaborate preparations. And on a bright summer day, he and the baroness and their daughter broke fast on a bit of bread and watered wine, and then walked out into the yard, where a covered carriage drawn by two chestnut horses awaited. As the ladies were helped up into the carriage, the baron issued final instructions to the servants who were staying behind, then climbed into the carriage himself.

They proceeded out through the castle gate and down into the town and out onto the King's Road. At the edge of Hereford they were met by a bodyguard of twenty knights and men-at-arms accompanied by nine wagons piled high with provisions, dishes and utensils, clothes and personal belongings; and four wagons filled with cooks, kitchen helpers, musicians, and sundry servants, all under the supervision of Remey, the baron's aged seneschal.

"God with you, Sire," said the baron's master-at-arms.

"God with you, Marshal Orval," returned the baron. "Is all well this morning?"

"All is well and in order, and awaiting your command," replied the marshal, making a small bow from the saddle. "If you will give the order, we will be on our way."

The baron glanced at the double rank of knights arrayed at the edge of the field beside the road. "Is this all you have mustered?" wondered the baron. "I thought there would be more."

"Indeed, Sire, yes," replied Marshal Orval, "there are as many more as you see here. I thought best to send the others on ahead to make certain the way is clear. We should encounter no trouble on the way."

"Very good, Marshal," agreed Neufmarché, satisfied at last. "Then you may give the signal and move out. We have a wedding to attend." With this last, he reached over and gave his daughter's hand a squeeze.

For her part, the young lady was suitably demure beneath a cap of pale blue silk with a veil that rested lightly over her long dark hair. In her lap she carried a posy of tiny white flowers bound in a bit of green cloth. She smiled at her father as the carriage lurched into motion, and said, "You have gone to far too much trouble—as I feared you might."

"Nonsense!" replied the baron. "Only what was necessary—nothing more."

"Nine wagons—necessary?" She laughed, not at all put out by her father's extravagance. "I'm not marrying the entire realm."

"*Au contraire, chérie,* but you are," insisted Bernard. "You will be queen and ruler of the realm—the woman all your male subjects will admire and all female subjects emulate."

"Your father is right," offered the baroness. "A future queen cannot be seen to hold herself too low, or she will lose the respect of those who must live beneath her rule."

"Nor would we care to be thought close-fisted on such an important occasion," continued the baron. "We must by all means demonstrate the prosperity we intend to cultivate in the realm. The people must see what it is that we intend for them."

"Not *all* the people, surely," said Sybil in mild derision. "I doubt I will have any dealings with the serfs."

"Do you not think so?" replied her mother. "Each and every one of your vassals will benefit from your rule—serfs as well as nobility. You must not allow yourself to become distant from those you rule. This is something that happens far too often in France, and I do not think it altogether a good thing."

This last pronouncement surprised the baron into silence. Coming from a bishop or cardinal such a sentiment would not seem out of place; but this—from the lips of a woman who, after fourteen years still did not know the names of the cook or any of the kitchen servants, and had yet to meet the porter, stabler, and grooms—it fair took his breath away.

Lady Agnes turned to him. *"Ce n'est pas, mon mari?"* she inquired with a lift of her eyebrow.

It took him a moment to realize she was speaking to him. "Oh! Indeed! Indeed, yes," he agreed hurriedly. "Sadly, it is much the way of things in France, but we have the opportunity to do better now." He smiled at the grave expression on his daughter's face. "But do not worry, *mon coeur*. It will soon be second nature to you." He glanced from his daughter to his wife, and added, "Why, you'll be surprised at how naturally it grows."

"And you will have your handmaids and servants to help—as well as a seneschal," Agnes continued. "A good seneschal is worth his weight in gold—and we shall make it a matter of some urgency to find one who knows what he's about. Your grandfather will have some ideas, I think; I will write to him and ask him to send two or three and you can choose the one that suits you best."

"A Welsh seneschal would be better, surely," ventured Sybil. "Because of the language . . ."

"Tch!" her mother countered. "That would never do. You would soon fall into the errors of their ways. As I said, it will be your duty—the duty of us all—to teach them."

They talked of this and other things, and the day passed with the countryside juddering slowly by. Because of all the wagons, they could not move with any speed, and as the sun dropped lower and ever lower in the west, Marshal Orval searched for and found a suitable place to make camp for the night. While the servants prepared a meal for all the entourage, the baron and baroness walked up to the top of the nearest hill to stretch their legs after riding in the carriage all day. In the distance they could see the dark, close-crowded hills of Wales, misty with the coming of night.

"What do you see?" asked Agnes.

The baron was thoughtful for a moment, then said, "I see wealth and power and a throne to rival England's." His naked declaration embarrassed him a little; he could feel Agnes's eyes on him, so he shrugged and added, "At least, it is closer now than it has ever been. The wedding will make a glorious beginning."

She returned his smile and took his hand. "That, *mon amour*, is exactly what I was thinking."

CHAPTER 4

It was five days of anxious travel before Bran and the Grellon reached Coed Cadw. Footsore, weary, and disheartened beyond measure, they sought the safety of their forest keep. As they moved into the lush, green-shadowed solitude of the Guardian Wood, the heat of the day dropped away and they walked a little easier and lighter of step. There among the trees the weary, heartsick band began to heal the wounded memories of the last days—the betrayal of the Ffreinc king, the treachery of the Black Abbot, the fierce and bloody battle, and their anxious flight.

Though they had escaped the battle without fatality—a few of the men suffered cuts and bruises, one a broken arm, and another a deep sword wound to the thigh—the carnage had exacted a toll that only became apparent in the days that followed. For most of the Grellon the panic and horror of that day was a plague that worked away on their souls, and they were infected with it.

Thus, soul-sick and exhausted they crept back into the solace of the greenwood to heal the raw, inflamed wounds of their memories, arriving at Cél Craidd to the great relief of those who had been left to look after the settlement in their absence.

The watchers had seen them on the road and hastened back to prepare a welcome: jars of cool water flavoured with elderflower blossoms and honey seed cakes to restore their strength. But the travellers were in no mood to rejoice, and their stark response to what should have been a glad homecoming soon dashed any notions of celebration. "Something is amiss, my lord," observed Henwydd delicately; an older man, he had been given the care of Cél Craidd in Bran's absence. "Forgive me if I speak in error, but the faces I see around me would be better suited to a funeral party, not a homecoming."

"How can it be otherwise?" said Bran, his voice thick with bitterness. "The black-hearted English king broke his promise. The realm belongs to the Ffreinc, and we are outlaws still."

"Sooner have milk from a stone," grumbled Iwan, following Bran, "than get satisfaction from a Norman."

Angharad arranged her wrinkled face into a sad smile. She thanked Henwydd and the others for their thoughtfulness and accepted a drink from the welcome cup. Then, taking her leave of Bran and the others, she shuffled slowly to her hut.

"Did Red William not redeem your throne?" asked another, pressing forward.

"He did not," answered Bran. "Count Falkes is banished to Normandie with his uncle the Baron de Braose, and Elfael is claimed by the king."

"Bloody Black Abbot Hugo and his gutless marshal, Gysburne, are placed over us for our *care* and *protection*," growled Siarles.

"Then we won't be going home," said Henwydd.

"No," Bran replied. "We stay here—for now, at least."

"Are we to remain in the forest forever?" asked Teleri, another who had remained behind. An older woman, she had lost all she had to the Ffreinc when the count took her house for the new church. There were tears in her eyes as the meaning of Bran's words broke upon her.

Mérian had come to stand beside Bran; she reached out and put her arm around the woman's shoulders to comfort her. "We have endured the forest this long," Mérian said, "what is another season or two?"

"Season or two?" said Henwydd, growing angry. "Why not ten or twenty?"

"If you have something to say," Bran replied sternly, "go on, say it. Speak your mind."

"We believed in you, my lord. We trusted you. I have suffered this outlaw life for the hope of the deliverance you promised. But I cannot abide another season scrabbling hand to mouth in the greenwood. It is no fit life, and I am too old."

Others, too, spoke out against the desperate life in the forest, with its darkness and dangers—exposure, privation, and the constant fear of discovery. If the Ffreinc didn't kill them, they said, the wolves would. They had followed Bran this far, but now that there was no hope of justice to be had from the Ffreinc, it was time to think what was best for themselves. "William the Red commands armies beyond number," one man said. "We cannot fight them all, and only a fool would try."

Bran glowered, but held his tongue.

"I am sorry, my lord," continued Henwydd, "but you see how it is. I beg leave to quit the forest. I have never asked anything of you, but I'm asking you now to grant me leave to depart."

"And where will you go?" asked Mérian.

"Well," considered the old man, "I have kinsmen still in Dyfed. It may be they will take me in. But whether they do or don't makes no matter, 'cause anywhere is better than here."

"There we have it," Bran said, eyes alight and voice cold. He turned and addressed the rest of the settlement. "Who else feels this way? Who else wants to leave the forest?" He swung around, his voice attacking. "Iwan? Will Scarlet? Siarles, what about you? Mérian— God knows you've wanted to leave often enough, why not go now?" He glared around at the ring of grim faces. None would meet his ferocious stare.

Mérian, standing beside Tuck, grasped the friar's hand. "Oh, no," she breathed, tears starting to her eyes. Tuck grasped her hand and gave it a squeeze.

"Who else is for leaving?" demanded Bran. "If you would go, speak up. All who wish to leave may go with my blessing. I do not force anyone to stay who would not do so gladly and of their own accord."

There was an instant commotion at this, and the forest-dwellers began arguing it over amongst themselves. Some were for leaving, others for staying, and all shouting to be heard and convince the rest. Bran let this continue until most had had a chance to speak out, then said, "Well? What say you? Anyone else want to go? Step up and take your place with Henwydd. For all saints bear witness, I do not care to stand with anyone who does not care to stand with me."

At first, no one moved, and then, one by one, others joined Henwydd until a group of seventeen men and women, some with children, stood together in a dismal clump.

"So, now," Bran, his face hard, addressed those who had chosen to leave. "Gather your things and make ready to depart—take whatever you need for your journey. If you would have my advice, wait until the sun goes down and make your way by night; you should avoid any Ffreinc and reach the borders of Elfael before sunrise tomorrow. I bid you God's speed, and may you all fare well."

With that, he turned and strode to his hut.

A shocked and dismayed Cél Craidd watched him go. Iwan and Siarles looked on aghast, and Scarlet and Mérian began to persuade those who had decided to leave that they were making a mistake— but thought better of it. The tight bond between King Raven and his proud Grellon was broken; the settlement was divided and there was nothing anyone could do.

Later, as twilight deepened the shadows in the wood, Friar Tuck called the people together for a prayer of thanks for their deliverance from the hands of the enemy and for a safe return, and for the future of the realm. He then led his discouraged flock in a hymn; he sang the first verses alone, but soon everyone joined in, lifting their voices and singing loudly as the moon rose in the pale blue sky. Neither Bran nor Angharad attended the prayer service, but the banfáith appeared after sundown when the first of those leaving the forest settlement were setting off. Gripping her staff, she offered blessings for the journey and safe arrivals for all who would travel that night.

The next morning after breaking fast, the remaining Grellon resumed their chores; there was more work now that a fair number of the most able-bodied had gone. As those who remained took stock of their numbers it was clear that others, unwilling to be seen by their friends, had departed silently during the night. Taking a silent tally, they soon realized that fewer than half their number remained.

With heavy hearts they set to and were just discussing how to divide the duties of the day and the days to come when Angharad called all Cél Craidd to gather at the Council Oak in the centre of the settlement. As the forest-dwellers assembled beneath the spreading boughs of the great, grey giant, they found Bran seated in his chair made of ash branches lashed together and covered by a bearskin. Bran looked like a Celtic king of old—an impression only strengthened by the long-beaked mask of King Raven that lay at his feet. Angharad stood behind her king, wearing the Bird Spirit cloak and holding a long, thin, rodlike staff in her right hand.

As soon as everyone had settled themselves close about this primitive throne, the banfáith raised the staff and said, "Heed the Head of Wisdom and attend her counsel. You are summoned here to uphold your king in his deliberations with strong consideration. Therefore, make keen your thoughts and carefully attend your words, for the course we determine here among us will be the life and death of many."

She paused, and Bran said, "If anyone here does not wish to bear this burden, you may leave now in peace. But if you stay, you will agree to abide by the decisions we shall make and pledge life, strength, and breath to fulfil them whatever they shall be."

Iwan, grim and deeply aggrieved, spoke for them all when he said, "Those who wanted to leave have gone, my lord, and God bless 'em. But those you see before you are with you to the end—and that end is to see you take your rightful throne and lead your people in peace and plenty."

"Hear him!" said Scarlet. "Hear him!"

"S'truth," added Siarles, and others shouted, "God wills it!"

Bran nodded to Angharad, who struck the bare earth three times with the end of her staff to silence the commotion. Then, raising her hand, palm outward, she tilted her face to the light slanting down through the leaf-laden branches. "Goodly Wise, Strong Upholder, Swift Sure Hand," she said in a queer chanting voice, "draw near to us; enter into our minds and hearts; be to us the voice that speaks the True Word. Be to us our rock and fortress, our shield and defender, our strength and courage. Go before us, Lord of Hosts, bare Your mighty arm, set Your face against our enemies, and as You destroyed the army of the wicked pharaoh in the sea, let fear swallow up those who raise their hands against us. These things we ask in the name of Blesséd Jesu, Our Hope and Redeemer, and Michael Militant the Terrible Sword of Your Righteousness." Her mouth moved silently for a moment longer; then she said, "Amen."

All gathered in the solemn assembly echoed. "Amen."

Bran turned his head and thanked his Wise Banfáith for her prayer. To the people gathered before him, he said, "We are here to decide how the war with the Ffreinc shall be pursued. On my most solemn vow, there will be an end to their rule in this realm . . . or there will be an end to me. For I will not tolerate their presence in the land of my fathers while there is yet a single breath in my body."

"I am with you, my lord!" cried Iwan, slapping his knee. "We will drive them from this realm—or die in the attempt."

Bran gave a downward jerk of his chin by way of acknowledgement of Iwan's pledge, and continued. "Let us speak freely now, holding nothing back. As we must stand together in the days to come, let us share our hearts and minds." He paused to let his listeners gather their thoughts. "So now." He spread his hands. "Who will begin?"

Tuck was first to find his voice. "To speak plain, I am grieved in heart, soul, and mind since the attack in the grove—and any man who said otherwise is a liar. Our King William has proven himself a greedy, grasping rogue and a stranger to all honour. If that was not a bitter enough brew to swallow, our Ffreinc overlords have shown us that they will attack with impunity, little respecting women and children—"

"Devil take them all," muttered Siarles.

"Nevertheless," the friar continued, raising a hand for silence, "I have bethought myself time and time again, and it seems to me that if our enemies have any tender feelings within reach of their cold hearts, it may be that they are even now sorely regretting that rash act."

"What are you saying, Tuck?" asked Bran softly.

"It would be well to send Abbot Hugo an offer of peace."

"Peace!" scoffed Bran. "On my father's grave, a moment's peace they will not have from me."

"I know! My lord, I know—they have earned damnation ten times over. Is there anyone here who does not know it? But, I pray you, do not dismiss the notion outright."

Tuck turned to appeal to those gathered beneath the oak boughs. "See here, it is not for our enemies that I make this plea—it is for *us* and for our good. The pursuit of war is a dire and terrible waste— of life and limb, blood and tears. It maims all it touches. Maybe we gain justice in the end, maybe not. No one knows how it will end. But, know you, we will lose much that we hold dear long 'ere we reach the end, and of that we can be more than certain."

"We have little to lose, it seems to me," remarked Iwan.

"True enough," Tuck allowed, "but it is always possible to lose even that little, is it not? Think you now—if war could be avoided, we might be spared that loss. By pursuing peace as readily as war, we might even gain the outcome we seek—and is that not a thing worth the risk of trying?"

Tuck's plea fell into silence even as he implored the others to at least consider what he had said. No one, so it appeared, shared his particular sentiment.

"Our priest is right to speak so," said Mérian, moving to stand beside the little cleric. "War with the Ffreinc will mean the deaths of many—maybe all of us. But if death and destruction can be avoided, we must by all means try—for the sake of those who will be hurt by what we decide today, we must make an offer of peace."

"Offer peace?" wondered Scarlet aloud. "That's begging for trouble with a dog and bowl."

"Aye, trouble and worse," growled Siarles. "If you have no stomach for the fight ahead, maybe you should both join Henwydd and his band of cowards. They're not so far ahead that you couldn't catch 'em up."

"Coward? Is that what you think?" asked Tuck, voicing the question to the whole gathering. "Is that what everyone thinks?"

"I don't say it is, I don't say it en't," replied Siarles. "But the shoe fits him who made it."

"Enough, both of you. Courage is not at issue here," Bran pointed out. "I was willing to swear fealty to William Rufus. Indeed, I encouraged my father to do so, and we would not be here now if he had listened to me and acted before it was too late . . ."

"Do you not see?" said Mérian. "You're in danger of becoming just like your father—too proud and stubborn for the good of your people. And, like your father, you will die at the end of a Norman spear." She put out a slender hand and softened her tone. "Red William is a false king; that is true. His decision was the ruin of all our hopes, and now everything has changed. Look around, my lord—only half of Cél Craidd remains. Even if we were mighty warriors, champions each and every one, we could not take back Elfael by force of arms alone."

Bran glared at her, his brow low and furrowed. Judging from the expressions on the faces around him, Mérian had won solid support for her opinion. "What do you suggest?" he said at last.

Mérian glanced at Tuck. "That is not for me to say, my lord."

"It seems to me you have said a great deal already, my lady. Why stop now?" He lifted his head to include the rest of the gathering. "Come, speak up, your lord is asking for your counsel. What do you advise?"

"If I may speak freely, my lord," began Tuck.

"I doubt anything in heaven or earth could prevent you," remarked Bran. "Speak, priest."

"Hardheaded Saxon that I am, I have always thought it a good thing that the clerics rule the church and kings rule the realm. That is the way God has ordained it, has He not? Render unto Caesar the things that are Caesar's, to be sure, but give to God the things that are God's. Like it or not, the Ffreinc—"

"Is there a point to this sermon, Friar?" interrupted Bran.

"Only that we must be prepared to compromise if we are to persuade the abbot and sheriff to accept the peace."

"Compromise," repeated Bran dully.

"What sort of compromise?" asked Siarles.

"That any Ffreinc who have settled should be allowed to remain in Elfael under your rule, and that Hugo will remain in charge of the spiritual concerns of the abbey."

"Let Hugo keep the abbey and I take the fortress—is that what you're saying?" said Bran.

"In a word, yes, my lord."

"Why in heaven's name would Hugo agree to that?"

"Because," suggested Tuck, "it would allow him to put his efforts into saving his abbey, which he will certainly lose if he continues to pursue this war. Lose the abbey and he has lost his place in the church—and I heartily doubt he'll ever get another one. Who'd have him?"

"Indeed," said Bran.

"You know what I mean," Tuck continued. "If he agrees to the peace, he will survive, and keep much that he will lose if the war continues."

"My lord, you would have to swear fealty to William," Will Scarlet pointed out.

"He has offered to do that already," Iwan reminded him. "Twice."

"What about the king? He has given the realm to Hugo."

"Then he can take it away again and give it back to its rightful ruler," said Tuck, adding, "of course, the abbot would have to agree to support you before the king."

"He'd never do it," said Siarles.

"Share my realm with that rank Ffreinc butcher?" wondered Bran, shaking his head. "My stomach churns at the very thought."

He glanced to Angharad for support, but the old woman admonished him, saying, "What the friar suggests has merit, Lord King. Think you: force has availed us nothing, nor has any other remedy offered a cure for this wasting blight. We hurt them in the grove, mind. Our enemies may be ready to listen to such an offer. It would be well to ponder the matter further."

"I bow to your judgment," allowed Bran grimly. Turning to the assembly, he said, "Let us suppose, for the moment, that we send an offer of peace to the abbot. What then?"

"Then it is for the Ffreinc to decide, is it not?" replied Tuck. "Either they accept and proceed according to your decree—"

"And if they don't?" wondered Siarles.

"We will be no worse off," suggested Mérian.

"But whatever happens will be on their heads," added Tuck. "At all events, it is our Christian duty to try for peace if it lays in our power."

Bran chewed his lip thoughtfully for a moment. Tuck thought he could see a chink of light shining in the darkness of Bran's bleak mood. "Lord Bran," the friar said, "I would like to take the message to Hugo myself and alone."

"Why alone?" said Bran.

"Priest to priest," replied Tuck. "That is how I mean to approach him—two men of God answerable to the Almighty. Blesséd are the peacemakers, are they not?"

"As Angharad suggests," put in Mérian, "the abbot may welcome the opportunity to be rid of this bloodshed."

"Hugo will welcome the opportunity to carve him like a Christmas ham," observed Scarlet. To Tuck, he said, "He'll roast your rump and feed it to his hounds."

"Nay," said Tuck. "He'll do no such thing. I am a brother cleric and a minister of the church. A rogue he may be, but he will receive me, as he must."

"While I do not expect the abbot to honour any offer we put before him," said Iwan, "I agree with our man Tuck—we should do what we can to avoid another bloodletting, as it may well be our blood next time instead of theirs. Try as I might, however, I can think of no other way to avoid it—our choices are that few. It is worth a try."

There was more talk then, as others added their voices to the discussion—some for the idea, others against. In the end, however, Tuck's proposition carried the day.

"Then it is decided," declared Bran when everyone had had their say. "In observance of our Christian duty, and for the sake of our people, we will make this offer of peace to Hugo and urge him by all means to accept it and to support me before King William."

"It is the right decision, my lord," said Mérian, pressing close. "If Hugo will listen to reason, then you'll have reclaimed what is rightfully yours without risking the lives of any more of your people."

"Right or wrong it makes no difference," Bran told her. "We are too weak to pursue the war further on our own." He declared the council at an end and said, "I will frame a message for Tuck to deliver to the abbot. If he accepts my offer, we will soon be out of the forest and back in our own lands."

"I'll believe it when it happens," grumbled Siarles.

"You're not alone there," Scarlet said. "Give 'em a year o' Sundays and a angel choir to show 'em the way, the bloody Ffreinc will never shift an English inch."

"Then pray God to change their hearts," Tuck said. "Do not think it impossible just because it has never happened."

CHAPTER 5

The council concluded, and as everyone dispersed Tuck lingered in Angharad's presence a little longer. Close to her, he was aware once again of a curious sensation—like that of standing beneath one of the venerable giants of the forest, an oak or elm of untold age. It was, he decided, the awareness that he was near something so large and calm and rooted to depths he could scarcely imagine. With her face a web of wrinkles and her thinning hair a haze of wisp on her head, she seemed the very image of age, yet commanded all she beheld with the keen intelligence of her deep-set, dark eyes. "I hope I have served him wisely," he told the old woman.

"So hope we all," she replied.

"I am afraid Siarles is right—offering peace is just begging for trouble."

"Trouble have we in abundance," the banfáith pointed out. "It is a most hardy crop."

"Too true," the friar agreed.

"Hear me, friend priest," she said, holding him with her deep-set, dark eyes. "This war began long ago; we merely join it now. The trouble is not of our making, but it is our portion and ours to endure."

"That does not cheer me much," sighed Tuck.

"Regrets, have you?"

"No, never," he answered. "That is the duty of any Christian."

"Then trust God with it and that which is given you, do."

"You are right, of course," he said at last.

Angharad regarded the friar with a kindly expression. The little priest with his rotund, bandy-legged form, his shaggy tonsure, his stained and tattered robe—smelling of smoke and sweat and who knows what else—there was that much like a donkey about him. And like the humble beast of burden, he was loyal and long-suffering, able to bear the heavy load of responsibility placed upon him now. "As God is our lord and leader," she said, "it is our portion to obey and follow. We trust him to lead us aright. As with our Heavenly Lord, so with Bran. More we cannot do just now, but we must do that at least."

"Ah, but earthly vessels are all too fragile, are they not? We trust them at our peril."

The old woman smiled gently. "Yet it is all we have."

"Too true," Tuck agreed.

"So we trust and pray—never knowing which is the more needful."

Tuck accepted her counsel and made his way to the edge of the forest settlement, where he found Bran and Mérian sitting knee to knee on stumps facing one another as if in contest, while Will, Noín, and Odo stood looking on. "They *know* we will fight," Mérian was saying. "If ever there was the smallest doubt, we showed them in the grove. But you *must* give them some assurance that we will not seek revenge if they accept your offer."

Bran nodded, conceding the point.

"They have to know that they are not simply cutting their own throats," she insisted.

"I understand," Bran replied. "And I agree. Go on."

"It must be something they can trust," she continued, "even if they don't trust *you*."

"Granted, Mérian," said Bran, exasperation edging into his voice. "What do you suggest?"

"Well"—she bit her lip—"I don't know."

"Maybe we could get the abbot at Saint Dyfrig's to oversee the truce," suggested Noín. "He is a good man, and they know him."

"After what happened in the square on Twelfth Night, I cannot think they would trust any of us any farther than they could spit a mouthful of nails," Scarlet said, shaking his head.

"It must be someone they know, someone they can rely on to be fair."

Mérian's face clenched in thought. "I know!" she said, glancing up quickly. "We could ask my father . . ."

"Your father—what possible reason could Hugo have for trusting him?"

"Because he is a loyal vassal of King William, as is the abbot himself . . ."

"No," said Bran, jumping up quickly. "This is absurd." He began stalking around the stump. "It won't work."

"Why—because *you* did not think of it?"

"Your father hates me," Bran said. "And that was *before* I abducted you! God alone knows what he thinks of me now. If that was not enough, Lord Cadwgan answers to Baron Neufmarché, his liege lord—and if the baron were to get wind of this there is no way we could keep him out of it."

"The Ffreinc would trust the baron," Mérian said.

"They might, but could *we*?" wondered Scarlet.

"Have you forgotten Neufmarché tried to kill me last time I went to him for help?" said Bran. "If it is all the same to you, I'd rather not give him another chance."

Mérian frowned. "That was unfortunate."

"Unfortunate!" cried Bran. "Woman, the man is a two-faced Judas. He betrayed me outright. Indeed, he betrayed us both. Your own life was none too secure, if you'll recall."

"What you say is true," she conceded. "I'll not argue. Still, he is a Ffreinc nobleman and if—together with my father, of course—we could convince him that it was in his own best interest to help us, I know he'd agree."

"Oh, he'd agree," Bran retorted, "agree to help empty Elfael of his rivals so he could have it all to himself. We'd just be exchanging one tyrant for an even bigger, more powerful tyrant." Bran gave a sharp chop of his hand, dismissing the suggestion. "No. If the Ffreinc require assurance that we will hold to our word, we will appeal to Abbot Daffyd to swear for us and they will have to accept that." He sat back down. "Now then, what do we want Tuck to tell them?"

They fell to discussing the substance of the message and soon hammered out a simple, straightforward appeal to meet and discuss the proposed offer of peace. By the time Siarles came to say that the horse was ready, the Ffreinc scribe, Odo, had schooled and corrected Tuck's creaky Latin so there would be no mistake. "I have some of the Norman tongue too," Tuck pointed out in French. "Picked up a fair bit in my years in Hereford."

"Not enough, God knows," snipped Odo.

"I understand far more than I can speak," said Tuck.

"Even so," allowed the scribe, "it is not what you understand that will lead you to difficulty, but what you are likely to *say*."

"Perhaps you should come with me, then," suggested Tuck. "To keep a poor friar from stumbling over the rocky places."

The colour drained from the already pasty face of the young cleric.

"I thought not," replied Tuck. "'Tis better I go alone."

"Ah!" said Odo. "I will write it down for you so the abbot can read it for himself if you go astray." He bustled off to find his writing utensils and a scrap of something to carry the ink.

"All is well?" asked Bran, seeing the scribe depart on the run.

"Right as rain in merry May," replied Tuck. "Odo is going to write it for me so if all else fails I have something to push under the abbot's nose."

"Scarlet is right—this is dangerous. Hugo could seize you and have you hung, or worse. You don't have to go. We can find another way to get a message through."

"The Lord is my shield and defender," replied Tuck. "Of whom shall I be afraid?"

"Well then," Bran concluded, "God with you, Tuck. Siarles and I will see you to the edge of the forest at least."

A short while later, the would-be peacemakers paused at the place where the King's Road crossed the ford and started down into the valley. Bran and Siarles were each armed with a bow and bag of arrows, and Tuck carried a new-made quarterstaff. In the distance they could see Caer Cadarn on its hump of rock, guarding the Vale of Elfael. "I do not expect the abbot will have let the fortress stand abandoned for long," Bran surmised. "He would have moved men into it as soon as Count Falkes had gone."

"If any should see me, they will only see a poor fat friar on a skinny horse making for town—nothing to alarm anyone."

"And if they should take exception and stop you?" asked Siarles.

"I will tell them I bring a word of greeting and hope to Abbot Hugo," replied Tuck. "And that is God's own truth."

"Then off with you," said Bran, "and hurry back. We'll wait for you here."

I t took Tuck longer to reach the town than he had reckoned, and the sun was already beginning its descent as he entered the market square—all but empty, with only a few folk about and no soldiers that he could see. Always before there had been soldiers. Indeed, the town had a tired, deserted air about it. He tied his mount to an iron ring set in a wall, drew a deep breath, hitched up his robe, and strode boldly across the square to stand before the whitewashed walls of the abbey. He pounded on the timber door with the flat of his hand and waited. A few moments later, the door opened, and the white-haired old porter peered out.

"Nous avons un message pour l'abbé," Tuck intoned politely. *"Je vous prie de l'apporter à lui toute de suite."*

Brother porter ducked his head respectfully and hurried away.

"Thank you, Lord," said Tuck, breathing a sigh of relief to have passed the first test.

Tuck waited, growing more and more uneasy with each passing

moment. Finally, the door in the abbey gate opened once more and the porter beckoned him to come inside, where he was led across the yard to the abbot's lodge. A few of the monks stopped to stare as he passed—perhaps, thought Tuck, recognizing him from their previous encounter in King William's yard not too many days ago.

Once inside, he was conducted through a dark corridor and brought to stand before a panelled door. The porter knocked and received the summons to enter. He pushed open the door and indicated that Tuck should go in.

The abbot was standing over a table on which was spread a simple supper. He was spearing a piece of cheese with a long fork as Tuck entered. Glancing up, Hugo stopped, his mouth agape. Then, collecting himself, he said in a low voice, *"Vous devez être fous de venir ici en cette manière. Que voulez-vous?"*

Tuck understood this to mean that the abbot thought he must be insane to come there, and demanded to know what he wanted.

At this, Tuck, speaking in measured tones and with many haltings as he searched for the words, began his prepared speech. He appealed to Abbot Hugo as a brother in their common calling as priests of the church, and thanked the abbot for allowing him to speak. He then said that he had come with an offer of peace from the forest-dwellers. When words began to fail, he took out the little scrap of parchment Odo had prepared for him, listing the central stipulations of the plan. The abbot's face grew red as he listened, but he held his tongue. Tuck concluded, saying, "You have until midday tomorrow to give your answer. If you accept Bran's offer, you will ring the abbey bell nine times—three peals of three. Then, come to the edge of the forest, where you will be told what to do next. Do you understand?"

To which the abbot replied, "I do not know which offends me

the more—your uncouth speech or the crudeness of your appearance." He waved a hand in front of his nose. "You smell worse than a stable hound."

Tuck bore the insult with a smile. He'd not expected an easy ride through enemy territory. "But you understand what I am saying?"

"Oh, I understand," confirmed Hugo. "However, I fail to see why I should dignify this ridiculous idea of sharing the governance of Elfael with a vile outlaw and rebel."

"Bran ap Brychan is neither outlaw nor rebel," Tuck replied evenly, hoping he had got the words right. "In truth, his family has ruled this realm for a hundred years or more. If you agree, you would be sharing the dominion of the cantref with the rightful heir to the throne of Elfael, who—no fault of his own—has been deprived of his kingship."

"And if I do not agree?"

"Then there will be a bloody price to pay."

"Is that supposed to frighten me?" asked Hugo, arching an eyebrow. "If so, forgive me if I refuse to take this threat of retribution seriously. It seems to me that *if* your Lord Bran could take this town by force, he would have done so long ere now, no?"

"He is giving you one last chance," said Tuck.

"One last chance."

"Yes, Abbot—this is the last and best chance you will receive."

"So, I am supposed to simply abandon the town and fortress to the outlaws and imprison myself in the abbey here—is that it?"

"You would not be held captive," said Tuck, struggling to make himself understood. "Bran would rule the realm as a liegeman of the king, and you would support him in this and . . . ah, *confine* . . . your activities to the work of the abbey."

"Non!" roared the abbot, throwing down the long-handled fork. *"C'est impossible!* The king has given me Elfael to rule as I see fit. I will in no wise share the governance of this realm with a low brigand." Hugo leaned on the table with his fists, his anger mounting. "I may not have enough men to drive your King Raven from his forest perch, but if he has the might to defeat me, then let him try."

Tuck stared at the abbot, his mind whirling as he tried to decipher this last outburst. "But you will consider the offer?"

"I think our talk is finished." The abbot made a dismissive gesture with his hand. "You may go, but if you ever come here again I will have you arrested to stand trial as a traitor to the crown. You can tell your friends that if I ever catch you or any of them your lives are forfeit."

Tuck stiffened at the insult. "I came here in good faith, Abbot, as a Christian priest. Even so, I don't expect you'll see me again."

"Out!"

"I am going," Tuck said, stepping towards the door. "But I urge you to seriously consider the offer of peace—pray, discuss it with your marshal and the sheriff. You have until midday tomorrow to decide, and if you accept—"

"Porter!" shouted the abbot. "Take this man away!"

Outside once more, Tuck returned to his mount, untied it, and heaved himself up into the saddle. As he lifted the reins he cast a backward look at the abbey and saw a monk flitting along the front of the church towards the guard tower.

He did not linger, but departed quickly lest the abbot betray his word and arrest him. He urged his mount to a trot and left the town, hastening back to the forest with the curious sensation that he had been given a valuable prize but could not remember what it was—something Abbot Hugo had said . . . but what?

In any event, he was satisfied that, as a priest of the church, he had done his duty. "Blesséd are the peacemakers," he murmured to himself. "And the Good Lord help us all."

CHAPTER 6

Saint Martin's

A s long as those outlaws hold the King's Road," complained Marshal Guy, swirling the wine in his cup, "nothing enters or leaves the forest without their notice. We lost good men in that ill-advised attack at Winchester and—"

"You need not whip that dead horse any longer, Marshal," growled Abbot Hugo, slamming down the pewter jar. Wine splashed out and spattered the table linen, leaving a deep crimson stain. "I am only too aware of the price we are paying to maintain this accursed realm."

"My point, Abbot, was that without hope of raising any more soldiers, the cantref is lost already. Sooner or later, the rogues will discover how few men we have, and when they do, they will attack and we will not be able to repel them. That, or they will simply wear us down. Either way, they win."

"Possibly." Hugo shook the wine from his hand, raised his cup, and drank.

"Their Raven King has made us an offer of peace—take it, I say, and let us be done with this godforsaken realm. I wish to heaven I'd never heard of it."

"Be that as it may," Hugo said, staring into his cup, "King William has given the governance of the realm to me, and I will not suffer that ridiculous King Raven and his scabrous minions to hold sway over it. They will be defeated."

"Have you heard a single word I've said?"

"I heard, Marshal, but I do not think you understand the depth of my resolve. For I propose we root out King Raven and his brood for once and all."

"Then just you tell me how do you *propose* we do that?" Guy de Gysburne glared at the abbot, daring him to put up something that could not be knocked down with a single blow. "As many times as we have gone against them, we have been forced to retreat. Swords and spears are no use against those infernal longbows because we cannot get close enough to use them. Pitched battle is no good: they will not stand and fight. They hide in the woods where our horses cannot go. They know the land hereabouts far better than we do, so they can sit back and slaughter us at will."

Abbot Hugo was in no mood to listen to yet another litany of Guy's complaints. They never advanced the cause and always fell back on the tired observation that unless they found a powerful patron to supply men and weapons, and provisions, the realm would fall. The battle in the grove had cost them more than either one of them cared to contemplate—though Guy had not allowed anyone within hearing distance to forget it. Of the thirty-three knights and men-at-arms left to them after the departure of the exiled Baron de Braose, only twenty-one remained. And Elfael, nestled in its valley and surrounded by forest on three sides, was far too vulnerable to the predation of Bran and his outlaw band, who had proven time and again that they could come and go as they pleased.

"If we cannot get to them," replied Hugo, adopting a more conciliatory air, "then we will bring the so-called Raven and his flock to us."

"Easier said than done," muttered Guy. "Our Raven is a canny bird. Not easy to trick, not easy to catch."

"Nor am I an adversary easily defeated." Hugo raised his cup to his mouth and took a deep draught before continuing. "Simply put, we will entice them, draw them out into the open where they cannot attack us from behind trees and such. Their bows will be no good to them at close quarters."

Guy stared at the abbot in amazement and shook his head. "The forest is their fortress. They will not leave it—not for any enticement you might offer."

"But I need offer nothing," the abbot remarked. "Don't you see? They have outwitted themselves this time. Under pretence of accepting the peace, we will lure them into the open. Once they have shown themselves, we will slice them to ribbons."

"Just like that?" scoffed the marshal, shaking his head.

"If you have a better plan, let us hear it," snapped the abbot. Growing weary of arguing with Gysburne at every turn, he decided to end the discussion. "Count Falkes was no match for the Welsh, as we all know. He paid the price for his mistakes and he is gone. I rule here now, and our enemies will find in me a more ruthless and cunning adversary than that de Braose ninny."

Clearly, they had reached an impasse, and Marshal Guy could think of nothing more to say. So he simply dashed the wine from his cup and took his leave.

"If all goes well, Marshal," said the abbot as Guy reached the door, "we will have that viper's nest cleaned out in three days' time."

How very optimistic," observed Sheriff de Glanville when the marshal told him what the abbot had said. "So far, in all our encounters with these brigands, we've always come off the worse—while *they* get away with neither scratch nor scrape."

"Putting more men in the field only gives them more targets for their accursed arrows," Guy pointed out.

"Precisely," granted the sheriff. He removed the leather hood from his falcon and blew gently on the bird's sleek head. With his free hand he picked up a gobbet of raw meat from a bowl on the table and flipped it to the keen-eyed bird on his glove. "Still, the abbot has a point—we might fare better if we could lure the outlaws from the wood. Have you any idea what the abbot has planned?"

"The outlaws have sent a message offering a truce of some kind."

"Have they indeed?"

"They have," confirmed Gysburne, "and the abbot thinks to use that to draw them out. He didn't say how it would be done."

The sheriff lifted a finger and gently stroked the falcon's head. "Well, I suppose there is no point in trying to guess what goes on in our devious abbot's mind. I have no doubt he'll tell us as soon as he is ready."

They did not have long to wait. At sundown, just after compline, the abbot summoned his two commanders to his private chambers, where he put forth his plan to rid the realm of King Raven and his flock.

"When the abbey bell goes," Abbot Hugo explained for the third time. "I want everyone in place. We don't know—"

"We don't know how many will come, so we must be ready for

anything," grumbled Marshal Gysburne irritably. "For the love of Peter, there is no need to hammer us over the head with it."

The abbot arched an eyebrow. "If I desire to lay stress upon the readiness—or lack of it—of your men," he replied tartly, "be assured that I think it necessary."

"The point is taken, Abbot," offered the sheriff, entering the fray, "and after what happened in the grove at Winchester I think a little prudence cannot go amiss."

Marshal Guy flinched at the insinuation. "You weren't there, Sheriff. Were you? Were you there?"

"You know very well that I was not."

"Then I will thank you to shut your stinking mouth. You don't know a thing about what happened that day."

"*Au contraire, mon ami,*" answered de Glanville with a cold, superior smile. "I know that you left eight good knights in that grove, and four more along the way. Twelve men died as a result, and we are no closer to ridding ourselves of these outlaws than we ever were."

The marshal regarded the sheriff from beneath lowered brows. "You smug swine," he muttered. "You dare sit in judgement of me?"

"Judge you?" inquired de Glanville innocently. "I merely state a fact. If that stings, then perhaps—"

"Enough!" said Abbot Hugo, slapping the arm of his chair with his palm. "Save your spite for the enemy."

Sheriff de Glanville gave the abbot a curt nod and said, "Forgive me, Abbot. As I was about to say, we will never have a better chance to take the enemy unawares. If the outlaws escape into the forest, it will be just like the massacre in the grove. We cannot allow that to happen. This is, I fear, our last best chance to take them. We must succeed this time, or all is lost."

"I agree, of course," replied the abbot. "That goes without saying."

"I beg your pardon, Abbot," remarked the sheriff, "but in matters of war, nothing *ever* goes without saying."

"Well then," sniffed Gysburne, "we have no worries there. You've seen to that—most abundantly."

"Get out of here—both of you," said the abbot. Rising abruptly, he flapped his hands at them as if driving away bothersome birds. "Go on. Just remember, I want you to have your men ready to attack the moment I draw the rogues out of hiding. And strike swiftly. I will not be made to stand waiting out there alone."

"You will not be alone, Abbot. Far from it," said de Glanville. "Gysburne and I will be hidden in the forest, and some of my men will be among your monks. We have thought of everything, I assure you."

"Just you match deed to word, Sheriff, and I will consider myself assured."

The two commanders left the abbey, each to look after his own preparations. Sometime later, when the moon was low and near to setting, but dawn was still a long way off, a company of soldiers departed Saint Martin's. Moving like slow shadows across the valley, ten mounted knights in two columns—their armour and horses' tack muffled with rags to prevent the slightest sound, their weapons dulled with sooted grease so that no glint or shine could betray them—rode in silence to the edge of the forest. Upon reaching the dark canopy of the trees, they dismounted and walked a short distance into the wood, hid their horses and themselves in the thick underbrush, then settled back to wait.

CHAPTER 7

Coed Cadw

With the approach of dawn, the forest awakened around the hidden soldiers—first with birdsong, and then with the furtive twitching and scratching of squirrels and mice and other small creatures. A light mist rose in the low places of the valley, pale and silvery in the early-morning light; it vanished as the sun warmed the ground, leaving a spray of glistening dew on the deep green grass. A family of wild pigs—a sow and six yearling piglets under the watchful eye of a hulking great boar—appeared at the margin of the trees to snuffle along the streambed and dig among the roots. The world began another day while the hidden soldiers dozed with their weapons in their hands. Slowly, the sun climbed higher in a cloud-ruffled sky.

And they waited.

Some little while before midday, there came a sound of movement further back in the forest—the rustling of leaves where there was no breeze, the slight creak of low branches, a sudden flight of sitting birds—and the soldiers who were awake clutched their weapons and nudged those still sleeping beside them. The ghosts of the greenwood were coming. King Raven would soon appear.

But the sounds died away. Nothing happened.

The sun continued its climb until it soared directly overhead. The soldiers, awake now and ready, strained their ears in the drowsy quiet of the wood as, above the whir and buzz of insects, the first faint chimes of a church bell sounded across the valley—far off, but distinct: three peals.

Then silence.

They listened, and they heard the signal repeated. After another lengthy pause, the sequence of three peals sounded for the third and last time.

After the second sequence had sounded, Marshal Gysburne, pressing himself to the ground, craned his neck from his hiding place behind an ash tree and looked down the long slope and into the bowl of the valley, where he saw a faint glimmering: Abbot Hugo and his white-robed monks making their way toward the forest. They came on, slow as snails it seemed to an increasingly impatient Gysburne, who like the other knights was sweating and stiff inside his armour. He inched back behind the tree and listened to the greenwood, hoping to catch any telltale sign of the outlaws' presence.

When at last the abbot's party came within arrow-flight of the edge of the wood, a call like that of a raven sounded from the upper branches of a massive elm tree. The party of white-robed monks surrounding the abbot heard it, too, and as if acting upon a previously agreed signal, stopped at once.

The raucous croak sounded twice more—not quite a bird's cry, Gysburne thought, but certainly not human, either. He scanned the upper branches for the source of the sound, and when he looked back, there, poised at the edge of the tree line, stood the slender young man known as Bran ap Brychan.

"Ah!" gasped Gysburne in surprise.

"Where the devil did he come from?" muttered Sergeant Jeremias from his place on the other side of the ash tree.

Dressed all in black, his dark hair lifting in the breeze, for an instant it seemed to the soldiers that he might indeed have been a raven dropped out of the sky to assume the form of a man. He stood motionless, clutching a longbow in his left hand; at his belt hung a bag of dark arrows.

"Had I one of those bows," Jeremias whispered, "I'd take him now, and save us all a load of bother."

"Shh!" hissed Gysburne in a tense whisper. "He'll hear you."

When the outlaw made no move to approach the group of monks, the abbot called out, *"Entendez-moi! Donc, ou a fait ce que vous avez demandé; qu'est-ce qui arrive maintenant?"*

Marshal Gysburne heard this with a sinking heart. *You old fool!* he thought, *the outlaws don't speak French. He'll have no idea what you're saying.*

But to the marshal's surprise, the young man answered, *"Attendez! Un moment!"*

He turned and gestured toward the wood behind him, and there was a rustling of leaves in the brush like a bear waking up; and out from the greenwood stepped the slump-shouldered Norman scribe— the one called Odo.

The two advanced a few more paces into the open, and then halted. At a nod from Bran, the scribe called out, "Have you come to swear peace?"

"I have come as requested," replied Abbot Hugo, "to hear what this man has proposed." Regarding the young scribe, he said, "Greetings, Odo. I suppose I should not be surprised to see you here—traitors and thieves flock together, eh?"

Odo cringed at his former master's abuse, but turned and explained to Bran what the abbot had said, received his lord's answer, and replied, "The proposal is simple. Lord Bran says that you will agree to the terms put to you, or he will pursue the war he has begun."

"Even if I were to agree," replied the abbot, "we must still discuss how the rule of Elfael is to be divided, and how we are to conduct the peace. Come, let us sit down together and talk as men."

Odo and Bran exchanged a quick word, then Odo replied, "First, my lord would have you swear a truce. You must promise to cease all aggression against himself and his people. Then he will *parler* with you."

The abbot and his monks held a quick consultation, and the abbot replied, "Come closer, if you please. My throat grows raw shouting like this."

"I am close enough," Bran replied. "Swear to the truce."

Abbot Hugo took a step forward, spreading his arms wide. "Come," he said, "let us be reasonable. Let us sit down together like reasonable men and discuss how best to fulfil your demands."

"First you must swear to the truce," answered Bran through Odo. "There will be no peace unless you pledge a sacred vow to uphold the truce."

Frowning, the abbot drew himself up and said, "In the name of Our Lord, I swear to uphold the truce, ceasing all aggression against the people of Elfael from this day hence."

"Then it is done," said Bran through Odo. "You may come forward—alone. Your monks are to stay where they are."

"A moment, pray," called the abbot. "There is more . . . I wish to—"

Bran halted. One of the monks behind Hugo dropped his hand to his side, and Bran caught the movement and glimpsed a solid shape beneath the folds of the monk's robe. Grabbing Odo by the arm, Bran whispered something, and the two began backing away.

"He's onto them!" whispered Sergeant Jeremias from his hiding place among the roots.

"I see that!" spat Gysburne. "What do you expect me to do?"

"Stop him!" urged the sergeant. "Stop him now before he reaches the wood."

"Wait!" cried Abbot Hugo from the clearing. "We need safe conduct back to the village. Send some of your men to guard us."

When Odo had relayed these words to Bran, the young man called over his shoulder and said, "You came here under guard—you can leave the same way. There is no truce."

The two outlaws started for the wood again, and again Hugo called out, but Bran took no further notice of him.

"Blast his cursed bones!" muttered Gysburne.

"Stop him!" urged Jeremias with a nudge in the marshal's ribs.

With a growl between his teeth, Guy rose from his hiding place and, stepping out from behind the ash tree, called out, "Halt! We would speak to you!"

At the sudden appearance of the marshal, Bran shoved Odo toward the nearest tree. Dropping to one knee, he raised his bow, the arrow already on the string. Gysburne had time but to throw himself to the ground as the missile streaked toward him. In the same moment, the nine knights hidden since midnight in anticipation of this moment rose with a shout, charging up out of the undergrowth.

Odo gave out a yelp of fright and stumbled backwards to where Bran was drawing aim on the wriggling figure of Gysburne as he snaked through the grass toward the safety of the bracken.

Swinging away from the marshal, Bran drew and let fly at the soldiers just then bolting from the wood to his left. His single arrow was miraculously multiplied as five more joined his single shaft in flight. Hidden since dawn in the upper branches of the great oaks and elms, the Grellon took aim and released a rain of whistling death on the knights scrambling below. Shields before them, the Ffreinc soldiers tried to keep themselves protected from the falling shafts. One knight stumbled, momentarily dropping his guard. An arrow flashed and the knight slewed wildly sideways, as if swatted down by a giant, unseen hand. A second arrow found its mark before the wounded man stopped rolling on the ground.

Three more knights were down just that quick, and the five remaining soldiers moved surprisingly fast in their mail and padded leather tunics. Ten running paces carried them across the open ground between the wood and the lone kneeling archer. Swords drawn, they roared their vengeance and fell upon him.

In the instant the soldiers raised their arms to strike, there came a sound like that of a hard slap of a gauntleted fist smashing into a leather saddle. Arrows streaked down from the upper branches of the surrounding trees, and the cracking thump was repeated so quickly the individual sounds merged to become one. The foremost knight seemed to rise and dangle on his tiptoes, as if jerked upright by a rope, only to crumple when his feet touched earth again. He collapsed in the grass, three arrows in his back.

A second knight threw his arms wide, his sword spinning from his grasp as he crashed to his knees and flopped face-first to the ground. A third knight paused in midstroke and glanced down at his chest, where he saw a rose-coloured stain spreading across his pale tunic; in the centre of the crimson stain, the steel tip of an arrowhead protruded. With a cry of pain and disbelief, he threw down his sword, grabbed at the lethal missile, and tried to pull it free even as he toppled.

The fourth knight took an arrow on his shield and was thrown onto his back as two more arrows ripped the autumn air, one of them striking the soldier a step or two ahead of him. The knight faltered, his legs tangling in midstep as the missile jolted into him, twisting his shoulders awkwardly. His shield banged against his knees, and he plunged onto his side at Bran's feet.

The sole remaining knight, still on the ground, covered his helmeted head with his shield and lay unmoving as the dead around him. Nocking another arrow to the string, Bran surveyed the battleground with a rapid sweep to the right and left. Several of the monks with Abbot Hugo had thrown off their robes to reveal mail shirts and swords, and others—five mounted soldiers including Sheriff Richard de Glanville—charged out from the nearest trees.

Stooping swiftly, Bran picked up Odo, dragging the frightened monk to his feet and driving him headlong into the safety of the greenwood. There came the sound of leaves rustling and branches thrashing in the forest nearby, and they were gone.

The mounted knights galloped to the edge of the wood and halted, listening.

All that could be heard were the groans of the wounded and dying. The marshal and Sergeant Jeremias ventured slowly out from behind their shields. "See to those men, Sergeant," ordered Gysburne. To the knight who lay unharmed among the bodies, he called, "Get up and find the horses."

"Are we going after the outlaws, Sire?" inquired the knight.

"Why, by the bloody rood?" cried the marshal. "To let them continue to practice their cursed archery on us? Think, man! They're hiding in the trees!"

"But I thought the abbot said——" began the knight.

"Obey your orders, de Tourneau!" snapped the marshal irritably. "Forget what the abbot said. Just do as you're told—and take Racienne with you."

The two knights clumped off together, and Gysburne turned to see Sheriff de Glanville and his bailiff turning back from the edge of the wood. "Have no fear," called the marshal. "The outlaws have gone. You are safe now."

The sheriff stiffened at the insinuation. "It was not for fear that we held back."

"No," granted the marshal, "of course not. Why would I think that? You merely mislaid your sword, perhaps, or I am certain you would have been in the fore rank, leading the charge."

"Enough, Gysburne," snarled the sheriff. "The last time I looked, you were crawling on your hands and knees like a baby."

The abbot shouted from the clearing, cutting short what promised to be a lively discussion. "De Glanville! Gysburne! Did you get him? Is he dead?"

"No," answered the marshal, "he got away." He promptly amended this, adding, "They got away. It was a trap; they were waiting for us."

Abbot Hugo turned his gaze to the bodies lying in the long grass. His face darkened. "Are you telling me you've lost four men and the outlaws have escaped again?" He swung around to face the marshal. "How did this happen?" he shouted.

"You ask the wrong man, Abbot," replied Gysburne coolly. "We did our part. It was the sheriff who failed to attack."

"*You* were supposed to draw them from hiding, Abbot, remember?" said the sheriff darkly. "Since you *failed* in the first order, no good purpose would be served by pursuing the second." He pointed to the bodies on the ground. "You can see what that accomplished. If I had attacked, it would have been at the cost of more men, and more lives wasted."

"If you had attacked as planned," the marshal said, his voice rising, "we could have taken him and we'd not be standing here now heaping blame on each other."

"There is plenty of blame to go around, it seems to me," retorted de Glanville angrily. "But I'll not own more than my share. The plan was flawed from the beginning. We should have anticipated that they would not be drawn out so easily. And now they know we have no intention of accepting their ridiculous peace offer. We've gained nothing." Turning away from the other two, he shouted for his men to load the bodies of the dead onto the backs of their horses and return to Saint Martin's. He climbed into the saddle, then called, "Gysburne! I turn my duties over to you while I am away. Bailiff will assist you."

De Glanville wheeled his horse.

"Where are you going?" demanded the marshal.

"To Londein," came the answer. "I am the king's man, and I require soldiers and supplies to deal with these outlaws."

"We should discuss this," Gysburne objected.

"There is nothing to discuss. We need more soldiers, and I'm going to get them. I should return within the fortnight."

Marshal Guy looked to the abbot. "Let him go," said Hugo. "He is right."

"I would not linger here any longer if I were you," called the sheriff. "We are finished, and it is not safe." He snapped the reins, and the big horse bounded off.

"Do not underestimate me, Sheriff," muttered Abbot Hugo, watching him go. "I am far from finished . . . very far from finished."

Marshal Guy de Gysburne walked over to where a knight had been slain; there was blood in the grass. He picked up the dead man's sword and stuck it in his belt. "You can stay if you like, Abbot, but they are probably watching from the forest."

Casting a hasty glance over his shoulder, the abbot hurried to rejoin his bodyguard and scuttled back to the abbey in undignified retreat.

PART TWO

Came Little John through the forest that morn,
    And chanc'd upon poor Rhiban Hud,
So high on his back he carries him to
    A priest on the edge of the woode.

"God save you, Fryer Tuck," quod John.
    "A handsome fish I've here.
His length's as longe from snout to tail
    As any I've seen this yere."

"Then don't delay, friend John," quod Tuck,
    "But lay him here on the hearthe.
Let's get him skinned and then get him cleaned
    And warmed up quick and smart."

Young Rhiban quickly mended himself
    At Fryer Tuck's strong, healing hands.
And when he had sense, the two hearde account
    Of the change that had passed in those lands.

"For twenty long summers," quoth Rhiban, "by God,
    My arrows I here have let fly.
Methinks it quite strange, that within the march,
    A reeve has more power than I.

"This forest and vale I consider my own,
And these folk a king think of me;
I therefore declare—and so solemnly swear:
    I will live to see each of them free."

"By t'rood, this is a most noble sport,"
    John Little did him proclaim.
"I'll stand with thee and fight 'til death!"
    "And I," quod Tuck, "The same!"

"Then send you bold captains to head up our men
    And meet in the greenwoode hereon:
Mérian, Llech-ley, and Alan a'Dale,
    Thomas, and Much Miller's son."

CHAPTER 8

Two riders picked their way carefully along the rock-lined riverbed, one in front of the other, silent, vigilant. Dressed in drab, faces hidden beneath wide-brimmed, shapeless hats, they might have been hunters hoping to raise some game along the river or, more likely, a party of merchants making for a distant market. Strange merchants, however—they shunned the nearby town, going out of their way to avoid it.

It was Bran's idea to appear as wayfarers simply passing through, in the hopes of attracting as little notice as possible. He watched the hilltops and ridgeways on either side of the valley, while Tuck remained alert to anyone approaching from the rear. Overhead, a brown buzzard soared through the empty air, its shadow rippling over the smooth, cloud-dappled slopes. Ahead the river forked into two branches: one wide and shallow, one little more than a rill snaking through a narrow, brush-choked defile. Upon reaching the place where the two streams divided, Bran paused.

"Which way?" Tuck said, reining in beside him. Odo halted a few paces behind.

"You ask me that?" replied Bran with a grin. "And still you call yourself a priest?"

"I am a priest," affirmed Tuck, "and I do ask you—for, all evidence to the contrary, I cannot read the minds of men, only their hearts." He regarded the two courses. "Which way do we go?"

"The narrow way, of course," answered Bran. "'Narrow is the way and hard the road that leads to salvation . . .' Isn't that the way it goes?"

"'Straight is the gate and narrow the way that leadeth to life, and there be few that find it,'" the friar corrected. "You should pay better attention when the Holy Script is read."

"We'll have to walk from here," Bran said, climbing down from the saddle. "But when we reach the end, we will be beyond the borders of Elfael and out of reach of de Glanville's soldiers." He glanced at Odo. The young priest had maintained a gloomy silence since climbing into the saddle. "Do either of you want to rest a little before we move on?"

"My thanks, but no—a chance to quit this saddle is all I need just now," Tuck said, easing himself down from the saddle. "Come, Odo. A change is as good as a rest, is it not?" He wiped the sweat from his face. "Although, to be sure, a jar of ale would not go amiss."

"When day is done," said Bran, starting into the gorge. "This way, you two."

They had left the forest before dawn, crossing the open ground to the south of the caer while it was still dark, quickly losing themselves in the seamed valleys of Elfael. They proceeded ever northward, keeping out of sight of the fortress and town until both were well behind them—and even then Bran continued with all caution. A chance encounter with a wayward Ffreinc party was to be avoided at all costs.

Leading the horses, they resumed their trek, picking their way along the stream. It was slow going because rocks, brush, and nettles filled the defile, making each step a small ordeal. The bowlegged priest struggled to keep up with his long-legged companions, scrambling over the rocks and dodging thorny branches, all the while ruing the turn of events that had made this journey necessary.

"We acted in good faith," Bran had declared in the council following the abbot's misguided ambush. "But Hugo sought to betray us—once again. It is only by God's favour that Odo and I escaped unharmed and none of our men were killed or wounded."

Bran and his archers had just returned from their encounter with the Ffreinc, and one glance at their scowling faces gave everyone to know that all was not well.

Tuck, with Mérian a close step behind, was there to meet the returning peace party. "God love you, Iwan, what happened?" Tuck asked, snagging hold of the big man's arm as he came through the blasted oak. "Did they fail to ring the bell?"

"Nay, Friar," answered the champion, shaking his head slowly. "They rang the bell for all to hear—but then attacked us anyway."

"They were lying in wait for us," said Siarles, joining them. "Hiding in the forest."

"Gysburne and his men showed themselves for the black devils they are," said Scarlet.

"Aye, and the sheriff too," added Siarles. "Dressed up as monks, some of 'em."

"Even so, we honoured our part," said Iwan. "We did not draw on them until they attacked Bran."

"Was anyone hurt?" Tuck glanced quickly at the other archers trooping into the settlement. There was no blood showing; all seemed to be in ruddy good health.

"No hurt to anyone but themselves," Scarlet pointed out. "A fella'd a thought they'd have learnt a little respect for a Welsh bowman by now. Seems they are a thick lot, these Ffreinc, say what you will."

The friar heard these words, and his heart fell like a stone dropped into a bottomless well. The slender hope that the abbot would accept the offered peace sank instantly, swallowed in the knowledge that Abbot Hugo would never be appeased. In light of this new outrage, he felt the fool for even imagining such a thing possible.

"You did what Christian duty required, and it will be accounted to your credit," Tuck assured them lamely. "God will yet reward you for remaining true to your part."

"No doubt, Friar," replied Siarles. "The same way he helps them who help themselves, methinks."

"I do not blame you for being disappointed," Tuck said, "but you should not place the failure at the Almighty's feet, when it—"

"Spare us, Tuck," snapped Bran. He and Odo, the last to arrive, passed the others as they stood talking. "I am not of a mind to hear it." Addressing the men, he said, "Get something to eat, all of you. Then I want my advisors to come to me and we will hold council again—this time it is a council of war."

The six archers moved off to find some food, leaving Tuck, Mérian, and the others looking on in dismay.

"I feared this might happen," said Mérian. "Still, we had to try." She looked to the friar for assurance. "We *did* have to try."

"We did," confirmed the priest. "And we were right." He glanced at the young woman beside him. How lovely she was; how noble of face and form. And how determined. A pang of regret pierced him to see her once-fine clothes now stained and growing threadbare from their hard use in the greenwood. She was made for finer things, to be sure, but had cast her lot with the outlaw band; and her fate, like all who called the forest home, was that of a fugitive.

"Ah, my soul," he sighed, feeling the weight of their failure settle upon him. "So much hardship and sadness could have been avoided if only that blasted abbot had agreed."

"I had my hopes, too, Friar," offered Mérian. "My father has ruled under Baron Neufmarché these many years—to the benefit of both, I think. It can be done—I know it can. But Hugo de Rainault is a wicked man, and there is no reasoning with him. He will never leave, never surrender an inch of ground until he is dead."

"Alas, I fear you've struck to the heart of it," confessed Tuck, shaking his head sadly. "No doubt that is where the trouble lies."

"Where, Friar?"

"In the hearts of ever-sinful men, my lady," he told her. "In the all-too-wicked human heart."

After the men had eaten, those who were counted among King Raven's advisors joined their lord in his hut. As they took their places around the fire ring, Bran said, "We need more men, and I am going to—"

More men, thought Tuck, and remembered what it was that he had learned from the abbot. "Good Lord!" he cried, starting up at the memory. "Forgive me," he said quickly as all eyes turned towards him, "but I have just remembered something that might be useful."

Bran regarded him, waiting for him to continue.

"It is just that—" Glancing around, he said to Iwan, "How many soldiers did you say the abbot and sheriff had with them?"

"No more'n twenty," replied the champion.

"At most," confirmed Siarles.

"Then that is all they have," said Tuck. "Twenty men—that is all that are left to them following the two attacks." He went on to explain about meeting with the abbot, and how Hugo had let slip that he no longer had enough men to defend the town. "So, unless I am much mistaken, those who attacked you are all that remain of the troops Baron de Braose left here."

"And there are fewer now," Siarles pointed out. "Maybe by four or five. He can have no more than fifteen or sixteen under his command." He turned wondering eyes towards Bran. "My lord, we can defeat them. We can drive them out."

"We can take back control of the cantref," echoed Iwan. "One more battle and it would be ours."

They fell to arguing how this might be accomplished, then, but arrived always at the same place where the discussion had begun.

"Gysburne may have only sixteen left," Bran pointed out. "But you can believe he won't be drawn into open battle with us. Nor can we take the town or the fortress, for all we are only six able-bodied bowmen. So, it comes to this: we need more men, and I am going to raise them." He paused. "First things first. Iwan, I want you and Owain and Rhoddi to watch the road—day and night. Nothing is to pass through the forest without our leave. All travellers are to be stopped. Any goods or weapons they carry will be taken from them."

"And if they refuse?" asked the champion.

"Use whatever force you deem necessary," Bran replied. "But only that and no more. All who comply willingly are to be sent on their way in peace."

"Nothing will get past us, my lord. I know what to do."

"Siarles," said Bran, "you and Tomas are to begin making arrows. We'll need as many as we can get—and we'll need bows too."

"And where will we be getting the wood for all these bows and arrows?" asked Siarles.

"Wood for bows, I know, and where to find it," Angharad said, speaking up from her place behind Bran's chair. "We will bring all you need, Gwion Bach and I."

Bran nodded. "The rest of the Grellon are to be trained to the longbow."

"Women too?" asked Mérian.

"Yes," confirmed Bran. "Women too." He turned to Will Scarlet. "Until your hand is healed, you will teach others what you know about the bow."

"That much is easily done," said Scarlet. "It's the trainin' that takes the time."

"Then start at once. Today."

Owain, one of the newer members of the council, asked, "You said you meant to raise more men. What is in your mind, my lord, if you don't mind my asking?"

"I have kinsmen among my mother's people in Gwynedd," replied Bran. "I mean to start there. Once the word spreads that we are gathering a force to overthrow the Ffreinc, I have no doubt we'll soon get all the warriors we need."

"There are warriors nearby that are yours for the asking," Mérian pointed out. "I have but to go to my father and——"

"No," said Bran firmly.

"The fact is, my father—"

"Your father is a vassal of Baron Neufmarché," Bran said in a pained tone, "a fact you seem determined to ignore."

Mérian opened her mouth to object, but Bran cut her off, saying, "That is the end of it."

Mérian glared at him from under lowered brows, but gave in without another word.

"Well then," said Bran, declaring himself satisfied with the preparations. "Be about your work, everyone. If all goes well, Tuck and I will return with a war band large enough to conquer the Ffreinc and force their surrender." As the others shuffled out, Bran called Tuck to him. "I will see to the horses, and you take care of the provisions—enough for four days, I make it."

The friar spent the rest of the day assembling the necessary provisions for their journey. While he was scraping together the few items they would need for making camp, Scarlet came to him. "I am worried about Odo," he said, sitting down on a nearby stump. "That scrape this morning has pitched the poor fella into the stew."

"Oh? I am sorry to hear it," replied Tuck. "Has he said anything?"

"Not so much," said Will. "He wouldn't. But if there was ever a creature ill fashioned for the wildwood, that's Odo through and through."

Tuck paused, considering what Scarlet was telling him. "What do you think we should do?"

"Well, seeing as you are heading north, I was wondering if it might be best for everyone if you took Odo along."

"To Gwynedd?"

"Aye," said Scarlet, "but only as far as that monastery with the old bishop."

"Saint Tewdrig's."

"That's the one. I know he'd fare better there, and no doubt the way things are with the folk so hard-pressed everywhere here-abouts, he'd be a better help there than here, if you see what I mean."

"He's suffering, you say."

"I've seen whipped dogs more cheerful."

"Well then," said Tuck. "I'll speak to Bran and see what we can do." He paused, then asked, "Why did you bring this to me?"

"I deemed it a priest thing—like confession," replied Scarlet, ris-ing. "And Odo would never be able to lift his head again if he thought Bran reckoned him a coward."

Tuck smiled. "You're a good friend, William Scatlocke. Consider it done, and Bran will think no ill of Brother Odo."

The travellers spent a last night in the forest, departing early enough to cross the Vale of Elfael before dawn.

Only Angharad was awake to see them off, which she did in her peculiar fashion. Raising her staff, she held it aloft, and blessed them with a prayer that put Tuck in mind of those he had heard as a child in the north country.

The three climbed into their saddles—Bran swinging up easily, Odo taking a bit more effort, and Tuck with the aid of a stump for a mounting block—and with a final farewell, quickly disappeared into the gloaming. By the time the sun was showing above the hori-zon, the riders had passed the Ffreinc-held Saint Martin's and were well on their way. Now, as the sun sailed high over head, they eked their way over bare rocks along the edge of the rill and, a little while later, passed beyond the borders of Elfael and into the neighbouring cantref of Builth.

It was well past midday when they came within sight of the monastery, and in a little while stood in the yard of Saint Tewdrig's introducing the young Ffreinc priest to Bishop Asaph, who professed himself overjoyed to receive an extra pair of hands. "As you see," he told them, "we are run off our feet day and night caring for the souls who come to us. We will put him to work straightaway, never fear." He fixed Bran with a look of deepest concern. "What is this I am hearing about you declaring war on Abbot Hugo?"

"It is true," Bran allowed, and explained how the English king had reneged on his promise to restore Bran's throne, appointing the abbot and sheriff as his regents instead. "We are on our way north to rally the tribes."

The ageing bishop shook his head sadly. "Is there no other way?"

"If there was," Bran conceded, "we are beyond recalling it now." He went on to tell how the Black Abbot had rebuffed his offer of peace. "That was Tuck's idea."

"We had to try," offered the friar. "For Jesus' sake we had to try."

"Indeed," sighed the bishop.

They stayed with the monks that night, and bidding Odo farewell, they departed early the next morning. They rode easily, passing the morning in a companionable silence until they came to a shady spot under a large outcrop of stone, where Bran decided to stop to rest and water the horses, and have a bite to eat before moving on once more. The going was slow, and the sun was disappearing beyond the hill line to the west when they at last began to search for a good place to make camp for the night—finding a secluded hollow beside a brook where an apple tree grew; the apples were green still, and tart, but hard to resist, and there was good water for the horses. While Bran gathered wood for the fire, Tuck tethered the animals so they could graze in the long grass around the tree, and then set about preparing a meal.

"We should reach Arwysteli tomorrow," Bran said, biting into a small green apple. The two had finished a supper of pork belly and beans, and were stretched out beneath the boughs bending with fruit. "And Powys the day after."

"Oh?" Tuck queried. "We are not stopping?"

"Perhaps on the way back," Bran said. "I am that keen to get on to Bangor. I know no one in these cantrefs, and it might be easier to get men if on our return we are accompanied by a sizeable host already."

This sounded reasonable to the friar. "How long has it been since you've seen your mother's people?" he asked.

Bran gnawed on his sour apple for a moment, then said, "Quite a long time—a year or two after my mother died, it must have been. My father wanted to return some of her things to her kinfolk, so we went up and I met them then."

"You were—what? Eight, nine years old?" Tuck ventured.

"Something like that," he allowed. "But it will make no difference. Once they have heard what we intend, they will join us, never fear."

They spent a quiet night and moved on at dawn, passing through Builth without seeing another living soul, and pressing quickly on into Arwysteli and Powys, where they stopped for the night in a settlement called Llanfawydden. Tuck was happy to see that the hamlet had a fine wooden church and a stone monk's cell set in a grove of beeches, though the village consisted of nothing more than a ring of wattle-and-mud houses encircling a common grazing area. After a brief word from the local priest, the chief of the village took them in and fed them at his table, and gave them a bed for the night. The chieftain and his wife and three sons slept on the floor beside the hearth.

The travellers found the family amiable enough. They fed them well, entertained them with news of local doings, and asked no questions about who their guests were, or what their business might be. However, when they were preparing to leave the next morning, one of the younger lads—upon learning that they had travelled from Elfael—could not help asking whether they knew anything about King Raven.

"I might have heard a tale or two," Bran allowed, smiling.

The boy persisted in his questions despite the frowns from his mother and brothers. "Is it true what they say? Is he a very bad creature?"

"Bad for the Ffreinc, it would seem," Bran said. "By all accounts King Raven does seem a most mysterious bird. Do you know him hereabouts?"

"Nay," replied the middle lad, shaking his head sadly. "Only what folk say."

One of his older brothers spoke up. "We heard he has killed more'n two hundred Ffreinc—"

"Swoops on 'em from the sky and *spears* 'em with his beak," added the one who had raised the subject in the first place.

"Boys!" said the mother, embarrassed by her sons' forthright enthusiasm. "You have said enough."

"No harm," chuckled Bran, much amused by this. "I don't know about spearing knights with his beak, but at least the Ffreinc are afraid of him—and that's good enough for me."

"They say he helps the Cymry," continued the younger one. "Gives 'em all the treasure."

"That he does," Tuck agreed. "Or, so I've heard."

The travellers took their leave of their hosts shortly after that, resuming their journey northward. The day was bright and fair, the breeze warm out of the south, and the track good. Bran and Tuck rode easily along, talking of this and that.

"Your fame is spreading," Tuck observed. "If they know King Raven here, they'll soon enough know him everywhere."

Bran dismissed the comment with a shrug. "Children are readily persuaded."

"Not at all," the friar insisted. "Where do children hear these things except from their elders? People know about King Raven. They are talking about him."

"For all the good it does," Bran pointed out. "King Raven may be better liked than William the Red, but it is the Red King's foot on our neck all the same. The Ffreinc may be wary of the Phantom of the Wood, but it hasn't changed a blessed thing."

"Perhaps not," Tuck granted, "but I was not thinking of the Ffreinc just now. I was thinking of the Cymry."

Bran gave an indifferent shrug.

"King Raven has given them hope," insisted Tuck. "He has shown them that the invaders can be resisted. You must be proud of your feathered creation."

"He had his uses," Bran admitted. "But, like all things, that usefulness has reached its end."

"Truly?"

"King Raven has done what he can do. Now it is time to take up bows and strap on swords, and join battle with the enemy openly, in the clear light of day."

"Perhaps," Tuck granted, "but do not think to hang up your feathered cloak and long-beaked mask just yet."

"There will be no more skulking around the greenwood like a ghost," Bran declared. "That is over."

"Certain of that, are you?" Tuck said. "Just you mark my words, Bran ap Brychan, King Raven will fly again before our cause is won."

CHAPTER 9

Long before Rome turned its eyes toward the Isle of the Mighty, Bangor, in the far north of Gwynedd, was an ancient and revered capital of kings. There, among the heavy overhanging boughs of venerable oaks, the druids taught their varied and subtle arts, establishing the first schools in the west. That was long ago. The druids were gone, but the schools remained; and now those aged trees sheltered one of the oldest monasteries in Britain, and for all anyone knew, all of Christendom. Indeed, the proud tribes of Gwynedd had sent a bishop and some priests to Emperor Constantine's great council half a world away in Nicea—as the inhabitants of north Wales never tired of boasting.

When Bran's father—Brychan ap Tewdwr, a prince of the south—found himself in want of a wife, it was to Gwynedd that he had come looking. And in Bangor he had discovered his queen: Rhian, a much-loved princess of her tribe. While she had lived, ties between the two kingdoms north and south had remained strong.

Thus, Bran expected to find a hearty welcome among his mother's kinsmen.

After three days on the road, the two travellers drew near the town and the pathways multiplied and diverged. So they stopped to ask directions from the first person they met—a squint-eyed shepherd sitting under a beech tree at the foot of a grassy hill.

"You'll be wanting to see your folk, I expect," observed the shepherd.

"It is the reason we came," Bran told him, a hint of exasperation colouring his tone. Having already explained that his mother had been the daughter of a local chieftain, he had asked if the fellow knew where any of her people might be found.

"Well," replied the shepherd. He craned his neck around to observe his sheep grazing on the hillside behind him, "you won't find any of 'em in town yonder."

"No?" wondered Bran. "Why not?"

"They en't there!" hooted the man, whistling through his few snaggled teeth.

"And why would that be?" wondered Bran. "If you know, perhaps I could persuade you to tell me."

"No mystery there, Brother," replied the shepherd. "They've all gone over to Aberffraw, en't they."

"Have they indeed," said Bran. "And why is that?"

"It's all to do with that Ffreinc earl, 'n' tryin' to stay out o' his reach, d'ye ken?"

"I think so," replied Bran doubtfully. "And where might this Aberffraw be?"

"Might be anywhere," the shepherd replied. His tanned, weather-beaten face cracked into a smile as he tapped his nose knowingly.

"Just what I was thinking," remarked Bran. "Even so, I'll wager that *you* know, and could tell me if you had a mind to."

"You'd win that wager, Brother, I do declare."

"And will you yet tell me?"

The shepherd became sly. "How much would you have wagered?"

"A penny."

"Then I'll be havin' o' that," the man replied.

Bran dug in his purse and brought out a silver coin. He held it up. "This for the benefit of your wide and extensive knowledge."

"Done!" cried the shepherd, delighted with his bargain. He snatched the coin from Bran's fingertips and said, "Aberffraw is on the Holy Isle, en't it. Just across the narrows there and hidden round t'other side o' the headland. You won't see it this side, for it is all hidden away neat-like."

Bran thanked the shepherd and wished him good fortune, but Tuck was not yet satisfied. "When was the last time you went to church, my friend?"

The shepherd scratched his grizzled jaw. "Well now, difficult to say, that."

"Difficult, no doubt, because it has been so long you don't remember," ventured Tuck. Without waiting for a reply, he said, "No matter. Kneel down and bow your head. Quickly now; I'll not spend all day at it."

The shamefaced shepherd complied readily enough, and Tuck said a prayer for him, blessed his flock, and rode on with the stern admonition for the herdsman to get himself to church next holy day without fail.

At Bangor, they stopped to rest and eat and gather what information they could about the state of affairs in the region. There was no tavern in the town, much less an inn, and Tuck was losing hope of finding a soothing libation when he glimpsed a clay jar hanging from a cord over the door of a house a few steps off the square. "There!" he cried, to his great relief, and made for the place, which turned out to be the house of a widowed alewife who served the little town a passing fair brew and simple fare. Tuck threw himself from his saddle and ducked inside, returning a moment later with generous bowls of bubbly brown ale in each hand and a round loaf of bread under his arm. "God is good," he said, passing a bowl to Bran. "Amen!"

The two travellers established themselves on the bench outside the door. Too early for the alewife's roast leg of lamb, they dulled their appetites with a few lumps of soft cheese fried in a pan with onions, into which they dipped their bread. While they ate and drank, they talked to some of the curious townsfolk who came along to greet the visitors—quickly informing them that they'd arrived at a bad time, owing to the overbearing presence of the Earl of Cestre, a Ffreinc nobleman by the name of Hugh d'Avranches.

"Wolf Hugh is a rough pile," said the ironsmith from the smithy across the square. He had seen the travellers ride in and had come to inquire if their horses needed shoeing or any tack needed mending.

"That he is," agreed his neighbour.

"You call him Wolf," observed Tuck. "How did he come by that?"

"You ever see a wolf that wasn't hungry?" said the smith. "Ravening beast like that'll devour everything in sight—same as the earl."

"He's a rough one, right enough," agreed his friend solemnly. "A rogue through and through."

"As you say," replied Bran. "Here's to hoping we don't meet up with him." He offered his bowl to the smith.

The smith nodded and raised the bowl. "Here's to hoping." He took a hearty draught and passed the bowl to his friend, who drained it.

When they had finished, Bran and Tuck made their way down to the small harbour below the town. A fair-sized stretch of timber and planking, the wharf was big enough to serve seagoing ships and boats plying the coastal waters between the mainland and Ynys Môn, known as Holy Island, just across the narrow channel. They found a boatman who agreed to ferry them and their horses to the island. It was no great distance, and they were soon on dry land and mounted again. They followed the rising path that led up behind the promontory, over the headland, and down to a very pleasant little valley on the other side: Aberffraw and, tucked into a fold between the encircling hills, the settlement of Celyn Garth.

Less a town than a large estate consisting of an enormous timber fortress and half a dozen houses—along with barns, cattle pens, granaries, and all surrounded by apple orchards and bean, turnip, and barley fields scraped from the ever-encroaching forest which blanketed the hills and headlands—it had become the royal seat of the northern Welsh and was, as the shepherd had suggested, perfectly suited to keeping out of the voracious earl's sight.

Bran and Tuck rode directly to the fortress and made themselves known to the short, thick-necked old man who appeared to serve the royal household as gateman and porter. With a voice like dry gravel, he invited them to enter the yard and asked them to wait while he informed his lord of their arrival.

Whatever life the kings of North Wales had known in earlier times, it was clear that it was much reduced now. As in England, the arrival of the Normans meant hardship and misery in draughts too great to swallow. The Cymry of the noble houses suffered along with the rest of the country, and Celyn Garth was proof of this. The yard was lumpy, rutted, and weedy; the roof of the king's hall sagged, its thatch ratty and mildewed; the gates and every other door on the nearly derelict outbuildings stood in need of hingeing and rehanging.

"I hope we find the king well," said Bran doubtfully.

"I hope we find him at his supper," said Tuck.

What they found was Llewelyn ap Owain, a swarthy, nimble Welshman who received them graciously and prevailed upon them to stay the night. But he was not the king.

"It's Gruffydd you're looking for, is it?" he said. "Aye, who else? It pains me, friend, to inform you that our king is a captive." Llewelyn explained over a hot supper of roast pork shanks and baked apples. They were seated at the hearth end of the near-empty hall. Their host sat at table with his guests, while his wife and daughters served the meal. "He's held prisoner by Earl Hugh, may God rot his teeth."

"Wolf Hugh?" asked Bran. "Is that the man?"

"Aye, Cousin, that's the fellow—Hugh d'Avranches, Earl of Cestre—devious as the devil, and cruel as Cain with a toothache. He's a miserable old spoiler, is our Hugh, with a heart full of torment for each and all he meets."

"How long has Gruffydd been captive?" wondered Tuck.

Llewelyn tapped his teeth as he reckoned the tally. "Must be eight years or more, I guess," he said. "Maybe nine already."

"Has anyone seen him since he was taken prisoner?" Tuck asked.

"Oh, aye," replied Llewelyn. "We send a priest most high holy days. The earl allows our Gruffydd to receive food and clothing and such since it whittles down the cost of keeping an expensive captive. We use those visits for what benefit we can get."

Bran nodded; he and Tuck shared a glance, and each could sense the sharp disappointment of the other. "Who's ruling in Gruffydd's place?" asked Bran, swallowing his frustration.

Llewelyn paused to consider.

It was a simple enough question, and Tuck wondered at their host's hesitation. "You must be looking at him, I reckon," Llewelyn confessed at last. "Although I make no claim myself, you understand." He spread his hands as if to express his innocence. "I merely keep the boards warm for Gruffydd, so to speak. I am loyal to my lord, while he lives, and would never usurp his authority."

"Which is why the Ffreinc keep him alive, no doubt," observed Bran. As long as Gruffydd drew breath, no one else could occupy his empty throne, much less gather his broken tribe.

"But people do come to me for counsel and guidance," Llewelyn offered, "and I see it my duty to oblige however I can."

"I understand," said Bran. He fell silent, contemplating the depth of his difficulty. The kingdom of Gwynedd, leaderless and adrift, was in no shape to supply a war host to help fight a war beyond its borders. He realized with increasing despair that he had come all this way for nothing.

"So then, I'll be sending for your relations," said Llewelyn, breaking the silence. "They'll be that glad to see you."

"And I them," replied Bran, and complimented his host on his thoughtfulness. "Thank you, Llewelyn; I am in your debt."

They finished supper, and the guests were given their own quarters so they would not have to share with the rest of Llewelyn's household, who mostly slept on benches and reed mats in the hall.

The next morning—on the counsel and guidance of their host—Bran and Tuck rode out to get the measure of the land and people of the northern part of Gwynedd, and to speak frankly without being overheard.

"This is going to be more difficult than I thought," Bran admitted when, after riding for a goodly time, they stopped to water the horses at a stream flowing down a rocky, gorse-covered hill and into Môr Iwerddon, the Sea of Ireland, gleaming blue under a fine early autumn sky.

"Raising an army of king's men with the king in an enemy prison?" Tuck queried. "What is difficult about that?"

"I don't think he even *has* an army."

"Well, that would make it slightly more tricky, I suppose," remarked Tuck.

"Yes," mused Bran. "Tricky." He walked a few paces away, then back. Glancing up suddenly, he grinned that twisted, roguish smile that Tuck knew meant trouble. More than that, however, it was the first time in many, many days that Tuck had seen him smile, and the friar had almost forgotten the magic of that lopsided grin—truly, it was as if a slumbering spirit had awakened in that instant to reanimate a young man only half-alive until now. He was once again himself, Rhi Bran y Hud, alive with mischief and alert to possibility. "That's it, friend friar—a trick!"

"Eh?"

"To raise a king's army from a king who is in prison."

Tuck caught his meaning at once.

Gathering up the reins, Bran stepped quickly to his horse, raised his foot to the stirrup, and swung up into the saddle. "Come, Tuck, why are you dragging your feet?"

Why, indeed? Tuck walked stiffly to his horse and, after leading it to a nearby rock big enough to serve as a mounting block, struggled into the saddle. "You'll get us killed, you know," the priest complained. "Me most of all."

Bran laughed. "A little more faith would become you, Friar."

"I have faith enough for any three—and I'll thump the man who says me nay. But you go jumping into a bear trap with both feet, and it'll not be faith you feel chomping on your leg bones!"

Grabbing up the reins, he raised his eyes towards heaven. "Is there no rest for the weary?" he sighed. By the time he regained the path, Bran was already racing away.

On their return to Celyn Garth, Bran secluded himself in his quarters and set Tuck to finding certain items that he needed. When they had assembled everything necessary, Bran went to work and the change was swiftly effected. It was nearly time for the evening meal when he emerged, and Tuck accompanied him to the hall where Llewelyn was waiting with some of Bran's relations he had invited especially to meet their long-lost kinsman. There were seven of them: three young men in the blue-and-red checked tunics of the north country; three of middling age in tall boots and leather jackets over their linen shirts; and one old man, bald as a bean, in a pale robe of undyed wool.

"Lead the way, Tuck," Bran murmured. "And remember, I speak no Cymry."

"Oh, I'll remember," Tuck retorted. "It's yourself you should be reminding."

Stepping into the hall, the little friar approached the long table where the men were already gathered over their welcome cups. Llewelyn took one look at the cleric and his companion and rose quickly.

"Friar Aethelfrith," he said, "I did not know you brought a guest. Come, sit down." To the unexpected visitor, he said, "Be welcome in this house. Pray, sit and share a cup with us."

Tuck kept his eyes on Llewelyn, who seemed to recognize something familiar in the young man beside him. But if the long black robes did not fully disguise him, then the sallow, sombre expression, the slightly hunched shoulders and inwardly bending frame, the close-shorn hair and gleaming white scalp of his tonsure, the large sad eyes, hesitant step, and almost timid way he held his head—taken all together, the appearance was so unlike Bran ap Brychan that Llewelyn did not trust his first impression and withheld judgement on the newcomer's identity.

For his part, Bran inclined his head in humble acceptance and offered, as it seemed to those looking on, a somewhat melancholy smile—as if the slender young man carried some secret grief within and it weighed heavily on his heart. He turned to Tuck, and the others also looked to the priest as for an explanation.

"My lords," said Tuck, "allow me to present to you my dear friend, Father Dominic."

CHAPTER 10

Speaking with the humble, yet confident authority that one would expect of a papal envoy, the slender young man introduced as Father Dominic charmed his listeners with tales of his travels in the service of the Holy Father and his dealings with kings and cardinals. It fell to Tuck, of course, to translate his stories for the benefit of his listeners since Bran spoke in the curious, chiefly meaningless jibber-jabber of broken Latin that passed for the language of the Italian nobility among folk who had never heard it. Tuck was able to keep one step ahead of his listeners by his many sudden consultations—to clarify some word or thought—where Bran, as Father Dominic, would then whisper the bare bones of what his struggling translator was to say next. Such was Father Dominic's winsome manner that Tuck found himself almost believing in the charming lies, even knowing them to be spun of purest nonsense and embellished by his own ready tongue.

Father Dominic revealed that he was on a mission from Rome,

and explained that he had come to the region to make acquaintance with churchmen among the tribes of Britain who remained outside Norman influence. This was announced in a casual way, but the subtlety was not lost on his listeners. Father Dominic, speaking through Tuck, told them that because of the delicate nature of his inquiry, he was pleased to travel without his usual large entourage to enable him to go where he would, unnoticed and unannounced. The Mother Church was reaching out to all her children in Britain, he said, the silent and suffering as well their noisier, more overbearing, and belligerent brothers.

All the while, their distracted host would glance towards the empty doorway. Finally, when Bran's absence could no longer be comfortably ignored, Llewelyn spoke up. "Forgive me for asking, Friar Aethelfrith, but I begin to worry about our cousin. Is he well? Perhaps he has fallen ill and requires attention."

Bran ap Brychan's kinsmen had done him the honour of travelling a considerable distance to greet their cousin from the south, and although beguiled by the unexpected arrival of a genuine emissary of the pope in Rome, they could not help but wonder about their cousin's puzzling absence. Father Dominic heard Llewelyn's question, too, and without giving any indication that he knew what had been said, he smiled, raised his hands in blessing to those who sat at the table with him, then begged to be excused, as he was feeling somewhat tired from his journey.

"Certainly, we understand," said Llewelyn, jumping to his feet. "I will have quarters prepared for you at once. If you will kindly wait but a moment—"

Father Dominic waved off his host, saying, through Tuck, "Pray do not trouble yourself. I shall find my own way."

With that he turned and, despite Llewelyn's continued protests, walked to the door of the hall, where he paused with his hand on the latch. He stood there for a moment. Then, with the others looking on, stepped back from the door, shook himself around and—wonder of wonders—seemed to grow both larger and stronger before the startled eyes of his audience. When he turned around it was no longer Father Dominic who stood before them, but Bran himself once more—albeit berobed as a priest, and with a shorn and shaven pate.

Llewelyn was speechless, and all around the board stared in astonishment at the deception so skilfully executed under their very noses. They looked at one another in baffled bemusement. When Llewelyn finally recovered his tongue, he contrived to sound angry— though his tone fell short by a long throw. "How now, Cousin? What is this devilment?"

"Forgive me if I have caused offence," said Bran, finding his own true voice at last, "but I knew no better way to convince you all."

"Convince?" wondered Llewelyn. "And what, pray, are we to be convinced of, Cousin?"

Bran shrugged off the black robe, resumed his place at the board, and poured himself a cup of ale, saying, "That I will tell, and gladly." Smiling broadly, he raised his cup to the men around the board. "First, I would know these kinsmen of mine a little better."

"As soon said as done," replied Llewelyn, some of his former goodwill returning. Indicating the elder man sitting beside him, he said, "This is Hywel Hen, Bishop of Bangor, and the granduncle of young Brocmael beside him; Hywel was brother to your mother's father. Next is Cynwrig, from Aberffraw, and his son Ifor. Then we have Trahaern, Meurig, and Llygad from Ynys Môn. Meurig is married to your mother's younger cousin, Myfanwy."

"God with you all," said Bran. "I know your names, and I see my dear mother in your faces. I am pleased to meet you all."

"We've met before, my boy," said Hywel Hen, "though I don't expect you to remember. You were but a bare-bottomed infant in your mother's arms at the time. I well remember your mother, of course— and your father. Fares the king well, does he?"

"If it lay in my power to bring you greetings from Lord Brychan, trust that nothing would please me more," replied Bran. "But such would come to you from beyond the grave."

The others took this in silence.

"My father is dead," Bran continued, "and all his war band with him. Killed by the Ffreinc who have invaded our lands in Elfael."

"Then it is true," said Meurig. "We heard that the Ffreinc are moving into the southlands." He shook his head. "I am sorry to hear of King Brychan's death."

"As are we all," said Trahaern, whose dark hair rippled across his head like the waves of a well-ordered sea. "As are we all. But tell us, young Bran, why did you put on the robes of a priest just now?"

"I cannot think it was for amusement," offered Meurig. "But if it was, let me assure you that I am not amused."

"Nor I," said Cynwrig. "Your jest failed, my friend."

"In truth, my lords, it was no jest," replied Bran. "I wanted you to see how easily men defer to a priest's robe and welcome him that wears it."

"You said it was to *convince* us," Llewelyn reminded him.

"Indeed." Hands on the table, Bran leaned forward. "If I had come to you saying that I intended to fetch King Gruffydd from Earl Hugh's prison, what would you have said?"

"That you were softheaded," chuckled Trahaern. "Or howling mad."

"Our king is held behind locked doors in a great rock of a fortress guarded by Wolf Hugh's own war band," declared Llygad, a thickset man with the ruddy face of one who likes his ale as much as it likes him. "It cannot be done."

"Not by Bran ap Brychan, perhaps," granted Bran amiably. "But Father Dominic—who you have just seen and welcomed at this very table—has been known to prise open doors barred to all others."

He looked to Tuck for confirmation of this fact. "It is true," the friar avowed with a solemn shaking of his round head. "I have seen it with my own eyes, have I not?"

"Why should you want to see our Rhi Gruffydd freed from prison?" asked Hywel, fingering the gold bishop's cross upon his chest. "What is that to you?"

Despite the bluntness of the question, the others looked to Bran for an answer, and the success of King Raven's northern venture seemed to balance on a knife edge.

"What is it to me?" repeated Bran, his tone half-mocking. "In truth, it is *everything* to me. I came here to ask your king to raise his war band and return with me to help lead them in the fight. Unless, of course, *you* would care to take the throne in his absence . . . ?" He regarded Hywel pointedly and then turned his gaze to the others around the board. No one volunteered to usurp the king's authority, prisoner though he was.

"I thought not," continued Bran. "It is true that I came here to ask your king to aid me in driving the Ffreinc from our homeland and freeing Elfael from the tyranny of their rule. But now that I know that my best hope lies rotting in a Ffreinc prison—for all he is my kinsman, too—I will not rest until I have freed him."

Bran's kinsmen stared at him in silence that was finally broken by Trahaern's sudden bark of laughter.

"You dream big," the dark Welshman laughed, slapping the table with the flat of his hand. "I like you."

The tension eased at once, and Tuck realized he had been holding his breath—nor was he the only one. The two younger Cymry, silent but watchful, sighed with relief and relaxed in their elders' pleasure.

"It will take more than a priest's robe to fetch Gruffydd from Wolf Hugh's prison," Meurig observed. "God knows, if that was all it took he'd be a free man long since."

The others nodded knowingly, and looked to Bran for his response.

"You have no idea," replied Bran, that slow, dangerous smile sliding across his scarred lips, "how much more there is to me than that."

CHAPTER II

Caer Rhodl

The wedding was all Baroness Neufmarché hoped it would be, conducted in regal pomp and elegance by Father Gervais, who had performed the marriage ceremony for herself and the baron all those years ago. Lady Sybil—resplendent in a satin gown of eggshell blue, her long brown hair plaited with tiny white flowers—made a lovely bride. And King Garran, his broad shoulders swathed in a long-sleeved, grey tunic falling to the knees and a golden belt around his lean waist, looked every inch a king worthy of the name. It was to Agnes's mind a fine match; they made a handsome couple, and seemed unusually happy in one another's company. Garran's French was not good, though better than Sybil's Welsh, but neither seemed to care; they communicated with smiling glances and flitting touches of fingers and hands.

The final prayer caught Lady Agnes somewhat by surprise.

When Sybil's attendants—several of the groom's young female cousins—stepped forward to hold the *carr* over the couple kneeling before Father Gervais, Agnes felt tears welling up in her eyes. The simple white square of cloth was the same one that had been stretched above her head the day she married the baron and which had swaddled the infant Sybil at her baptism. Now it sheltered her daughter on her wedding day, and would, please God, wrap Sybil's baby in turn. This potent reminder of the continuity of life and the rich depth of family and tradition touched the baroness's heart and moved her unexpectedly. She stifled a sob.

"My love," whispered the baron beside her, "are you well?"

Unable to speak, she simply nodded.

"Never mind," he said. "It is soon over."

No, she thought, *it is only beginning. It all begins again.*

After the service in the rush-strewn hall, the wedding feast began. Trestles and boards, tables, chairs, and benches filled the courtyard where a pit had been dug to roast a dozen each of spring lambs and suckling pigs; vats of ale sat upon stumps, and tuns of wine nestled in cradles; the aroma of baking bread mingled with that of the roasting meat in the warm, sun-washed air. As the newly wedded couple emerged from the hall, the musicians began to play. The bride and groom were led by their attendants in stately procession around the perimeter of the yard, walking slowly in opposite directions, pausing to distribute silver coins among the guests, who waved hazel branches at the royal pair.

After the third circuit of the yard, Garran and Sybil were brought to the high table and enthroned beneath a red-and-blue striped canopy where they began receiving gifts from their subjects: special loaves of bread or jars of mead from humbler households; and from the more well-to-do households, items of furniture, artfully woven cloth, and a matched pair of colts. Visitors who had made the journey from the baron's holdings in France brought more exotic gifts: crystal bowls, engraved pewter platters, a gilded cross, soft leather shoes and gloves, and jeweled rings with golden bands. Having given their gifts, the celebrants took their places at the long tables. When everyone was seated, the servants filled the cups and bowls with wine, and the first of many healths were raised to the married couple, often accompanied by a word or two in Welsh that none of the Ffreinc understood, but which brought bursts of laughter from all the Britons.

Then, as the servants began carrying platters of food to the tables, some of the groom's men seized the instruments from the minstrels and, with great enthusiasm, began playing and singing as loudly as they could. Their zeal, though commendable, was far in excess of their abilities, Lady Agnes considered; however, they were soon joined by others of the wedding party, and before a bite of food was touched the entire Welsh gathering was up on their feet dancing. Some of the groom's men hoisted the bride in her chair and carried it around the yard, and three of the bride's maids descended on the groom and pulled him into the dance. The servants attempting to bring food to the tables quickly abandoned the task since it was all but impossible to carry fully laden trenchers and platters through the gyrating crowd.

Lady Agnes, at first appalled by the display, quickly found herself enjoying the spectacle. "Have you ever seen the like?" asked the baron, smiling and shaking his head.

"Never," confessed the baroness, tapping her foot in time to the music. "Is it not . . ."

"Outrageous?" suggested the baron, supplying the word for her.

"Glorious!" she corrected. Rising from her place, she held out her hands to her husband. "Come, *mon chére*, it is a long time since we shared a dance together."

Baron Neufmarché, incredulous at his wife's eagerness to embrace the raucous proceedings, regarded her with a baffled amazement she mistook for reluctance. "Bernard," said Lady Agnes, seizing his hand, "if you cannot dance at a wedding, when will you dance?"

The baron allowed himself to be pulled from his chair and into the melee and was very soon enjoying himself with enormous great pleasure, just one of the many revellers lost in the celebration. Amidst the gleeful clatter, he became aware that his wife was speaking to him. "There it is again," she said.

"What?" he asked, looking around. "Where?"

"There!" she said, pointing at his face. "That smile."

"My dear?" he said, puzzled.

She laughed, and it was such a thrilling sound to his ears that he wondered how he had lived without it for so long. "I haven't seen that smile for many years," she declared. "I had all but forgotten it."

The music stopped and the dance ended.

"Has it been all that rare?" Bernard asked, falling breathless back into his chair.

"As rare, perhaps, as my own," replied the baroness.

He suddenly felt a little giddy, although he had only had a mouthful or two of wine. "Then we shall have to do something about that," he said, and reaching out, pulled his wife to him and gave her a kiss on the cheek.

"Tonight, *mon cher*," she whispered, her lips next to his ear, "we shall discover what else we have forgotten."

The feast resumed in earnest then, and the happy celebrants sat down to their meal, and the day stretched long into the twilight. As the shadows began to deepen across the yard and the first pale stars winked on in the sky, torches were lit and the ale vats and wine tuns replenished. There was more singing and dancing, and one of King Garran's lords rose to great acclaim to tell a long and, judging from the laughter of his listeners, boisterously entertaining story. Lady Agnes laughed too, although she had not the slightest idea what the story might have been about; it did not matter. Her laughter was merely the overflowing of an uncontainable abundance of joy from a truly happy heart.

As the festivities continued into the night, Lady Agnes noticed that some of the groom's men had taken up places by the gate—three on each side—and as the musicians began another lively dance, she saw two more of the groom's men creeping along the far wall. She stiffened to a tingle of fear in the knowledge that something was about to happen—treachery of some kind? Perhaps an ambush?

She nudged the baron with her elbow; he was leaning back in his chair, nodding, tapping his hands on the armrests in time to the music. "Bernard!" she hissed, and nodded towards the gate. The two groom's men had reached the gate. "Something is happening."

He looked where she indicated and saw the gathered men. He could make out the forms of horses standing ready just outside the gate. He glanced hurriedly around for his knights. All that he could see were either dancing or drinking, and some had coaxed Welsh girls onto their laps.

Before he could summon them, one of the men at the gate raised a horn and blew a sharp blast. Instantly, a hush fell upon the revellers. "My cymbrogi!" the man called. "Kinsmen and countrymen all!"

"Wait! That's Garran," said Baron Bernard.

"Shh! What's he saying?"

He spoke in Welsh first, and then again in French, saying, "I thank you for your attendance this day, and pray let the celebration continue. My wife and I will join you again tomorrow. You have had the day, but the night belongs to us. Farewell!"

The second groom's man turned, and Agnes saw her daughter— with a man's dull cloak pulled over her glistening gown—raise her hand and fling a great handful of silver coins into the crowd. With a shout, the people dashed for the coins, and the newly wedded couple darted through the doorway towards the waiting horses. The groom's men shut the gate with a resounding thump and took up places before it so that no one could give chase; the music resumed and the festivity commenced once more.

"Extraordinary," remarked Baron Neufmarché with a laugh. "I wish I had thought of that on my wedding day. It would have saved all that commotion."

"You *loved* the commotion, as I recall," his wife pointed out.

"I loved *you*," he said, raising her hand to his lips. "Then—as I love you now."

Perhaps it was the wine and song making him feel especially expansive, or the music and contagious spirit of the celebration; but it was the first time in many years that Bernard had said those words to his wife. Yet, even as he spoke them he knew them to be true. He *did* love Agnes. And he wondered why he had allowed so many other concerns—and women—to intrude upon his love for her, to wither it and debase it. Now, in this moment, all else faded in importance, growing dim and inconsequential beside his life with Agnes. In that moment, he vowed within himself to make up for those years of waste and the pain his neglect and infidelity must have caused her.

The baron stood. "Come, my dear, the revelry will continue, but I grow weary of the throng. Let us go to our rest." He held out his hand to his wife; she took it and he pulled her to her feet. The celebration did continue far into the night, the revellers pausing to rest only when dawnlight pearled the sky in the east.

For three days the wedding festivities continued. On the fourth day people began taking their leave of the bride and groom, paying homage to both as their king and queen before departing for home. Baron Neufmarché, well satisfied that he had done all he could to strengthen his client king and provide for his daughter, turned his thoughts to Hereford and the many pressing concerns waiting for him there.

"My dear," he announced on the morning of the fifth day after the wedding, "it is time we were away. I have ordered the horses to be saddled and the wagon made ready. We can depart as soon as we have paid our respects to the dowager queen, and said our farewells."

Lady Agnes nodded absently. "I suppose . . ." she said mildly.

The baron caught the hesitancy in her tone. "Yes? What are you thinking?"

"I am thinking of staying," she said.

"Stay here?"

"Where else?"

"In Wales?"

"Why not?" she countered. "I am happy here, and I can help Sybil begin her reign. She still has much to learn, you know. You could stay, too, *mon cher*." She reached for his hand and squeezed it. "We could be together."

The baron frowned.

"Oh, Bernard," she said, taking his arm, "I am happy for the first time in many years—truly happy. Do not take that away from me, I beg you."

"No," he said, "you need not beg. You can stay, of course—if that is what you want. I only wish I could stay with you. I'd like nothing more than to see the building work on the new castle properly begun. Alas, I am needed back in Hereford. I must go."

Agnes sympathized. "But of course, *mon cher*. You go and tend to your affairs. I will remain here and do what I can to help. When you have finished, you can return." She smiled and kissed him on the cheek. "Perhaps we will winter here."

"I would like that." He leaned close and kissed her gently. "I shall return as soon as may be."

So, that was that. Lady Agnes stayed at Caer Rhodl, and the baron returned to Hereford, leaving behind his wife and daughter and, to his own great surprise, a piece of his heart.

CHAPTER 12

While Bran continued to court the confidence of Llewelyn and the lords of Gwynedd, slowly converting them to his scheme, Tuck was given the chore of gleaning all the information and gossip he could discover about Earl Hugh d'Avranches. He begged a ride across the strait in one of the local fishing boats to the busy dockyards at Bangor, where he spent a goodly while talking to the seamen of various stripes; all had strong opinions, but were weak on actual facts. When he reckoned he had gleaned all that could be learned on the docks, he moved on to the market square and strolled among the stalls, listening to the merchants and their customers, and stumping up the cost of a jar or two to share when he found someone whose opinions seemed worth his while to hear. As the day began to fade toward evening, he took shelter at the monastery, sat with the monks at table, and talked to the porter, kitchener, and secnab.

In this way, Tuck had collected a tidy heap of tittle-tattle and, after sifting everything well and wisely, it came to this: Hugh d'Avranches had come to England with the invading forces of the Duke of Normandy—William the Conqueror to some, Willy Bastard to others, father of the present King of England, William Rufus. And although Hugh did not actually fight at Hastings against Good King Harold, the Norman nobleman was nevertheless granted generous swathes of land in the north of England as a reward for his loyalty and support. Why was this? He had ships.

It was said that if not for Hugh d'Avranches' ships, the invasion of England would never have taken place. The master of upwards of sixty seaworthy vessels, he lent them to Duke William to carry the Ffreinc army across the Narrow Sea to Britain's green and pleasant shores, thereby earning himself an earldom. Most of the Cymry knew Earl Hugh as a fierce adversary well deserving of his wolfish nickname; more extreme views considered him little more than a boot-licking toady to his bloat-gut royal master, and called him Hw Fras, or Hugh the Fat. In either case, the Cymry of the region had long since come to know and loathe him as a ruler who made life a torrent of misery for all who lived within his reach, and a very long reach it was.

From his sprawling fortress at Caer Cestre on the northern border between England and Wales, Earl Hugh harrowed the land: raiding, thieving, spoiling, feuding, burning, and wreaking whatever havoc he might on any and all beyond the borders of his realm. Forever a thorn in the side of the local Cymry, he pricked them painfully whenever he got the chance.

It went without saying that it fell to King Gruffydd of Gwynedd to make a stand against this rapacious tyrant. Time and again Gruffydd's warriors and the earl's—or those of the earl's blood-lusting kinsman, Robert of Rhuddlan—tangled and fought. Sometimes the Cymry bloodied the Norman noses, but more often it went the other way. On one disastrous day, however, King Gruffydd ap Cynan had been captured. Earl Robert had bound his prize in chains and hauled him to Caer Cestre, where Gruffydd was cast into Fat Hugh's hostage pit. That was eight years ago, and he was still there, kept alive at Hugh's pleasure to torment and torture as whim moved him. It was thought that the Welsh king would rot in captivity. Hugh had no intention of releasing him and had refused to set either a ransom or a day of execution, but the earl did allow the Welsh king's kinsmen to pay their respects on high holy days, when a selected few were admitted to the danksome keep with carefully inspected parcels of food, clothing, candles, and other necessaries for their captive king.

The earl's fortress at Caer Cestre was a squat square lump of ruddy stone with thick walls and towers at each corner and over the gate, and the whole surrounded by a swampy, stinking ditch. It had been constructed on the remains of a stout Saxon stronghold which was itself built on foundations the Romans had erected on the banks of the River Dee. The town was also walled, and those walls made of stone the Roman masons cut from the red cliffs along the river. The caer, it was said, could not be conquered by force.

These and other things Tuck learned and reported it all to Bran.

"He likes his whoring and hunting, our Hugh," he reported. They were sitting in the courtyard of Llewelyn's house, sharing a jug of cool brown ale. A golden afternoon sun was slanting down, warming the little yard agreeably, and the air was soft and drowsy with the buzz of bees from the hives on the other side of the wall. "They say he likes his mistresses better than his money box, his falcons better than his mistresses, and his hounds better than his falcons."

"Thinks himself a mighty hunter, does he?" mused Bran with his nose in the jar. He took a sip and passed it to Tuck.

"That he does," the friar affirmed. "He spends more on his dogs and birds than he does on himself—and he's never been known to spare a penny there, either."

"Does he owe anyone money?" wondered Bran.

"That I cannot say," Tuck told him. "But it seems he spends it as fast as he gets it. Musicians, jugglers, horses, hounds, clothes from Spain and Italy, wine from France—he demands and gets the best of whatever he wants. The way people talk, a fella'd think Fat Hugh was one enormous appetite got up in satin trousers."

Bran chuckled. He took back the jar and raised it. "A man who is slave to his appetites," he said, taking another drink, "has a brute for a master."

"Aye, truly. That he has," the friar agreed cheerfully. "Here now! Save a bit o' that for me!"

Bran passed the jar to the friar, who upended it and drained it in a gulp, froth pouring down his chin, which he wiped on a ready sleeve.

When Tuck handed the empty jar back, Bran peered inside and declared, somewhat cryptically, "It is the master we shall woo, not the slave."

What he meant by this, Tuck was not to discover for several days. But Bran set himself to preparing his plan and acquiring the goods he needed, and also pressed his two young cousins, Brocmael and Ifor, into his service. He spent an entire day instructing the pair in how to comport themselves as members of his company. Of course, Tuck was given a prime part in the grand scheme as well, so the bowlegged little friar was arrayed accordingly in some of Bishop Hywel Hen's best Holy Day vestments borrowed for the purpose.

At last, Bran declared himself satisfied with all his preparations. The company gathered in Llewelyn's hall to eat and drink and partake of their host's hospitality before the fire-bright hearth. Llewelyn's wife and her maids tended table, and two men from the tribe regaled the visitors and their host with song, playing music on the harp and pipes while Llewelyn's daughters danced with each other and anyone else they could coax from their places at the board. Some of the noblemen had brought their families, too, swelling the ranks of the gathering and making the company's last night a glad and festive time.

The next morning, after breaking fast on a little bread soaked in milk, Bran repeated his instructions to Llewelyn, Trahaern, and Cynwrig. Then, mounting their horses, the four set off for the docks in search of a boat heading north. Caer Cestre sat happily on the Afon Dyfrdwy, which Tuck knew as the River Dee. All told, Earl Hugh's castle was no great distance—it seemed to Tuck that they could have reached it easily in three easy days of riding—but Bran did not wish to slope unnoticed into town like a fox slinking into the dove cote. He would have it no other way but that they would arrive by ship and make as big an occasion of their landing as could be. When Bran came to Caer Cestre, he wanted everyone from the stablehand to the seneschal to know it.

CHAPTER 13

L ord love us," said Tuck, a little breathless from his ride to the
caer, "It's an Iberian trading vessel on its way to Caer Cestre.
The ship's master has agreed to take us on board, but they are leaving on the tide flow."

"Tuck, my friend, I do believe things are going our way at last,"
declared Bran happily. "Fetch young Ifor and Brocmael. I'll give
Llewelyn our regards and meet you at the dock. Just you get yourself
on board and make sure they don't leave without us."

The travelling party arrived wharfside just as the tide was beginning to turn and got themselves to the ship with little time to spare.
As the last horse was brought aboard and secured under the keen
gaze of the ship's master—a short, swarthy man with a face burned
by wind and sun until it was creased and brown as Spanish leather—
Captain Armando gave the order to up anchor and push away from
the dock. A good-natured fellow, Armando contented himself with
the money Bran paid him for their passage, asking no questions and

treating his passengers like the nobility they purported to be. The ship itself was broad abeam and shallow drafted, built for coasting and river travel. It carried a cargo of olive oil and wine in an assortment of barrels and casks; bags of dried beans and black pepper, rolls of copper and tin, and jars of coloured glass. And for the noblemen of England and France: swords, daggers, and helmets of good Spanish steel; and also rich garments of the finest cloth, including silks and satins from the Andalus, and wool from the famous Spanish merinos. The four travellers ate well on board, and their quarters, though cramped—"a body cannot turn around for tripping over his own feet," complained Tuck—were nevertheless clean enough. At all events it was but a short voyage and easily endured. Mostly, the passengers just leaned on the rail and watched shoreline and riverbank slide slowly by, now and again so close they could almost snatch leaves from the passing branches.

On the third day, having skirted the north coast of Wales and then proceeded inland by way of the River Dee, the ship and its passengers and cargo reached the wharf at Caer Cestre. After changing their clothes for the finery bought at some expense in Bangor, the four prepared to disembark.

All during the voyage, Bran had laboured over the tale they were to tell, and all knew well what was expected of them. "Not a cleric this time," Bran had decided on the morning of the second day out. He had been observing the ship's master and was in thrall of a new and, he considered, better idea.

"God love you, man," sighed Tuck. "Changing horses in the middle of the stream—is this a good idea, I ask myself?"

"From what you say, Friar," replied Bran, "Wolf Hugh is no respecter of the church. Good Father Dominic may not receive the welcome he so rightly deserves."

"Who would fare better?" wondered Tuck.

"Count Rexindo!" announced Bran, taking the name of a Spanish nobleman mentioned by the ship's master.

Tuck moaned. "All very well for you, my lord. You can change like water as mood and whim and fits of fancy take you. God knows you enjoy it."

"I confess I do," agreed Bran, his twisted smile widening even more.

"I, on the other hand, am a very big fish out of water. For all, I am a poor, humble mendicant whom God has seen fit to bless with a stooped back, a face that frightens young 'uns, and knees that have never had fellowship one with the other. I am not used to such high-flown japes, and it makes me that uneasy—strutting about in someone else's robes, making airs like a blue-feathered popinjay."

"No one would think you a popinjay," countered Bran. "You worry too much, Tuck."

"And you not enough, Rhi Bran."

"All will be well. You'll see."

Now, as they waited for the horses to be taken off, Bran gathered his crew close. "Look at you—if a fella knew no better," he said, "he'd think you had just sailed in from Spain. Is everyone ready?" Receiving the nodded affirmation from each in turn, he declared, "Good. Let the chase begin."

"And may God have mercy on us all," Tuck added and, bidding their captain and crew farewell, turned and led the landing party down the gangplank. Bran came on a step or two behind, and the two young Welshmen, doing their best to look sombre and unimpressed with their surroundings, came along behind, leading the horses.

Their time aboard the Spanish ship had served Bran well, it had to be admitted. The moment his feet touched the timber planks on the landing dock, Bran was a man transformed. Dressed in his finery—improved by garments he'd purchased from the trading stock Captain Armando carried—he appeared every inch the Spanish nobleman. Tuck marvelled to see him, as did the two young noblemen who were inspired to adopt some of Bran's lofty ways so that to the unsuspecting folk of Caer Cestre, they did appear to be a company of foreign noblemen. They were marked accordingly and soon drew a veritable crowd of volunteers eager to offer their services as guides for a price.

"French!" called Tuck above the clamour. "Anyone here speak French?"

No one did, it seemed; despite the years of Norman domination, Caer Cestre remained an English-speaking town. The disappointed crowd began to thin as people fell away.

"We'll probably have better luck in the town," said Bran. "But offer a penny or two."

So they proceeded up the steep street leading to the town square, and Tuck amended his cry accordingly. "A penny! A penny to anyone who speaks French," he called at the top of his voice. "A penny for a French speaker! A penny!"

At the end of the street stood two great stone pillars, ancient things that at one time had belonged to a basilica or some such edifice but now served as the entrance to the market square. Though it was not market day, there were still many people around, most paying visits to the butcher or baker or ironmonger who kept stalls on the square. A tired old dog lay beside the butcher's hut, and two plough horses stood with drooping heads outside a blacksmith's forge at the far end of the square, giving the place a deceptively sleepy air.

Tuck strode boldly out into the open square, offering silver for service, and his cry was finally answered. "Here! Here, now! What are you on about?"

Looking around, he saw a man in a tattered green cloak, much faded and bedraggled with mud and muck; he was sitting on the ground with his back against the far side of the butcher hut and his cap in his hands as if he would beg a coin from those who passed by. At Tuck's call, he jumped up and hurried towards the strangers. "Here! What for ye need a Frankish man?"

Tuck regarded him with a dubious frown. The fellow's hair was a mass of filthy tangles hanging down in his face, and his straggling beard looked as if mice had been at it. The eyes that peered out from under the ropy mass were watery and red from too much strong drink the night before, and he reeked of piss and vomit. Unshorn and unkempt he was, Tuck considered—not the sort of person they had in mind for this special chore. "We have business in this town," Tuck explained brusquely, "and we do not speak French."

"I does," the beggar boasted. "Anglish and Frenchy, both alike. What's yer sayin' of a penny, then?"

"We have a penny for anyone who agrees to bear a message of introduction for us," Tuck replied.

"I'm t'man fer ye," the beggar chirped, holding out a filthy hand to receive his pay.

"All in good time, friend," Tuck told him. "I've heard you speak English, but how do I know you can speak French?"

"Speaks it like t'were me ine mither tongue," he replied, still holding out his hand. "*Naturellement, je parle français*, ye ken?"

"Well?" said Bran, stepping up beside them. "What's he say?"

Tuck hesitated. "This fellow says he'll help us, but if his French is as poor as his English, then I expect we're better off asking the butcher's dog over there."

Bran looked around. Seeing as no one else had come forward, and the day was getting on, he said, "Had we a better choice . . . but"—Bran shrugged—"he will have to serve. All the same, tell him we'll give him an extra penny if he will wash and brush before we go."

Tuck told the scruffy fellow what Bran had said, and he readily agreed. "Go then," Tuck ordered. "And be quick about it. Don't make us wait too long, or I'll find someone else."

The beggar dipped his head and scampered off to find a trough in which to bathe himself. Tuck watched him go, still nursing deep misgivings about their rough guide; but since they only needed some-one to make introduction, he let the matter rest.

While they waited for the beggar to return, Bran rehearsed once again the next portion of his plan with the two young noblemen so they might keep in mind what to expect and how to comport them-selves. "Ifor, you know some Ffreinc."

"A little," admitted Ifor. A slender young man with dark hair and wary eyes beneath a smooth, low brow, he was that much like Bran anyone could well see the family resemblance, however distant it might have been. Blood tells, thought Tuck, so it does. "Not as much as Brocmael, though."

"We hear it at the market in Bangor sometimes," Brocmael explained. Slightly older than Ifor, he had much about him of a good badger dog.

"You may find it difficult to pretend otherwise," Bran told them, "but you must not let on. Keep it to yourselves. The Ffreinc will not be expecting you to understand them, and so you may well hear things to our advantage from time to time." He smiled at their dour expressions. "Don't worry. It's easy—just keep remembering who you are."

The two nodded solemnly. Neither one shared Bran's easy confidence, and both were nearly overwhelmed by their arrival in a Norman town and the deception they meant to work—not to say frightened by the prospect of delivering themselves into their chief enemy's hands. Truth be told, Tuck felt much the same way. The sun climbed a little higher, and the day grew warmer accordingly. Bran decided that they should get a bite to eat, and Tuck, never one to forego a meal if it could be helped, readily agreed. "Unless my nose mistakes me," he said, "the baker is taking out fresh pies as we speak."

"Just what I was thinking," said Bran. Turning to his young attendants, he said, "Here is a good time to test your mettle. Remember who we are." He pulled a leather bag from his belt and handed it to Ifor. "Get us some pies—one for each and one for our guide, too, when he returns. He looks like he could use a meal."

"And, lads, see if there is any beer," Tuck added. "A jug or two would be most welcome. This old throat is dry as Moses' in the wilderness."

They accepted the purse, turned, and with the air of men mounting to the gibbet, moved off to the baker's stall. "They'll be all right," observed Bran, more in hope than conviction.

"Oh, aye," Tuck agreed with equal misgiving. "Right as a miller's scale."

The presence of wealthy foreign strangers in the square was attracting some interest. A few of the idlers who had been standing at the well across the square were staring at them now and nodding in their direction. "You wanted to be noticed," Tuck said, smiling through his teeth. "But I don't think those fellas like what they're seeing."

"You surprise me, Tuck. This is just what we want. If word of our arrival reaches the earl before we do, so much the better. See there?" He indicated two of the men just then hurrying away. "The news is on its way. Be at ease, and remember—as highborn Spanish noblemen it is beneath us to pay them heed."

"*You* may be the king of Spain for all Caer Cestre knows," Tuck declared, "but these rich clothes fit me ill, for all I am a simple Saxon monk."

"A simple Saxon worrier it seems to me," Bran corrected. "There is nothing to fear, I tell you."

Brocmael and Ifor returned a short while later with pies and ale for all. Their errand had settled them somewhat and raised their confidence a rung or two. The four ate in the shade of the pillar at the side of the square and were just finishing when three of the idlers approached from the well.

"Here's trouble," muttered Tuck. "Keep your wits about you, lads."

But before any of them could speak, the beggar returned. He came charging across the square and accosted the men in blunt English. Bran and the others watched in amazement as the idlers halted, hesitated, then returned to their places at the well.

"A man after my own heart," said Tuck. He looked their reprobate guide up and down. "Here now, I hardly know you."

Not only had he washed himself head to toe, but he had cleaned his clothes with a bristle brush, cut his hair, and trimmed his beard. He had even found a feather to stick in his threadbare hat. Beaming with somewhat bleary good pleasure, he strode to where Bran was standing and with a low bow swept his cap from his head and proclaimed in the accent of an English nobleman, "Alan a'Dale at your service, my lord. May God bless you right well."

"Well, Tuck," remarked Bran, much impressed, "he's brushed up a treat. Tell him that I mean no offence when I say that I'd not mark him for the same man."

The man laughed, the sound full and easy. "The Alan you see is the Alan that is," he said. "Take 'im or leave 'im, friend, 'cause there en't no ither, ye ken?"

When Tuck had translated, Bran smiled and said, "We'll take you at your word, Alan." To Tuck, he said, "Give him his pennies and tell him what we want him to do."

"That is for the wash," said Tuck, placing a silver penny in Alan's pink-scrubbed palm, "and this is for leading us to Earl Hugh's castle. Now, sir, when we get there we want you to send for the earl's seneschal and tell him to announce us to the earl. Do that, and do it well—there's another penny for you when you're finished."

"Too kind, you are, my friend," said Alan, closing his fist over the coins and whisking them out of sight.

"And here's a pie for you," Tuck told him. The pie was still warm, its golden crust clean and unbroken.

"For me?" Alan was genuinely mystified by this small courtesy. He looked from Tuck to Bran and then at the younger members of their party. His hand was shaking as he reached out to take the pie. "For me?" he said again, as one who could not quite believe his good fortune. It seemed to mean more to him than the silver he had just been given.

"All for you, and we saved a little ale too," Tuck told him. "Eat now, and we will go as soon as you've finished."

"Bless you, Father," he said, grabbing Tuck's hand and raising it to his lips. "May the Good Lord repay your kindness a thousand times."

It happened so fast the little friar had no time to snatch his hand away again before the teary-eyed fellow had kissed it. "Here now! Stop that!"

"Bless you, good gents all," he said, lapsing into the accents of the street once more. "Alan a'Dale en't one to fergit a good turn."

He sat down on the ground at the base of the pillar and began to eat, stuffing his mouth hungrily and smacking his lips with each bite. Bran sent Ifor and Brocmael to water the horses while they waited, and then asked Tuck to find out what he could from their hungry guide. "Tell him who we are, Tuck, and let's see how he takes it."

"My lord wants you to know that you are in the service of an esteemed and wealthy foreign nobleman in need of your aid. Perform your service well and you will be amply rewarded. He gives you good greeting."

At this, Alan carefully laid his pie aside, rose to his knees, swiped off his hat, and bowed his head. "You honour your servant, m'lord. May God be good to you."

"Give him our thanks," Bran said, "and ask him how long he's been in the town, and what news of the earl and his court."

Turning to Alan, Tuck relayed Bran's question. "My lord thanks you and wishes to know how long you have sojourned in this place."

Alan raised his eyes heavenward, his lips moving as he made his calculations. "In all, three year—give or take. No more than four."

"And how do you find the lord here—Earl Hugh?" Tuck asked, then added, "Please, finish your meal. We will talk while you eat."

"Aye, that's him," replied their guide, settling himself against the pillar once more. He picked up the pie and bit into it. "Fat Hugh, they call him—aye, and well-named, he. There's one hog wants the whole wallow all to himself, if ye ken."

"A greedy man?"

"Greedy?" he mused, taking another bite and chewing thought-fully. "If a pig be greedy, then he's the Emperor o' Swine."

"Is he now?" Tuck replied, and translated his words for the Cymry speakers, who chuckled at the thought.

"That tallies with what we've heard already," replied Bran. "Ask him if he knows the castle—has he ever been inside it?"

"Aye," nodded Alan when Tuck finished. "I ken the bloody heap right well. Lord have mercy, I been up there a few times." He crinkled up his eyes and asked, "Why would a bunch o' God fearin' folk like yerselves want to go up there anyway?"

"We have a little business with the earl," explained Tuck.

"Bad business, then," observed Alan. "Still, I don't suppose you can be blamed for not knowing what goes on hereabouts . . ." He tutted to himself. "Mark me, you'd be better off forgetting you ever heard of Wolf d'Avranches."

"If it's as bad as all that," Tuck ventured, "then why did you agree to take us there so quickly?"

"I didn't ken ye was God-fearin' gents right off, did I?" he said. "I maybe thought you were like his nibs up there, an' ye'd give as good as get, ye ken?"

"And now?"

"Now I ken different-like. Ye en't like them rascals up t'castle. Devil take 'em, but even Ol' Scratch won't have 'em, I daresay." Alan gazed at the strangers with pleading eyes. "Ye sure ye want to go up there?"

"We thank you for the warning. If we had any other choice, no doubt we'd take your advice," Tuck told him. "But circumstances force us to go, and go we must."

"Well, don't ye worry," said Alan, brushing crumbs from his clothes as he climbed to his feet. "I'll still see ye right, no matter. An' what's more, I'll say a prayer for yer safe return."

"Thank you, Alan," Tuck said. "That's most thoughtful."

"Hold tight to yer thanks," he replied. "For ye might soon be a'thinkin' otherwise."

With that subtle warning still hanging in the air, the visitors and their rascal of a guide set off.

PART THREE

"But where is Will Scadlocke?" quod Rhiban to John,
    When he had rallied them all to the forest,
"One of these ten score is missing who should
    Be stood at the fore with the best."

"Of Scadlocke," spoke young Much, "sad tidings I give,
    For I ween now in prison he lay;
The sherif's men fowle have set him a trap,
    And now taken the rascal away.

"Ay, and to-morrow he hangéd must be,
    As soon as ere it comes day.
But before the sheriff this victory could get,
    Four men did Will Scadlocke slay!"

When Rhiban heard this loathly report,
    O, he was grievéd full sore!
He marshalled up his fine merrye men
    Who one and together all swore:

That William Scadlocke rescued should be,
    And brought in safe once again;
Or else should many a fayre gallant wight
    For his sake there would be slain.

"Our mantles and cloaks, of deep Lincoln green,
    Shall we behind us here leave;
We'll dress us six up as mendicant monks—
    And I whist they'll not Rhiban perceive."

So donned they each one of them habits of black,
    Like masse-priests as such are from Spayne.
And thus it fell out unknowingly, that,
    Rhiban the reeve entertain'd.

To the sherif bold Rhiban proposéd a sport,
    For full confidence he had achiev'd.
If Will could outshoot monk Rhiban, disguised,
    The prisoner should earn a reprieve.

This sheriff was loath but at length did agree
    For a trick on the prisoner he planned.
Before William Scadlocke had taken his turn,
    The sheriff had twisted Will's hand.

CHAPTER 14

Earl Hugh's castle was built on the ancient foundations of the old Roman fort, partly of timber and partly of the same bloodred stone the Roman masons carved from the bluffs above the river so long ago. It loomed over the town like a livid, unsightly blemish: inflamed and angry, asquat its low hilltop.

For all the brightness of the day, the place seemed to breathe a dark and doomful air, and Tuck shivered with a sudden chill as they passed through the gate—as if the frost of bitter winter clung to the old stone, refusing to warm beneath the autumn sun. And although it was but a short distance from the town which carried its name, Caer Cestre remained as remote behind its walls as any Ffreinc stronghold across the sea.

This impression was due in part to the unseemly number of Ffreinc soldiers loitering in the courtyard—some in padded armour with wooden practice weapons, others standing about in clumps looking on, and still others sitting or reclining in the sun. There must have been twenty or more men in all, and a good few women too; and from the way they minced about the perimeter of the yard, smirking and winking at each and all, Tuck did not imagine they were wives of the soldiers. A heap of sleeping hounds lay in one corner of the yard, dozing in the sun, while nearby a group of stablehands worked at grooming four large chestnut-coloured hunting horses— big, raw-boned heavy-footed beasts of the kind much favoured by the Ffreinc.

Striding along after the porter who conducted them to the hall, the small procession consisting of two young foreigners, a rotund priest, their noble leader, and a local guide caused nary a ripple of interest from anyone they passed. Upon entering the vestibule, they were shortly brought to stand before the seneschal. Alan a'Dale, despite his many shortcomings, performed the service of interpreter surprisingly well, and they were admitted into the hall without the slightest difficulty whatever. Tuck breathed a prayer as they entered Wolf Hugh's den: a noisy and noisome room filled with rough board benches and tables at which men and women, and even a few children, appeared to be entering the final progressions of a night's debauch—even though the sun had yet to quarter the sky. The roil of eating and drinking, dicing and dancing, flirting and fighting amidst gales of coarse laughter and musicians doggedly trying to make themselves heard above the revellers greeted the visitors like the roll and heave of a storm-fretted sea. In one corner, dirty-faced boys tormented a cat; in another, an amorous couple fumbled; here, a man already deep in his cups shouted for more wine; there, a fellow poked at a performing juggler with a fire iron. Hounds stalked among the benches and beneath the tables, quarrelling over bones and scraps of meat. There was even a young pig, garlanded and beribboned, wandering about with its snout in the rushes underfoot.

Crossing the threshold, Bran paused to take in the tumult, collected himself, and then waded into the maelstrom. Here Bran's special genius was revealed, for he strode into the great, loud room with the look of a man for whom all that passed beneath his gaze in this riotous place was but dreary commonplace. His arrival did not go unnoticed, and when he judged he had gathered enough attention, he paused, his dark eyes scanning the ungainly crowd, as if to discern which of the roisterers before him might be the earl.

"By Peter's beard," muttered Tuck, unable to believe that anyone entering the castle could experience so much as a fleeting doubt about which of the men at table was Fat Hugh. *Only look for the biggest, loudest, most slovenly and uncouth brigand in the place,* he thought, *and that's the man. And yet . . . here's our Bran, standing straight and tall and searching each and every as if he could not see what was plain before his nose. Oh, this shows a bit of sass, does it not?*

What is more, Tuck could tell from the curious look on the earl's face that Hugh was more than a little taken aback at the tall dark figure standing before him. For there he was, a very king in his own kingdom, the infamous Wolf d'Avranches renowned and feared throughout his realm, and who was this that did not know him? And here was Bran without so much as a word or gesture, taking the overbearing lord down a peg or two, showing him that he was nothing more than a wobble-jowled ruffian who could not be distinguished from one of his own stablehands.

Oh, our canny King Raven is that shrewd, Tuck considered, a little courage seeping back into his own step. He glanced at Ifor and Brocmael and saw from the frozen expressions on their faces that the two Cymry, appalled by what they saw, were nevertheless struggling to maintain any semblance of calm and dignified detachment. "Steady on, lads," Tuck whispered.

Alan a'Dale, however, seemed at ease, comfortable even, walking easily beside Tuck, smiling even. At the friar's wondering glance, he said, "Been here before, ye ken."

"Often?"

"Once or twice. I sing here of a time."

"You sing, Alan?"

"Oh, aye."

Bran silenced them with a look and turned to address the onlooking crowd. *"Qua est vir?"* Bran announced in that curious broken Latin that passed for Spanish among folk who knew no better. *"Qua est ut accersitus Señor Hugh?"*

The seneschal, not understanding him, looked to Alan for explanation. He conferred with Tuck, then replied, "My lord wishes to know where is he that is called Earl Hugh?"

"But he is *there*," answered the chief servant as if that should be every whit as obvious as it was. He indicated the high table where, surrounded by perhaps six or eight ladies of the sort already glimpsed in the courtyard, sat a huge man with a broad, flat face and hanging dewlaps like a barnyard boar. Swathed in pale sea-green satin so well filled one could see the wavelike ripples of flesh beneath the tight-stretched fabric, he occupied the full breadth of a thronelike chair which was draped in red satin lined with ermine. Dull brown hair hung in long, ropy curls around his head, and a lumpy, misshapen wart besmirched one cheek. He held a drinking horn half raised, his wide, full-lipped mouth agape as he stared at the strange visitors with small, inquisitive eyes.

"I present my Lord Hugh d'Avranches," proclaimed the seneschal, his voice striving above the commotion of the great room.

Alan passed this along to Bran, who made a sour face as if he suddenly smelled something foul. *"Et? Et?"* he said. *That?*

Even the seneschal understood him then. "Of course," he said, stiffly. "Who else?"

Without another word, Bran approached the table where the earl sat drinking with his women. A strained silence fell at his approach as attention turned to the newcomers. Bran inclined his head in the slightest of bows and waved both Tuck and Alan to his side. *"Adveho, sto hic. Dico lo quis ego detto,"* he said grandly, and Tuck relayed his words to Alan, who offered: "His estimable lord Count Rexindo greets you in the name of his father, Ranemiro, Duke of Navarre, who wishes you well."

"Mon Dieu!" exclaimed the earl, his astonishment manifest.

Bran, looking every inch a Spanish nobleman, made another slight bow and spoke again. When he finished, he nodded at Tuck, who said, speaking through Alan, "Count Rexindo wants you to know that word of your fame has reached him in his travels, and he requests the honour of a private audience with you."

"Duke of Navarre, eh?" said Earl Hugh. "Never heard of him. Where is that?"

"It is a province in Spain, my lord," explained Alan politely. "The duke is brother to King Carlos, who is——"

"I know who King Carlos is, by the rood," interrupted the earl. "Heard of him." He passed an appraising eye over the tall man before him, then at his companions, evidently finding them acceptable. "Nephew of the king of Spain, eh? However did you find your way to a godforsaken wilderness like this?"

Tuck and Count Rexindo conferred, whereupon Alan replied, "The count has been visiting the royal court, and heard about the hunting here in the north."

"Eh? Hunting?" grunted the earl. He seemed to remember that he held a cup in his hand and finished raising it to his mouth. He guzzled down a long draught, then wiped his lips on the sleeve of his green satin shirt.

As if this was the signal the room had been awaiting, the hall lurched into boisterous life once more. The earl slapped his hand on the board before him, rattling the empty jars. "Here! Clear him a place." He began shoving his cups and companions aside to make room for his new guests. "Sit! All of you! We'll share a drink—you and your men—and you can tell me about this hunting, eh?"

By Saint Mewan's toe, thought Tuck, *he's done it! Our Bran has done it!*

Earl Hugh filled some empty cups from a jar and sent one of the women to fetch bread and meat for his new guests. Turning to regard his visitors from across the table, he observed, "Spaniard, eh? You're a long way from home."

Bran gazed placidly back at him as Alan, translating Tuck's hurried whispers, relayed his words.

"That is so, may it please God," replied Count Rexindo. Even speaking through two interpreters his highborn courtesy was clear to see. "We have heard that the hunting in England is considered the best in the world. This, I had to see for myself." He smiled and spread his hands. "So, here I am."

The count drank from his cup while his words were translated for the earl, smiling, looking for all the world like a man at utter ease with himself and his fellows. The women at the board seemed to find his dark looks attractive; they vied for his notice with winks and none-too-subtle smiles. When Alan finished, Count Rexindo indicated his companions and conferred with his interpreter, who said, "Pray allow me to introduce the count's companions. I present to you Father Balthus, Bishop of Pamplona," he said, and Tuck dipped his head in modest acknowledgement. "Also, I give you Lord Galindo of Tolosa"—and here he indicated Ifor—"and next to him is Lord Ramiero of Petilla." Brocmael, solemn as the tomb, inclined his head. "They are favourites among the count's many cousins."

If Alan suspected that he was part of a cunning deception, he did not let it show in the slightest. On the contrary, the further into the tale he delved, the more comfortable he became, and the more his admiration for the dark-haired young nobleman grew. Bran, as Count Rexindo, was a very marvel: his manner, his air, his being—everything about him had changed since entering that den of rogues; even his voice had taken on a subtle quality of refinement and restraint.

Tuck, too, was impressed, for when Bran spoke his made-up Spanish, it was with the light, soft lisping tone of Hibernia that Tuck recalled in their friend from Saint Dyfrig's, the stately Brother Jago. Slow boat that he was, it finally occurred to the friar that this was where Bran had got the names and titles and all the rest for them all. All that time spent travelling together last spring, Bran had had plenty of time to learn all that and more besides from the Spanish monk.

"You like to hunt, eh?" mused Earl Hugh into his cup. "So do I, by the bloody rood! So do I."

A brief conference between Tuck, Alan, and Bran set the course for the next part of the plan. "Give him to know that in Spain I am renowned as a great hunter, and that my father keeps a stable of the best horses in the realm. There is nothing I have not hunted." Bran nodded. "Make a good tale of it, Tuck, but be sure to remember what you have said so you can tell me after."

Tuck relayed to Alan what Bran had said, and added his own warning, "And don't over-egg the pudding, boyo," he said. "I'll be listening, mind, so keep it pure and simple."

"Never fear," replied Alan, who then turned to Earl Hugh and said, "My apologies, Lord. The count is embarrassed by his lack of French. But he wishes you to know that in his home country, he is a very champion among hunters and has ridden to the hunt throughout Spain. His father, the duke, keeps a stable of the finest horses to be found anywhere in the realm."

The earl listened, his interest piqued. "No finer horses than mine, I'll warrant," he suggested when Alan finished. "I'd like to see them. Did you bring any with you?"

"Alas no, Lord," answered Alan, without waiting to consult his master. "They are very valuable animals, as you must imagine, and could not be allowed to make a voyage, however short."

"A pity," replied Hugh. "I should like to have seen them in the flesh. My own horses have been praised by those who know a good animal when they see one. I'll show them to you, eh?"

Alan turned his head to receive the count's decision, then said, "My lord would like nothing more than to have the pleasure of viewing your excellent animals."

"Then let's be at it!" said Hugh, hoisting himself from his chair with the aid of the board before him. Calling for his seneschal, he motioned his visitors to follow and bowled from the hall with a lurching, unsteady gait.

"We're well on our way, men," Bran whispered. To Ifor and Brocmael, he said, "This next part will be in your hands. Are you ready?" Both young men nodded. "Good." To Tuck, he added, "Tell Alan—"

"My lord," said Alan, with a fishy grin at Tuck, "it is not necessary, as I speak a fair bit of Cymry, too, ye ken?"

"You do amaze me," Bran confessed. "I begin to believe you were born to this."

"Just where *did* you learn to speak like that?" Tuck wondered. "I mean no offence, but you spoke like a roadside beggar before we passed through these gates."

Alan lifted one shoulder in a halfhearted shrug. "It is useful for the earnin' o' a penny or two," he said, putting on the rough speech again as easily as a man putting on a hat. "A wanderin' musician is a pitiful lump without his harp."

"Wandering musician," echoed Tuck. "A minstrel?"

"If ye like," said Alan.

"How did you lose your harp?" the friar asked.

"Let's just say some lords appreciate a jest more'n others, ye ken?"

Bran laughed and clapped him on the shoulder. "I want you to stay with us while we're here—will you do that? I'll reward you well. Perhaps when this is over we can even find you a harp."

"I am honoured, Sire," the beggar answered.

"Here now!" called Earl Hugh from a doorway across the way. "This way to the stables."

"Let the hunt begin," said Bran, and the four Spanish noblemen and their interpreter hurried to join their host.

CHAPTER 15

Cél Craidd

Mérian held the long smooth length of ash between her fingers and carefully wrapped the thin rawhide strap in a tight spiral around the end, placing the clipped halves of stripped feathers from a goose's wing just so as she slowly turned the rounded shaft. Half her mind was on her task—fletching arrows required patience and dexterity, but consumed little thought—and the other half of her mind was on the worrying news that had reached them the night before.

The news had come after nightfall. Mérian and Noín and two of the other women were tending to the evening meal, and the rest of Cél Craidd was still at work: some trimming and shaping branches of ash and yew for war bows, or assisting Siarles in splitting narrow lengths of oak for arrows; two of the women were weaving hemp and linen for strings, and Tomas was helping Angharad affix the steel points. Scarlet and his small host of warriors—two of the younger women and three of the older children—were hard at work training to the longbow—they would practice until it was too dark to see. And any who were not busy with either bows or arrows were tending the bean field. The forest round about was sinking into a peaceful and pleasant autumn twilight.

And then they heard the long, low whistle that signalled the return of the scouts—those who had been away all day watching the King's Road. A few moments later, Rhoddi and Owain tumbled breathless down the bank and into the settlement bearing the news: Sheriff de Glanville had returned with upwards of fifty knights.

"They came quick and they came quiet," Rhoddi said when he had swallowed a few mouthfuls of water and splashed a cup over his head. "It was already getting dark, and they were on us before we knew it or we would have prepared a welcome for them."

"Where's Iwan?" asked Siarles, already halfway to flying off to his aid.

"He stayed to watch and see if any more came along," explained Owain. "He sent us on ahead." Catching Siarles's disapproving glance, the young warrior added, "There was nothing we could do. There were just too many, and we didn't have men or arrows enough to take 'em on."

"We thought better to let be this once," offered Rhoddi.

"Rhi Bran would have fought 'em," said Siarles.

"Given men enough and clear warning to get set in place, aye," agreed Rhoddi, "King Raven would have taken 'em on and no doubt won the day. But we en't Bran, and we didn't have men enough or time."

Iwan had returned a little while later to confirm what the others had said. "So now, Bloody Hugo has fifty more knights to throw at us. I hope Bran and Tuck fare well on their errand—we'll need all the help we can get. I just wish there was some way to get word to them."

Now, as the sun beat down brightly upon their wildwood settlement, Mérian looked around at the quiet industry around her, Iwan's words circling in her mind like restless birds. *I might not be able to get word to Bran*, she thought, *but I can do better than that—I can raise troops myself.* In that moment, she knew what she had to do: she would go to her father and persuade him to join Bran in the battle to drive the Ffreinc out of Elfael. Her father could command thirty, perhaps forty men, and each one trained to the longbow. Experienced archers would be more than welcome and, added to however many men Bran was able to raise, would form the beginnings of a fair army. She knew Bran's feelings about involving her father, but he was wrong. She'd tried to persuade him otherwise and met with a stubborn— nay, prideful—resistance. But in this matter of life and death, she considered, the outcome was just too important to allow such petty concerns to cloud good judgement. They needed troops, her father had them, and that was that.

Bran, she knew, would forgive her when he saw the men she would bring. Moreover, if she left at once, she could be back in Cél Craidd with the promise of warriors or better, the warriors themselves, before Bran returned.

Having made up her mind, the urge to go reared up like a wild horse and she was borne along like a helpless rider clinging to its neck. She made short work of the arrow she was fletching, set it aside, and rose, brushing bits of feather from her lap. *I can't be wearing this home to meet my family*, she decided, looking down at her stained and threadbare gown. Hurrying to her hut, she went inside and drew a bundle down from the rafters, untied it, and shook out the gown she had worn as an Italian noblewoman when accompanying Bran on the mission to rescue Will Scarlet. Though of the finest quality, the material was dark and heavy and made her look like an old woman; nevertheless, it was all she had and it would have to do. As she changed into the gown, she thought about what she would say to the family she had not seen for . . . how long had it been? Two years? Three? Too long, to be sure.

She brushed her hair and washed her face, and then hurried off to prepare a little something to eat on the way, and to ready a horse. Caer Rhodl was no great distance. It was still early; if she left at once and did not stop on the way, she could be there before nightfall.

"Are you certain, my lady?" said Noín with a frown when Mérian explained why she was saddling a horse while wearing her Italian gown. "Perhaps you should wait and speak to Iwan. Tell him what you plan."

"I am only going to visit my family," replied Mérian lightly. "Nothing ill can come of it."

"Then tell Angharad. She should—" Mérian was already shaking her head. "But you must tell *someone*."

"I am," said Mérian. "I'm telling *you*, Noín. But I want you to promise me you won't tell anyone else until this evening when I'm sure to be missed. Promise me."

"Not even Will?"

"No," said Mérian, "not a word to anyone—even Will. I should be at Caer Rhodl by the time anyone thinks to come looking for me, and by then there will be no need."

"Take someone with you, at least," suggested Noín, her voice taking on a note of pleading. "We could tell Will, and he could go with you."

"He is needed here," answered Mérian, brushing aside the offer. "Besides, I will be safe home before anyone knows it."

Noín's frown deepened; a crease appeared between her lowered brows. "There are dangerous folk about," she protested weakly.

"I shouldn't worry," replied Mérian, a smile curving her lips. "The only dangerous folk here about are *us*." She took the other woman's hand and pressed it firmly. "I'll be fine."

With that, she took up her small cloth bag, mounted quickly into the saddle, and was gone.

She struck off along a familiar path—it seemed as if she had lived a lifetime in this forest; were there any paths she didn't know?—and with swift, certain strides soon reached the King's Road. There she paused to take a drink of water from her stoppered jar and listen for anyone moving in the greenwood. Satisfied there was no one else about, she crossed the road, flitting quickly as a bird darting from one leafy shelter to another, and rode quickly on.

Just after midday, the trail divided and she took the southern turning, which, if she remembered correctly, would lead to her father's lands in Eiwas. The day was warm now, and she was sweating through her clothes; she drank some more water and moved along once more, riding a little slower now; she was well away from Cél Craidd, and there had been no sign of anyone following her. Except for a few stands of nettles and some brambles to be avoided, the path was clear and bright and easy underfoot. When she grew hungry, she ate from the bag slung under her arm, but she did not stop until finally reaching the forest's southwestern border.

Here, at the edge of the great wood that formed the boundary of the March, the land fell away to the south in gentle, sloping runs of low, grassy hills and wooded valleys—the land of her home. As she gazed out upon it now, Mérian was lifted up and swept away on wave after wave of guilt: it was so close! And all this time it had been awaiting her return—her *family* had been awaiting her return.

Stepping from the forest, she started down the broad face of a long hill towards the small, winding track she knew would lead her home—the same track Bran had used so often in the past when he came calling, usually in the dead of night. The thought sent another pang through her. Why, oh why, had she never tried to get home sooner?

It was no good telling herself that she had been taken prisoner and held against her will. That had been true for only the first few moments of her captivity. Events had proven Bran right: Baron Neufmarché was a sly, deceitful enemy, and no friend of hers or her family's. He had shown neither qualm nor hesitation in sending men to kill them following their escape. Once she understood that, she had stopped trying to get away. In fact, she had been more than content to remain at Bran's side in his struggle to save Elfael. And after that first season, the greenwood had become her home, and truth be told, she had rarely spared a passing thought for Eiwas or her family since.

The reason was, she decided, because in her heart of hearts she knew there was nothing waiting for her at Caer Rhodl except marriage—most likely to an insufferable Ffreinc nobleman of her father's choosing in order to advance her family's fortunes and keep the cantref safe. As true as that may have been, it was still only part of the tale. Partly, too, her lack of interest in returning home was due to the fact that in the months following her abduction she had become a trusted member of King Raven's council. In Cél Craidd she was honoured and her presence esteemed by all, and not merely some chattel to be packed off to the first Norman with a title that her father deemed advantageous to befriend. Mérian did not mean to condemn her father, but in the precarious world her family inhabited that was the way things were.

In short, with Bran she had a place—a place where she was needed, valued, and loved, a place she did not have without him. And that, more than anything else, had prevented her from leaving.

Now Bran needed her more than ever, if he only knew it. Stubborn as an old plough horse, Bran had refused to even consider asking her father for aid. They needed warriors; Lord Cadwgan had them. The solution was simple, and Mérian was not so childish as to allow anything so inconsequential as stubbornness or pride or a misplaced sense of honour to stand in the way of obtaining the aid her people so desperately needed.

Oh, there was a question: when, exactly, had she begun thinking of them as *her people*?

Mérian continued along the well-trod trail, her mind ranging far and wide as her mount carried her unerringly home. Once she passed a farmer and his wife working in a turnip field; they exchanged greetings, but she did not turn aside to talk to them. In fact, she stopped only once for a short rest in a little shady nook beside the road; she watered the horse, then drank some herself, and splashed some water on her face before moving on again. The sun quartered the sky, eventually beginning its long descent.

The sun was well down and the first stars were alight in the east when Mérian came in sight of Caer Rhodl. The old fortress with its timber walls stood tall and upright on the hill, the little wooden church quiet in the valley below. The place breathed an air of peace and contentment. In fact, nothing about the settlement had changed that she could see. Everything was still just the same as she remembered it.

This thought gave her heart a lift as she hurried on, reaching the long ramp leading to the gate, which stood open as if awaiting her arrival. A few more quick steps brought her through the gate and into the yard, where Mérian paused to look around.

Across the way, two grooms were leading horses to the stables; the horses were lathered, lately ridden—and at some distance and speed. Odd, she had not seen them on the road.

And then she saw Garran, her brother. Mérian had only the briefest glimpse of him as he disappeared through the entrance to the hall, but she thought he was in the company of a young woman. With a shout, she called his name and started across the yard. Three men and several women stood talking near the kitchen; they turned at Mérian's cry and saw a dark-haired young woman in a long dark gown flitting across the yard.

"Here! You!" shouted one of the men, moving forward. "Stop!"

When Mérian gave no sign that she had heard him, he cried out again, and moved to catch her before she reached the hall.

"Here, now!" he called, stepping into her path. "Where might you be going, young miss?"

So intent was she that it was not until the man took hold of her arm that she noticed him. "What?" she said. Feeling the man's hand tighten around her arm, she tried to pull away. "Let me go!" Looking towards the door to the hall, she cried, "Garran! Garran, it's me!"

"Be still," said the man, pulling her back. "You just stop that now. We're going to have a talk."

"Let me go!" She turned to face her captor, and recognized him as one of her father's men. "Luc?"

"Here, now," he said, his eyes narrowing in suspicion. "How do you know my name?"

"Luc, it's Mérian," she said. "*Mérian*—do you not know me?"

A figure appeared in the doorway behind Luc. "What's this?"

Mérian's gaze shifted to the hall entrance. "Garran!"

"I warned you," said her father's man, pulling her away. "Come along. You're going to——"

"Release me!" Mérian wriggled in his grasp.

"Mérian?"

She turned to find herself looking into the face of her very astonished brother.

"Saints and angels, Mérian," he gasped, "is it really you?"

"Oh, Garran—thank God, you're here. I—I . . ." she began, and suddenly could not speak for the lump in her throat.

"Lady Mérian," said Luc, "forgive me. On my word I didn't recognize you." He turned and called to the others who stood looking on. "El! Rhys! It's Lady Mérian come home!"

The others surged forward, clamouring all at once. Garran silenced them with a wave of his hand. "Look at you," he said, lifting her face with a thumb and finger. "Where have you been all this time?"

"Father and Mother—are they here? Of course they are," she said, finding her voice again. She started towards the hall. "I'm longing to see them. Come, Garran, you can present me to the king." When her brother did not move, she turned to him again. The solemn look on his face stopped her. "Why? What is it?"

"Father is dead, Mérian."

She heard what he said, but did not credit the words. "Where?" she asked. "Come along, I'm certain they—"

"Mérian, no," said Garran firmly. "Listen to me. Father is dead."

"He was sick for a very long time, my lady," offered Luc. "My lord Cadwgan died last spring."

"Father . . . dead?" Her stomach tightened into a knot, and her breath came in a gasp as the full weight of this new reality broke upon her. "It can't be . . ."

Garran nodded. "I'm the king now."

"And mother?" she asked, fearing the answer.

"She is well," replied Garran. "Although, when she sees you . . ."

Some of the others who had gathered around spoke up. "Where have you been?" they asked. "We were told you had been killed. We thought you dead long ago."

"I was taken captive," Mérian explained. "I was not harmed."

"Who did this to you?" demanded Luc. "Tell us and we will avenge you, my lady. This outrage cannot be allowed to stand—"

"Peace, Luc," Garran interrupted. "That is enough. We will discuss this later. Now I want to take my sister inside and let her get washed. You and Rhys spread the news. Tell everyone that Lady Mérian has come home."

"Gladly, Sire," replied Rhys, who hurried off to tell the women standing a little way off.

Rhi Garran led the way into the hall, and Mérian followed, walking across the near-empty hall on stiff legs. She was brought to her father's chamber at the far end of the hall and paused to smooth her clothes and hair with her fingers before allowing Garran to open the door. She gave him a nod, whereupon he knocked on the door, lifted the latch, and pushed it open.

The dowager queen sat alone in a chair with an embroidery frame on a stand before her. With a needle in one hand and the other resting on the taut surface of the stretched fabric, she hummed to herself as she bent over her work.

"Mother?" said Mérian, stepping slowly into the room as if entering a dream where anything might happen.

"Dear God in heaven!" shrieked Queen Anora, glancing up to see who it was that had entered the room.

"Mother, I—"

"Mérian!" Anora cried, leaping up so quickly she overturned the embroidery frame. She stretched out her arms to the daughter she had never hoped to see again. "Oh, Mérian. Come here, child."

Mérian stepped hesitantly at first, then ran, and was gathered into her mother's embrace. "Oh, oh, I—" she began, and found she could not speak. Tears welled in her eyes and began to run down her cheeks. She felt her mother's hands on her face and her lips on her cheek.

"There now, dear heart," her mother said soothingly. "All is well now you're home."

"Oh, Mother, I-I'm so sorry," she sobbed, burying her face in the hollow of her mother's throat. "There are so many times I would have come to you—so many times I *should* have come . . ."

"Hush, dearest one," whispered Queen Anora, stroking her daughter's hair. "You are here now and nothing else matters." She held Mérian for a time without speaking, then said, "I only wish your father could have seen this day."

Mérian, overcome with grief and guilt, wept all the more. "I'm so sorry," she murmured again. "So very sorry."

"Never mind," Anora sighed after a moment. "You're home now.

Nothing else matters." She held her daughter at arm's length and cast her eyes over her, as if at a gown or tunic she had just finished sewing. "You're half starved. Look at you, Mérian: you're thin as a wraith."

Mérian stepped back a little and looked down the length of her body, smoothing her bedraggled clothing with her hands. "We have many mouths to feed, and there is not always enough," she began.

There was a movement behind her, and a voice said, *"Qu'est-ce que c'est?"*

Mérian's shock at hearing the news of her father's death was only slightly greater than that of seeing the women who had entered the room. "Sybil!" gasped Mérian. "Baroness Neufmarché!"

At the sight of Mérian, Lady Agnes Neufmarché put her hands to her face in amazement. *"Mon Dieu!"*

"Mérianne," said Sybil, echoing her mother's astonishment.

Prince Garran stood to one side, a half smile on his face, enjoying the women's surprise at seeing one another again so unexpectedly.

Mérian saw his smile and instantly turned on him. "What are *they* doing here?" she hissed.

The baroness crossed quickly to her. *"Ma chère,"* she cooed, placing a hand on her shoulder. "How you must have suffered, *non?"*

Mérian reacted as if she had been burned by the touch. She gave a start and shook off Lady Agnes's hand. "You!" she snarled. "Don't touch me!"

"Mérian!" said Garran. "Have you gone mad?"

"Why are they here?" demanded Mérian, her voice quivering with pent rage. "Tell me why they're here!"

Lady Agnes stepped back, her expression at once worried and offended.

"Darling, what do you mean?" asked her mother. "They are living here."

Mérian shook her head. "No," she said, backing away a step. "That cannot be . . . it can't."

"Listen to you," replied the queen gently. "Why ever not? Garran is married now. Sybil is his queen. The baroness is spending the winter here helping Sybil settle in and begin her reign."

Mérian's horrified gaze swung from the baroness to the slender young queen standing mute and concerned beside her. Garran moved to take Sybil's hand, and she leaned toward him. "It is true, Mérian," said Garran. "We were married four months ago. I'm sorry if we failed to seek your approval," he added, sarcasm dripping from his voice.

"My lord," said Anora, her tone sharp. "That was not worthy of you."

"Forgive me, Mother," Garran said, inclining his head. "I think the excitement of this meeting has put us all a little out of humour. Come, Mérian, you are distraught. Be at peace, you are among friends now."

"Friends, is it?" scoffed Mérian. "Some friends. The last time we met they tried to kill me!"

CHAPTER 16

"On your mettle, my lords," said Alan a'Dale, glancing over Bran's shoulder across the yard, where the earl of Cestre had just appeared at the stable door.

"Everyone ready?" asked Bran. Ifor and Brocmael nodded, their brows lowered with the weight of responsibility that had been laid upon them. "When we get into the forest," Bran continued, "find your place and mark it well. If we should become separated, go back to the head of the run and wait for us there. Whatever happens, don't linger in the run waiting for one of Hugh's men to see you."

"We know what to do," said Ifor, speaking up for the first time since entering the Ffreinc stronghold.

"Count on us," added Brocmael, finding his voice at last. "We won't fail."

"Just you and Alan keep the earl busy, my lord," the friar said. "Let Tuck and his young friends here worry about the rest. If any of the earl's men come looking for us, I'll make sure they don't twig to the lads' doings here, never fear."

Bran nodded and drew a deep breath. He arranged his features into the curiously empty-eyed, slightly bored guise of Count Rexindo, then turned to greet the earl with his customary short bow and, *"Pax vobiscum."*

Earl Hugh, waddling like a barnyard sow, came puffing up already red faced and sweating with the exertion of walking across the courtyard. Accompanying him were two of his men: rough fellows in once-fine tunics spattered with wine stains and grease spots, each with a large dagger thrust into his leather belt—nasty brutes by both look and smell. Behind these two trailed three more stout Ffreinc in leather jerkins and short trows with high leather leggings; they wore soft leather caps on their heads and leather gauntlets on their hands with which they grasped the leashes of three hunting hounds. The dogs were grey, long-legged beasts with narrow heads and chests and powerful haunches; each looked fully capable of bringing down a stag or boar all on its own strength.

"Pax! Pax!" said Hugh as Bran stepped to meet him. "Good day for a chase, eh?"

"Indeed," replied Bran, speaking directly through Alan now. "I am keen to see if the trails of England can match those of Spain."

"Ho!" cried the earl in joyous derision. "My hunting runs are second to none—better even than Angevin, which are renowned the world over."

Count Rexindo sniffed, unimpressed when the earl's boast was relayed to him. He turned his attention to the dogs, walking to the animals and wading in amongst them, his hands outstretched to let them get his scent. It did not hurt that he had rubbed his palms and fingers with the meat he had filched from the supper platter the previous night. The hounds nuzzled his hands with ravenous enthusiasm, licking his fingers and jostling one another to get a taste. Bran smiled and stroked their sleek heads and silken muzzles, letting the animals mark and befriend him.

"Very unusual, these dogs," he said through Alan. "What breed are they?"

"Ah, yes," said Hugh, rubbing his plump palms together. "These are my boys—a breed of my own devising," he declared proudly. "There are none like them in all England. Not even King William has hounds as fine as these."

This required a small conference, whereupon the count replied through his translator. "No doubt your king must spare a thought for more important matters," allowed Count Rexindo with a lazy smile. "But never fear, my lord earl. If your dogs are even half as good as you say, I will not hold your boast against you."

The earl flinched at the slight. "You will not be disappointed, Count," replied Hugh. He called for the horses to be brought out— large, well-muscled beasts, heavy through the chest and haunches. Hugh's own mount was a veritable mountain of horseflesh, with a powerful neck and thick, solid legs. With the help of a specially made mounting stool and the ready arms of his two noblemen, Fat Hugh hefted himself into the saddle. But when the earl saw Bishop Balthus likewise struggling to mount, he called out in Ffreinc, "You there! Priest." Tuck paused and regarded him with benign curiosity. "This hunt is not for you. You stay here."

Although Tuck understood well enough what was said, he appealed to Alan, giving himself time to think and alerting Bran to the problem. Once it was explained to him, Bran reacted quickly.

"My lord Balthus rides today, or I do not," he informed the earl through Alan; he tossed aside the reins and made as if preparing to dismount.

Alan softened this blunt declaration by adding, "Pray allow me to explain, my lord."

The earl, frowning mightily now, gave his permission with an irritated flick of his hand.

"You see," Alan continued, "it seems Count Rexindo's father required Bishop Balthus to make a sacred vow never to allow the count out of his sight during his sojourn in England."

"Eh?" wondered the earl at this odd revelation.

"Truly, my lord," confessed Alan. He leaned forward in the saddle and confided, "I think my lord the duke believes his son a little too . . . ah, *spirited* for his own good. He is the duke's only heir, you understand. It is the bishop's head if anything ill should befall the count."

Earl Hugh's glower lightened somewhat as he considered the implications of what he had just been told. "Let him come, then," said the earl, changing his mind. "So long as he can keep his saddle— the same as goes for anyone who rides with me."

Alan explained this to Count Rexindo, who picked up the reins once more. *"Gracias, señor,"* he said.

The dog handlers departed from the castle first, and after a few rounds of the saddle cup, the riders followed. Hugh and Count Rexindo led the way, followed by the earl's two knights; the two young Spanish lords, Ramiero and Galindo, followed them, and Bishop Balthus fell into line behind the others, thinking that if he was last from the start no one would mark him dawdling along behind. "Wish us God's speed, Alan," he said as he kicked his mount to life.

"Godspeed you, my lord," replied Alan, raising his hand in farewell, "and send you his own good luck."

Out through the castle's rear gate they rode. A fair number of the earl's vassals were at work in his fields, and from his vantage point at the rear of the procession, Tuck could not help noticing the looks they got from the folk they passed: some glared and others spat; one or two thumbed the nose or made other rude gestures behind the backs of the earl and his men. It was sobering to see the naked hostility flickering in those pinched faces, and Tuck, mindful of his bishop's robes, smiled and raised his hand, blessing those few who seemed to expect it.

Once beyond the castle fields, the hunting party entered a rough countryside of small holdings and grazing lands, hedged about by dense woodland through which wide trails had been clear cut—Earl Hugh's vaunted hunting runs. Wide enough to let a horse run at full gallop without getting slapped by branches either side, they pursued a lazy curving pattern into the close-grown wood; a few hundred paces inside the entrance the dense foliage closed in, cutting off all sight and sound of the wider world. This, Tuck considered, would serve their purpose right fair—*if* Ifor and Brocmael could keep their wits about them in the tangle of bramble thickets and scrub wood brush that cloaked the edges of the run.

The party rode deeper into the wood, and Tuck listened to the soft plod of the horses' hooves on the damp turf and breathed the warm air deep. As the sun rose and the greenwood warmed, he began to sweat in his heavy robes. He allowed himself to drop a little farther behind the others, and noticed that the two young Welshmen had likewise fallen behind the leaders.

The search has begun, thought Tuck.

Soon the others were some distance ahead. Tuck picked up a little speed and drew up even with the Welshmen. "Be about your business, lads," he said as he passed by them. "I'll go ahead and keep watch and give a shout if Hugh or his men come back this way."

Ifor and Brocmael stopped then, and Tuck rode on, still taking his time, keeping his eye on Bran and Earl Hugh and the others now fading into the dappled shadow of the trail far ahead. When he had put enough distance between himself and the two behind him, the friar reined his mount to a stop and waited, listening. He heard only the light flutter of the breeze lifting the leaves of the upper branches and the tiny tick and click of beetles in the long grass.

He had almost decided that Hugh and the others had forgotten about them when he heard the sound of returning hoofbeats. In a moment, he saw two horses emerge from the shadowed pathway ahead. The earl had sent his knights back to see what had happened to the stragglers.

Glancing quickly behind him, Tuck searched for a sign of his two young comrades, but saw nothing. "Hurry, lads," he muttered between his teeth. "The wolf's pups are nosing about."

Then, as the two Ffreinc knights neared, Tuck squirmed ungracefully from the saddle and, stooping to the right foreleg of his mount, lifted the animal's leg and began examining the hoof. There was nothing wrong with it, of course, but he made as if the beast might have picked up a stone or a thorn. As the two hailed him in French, he let them see him digging at the underside of the hoof with his fingers. One of the knights directed a question at him as much as to say, "What goes here?"

"*Mon cheval est . . .*" Tuck began. He pretended not to know the word for *lame*, or *limping* either, so just shrugged and indicated the hoof. The two exchanged a word, and then the second knight dismounted and crossed to where he stood. He bent and raised the hoof to examine it. Tuck stole a quick glance behind; the two tardy Welshmen were nowhere in sight. Sending up a prayer for them to hurry, he cleared his throat and laid his finger to the hoof in the huntsman's hand, pointing to a place where he had been digging with his finger. *"Une pierre,"* he said. That the animal had picked up a pebble was perhaps the most likely explanation, and the knight seemed happy with that.

"Boiteux?" he asked.

Tuck shrugged and smiled his incomprehension. The knight released the hoof and took hold of the bridle, and walked the animal in a circle around him, studying the leg all the while. Finally, satisfied that whatever had been wrong was no longer troubling the beast, he handed the reins back to Tuck, saying, *"On y va!"*

Tuck took his time gathering his bishop's skirts and, with the help of the knight to boost him, fought his way back onto the high horse. Taking up the reins once more, he heard the sound of hoofbeats thudding on the trail behind. He turned in the saddle to see Ifor and Brocmael trotting towards them. Tuck hailed them and, satisfied now that the stragglers were all together once more, the Ffreinc knights led them up the game run to rejoin the others.

They soon came to a small clearing where Count Rexindo and Earl Hugh were waiting. At that moment, the hounds gave voice. *"La chasse commence!"* cried the earl and, lashing his horse, galloped away, followed by his knights.

Bran wheeled his mount but lingered a moment to ask, "Success?"

"Just as we planned, my lord," replied Ifor.

Brocmael made a furtive gesture, indicating the empty lance holder attached to his saddle, and said, "Never fear; we were not seen."

"Well done," said Bran. "Now we hunt, and pray we sight the game before our beefy host. Nothing would please me more than to steal the prize from under Hugh's long Ffreinc nose."

CHAPTER 17

hree days of hunting from earliest daylight to evening dusk, and each day Bran, having taken a great interest in the earl's hounds, greeted the dogs with morsels of food he had saved from the previous night's supper board—gobbets of meat he kept in a little bag. Tuck watched the process with fascination and admiring approval as Earl Hugh swallowed the bait in a manner not at all unlike his hounds: and all because Count Rexindo let it be known that he wanted to buy three or four of the animals to take back to Spain as a gift for his father, the duke. The ever-greedy earl welcomed the sale, of course, fixing the price at a princely thirty marks—a price that made Tuck's eyes water. He could never have brought himself to buy three smelly hounds when he might have built an entire church—altar to steeple and everything in between—and had money left over.

Having favoured the hounds, they mounted their horses and all rode out to spend the day working the runs—to be followed by a night's drinking and roister in the hall. By the fourth day, Earl Hugh's nightly feasting began to tell on them all—everyone except Bran. Somehow Bran seemed to bear up under the strain of these all-night revels, awaking the next morning none the worse for his excesses. Indeed, Tuck began to think him blessed with the fortitude of Samson himself until he noticed the trick. Friar Tuck—himself an enthusiastic consumer of the earl's good wine and fortifying meat—happened to discover Bran's secret the second night. Bran quaffed as readily as the next man; however, the instant their host's attention wandered elsewhere, quick as a blink Bran's cup dipped below the board and the contents were dashed onto the soiled rushes under their feet. Thereafter, he drank from an empty vessel until it was filled again, and the process was repeated.

From then on, Tuck did the same himself even though it pained him to throw away good drink.

Wolf Hugh himself was ragged and mean of a morning, sore-headed, stinking of stale wine and urine, his eyes red and his nose running as he shuffled from his chambers bellowing for food and drink to drive the demons from head and belly. Still he seemed to possess unusual powers of recovery, and by the time the sun had breached the castle walls, the earl was ready to ride to his hounds once more, steady as a stone and keen for the chase. On the third day, Tuck freely complained that the nightly debauch was too much for him, and begged Bran to let him observe the hunt from the rails of his bed; but Bran insisted that they must go on as they had started. Ifor and Brocmael had youth on their side, and tolerated the revelry, but were increasingly reticent participants. Alan a'Dale fared less well and was laid low of a morning.

On the fourth day, the earl decided to rest the horses and

hounds. He had business to attend to with some of his nobles, leaving his guests free to take their ease and amuse themselves as they would. Bran let it be known that he wanted to go into the town and attend the market, and so they did. A hundred paces beyond sight of the castle gate, he gathered his crew around him and said, "You are doing very well, lads. I beg but a little more patience and we are done. We will not abide here much longer."

"How much longer?" asked Alan a'Dale.

"Next time we ride."

"That might be tomorrow," Brocmael pointed out.

Bran nodded. "Then we best make certain everything is ready today."

The two young men glanced at one another. "Do you think the earl will tumble?" Ifor wondered.

"Why not?" replied Bran. "He suspects nothing. If all goes well, we should be far away from here before he learns what has happened . . ." Regarding the solemn expressions on the faces of his two young comrades, he gave them his slightly twisted smile. ". . . if he ever learns—and I strongly suspect he never will."

Bran resumed his stroll into the town with Alan at his side, leaving Tuck and the two young lords to reckon what had just been said. "Don't you worry, lads," Tuck said, trying to bank their courage a little higher. "By tomorrow night we'll be well on our way back to Wales with our prize, and beyond the claws and teeth of Wolf d'Avranches."

A short while later they entered a fair-sized market in full cry; merchants shouting for custom, animals bawling, dogs barking. Bran paused and surveyed the comely chaos for a moment. "Good," he said, "there are enough people about that we should not draw undue attention to ourselves. You all know what to do?"

Brocmael and Ifor nodded grimly. Bran opened his purse and fished out a few pennies. "This should be enough," he told them. "We are not clothing him for his coronation, mind."

"We know what to do," said Ifor.

"Then off you go. Return here when you are finished and wait for us."

When they had gone, Bran, Tuck, and Alan commenced their own particular quest. "Have you given any thought to my idea?" asked Bran as they began to stroll among the stalls and booths of the busy market.

"That I have," Tuck replied.

"And?"

"Oh, I think it should work—although I am no dog-handler. It seems a simple enough matter, does it not? We will require a little oil and perhaps an herb or two to mix with it—something strong, but not too offensive. No doubt if Angharad were here she would know better."

"But she is not here, so we look to you now," Bran said. "What do you suggest?"

"Essence of angelica for the oil," Tuck answered after a moment's consideration. "It is light, yet easily stains a cloth. Get it on your skin and it lingers long, even after you wash."

"Excellent! Just the thing," said Bran. He gazed around at the seething crowd of people and animals. "What do you say, Alan? Will we find what we need here?"

"I expect so, my lord. I know of a 'pothecary who comes to market most days."

"And the herbs?" he asked. "What are we looking for?"

"There are several—any one of which will suffice," Tuck mused aloud. "Lavender is strong, but not unpleasant. It is distinctive and not to be mistaken for anything else. There is also thyme, marjoram, or sage. Any of those, I think. Or all of them, come to that."

Bran commended his cleric happily. "Splendid! One day Alan here will laud your native Saxon cunning from one end of this island to the other."

"Lord help us, I don't want to be lauded," Tuck told him. "I'd as soon settle for a month of peace and quiet in my own snug oratory with nary a king or earl in sight." He paused, considering. "I think about that, do I not?" He caught Bran's expression and said, "I do! Sometimes."

Bran shook his head. "Ah, Tuck, my man, you were born for greater things."

"So you say. The world and his wife says different, methinks."

The three waded into the busy square and made short work of purchasing the items required. Alan prevailed upon the apothecary to mix the lavender and angelica oil for them, and add in the herbs. This made a fairly sticky concoction with a strong odour which seemed right for the purpose. They also bought a stout hemp bag with a good leather cord to close it, and then wound their way back to meet their two young companions and see how they had fared.

"We bought these," said Brocmael, offering up the bundle of goods they had purchased. "Not new, mind, but good quality." Still looking doubtful, he added, "I would wear them."

"It cost but a penny," Ifor explained. "So we bought a cloak as well." He shook out a hooded cloak and held it up. It was heavy wool of a tight weave, dyed green. It had once been a handsome thing, made perhaps for a nobleman. It was slightly faded now and patched in several places, but well-mended and clean. "No doubt he'd choose a better one," Ifor admitted, looking to Bran for approval, "but needs must, and this is better for hiding."

"He will be glad of it," Bran assured him. "You've done well—both of you. So now"—he looked around with the air of a man about to depart for territories unknown—"I think we are ready at last."

With that, the party began making their way back to the castle. The day had turned fair and bright; the breeze coming inland from the sea was warm and lightly scented with the salt-and-seaweed smell of the bay. They walked along in silence as thoughts turned to the danger of what lay ahead. All at once, Bran stopped and said, "We should not go on this way."

"Which way should we go?" Alan said. "This is the shortest way back to the castle."

"I mean," Bran explained, "it will not do to rouse the wolf in his den."

Tuck puzzled over this a moment, and said, "Dunce that I am, your meaning eludes me, I fear."

"If we return to the caer like this—all long-faced and fretful—it might put the earl on edge. Tonight of all nights we need the wolf to sleep soundly while we work."

"I agree, of course," Tuck replied. "So, pray, what is in your mind?"

"A drink with my friends," Bran said. "Come, Alan, I daresay you know an inn or public house where we can sit together over a jar or two."

"Right you are there, m'lord. I'm the man fer ye!" he declared, lapsing once more into that curious beggar cant he adopted from time to time. "Fret ye not whit nor tiddle, there's ale aplenty in Caer Cestre. Jist pick up yer feet an' follow Alan."

He turned and led the little group back down the street towards the centre of the town. It is a commonplace among settlements of a certain size that the better alehouses will be found fronting the square so as to attract and serve the buyers and sellers on market days. And although the Normans ruled the town of late, it was still Saxon at heart, which meant, if nothing else, that there would be ale and pies.

Alan pointed out two acceptable alehouses, and they decided on the one that had a few little tables and stools set up outside in the sun. There were barrels stacked up to one side of the doorway, form ing a low wall to separate the tables from the bustle of the square. They sat down and soon had jars of sweet dark ale in their fists and a plate of pies to share amongst them.

"I would not insult you by repeating your instructions yet again," Bran said, setting his jar aside. "You all know what to do and need no reminding how important it is." He looked each in the eye as he spoke, one after the other as if to see if there might be a weakening of will to be glimpsed there. "But if any of you have any questions about what is to come, ask them now. It will be the last time we are together until we cross the river."

Bran, mindful of the trust he was placing on such young and untried shoulders, wanted to give the two Welshmen a last opportunity to ease their minds of any burdens they might be carrying. But each returned his gaze with studied determination, and it was clear the group was of one accord and each one ready to play his part to the last. Nor did anyone have any questions . . . save only their guide and interpreter.

"There is something I've been thinking these last few days, m'lord," Alan said after a slight hesitation, "and maybe now is a good time to ask."

"As good a time as any," agreed Bran. "What is in your mind, Alan?"

"It is this," he said, lowering his eyes to the table as if suddenly embarrassed to speak, "when you leave this place, will you take me with you?"

Bran was silent, watching the man across the table from him. He broke off a bit of crust from a pie and popped it into his mouth. "You want to come with us?" Bran said, keeping his voice light.

"That I do," Alan said. "I know I'm not a fighting man, and of no great account by any books—"

"Who would say a thing like that?" teased Bran.

"I know what I know," insisted Alan seriously. "But I can read and write, and I know good French and English, some Welsh, and a little Latin. I can make myself useful—as I think I've been useful to you till now. I may not be all—"

"If that is what you want," said Bran, breaking into Alan's carefully prepared speech. "You've served us well, Alan, and we could not have come this far without you. If we succeed, we will have you to thank." Bran reached out his hand. "Yes, we'll take you with us when we leave."

Alan stared at Bran's offered hand for a moment, then seized it in his own and shook it vigorously. "You will not be sorry, m'lord. I am your man."

So, the five sat for a while in peace, enjoying the ale and the warmth of the day, talking of this and that—but not another word of what was to come. When they rose a little later to resume their walk back to Castle d'Avranches, it was with lighter hearts than when they had sat down.

They slipped back into the castle and went to their separate quarters to prepare for the next day's activities. That night at supper, Bran baited and set the snare to catch Wolf Hugh.

CHAPTER 18

"Ah, there you are!" cried Earl Hugh as his Spanish guests trooped into the hall. With him at the table were several of his courtiers, six or seven of the women he kept, and, new to the proceedings, five Ffreinc noblemen the others had not seen before— large looming, well-fleshed Normans of dour demeanour. Judging from the cut and weave of their short red woollen cloaks, white linen tunics and fine leather boots, curled hair and clean-shaven faces, they were more than likely fresh off the boat from France. Their smiles were tight—almost grimaces—and their eyes kept roaming around the hall as if they could not quite credit their surroundings. Indeed, they gave every appearance of men who had awakened from a pleasant dream to find themselves not in paradise, but in perdition.

"Here's trouble," whispered Bran through his smile. "Not one Norman to fleece, but five more as well. We may have to hold off for tonight."

"No doubt you know best," Tuck said softly; and even as he

spoke, an idea sprang full-bloomed into his round Saxon head. "Yet, here may be a godsend staring us dead in the eye."

"What do you see?" Bran said, still smiling at the Ffreinc, who were watching from their places at the board. He motioned Alan and the others to continue on, saying, "Keep your wits about you, every-one—especially you, Alan. Remember, this is why we came." Turning once more to Tuck, he said, "Speak it out, and be quick. What is it?"

"It just came to me that this is like John the Baptiser in Herod's pit."

Bran's mouth turned down in an expression of exasperated incomprehension. "We don't have time for a sermon just now, Friar. If you have something to say—"

"King Gruffydd is John," Tuck whispered. "And Earl Hugh is Herod."

"And who am I, then?"

"It is obvious, is it not?"

"Not to me," Bran muttered. He gestured to the earl as if to beg a moment's grace so that he might confer a little longer.

"Lord bless you." Tuck sighed. "Do you never pay attention when the Holy Writ is read out? Still, I'd have thought some smat-tering of the tale would have stuck by you."

"Tuck! Tell me quick or shut up," Bran rasped in a strained whis-per. "We're being watched."

"You're Solomé, of course."

"Refresh my memory."

"The dancing girl!"

Bran gave him a frustrated glare and turned away once more. "Just you be on your guard."

The two approached the board where the earl and his noble

visitors were waiting. Alan, standing ready, smiled broadly for the Normans and made an elaborate bow. "My lords, I give you greetings in the name of Count Rexindo of Spain"—he paused so that Bran might make his own gesture of greeting to the assembled lords—"and with him, Lord Galindo and Lord Ramiero"—he paused again as the two young Welshmen bowed—"and Father Balthus, Bishop of Pamplona." Tuck stepped forward and, thinking it appropriate, made the sign of the cross over the table.

"Welcome, friends!" bellowed Earl Hugh, already deeply into his cups. "Sit! Sit and drink with us. Tonight, we are celebrating my good fortune! My lords here"—he gestured vaguely at the five newcomers—"bring word from Normandie, that my brother has died and his estates have passed to me. I am to be a baron. Baron d'Avranches—think of that, eh!"

"My sympathies for the loss of your brother," replied the count.

"He was a rascal and won't be missed or mourned," sniffed the earl. "But he leaves me the family estates, for which I am grateful."

"A fine excuse for a drink, then," remarked Count Rexindo through his able interpreter. "I can think of none better than sudden and unexpected wealth." Bran sent up a silent prayer that none of the earl's new guests could speak Spanish and took his place on the nearest bench; the rest of his company filled in around him. Two of the women—one of whom had been openly preening for the count's attention ever since he stepped across the threshold—brought a jar and some cups. She placed these before Bran, and then bent near to fill them—bending lower and nearer than strictly necessary. The count smiled at her obvious attentions, and gave her a wink for her effort. Such blatant flirtation was shameless as it was bold. But then, Tuck reflected, shame was certainly an oddity in Earl Hugh d'Avranches's court, and quite possibly unknown. Nevertheless, as Bishop Balthus, Tuck felt he should give the brazen woman a stiff frown to show his clerical displeasure; he did so and marked that it did nothing to chasten her. Nor did it prevent her from insinuating herself between him and the handsome count. *Oh well*, thought Tuck as he slid aside to make room for her, *with a toothsome prize in sight folk are blind to all they should beware of—and that has been true since Adam first tasted apple juice.*

The jars went round and round, filling cups and bowls and goblets, and then filling them again. Earl Hugh, in a high and happy mood, called a feast to be laid for this impromptu celebration of his windfall of good fortune. His musicians were summoned, and as the kitchen servants began laying a meal of roast venison on the haunch, loaves of bread, rounds of cheese, and bowls of boiled greens, a gang of rowdy minstrels entered the hall and commenced perpetrating the most awful screech and clatter, pushing an already boisterous gathering into a barely restrained chaos. Tuck viewed the convivial tumult as a very godsend, for it offered a mighty distraction to lull suspicious minds. He glanced around the board at his nearest companions: Alan seemed to be watching the roister in an agony of want as jar after jar passed him by. Yet, Lord bless him, he resisted the temptation to down as many as might be poured, and contented himself with coddling his one small cup; Ifor and Brocmael, true to their duty, resisted the temptation to indulge and passed the jars along without adding anything to their cups.

Bran, as Count Rexindo, on the other hand became more expansive and jolly as the evening drew on. He not only filled his own cup liberally, but was seen to fill others' as well—including those of the earl and the hovering women. Engaging the visiting Norman lords in loud conversation about hunting and fighting and the like—with the aid of Alan's ready tongue—he drew them out of their stony shells and coaxed a laugh a time or two. Therefore, no one was the least surprised when he rose from his seat and hoisted his cup high and announced, again through Alan, "I drink to our esteemed and honoured host! Who is with me?"

Of course, everyone stood with him then—as who would not?— and raised their cups, shouting, *"Bravo!"*

The Spanish count tipped down a great draught of wine, wiped his mouth, and said, speaking loudly and with some little passion, "My friends and I have enjoyed our sojourn here in your realm, my lord earl. Your hospitality is as expansive as your girth—"

The earl looked puzzled as this was spoken, and Alan quickly corrected the count's meaning, saying, "—generosity . . . as expansive as your generosity, my lord. Please excuse my poor translation. He means your hospitality is as great as your generosity."

"It is nothing," replied Earl Hugh grandly. "Nothing at all!"

"I must beg your pardon, my good earl," replied Count Rexindo a little blearily, "but it is *not* nothing to me. In Spain, where all the virtues are accorded great regard, none sits higher in our esteem than the welcome given to kin and countrymen, and the strangers in our midst." His words came across a little slurred through the wine, though Alan cleaned them up. "As one who knows something of this, I can say with all confidence that your hospitality is worthy of its great renown." He lifted his cup once more. "I drink to you, most worthy and esti . . . estimable lord."

"To Earl Hugh!" came the chorused acclaim.

All drank, and everyone sat down again and made to resume the meal, but Count Rexindo was not finished yet. "Alas, the time has come for us to leave. Tomorrow's hunt will be my last, but it will be memorable . . ." He paused to allow these words to penetrate the haze of drink and food befogging his listeners' heads. "Indeed, all the more if our exalted earl will allow me to suggest a certain refinement to tomorrow's ride."

"Of course! Of course!" cried the earl, his spirits lofty, goodwill overflowing like the wine sloshing over the rim of his cup. "Anything you desire," he said with an airy wave of his hand. "Anything at all." He smiled, his ruddy face beaming with pride at the way he'd been feted and flattered by the young count in the presence of his visiting noblemen.

"How very gracious of you, my lord. In truth, I expected nothing less from one whose largesse is legendary," Count Rexindo replied, beaming happily.

"Come, man!" bellowed the earl, thumping the table with his hand. "What is it that you want? Name it and it is done."

Count Rexindo, all smiles and benevolence, gave a little bow and said, "In my country, when a lord wishes to make a special hunt in honour of his guests he releases a prisoner into the wild. I can assure you that it is sport second to none."

Ah, there it is, thought Tuck. *Our Bran has remembered his Bible story at last.*

It took a moment for the earl and the others to work out what had just been suggested. "Hunt a *man*?" said the earl, his smile growing stiff.

"Yes, my lord," agreed the count, still standing, still commanding the proceedings. "A criminal or some other prisoner—someone of no account. It makes for a very good chase."

"But . . ." began the earl, glancing around the table quickly. He saw his other guests looking to him expectantly. Tuck saw the hesitation and, instantly, the distress that followed, and knew the earl was well and truly caught in Bran's trap. "Surely, that is unworthy of your attention," Hugh replied lamely. "Why not choose something else?"

"I see I have overreached myself," the count said, sitting down at last. "I understand if you have no appetite for such rich sport . . ."

"No, no," Earl Hugh said quickly, seeing the frowns appear on the faces of his gathered noblemen. Having accepted the count's effusive praise for his untethered largesse, how could he now refuse to grant Rexindo's wish? He had no wish to appear tightfisted and mean before his noblemen. So, like a ferret trapped in a snare, squirm though he might he could not get free without gnawing off one of his own legs. "Did I say no? I am intrigued by your suggestion," he offered, "and would be eager to try it myself. It is just that I keep no criminals here. As it is, I have only one captive in my keep . . ."

"And he is too valuable," concluded Count Rexindo, his disappointment barely contained. "I understand."

The earl glanced around at his noblemen as if to explain, saw their frowns growing and his own reputation diminishing in their eyes, and hastily reconsidered. "However, it seems to me that this prisoner would be well worthy of our sport—a king in his own country who has enjoyed my hospitality far too long already."

"*Splendido!*" cried the count. Through Alan, he continued, "It will give me a chance to try the hounds I am buying."

Again, a slight hint of a grimace crossed the earl's face. He did not like the idea of using valuable dogs for such dangerous sport—especially, considered Tuck, dogs that had not yet been purchased. But, rising to the bait, the earl shrugged off his misgivings. "Why not?" he roared, stirring the feast to life once more. "Why not, I say! Here! Let us drink to the count, and to tomorrow's sport!"

Thus, the trap was set and sprung, and the prey neatly captured. Tuck waited until the festivity slowly resumed, and when the music and drink were once again in full spate, he rose. Bowing to their host, who had recovered his good cheer, he approached the earl's chair and, with Alan's help, declared, "This game you propose sits ill with me, I do confess, my lord."

"Does it?" he replied lazily. "Does it indeed? How so, pray?"

"The hunting of men is an abomination before the throne of God." Before the earl could reply, he added, "True, it is a custom long honoured in Spain and elsewhere, but one that the church does not endorse."

This rocked the old wolf back a step or two. He frowned and swirled the wine in his cup. "If I told you that this rogue of a prisoner has earned his death ten times over, would that make it sit more comfortably with you?"

"Perhaps," Tuck allowed. "Though I would still wish to give the wretch the benefit of absolution. By your leave, Earl, I will hear his confession and shrive him now. Then he will be ready to face his ordeal with a clear mind and clean soul."

Seeing that Bishop Balthus was determined, and he equally anxious to maintain his top-lofty dignity in the eyes of his guests, Earl Hugh agreed. "Then do so," he said, as if it had been his own idea all along. He put his nose in his cup once more. "Do so by all means, if it pleases you. One of my men will take you down to him."

Tuck thanked him, begged his dinner companions to excuse his absence, and then departed. In the company of the earl's seneschal, who was standing at the door, the friar made his way down and down into the low-vaulted under-castle, to the hostage pit, to see for the first time the man they had come to free. Leaving the hall and its uproar behind, they passed along a dark, narrow corridor to an even darker, more narrow passage through the castle inner wall to a round chamber below what must have been the guardhouse. *"Attendez ici, s'il vous plaît,"* said the seneschal, who disappeared up the steps to the room above, returning a few moments later with a dishevelled man who had very obviously been drug from his bed. Yawning, the guard applied a key to an iron grate that covered a hole in the floor, unlocked it, and pulled back the grate. He took up a torch from a basket on the floor, lit it from the candle in the seneschal's hand, and beckoned Bishop Balthus to follow. A short flight of spiral steps led them to another passage, at the end of which stood another iron grate which formed the door of a cell. Upon reaching the door, the guard thrust his torch closer, and in the fitful light of it Tuck saw the prisoner slumped against the wall with his head down, legs splayed before him, hands limp at his sides, palms upward. With his thick and matted tangle of hair and beard, he looked more like a bear dressed up in filthy rags than a man.

Once again, the guard plied the key, and after a few moments huffing and puffing, the lock gave and the door swung open, squealing on its rusted hinges like a tortured rat. The prisoner started at the sound, then looked around slowly, hardly raising his head. But he made no other move or sound.

Stepping past the gaoler, Tuck pushed the door open farther and, relieving the porter of his torch, entered the cell. It was a small, square room of unfinished stone with a wooden stool, a three-legged table, and a pile of rancid rushes in one corner for a bed. Although it stank of the slop bucket standing open beside the door, and vermin crawled in the mildewed rushes, the room was dry enough. Two bars of solid iron covered a square window near the top of one wall, and an iron ring was set into the opposite wall. To this ring was attached a heavy chain which was, in turn, clamped to the prisoner's leg.

"I will shrive him now," Tuck said to the guard.

The fellow settled himself to wait, leaning against the corridor wall. He picked his teeth and waited for the bishop to begin.

"You are welcome to stay, of course," said Tuck, speaking as the bishop. "Kneel down. I will shrive you too."

Understanding came slowly to the guard, but when it did he opened his mouth to protest.

"Come!" insisted the smiling bishop. "We all need shriving from time to time. Kneel down," he directed. "Or leave us in peace."

The gaoler regarded the prisoner, shrugged, and departed, taking the key with him. Tuck waited, and when he could no longer hear the man's footsteps on the stairs outside, he knelt down before the prisoner and declared in a loud voice, sure to be overheard, *"Pax vobiscum."*

The prisoner made no reply, nor gave any sign that he had heard.

"Lord Gruffydd, can you hear me? Are you well?" Tuck asked, his voice hushed.

At the sound of these words spoken in his own language by a priest, the king raised his head a little and, in a voice grown creaky from disuse, asked, "Who are you?"

"Friar Aethelfrith," Tuck replied softly. "I am with some others, and we have come to free you."

Gruffydd stared at him as if he could not make sense of what he had been told. "Free me?"

"Yes."

The captive king pondered this a moment, then asked, "How many are with you?"

"Three," Tuck said.

"It cannot be done," Gruffydd replied. His head sank down again. "Not with three hundred, much less three."

"Take heart," Tuck told him. "Do as I say and you will soon gain your freedom. Rouse yourself, and pay me heed now. I must tell you what to do, and we do not have much time."

CHAPTER 19

Count Rexindo and his entourage assembled in the yard to await the appearance of the earl and his men. The stablehands and idlers in the yard—many who had been in the hall the night before—watched them with an interest they had not shown in several days. Word of the day's unusual sport had spread throughout the castle, and those who could had come to observe the spectacle for themselves. Under the gaze of the earl's court, Bran gathered his company at a mounting block near the stables and traced out the steps of his plan one last time. All listened intently, keenly aware of the grave importance of what lay before them. When he finished, Bran asked, "You gave Lord Gruffydd the oil, Tuck?"

"I did," the friar answered, "and Brocmael here has the clothes we bought."

Bran glanced at the young man, who patted a bulge beneath his cloak.

"Alan, you know what to say?" he asked, placing his hand on the fellow's shoulder and searching his face with his eyes.

"That I do, my lord. Come what may, I am ready. Never let it be said Alan a'Dale was ever at a loss for words."

"Well then," Bran said, gazing around the ring of faces. "It's going to be a long and dangerous day, God knows. But with the Good Lord's help we'll come through it none the worse."

"And the hounds?" asked Ifor.

"Leave them to me," answered Bran. There was a noise in the yard as the earl and his company—including the five Ffreinc noblemen they had feasted with the previous night—emerged from the doorway across the yard. He gave Brocmael and Ifor an encouraging slap on the back and sent them on their way. "To the horses, lads. See you keep your wits about you and all will be well."

As the two young Welshmen moved off to fetch their mounts, Bran composed himself as Count Rexindo; then, straightening himself, he turned, smiled, and offered a good-natured salute to Earl Hugh. Out of the side of his mouth, he said, "Pray for all you're worth, good friar. I would have God's aid and comfort on this day."

"Hey now," Tuck replied, "it's potent prayers I'm praying since first light this morning, am I not? Trust in the Lord. Our cause is just and we cannot fail."

The earl and his company came into earshot then, and the count, piping up, said, *"Pax vobiscum, mes amis."* Alan added his greeting and gave the earl a low bow he did not in any way deserve.

"Pax," said Hugh. He rubbed his fat hands and glanced quickly around the yard, looking for his hounds and handlers. The lately arrived Ffreinc noblemen stood a little apart, stiff-legged and yawning; with faces unshaven and eyes rimmed red, they appeared ill-

rested and queasy in the soft morning light. Clearly, they were not accustomed to the roister and revel such as took place in Castle Cestre of an evening. The earl shouted across the empty yard, his voice echoing off the stone walls. In response to his call, a narrow door opened at the far end of the stable block and the porter entered the yard, pulling a very reluctant prisoner at the end of a chain behind him. "Here! Here!" said Hugh.

A moment later, from a door at the other end of the stables, the hounds and their handlers entered the yard. The hounds, seeing the horses and men assembled and waiting, began yapping with eager anticipation of the trail as hounds will. Count Rexindo, however, took one look at the chained captive and began shaking his head gravely.

"This is very bad," he said, speaking through Alan, who made a sour face as he spoke—so as to emphasize the count's displeasure. "No good at all."

In truth, it *was* very bad. Years of captivity had reduced the Welsh king to little more than a rank sack of hair and bone. His limbs, wasted through disuse, were but spindles, and his skin dull and grey with the pallor of the prison cell. The bright morning light made him squint, and his eyes watered. Although he was so hunched he could hardly hold himself erect, Gruffydd nevertheless attempted to display what scraps of dignity he still possessed. This served only to make him appear all the more pathetic.

"My lord the count says that this prisoner will not serve," Alan informed the earl.

"Why not?" wondered Hugh. "What is wrong with him?"

The Spanish count flicked a dismissive hand at the shambling, ragged baggage before him and conferred with his interpreter, who said, "This man is in such wretched condition, the count fears it will be poor sport for us. The hunt will be over before it has begun." The count shook his head haughtily. "Please, get another prisoner."

"But this is the only one I have, God love you!" retorted the earl, although he too peered at the captive doubtfully.

Tuck wondered wonder how long it had been since the earl had last laid eyes on the Welsh lord—several months at least, he reckoned, perhaps years.

"I say he will serve," Hugh said stiffly. "In any event, he must, for there is no other."

Alan and Count Rexindo held a short consultation, whereupon Alan turned and said, "Begging your pardon, Lord Earl, but the man is clearly unwell. If he cannot give good chase there is little point in pursuing him. We regret that the hunt must be abandoned. With your permission, we will bid you farewell and prepare instead to take our leave."

The earl frowned mightily. He was that unused to having his will thwarted that he became all the more adamant that the hunt should take place as planned. He argued with such vehemence it soon became clear to the others that the earl and his visiting noblemen had wagered on the outcome of the day's hunt—or, more likely, which among them would draw first blood. Having set such great store by his prowess, he was now loath to see that particular prize elude him.

"The hunt will go ahead," he declared flatly, and motioned for the porter to remove the chains from the prisoner. "This was *your* idea, after all, Count. We will make what sport of it we can."

Count Rexindo accepted the earl's decision with good grace. He seemed to brighten then and said something to Alan, who translated, "Let it be as you say, Lord Earl. As it happens, the count has thought of a way to make a better game of it. We will not use the dogs, and this will give our quarry a fighting chance."

"Not use the dogs?" scoffed the earl. "But, see here, I thought you wished to try them one last time before the purchase."

Alan and the count held a brief discussion, and Alan replied, "It is not done this way in Spain," he explained. "However, the count allows that you know your realm best. Might he suggest using just one hound? If you agree, the count would like to use one of the dogs he will buy. Moreover, he is prepared to wager that he will make the kill today."

"How much will he wager?" wondered Hugh, his pig eyes brightening at the thought.

"Whatever you like," answered Alan. "It makes no difference to the count."

"One hundred marks," answered the earl quickly.

Alan relayed this to Rexindo, who nodded appreciatively.

"Done!" shouted the earl. Turning to Bishop Balthus, he said, "You! Priest! Mark this. You are a witness to the wager—one hundred marks silver to the one who makes the kill."

Tuck gave him a nod of acceptance, wondering where on God's green earth Bran imagined he would find such a princely sum *if*—heaven forbid it!—he should lose the wager.

Meanwhile, Bran, ignoring the stare of the captive king who stood shivering but a few paces away, instead approached the hounds and walked in amongst them, holding out his hands, as he was wont to do, allowing the dogs to lick his fingers and palms. He chose one from among those he had marked to buy—a big, sleek, shaggy grey creature—and rubbed the animal's muzzle affectionately. Reaching into the pouch at his belt, he brought out a morsel he'd filched from last night's meal and fed it to the hound, rubbing the dog's nose and muzzle all the while. "This one," he said through Alan. "Let us take this one with us and leave the others."

The earl, happy with the choice—all the more so since it meant he would not risk his other hounds developing a taste for this unusual game—agreed readily. Count Rexindo then gestured to his two young attendants and directed them to take charge of the prisoner. *"Relâchez le captif,"* Alan said to the gaoler, who began fumbling at his belt for the key to the shackles.

The earl frowned again as the chains fell away, and it appeared he might have second thoughts about disposing of such a valuable prisoner in this way. The hound was given to sniff the captive's clothing, and as the two young nobles began marching the prisoner away, he protested, "Here now! What goes?"

Alan explained. "The count has ordered his men to take the wretch to the head of the hunting run and release him. They are to ride back here and tell us as soon as it is done, and then the chase will begin." He paused, regarding the Ffreinc noblemen, then added, "With this many hunters there will surely be no sport unless the prey is given a fair start."

"Go then," directed Earl Hugh, "and hurry back all the sooner." Spying one of the servants just then creeping across the yard, he shouted, "Tremar! Bring us a saddle cup!" The man seized up like a thief caught with his hand in the satchel, then spun about and ran for the hall entrance. "Two of them!" roared Hugh as the man disappeared. To his noblemen, he added, "Hunting is such thirsty business."

When Count Rexindo finished with the hounds, he turned and walked back to where Bishop Balthus stood, and the cleric saw the count slip his fingers back into the pouch at his belt, replacing the rag that had been liberally doused with herb oil, and with which he had smeared his palm—the same that had stroked the dog's nose and muzzle.

"Do you think it will work?" Tuck whispered as the grooms brought out the horses. "Or are we mad?"

"We can but pray. Still, if Gruffydd has followed your instruction," he said, "we have a chance at least—*if* he can endure the hunt." He motioned Alan to him and said, "You had best come with us today; we may need you. Tell the earl that Count Rexindo requires the aid of his servant and to bring a horse for you. Can you ride?"

"I can keep a saddle, my lord," he answered.

"Good man."

As Alan arranged for himself to accompany the hunt, a servant appeared with two saddle cups overflowing, and these were passed hand to hand around the ring of gathered hunters. The Ffreinc noblemen revived somewhat with the application of a little wine, and were soon showing themselves as keen as the earl to begin the day's amusement.

"Watch them," muttered Bran as he passed the cup to Tuck and Alan once more. "We have the measure of Hugh, but as for these—we don't know them and cannot tell how they will behave once we're on the trail. They may be trouble."

"I will keep my eye on them, never fear," Tuck told him.

The grooms brought the horses then, and to pass the time the hunters examined the tack and weapons. It had been decided that each would have two spears and a knife: ample weapons to bring down a defenceless prey. By the time the count's two young attendants returned from their errand, the earl was in a fever to begin the pursuit. Despite any lingering misgivings about losing a valuable captive, the idea of hunting a man had begun to work a spell in him, and like the hounds he cherished so much, waiting chafed him raw. At the earl's cry, the company took to their saddles and clattered from the yard. Earl Hugh sang out for Count Rexindo to ride with him—which, of course, Bran was only too happy to do—and they were off.

At first, Ifor and Brocmael and Tuck pretended to be as eager for the pursuit as those around them. They kept pace, staying only a little behind the earl, who was leading the chase; the Ffreinc noblemen thundered along behind—so close that Tuck could have sworn he could hear the bloodlust drumming in their veins.

They reached the head of the game run at the gallop and entered the long, leafy avenue in full flight. Rather than wait for the hound and handler to catch up, Earl Hugh proceeded headlong down the run with Count Rexindo right beside. After a few hundred yards or so, the count swerved to the right as if to begin searching that side of the run. Two of the Ffreinc noblemen went with him, and the rest followed the earl. However, no one turned up a trail, so the party slowed, eventually coming to a halt. There was nothing for it but to return to the head of the run and await the hound, which was not long in coming.

Nor was the animal slow in raising the scent of the fugitive. Only a few hundred paces into the run, the great grey beast gave out with a loud baying yelp and leapt ahead, straining at the leash—and the party was away once more. This time, they were led directly to the tree where Ifor and Brocmael had hidden Brocmael's spear a few days earlier, the hound bawling and barking all the way. Upon arrival, the hunters discovered a heap of filthy rags—the prisoner's ratty clothes, now cast aside.

The dog handler picked up the heap of rags and showed it to the earl, whose eyes narrowed. "He is smart, this one," he said with grudging appreciation. "But it will take more than that to throw one of my dogs off the scent." To the handler, he said, "Give him to mark."

The handler shoved the bundle against the dog's muzzle to renew the scent, and the hound began circling the tree to raise the trail. Once, and again, and then three more times—but each time the beast stopped in the place where the clothes had lain, confusing himself the more and frustrating his handler.

"We must raise another scent, my lord," reported the handler at last. "This trail is tainted."

"Tainted!" growled Hugh. "The man shed his clothes is all. Give the hound his head and he will yet raise the trail."

The handler loosed the hound from the leash and urged it to search a wider area around the tree. This time the dutiful hound came to stand before Count Rexindo, who gazed placidly down from his saddle as the dog bayed at him. *"Lontano!"* said the count, waving the dog away.

The handler pulled the animal off, but time and again, the fuddled dog ran between the heap of clothing on the ground and Count Rexindo on his horse. Finally, the handler picked up some of the rags and gave them a sniff himself. Then, approaching the earl, he handed up the rags. "There is some mischief here, Sire," he said. "As you will see."

The earl gave the scraps a sniff and straightened in the saddle. "What?" He sniffed again. "What is that?"

"Lavender, methinks," replied the handler. "Tainted, as I said."

The earl looked around suspiciously. "How in the devil's name . . . ?"

Count Rexindo, impatient and keen to be off, spoke up, and Alan offered, "The count says that clearly the dog is useless. Our prey cannot be far away. He suggests we spread out and raise the trail ourselves."

"Yes, yes," replied Earl Hugh. "You heard him, eh?" he said to the Ffreinc noblemen. "Go to it—and give a shout when you find the trail."

So all scattered, each a separate way. The count led the search farther down the run, and several of the Ffreinc followed that way. Bishop Balthus led lords Galindo and Ramiero to the opposite side of the run and began searching there—all of them knowing full well that Gruffydd would not be found.

CHAPTER 20

Caer Rhodl

Mérian's fingernails dug deep grooves in her palm, and she fought to control the rage she felt roiling inside her. She did not expect the ladies Neufmarché to understand, much less accept the least part of what she had to tell them. They would refuse to listen, call her liar, heap scorn upon her. So be it.

Her mother and brother, however, could be counted on to support her. Once she had explained what had happened the day she was abducted—as well as all that had happened since—she knew they would rally to her aid without question. She drew a calming breath and organized her thoughts, deciding how she would relate the events of the past two years in the greenwood. Then, raising her head, she squared her shoulders and put her hand to the latch. She pushed open the door to the hall and stepped inside. They were all assembled to hear her: Lady Agnes beside her daughter, Queen Sybil, and in the next seat, her brother, Garran; beside him sat her mother, the dowager Queen Anora. The two Ffreinc women sat erect, grim-faced, clearly unhappy; they had heard the accusations Mérian had laid at their feet. Her brother, the king, appeared no happier; drawn and somewhat haggard, he was torn between his own family and that of his new bride. Only her mother looked at all sympathetic, offering her a sad smile, and saying, "Do come along, Mérian. We have been waiting for you."

"Pray forgive me," she said, moving farther into the room. She saw there was no chair for herself. Very well, she would stand; it was better this way. Taking her place before them, she folded her hands and glanced at each in turn. "I see you have been discussing the problem of Mérian already."

"You're not a problem to be solved, my dear," her mother replied. "But we thought it wise to talk a little among ourselves before seeing you again. You will appreciate how awkward—"

"Some of the things you have said," said Lady Agnes. "These *allégations*—"

"If it please you, my lady," interrupted Garran, "we will yet come to that. First," he declared, turning to face his sister, "I want you to know that these are grave charges you have made, and we are taking them very seriously."

"Naturally," replied Mérian, feeling more and more like a criminal with each passing moment. She rankled against the feeling. "Be assured, Brother, I would not have declared them if they were not true."

"We do not doubt you, Mérian," her mother put in quickly. "But you must see how difficult this has become—"

"Difficult?" Mérian snapped, her voice instantly sharp. "Mother, you have no idea. Living in the greenwood with the dispossessed who have been driven from their homes and lands, whose hands have been cut off or eyes gouged out for petty offences and imaginary crimes, is difficult. Living in a hovel made of sticks and mud and covered with animal skins in deep forest where the sun cannot penetrate and stifling every stray sound for fear of discovery is difficult. Creeping place to place, careful to stay out of sight lest the Ffreinc soldiers see you is difficult. Hiding day on day from a sheriff who slaughters any unfortunate who happens to cross his path—*that* is difficult. Grubbing in the dirt for roots and berries to feed—"

"Enough, Mérian!" snapped her brother, his tone matching hers. "We know you've suffered, but you are home now and safe. There is no one in this room who wishes you harm. Mind your tongue and we will all fare the better for it."

"Your brother is right, *ma chère*," said Agnes Neufmarché, controlling her tone. Her Welsh was fair, if simple; that she was able to speak it at all Mérian considered a revelation. "We are your family now. We seek nothing but your good."

"How kind," Mérian retorted. "And was it for *my good* that your husband the baron pursued me and tried to kill me?"

"Of course, you have endured the ordeal terrible," Agnes granted loftily. "Yet, knowing my husband as I do, I cannot . . . *accepter*? . . . accept this as the truth."

Mérian stiffened. She had been expecting this. "You would call me liar?"

"*Pas de tout!*" said the baroness. "I suggest only that perhaps in your fear you mistook the baron's, ah . . . *action* as the *assaut* . . ."

She glanced to her daughter, who supplied the proper word. "As an attack," said Sybil.

"Is that what you think?" challenged Mérian. "You were there that day, Sybil. You saw what happened. Is that what you think? Bran was forced to flee for his life. He took me with him, yes—at first I thought he meant to abduct me for ransom, but it was to save me. He saw the danger I was in before I did, and he acted. When the baron discovered our escape he sent men to kill us both."

"Very well!" said Garran irritably. "Granting what you say is true, what can be done about it now?" He stared at his sister, his lips bent in a frown of deep dissatisfaction. "It's been two years, Mérian. Things have changed. What do you want me to do?"

There it was: the question she had been anticipating, her sole reason for coming. "I want," she replied, taking time to choose her words carefully, "I want you to join with us. I want you to raise a war band and come help us recover Elfael."

"Us?" wondered Garran. It was not a response Mérian had anticipated. "Have you lived so long among the outlaws that you no longer know where your true loyalties lie?"

"*My* loyalties?" She blinked at him in confusion. "I don't understand."

"What your brother is saying," offered Anora, "is that the affairs of Elfael are nothing to do with us. You are safe now. You are home. What is past is past."

"But the fate of Elfael *is* my worry, Mother—as it is for all Cymry who would live free in their own country." She turned to her brother, the king, and his nervous young queen beside him. "*That* is where my loyalties lie, Brother—and where yours should lie too. Unless that bit of French fluff beside you has addled your mind, you would know this."

Her brother bristled. "Careful, Mérian dear, you will go too far."

"I am sorry," she said, changing her tone from haughty self-righteousness to appeal. She smoothed the front of her gown beneath her hands and began again. "I truly do not mean to offend. But if I cannot speak my mind here in this room among those who know me best, then perhaps I do not belong here anymore. In any event, the urgency of my errand leaves me little choice." She licked her lips. "Baron de Braose has been banished from his lands and holdings in England and Wales, as you may have heard by now. Elfael is in the hands of Abbot Hugo de Rainault and the king's sheriff, Richard de Glanville. Without the baron to back them up, they are weak. This is the best chance we've had in many years to drive the invaders from our land—but we must strike soon. The sheriff has brought more men, and we must act quickly if we are to keep our advantage. If you were to—"

"We know all this," her brother interrupted. "Elfael belongs to the king now. I should not have to remind you that to go against Red William is treason. To raise rebellion against him will get you drawn and quartered at the White Tower and your pretty head fixed to a pike above the gates."

"De Braose *stole* the land from Bran and his people. King William promised justice, but betrayed Bran and kept the land for himself."

"He is the king," countered Garran. "It is his right to do with it what pleases him."

"Oh? Truly?" said Mérian, growing angry again. "Is that what you think? You would sing a different song if the king's greedy eye was on *your* throne, brother mine. Or has Baron Neufmarché already bought your throne for the price of a wife?"

"Mérian!" warned her mother. "That is beneath you."

"*Non! S'il vous plaît,*" put in the baroness. "Do not tax her so. She has had the . . . *traumatisme,* yes? She is not herself. In time she will see that the *famille* Neufmarché means only good for the people of this realm."

"Thank you, Lady Agnes," said Garran. "As always your judgement is most welcome." To Mérian, he said, "Bran's affairs are nothing to do with us. He has become an outlaw and a rebel and will pay with his life for his crimes. Of that I have no doubt."

"Do not speak to me of crimes," Mérian said, her face flushing hot. "Abbot Hugo and the sheriff rule with blood and terror. They hang the innocent and subject the Cymry living beneath their rule to all manner of torment and starvation. They are the real criminals, and chief among them is King William himself." She tried one last desperate appeal. "Listen to me, please. Bran and his people are preparing for war. They mean to take the fight to the invaders, and there is every chance they can succeed, but they need help." Glancing at Queen Sybil, whose face appeared unnaturally white and pinched with worry, she said, "Join us. Help us overthrow this wicked throne and restore the rightful king to Elfael."

"No," said her brother. "We will speak no more about it."

"Then there is nothing more to say." Mérian turned on her heel and prepared to walk from the hall and out through the gates. Stunned by her brother's outright rejection, the only thing she could think was returning to Cél Craidd, and that if she hurried, she might make it back before the night had passed.

"Where do you think to go, Mérian?" King Garran called after her.

"To the greenwood," she said. "I am needed there. It is plain to me now that I have no place here."

"You will not leave the caer," Garran informed her.

She spun around and stormed back to confront her brother. "Who are you to tell me where I will or will not go?"

"Father is dead," Garran replied. "Until you are wed and have a husband, I am your guardian. Moreover I am king and you are a member of my household. You will obey me in this."

"My guardian! When did you ever lift a finger to help me, dear brother?" demanded Mérian. Her defiance gave her a terrible aspect, but Garran stood his ground. "I am a lady in my own right, and I will not submit to your ridiculous rule."

"You will never see those outlaws again," Garran told her with icy calm. "Never. You will remain here for your own protection."

The audacity of the command stole the warm breath from her body. "How dare you!"

"It is for your own good, Mérian," said her mother, trying to soften the blow. "You will see."

"I see very clearly already, Mother," Mérian retorted. "I see I was wrong to come here. I see that you have all made your bed with the enemy. Where once there was a family, I see only strangers. Mark me, you will yet curse this day."

"You are much mistaken, Sister," Garran said.

"Oh, indeed," agreed Mérian. She began backing away. "Thinking my own flesh and blood would understand and want to help—that was my mistake." She turned once more toward the door. "But do not worry, dear hearts. It is not a mistake I will make again."

She pulled open the heavy door, stepped through, and slammed it shut behind her with a resounding crack. She marched out into the yard, her heart roiling with anger at the unfeeling hardness of her own nearest kin. How could they fail to see the need and refuse her plea for help? Their intimate contact with the Ffreinc had corrupted them, poisoned their judgement and tainted their reason. That was the only explanation. Mérian shuddered. She, too, had come very close to succumbing to that same corruption once. If Bran had not rescued her she would be like her brother now—perhaps married off to some odious Norman nobleman or other. She would rather be dead.

Mérian strode to the stable, brought out her horse, and led it to the gate—only to find it closed. "Open it, please," she said to the gateman, a young man with a bad limp.

"Forgive me, my lady—" he began.

"Spare me!" she snapped. "Open the gate at once. I am leaving."

"Lord help me, I cannot."

"Why?" she demanded. "Why not?"

"My lord King Garran said I was to keep it locked and let no one in or out until he told me otherwise."

"Oh, he did?" she said. "Well, I am sure he did not mean me. Open the gate at once."

"Sorry, my lady. He mentioned you especially—said it was more than my life was worth to let you pass." The young man crossed his arms across his chest and stood his ground.

Mérian stepped around him and moved to the gate. At that moment there came a call from across the yard, and three men-at-arms issued from the hall and ran to apprehend her. "Now, now, Lady Mérian, come away from there," said the first to reach her. "You are to follow us—king's orders."

"And if I should refuse?"

The warrior made no reply, but simply wrapped his arms around her waist and hoisted her off her feet. She shrieked her outrage and kicked at his legs. The remaining two warriors joined the first, and all three laid hold; Mérian was hauled back to the hall in a spitting rage and thrown into her room.

No sooner had the door been shut than she began hammering on it with her fists, shouting to be let out.

"Scream all you like; it will avail you nothing," came the voice of her brother through the planking of the door.

"Let me out!" she cried.

"When you are prepared to listen to reason," he replied blandly, "and pledge to rejoin your true family."

"To the devil with you!"

Her only reply was the sound of the heavy iron bar dropping into place outside, and her brother's retreating footsteps.

CHAPTER 21

When a painstaking search of the hunting run and woodland surrounding the tree where the captive's cast-off clothing had been found failed to turn up any trace of their human prey, the hunters moved down the run and deeper into the forest. Owing greatly to Count Rexindo's many wrongheaded interventions, the company was subtly led farther and farther away from any path Gruffydd might have taken, thus spending the entire day without discovering their quarry or raising even so much as a whiff of his trail. As twilight began to glaze the trails with shadow, the frustrated company was forced to conclude that the captive king had miraculously eluded their pursuit. It appeared that Bran's audacious plan had worked; all that remained was to suffer the wrath of a very angry earl and then they, too, would be free.

The Spanish visitors endured an extremely acrimonious ride back to the fortress, the earl fretting and fuming all the way, cursing everything that came to mind—most especially, Count Rexindo's ineptitude and the incompetence of Spaniards in general, as well as his own misguided complicity in a fool-bait scheme which had not only cost him a very valuable prisoner, but also had returned a powerful enemy to the battlefield. "Courage, men," counselled Bran as they paused before the doors of the hall. "It is soon over." To Ifor and Brocmael, he said, "Are the horses ready?"

The young men nodded.

"Good. Whatever happens, be ready to depart on my signal. We may have to bolt."

They entered a hall much subdued from the previous night; where before the walls had reverberated with song and laughter, this night's supper was taken in sullen silence and bitter resentment. Count Rexindo and his retinue braved the blast of ill-will with stoic silence as they listened to Hugh d'Avranches alternately berating one and all for their gross failure and bemoaning the loss of his captive. As the drink took hold of him, the livid, simmering anger gave way to morose distemper, with the earl declaring loudly for all to hear that he wished he had never laid eyes on Count Rexindo and his miserable company. This, then, was the signal for the visitors to make their farewells and remove themselves from the castle.

The count, having been seen to bear the earl's complaints and abuse with the good grace of one who could not grasp the more subtle nuances of insult in a foreign tongue, rose from his seat and with the aid of his able interpreter, said, "No one is more sorry than I that we have failed today. Still, it is in the nature of things that the hunter is sometimes outwitted by his prey and must return to his hearth empty-handed." He gave a slight shrug. "I, myself, blame no one. It happens. We live to hunt another day. But a man would be a fool to remain where his friendship is no longer welcome or valued.

Therefore, I thank you for your hospitality, my lord, and bid you farewell."

Oh, well done, thought Tuck, rising at Bran's gesture. As bishop, he gave the earl a small, benedictory flourish and, turning, followed the count from the hall.

"What about the hounds?" cried Hugh after the departing count. Too late he remembered the money he hoped to make on the sale of his expensive animals.

Alan, taking the count's elbow, restrained him and whispered into his ear. Rexindo shook his head, gave a final gesture of farewell, and stepped through the door. "I am sorry, my lord," Alan said, standing with his hand on the latch, "but the count says that he could not possibly consider buying such ill-trained and ungovernable beasts as the one he witnessed today. He has withdrawn his offer. You may keep your dogs."

With that, Alan disappeared, following Bishop Balthus, Lord Galindo, and Lord Ramiero across the threshold and into the corridor beyond. As soon as the heavy door shut behind them, they fairly flew to the stable and relieved the grooms of the care of their horses. Rexindo, true to his noble Spanish character, paid the grooms a few silver pennies each—as much to buy their aid as for their unwitting diligence—and with kind words and praise, bade them farewell. The chief groomsman, pleased and charmed by the count's noble treatment, led the company from the yard and opened the gate for them himself.

As they mounted their horses, Bran reached down a hand to Alan. "If you still want to come with me," he said. Without hesitation, Alan a'Dale grabbed the offered hand, and Bran pulled him up to sit behind him.

At last, having successfully skinned the wolf in his den, the short ride to Caer Cestre became a jubilant race. In the fading evening light, the company came clattering into a nearly deserted town square, where they dismounted and quickly made their way to the docks to meet King Gruffydd. When a cursory search failed to find him, they split up and, each taking a separate street, began combing the town. This, too, failed. "Perhaps he is waiting at one of the inns," suggested Alan.

Bran commended the idea and said, "You and Tuck go look there. Ifor, Brocmael, and I will wait for you at the wharf in case he should come there."

The two hurried off and were soon approaching the first of the river town's three inns—a place called the Crown and Keys. Despite the somewhat lofty ambitions of its name, it was a low place, smuggy with smoke from a faulty chimney and poorly lit. A cushion of damp reeds carpeted the uneven floor upon which rested one long table down the centre of the room with benches on either side. Four men sat at the table, and the brewmistress stood nearby to fetch the necessaries for her patrons. One glance into the room told them they must pursue their search elsewhere.

The next inn—The Star—was the place where they'd sat outside in the sun and enjoyed a jar on a day that now seemed years ago. Inside, the single large room was full of travellers and townsfolk; pipers had taken up residence beside the great hearth, and the skirl of pipes lent a festive atmosphere to the room. It took them longer here to look among the tables and investigate all the corners. Alan asked the alewife if anyone answering Gruffydd's description had been seen in or about the place that day. "Nay—no one like that. It's been a quiet day all told," she said, shouting over the pipers. "Not being a market day, ye ken?"

They had another look around the room and then moved on to the last of the town's inns—a mean place only a rung or two up from a cattle stall; with a few small tables and a few nooks with benches, it had little to recommend it but its ready supply of ale, which many of the boat trade seemed to prefer, judging from the number of sea-farers in the place. Again, they quickly gleaned that not only was King Gruffydd not in the room, but no one answering his description had been seen that day or any other. Tuck thanked the owner, and he and Alan hurried back to rejoin Bran and the others at the dock.

"What now?" asked Ifor when Alan finished his report. "We've looked everywhere."

"I told him where to go," said Tuck. "I made certain he under-stood."

"Maybe he's hiding in a barn or byre somewhere," suggested Alan.

"When you took him out to the hunting run," said Bran, "what did you tell him?"

"To come to the dock in town and wait for us there," said Ifor. "He said he would."

"Then, I think we must assume he is not in the town at all," sug-gested Bran. "Otherwise he'd be here."

Tuck considered this. "He never made it, you mean?"

"Either that," confirmed Bran, "or he took matters into his own hands and fled elsewhere."

"You think he didn't trust us to get him away safely?" said Brocmael.

Ifor countered this, saying, "He knew we were kinsmen, and he was keen as the blade in my belt to be leaving Caer Cestre at last. He said he'd reward us right well for helping him."

"Did he say anything else?" asked Tuck.

"He kept asking about Lord Bran—about why he would risk so much to free him."

"What did you tell him?" Bran asked.

"We told him he would have to speak to you, my lord. Your reasons were your own."

"It does not seem as if he feared to trust us," remarked Tuck. "Something ill must have befallen him."

"What now?" asked Alan again.

"It's back to foul Hugh's hunting run," Bran decided. "We must try to raise Gruffydd's trail and track him down—this time in earnest. We'll get what rest we can tonight and ride as soon as it is light enough to see the trail beneath our feet." He hesitated, then added, "In any event, finding Gruffydd might be the least of our worries . . ."

"Why?" said Tuck. "What else?"

"The ship is gone."

Only then did it occur to Tuck to look among the vessels at anchor along the dock and in the central stream of the river. It was true; the Iberian boat that had brought them was no longer to be seen. "I thought he said he'd wait for us."

"He said his business would take him no more than a week," Bran corrected. "Maybe he finished sooner than he expected."

"Or, it's taken longer," Alan pointed out.

The two young noblemen shared a worried glance, and Tuck sighed, "Bless me, when it rains, it pours."

"Never mind," said Bran. "So long as we stay out of sight of the earl, we'll make good our escape. The Welsh border is only a day and a half away. We can always ride if need be."

They found a dry place on the dock among piles of casks and rope, and settled down for a restless night. It was warm enough, but as night drew on, clouds drifted in, bringing rain with the approach of dawn. Tuck awoke when his face grew wet and then could not get back to sleep, so contented himself with saying the Psalms until the others rose and they departed once more, leaving Alan a'Dale behind in case the Iberian ship should return.

Skirting the earl's stronghold, they made for the hunting run. By the time they reached the place where Gruffydd had shed his prison rags for those supplied by his rescuers, the sky was light enough and they could begin making out marks on the trail. Ifor and Brocmael dismounted and, on hands and knees, began searching the soft earth in the undergrowth around the tree where the clothes had been hidden. Ifor found a mark which he thought could have been made by the butt of a spear being used as a staff, and before Bran and Tuck could see it for themselves, Brocmael, working a little farther on, called out that he had found a half-print of a shoe.

Bran and Tuck dismounted and hurried to where the dark-haired young nobleman was waiting. "It is a footprint, no doubt," agreed Tuck when he saw it. "But is it our man? Or one of the Ffreinc handlers? That is the question, is it not?"

"Follow it," instructed Bran. "See if you can find out where it leads."

The trail was slight and difficult to follow, which made the going slow. Meanwhile, the sky flamed to sunrise in the east. By the time they had determined that the tracks they were finding did indeed belong to King Gruffydd, the sun was up and casting shadows across the many-stranded pathways of the wood.

"This is not good," observed Bran, gazing upwards at the cloud-swept heavens.

"My lord?" said Tuck, following his glance. "What do you see?"

"He's going the wrong way," Bran pointed out. "We're being led deeper into the wood and away from the town."

So they were. But there was nothing for it. They had to follow the trail wherever it led, and eventually arrived at a sizeable clearing on the south-facing slope of a hill, in the centre of which was a small house made of mud and wattles; brush and beech saplings and small elm trees were growing up around the hovel, and the grass was long. Clearly, the steading had been abandoned some few years ago—no doubt when the earl became its nearest neighbour. The surrounding wood was actively reclaiming the clearing and had long since begun to encroach on what once had been fine, well-drained fields. The grass still bore the faint trace of a path: someone had walked through the place not long ago.

At the edge of the clearing, the searchers paused to observe the house. "Do you think he's down there, my lord?" asked Ifor.

"He is," affirmed Bran, "or was. Let's find out." He lifted the reins and proceeded into the old field. The house was decrepit—two of the four walls were in slow, dissolving collapse—but the upright posts still stood strong, and stout crossbeams supported what was left of the roof. "Go and see," he told Ifor. "The rest of us will wait here so that we don't make more of a trail than is here already."

The young man hurried off, and the others watched his progress across the field until he disappeared around the far side of the house. They waited, and Ifor reappeared a moment later, signalling them to come on ahead. By the time the others reached the house, they found a very groggy King Gruffydd sitting on a stump outside the ruined doorway and Ifor sprawled on the ground clutching his head.

"I nearly did for your man, here," said Gruffydd, looking up as Bran, swiftly dismounting, came to stand over him. "He woke me up and I thought he was a Ffreinc come to take me back."

"You hit him?" said Tuck, kneeling beside the injured Ifor.

"Aye," admitted the king, "I did, and for that I am heartily sorry."

Tuck jostled the young man's shoulder. "Are you well, Ifor?"

Ifor groaned. "Well enough," he grunted between clenched teeth. "I think he broke my skull."

"I said I was sorry, lad," offered Gruffydd somewhat testily. "Have you brought anything to eat?"

"What are you doing here?" Bran asked. "We waited for you in the town. Why didn't you come?"

The grizzled king frowned as he watched Tuck gently probing the young man's head. "I got lost."

Bran stared at the man, unable to think of anything to say.

"It's eight years since I was beyond the walls of that vile place," Gruffydd explained. "I must have got muddled and turned around. And the air made me tired."

"The air," repeated Bran dully.

"I expect that's so," offered Tuck. "Considering his lordship hasn't been out of that cramped cell in a good long while, his endurance might have suffered in that time. It makes sense."

"I apologize, my lord," said Bran then. "It never occurred to me that your strength would be impaired."

"I'm *not* impaired, curse your lying tongue," growled the king. "I was just a little tired is all." He made to stand and tottered as he came to his feet. He swayed so much Tuck put out a hand to steady him, then thought better of it and pulled it away again. "Have you brought me a horse?"

"We had no time to get you one," Bran replied. "But it isn't far—you can share with one of us."

"I will not ride behind anyone!" the king asserted stiffly.

"You can have my horse, Sire," volunteered Brocmael. "Ifor and I will share. For all it's only back to town."

Bran nodded. "We best be on our way. I want to be as far from here as possible when Wolf Hugh realizes what has been done to him—if he hasn't guessed already."

Dismounting quickly, Brocmael gave over the reins of his horse and helped his king into the saddle; then he vaulted up behind Ifor and the party set off.

The fastest way to the town was along one of the hunting runs towards the castle. As the morning was still fresh, Bran decided the need for a speedy retreat outweighed the concern of being seen, so they made their way to the nearest hunting run and headed back the way they had come. They passed along the slightly undulating green-walled corridor, eyes searching the way ahead, alert to the barest hint of danger.

Even so, danger took them unawares. They had just rounded a blind bend, and as the leaf-bounded tunnel of the run came straight they saw, in the near distance, a hunting party riding towards them. Without a word, the four fugitives urged their mounts into the brake and were soon concealed in the heavier undergrowth amongst the trees. "Do you think they saw us?" asked Ifor, drawing up beside Bran.

"Impossible to say," replied Bran. Dismounting, he darted back toward the run. "Stay here, everyone, and keep the horses quiet."

"Do as he says," instructed Tuck, sliding from the saddle. He followed Bran, and found him crouched in the bracken, peering out from beneath low-hanging yew branches onto the run.

"Any sign of them?" he said, creeping up beside Bran.

"Not yet," whispered Bran, laying a finger to his lips.

In a moment, they heard the light jingling of the Ffreinc horses' tack and the faint thump of hooves on the soft earth as they came. Bran flattened himself to the ground, and Tuck likewise. They waited, holding their breath.

The first of the riders passed—one of the visiting Ffreinc noblemen who had ridden with them the previous day—scouting ahead of the others. At that moment, there was a rustling of brush behind them and King Gruffydd appeared.

"Is it him?" demanded Gruffydd. "Is it Wolf d'Avranches?"

"Shh!" Bran hissed. "Get down."

Just then the main body of hunters passed: four knights and Earl Hugh, riding easily in the early morning. "There he is!" said Gruffydd, starting up again.

"Quiet!" said Bran.

"That vile gut-bucket—I'll have him!" growled Gruffydd, charging out of the brake. Bran made a grab for the king, caught him by the leg and pulled. Gruffydd kicked out, shaking Bran off, and stumbled out onto the run. The riders were but a hundred paces down the run when the Welsh king appeared out on the open track behind them. He gave a shout, and one of the riders turned, saw him, and jerked hard on the reins. *"Ici! Arrêtez!"* he cried, wheeling his horse.

"He's insane!" snarled Bran. Out from the wood he leaped, snagged the king by the neck of his cloak, and yanked him back under the bough of the yew tree.

"Release me!" shouted the king, wrestling in his grasp.

"You'll get us all killed!" growled Bran, dragging him farther into the wood.

"Let them come!" sneered Gruffydd, shrugging off Bran's hands. "I'm not afraid."

"Jesu forgive," said Tuck to himself. Stepping quickly behind the king, he tapped him on the shoulder. Gruffydd turned, and the friar brought the thick end of a stout stick down on the top of his head with a crack. The king staggered back a step, then lurched forward, hands grasping for the priest. Tuck gave him another smart tap, and the king's eyes fluttered back in his head and he fell to his knees.

"Good work, Tuck," said Bran, catching Gruffydd as he toppled to the ground. From the hunting run there came a sound that set their hearts beating all the faster: hounds. The first dog gave voice, followed by two others. "Hurry! Get back to the horses."

Dragging the half-conscious king between them, they fought through the bracken and tangled vines of ivy to where Ifor and Brocmael were waiting with the horses. "Get his clothes off him," directed Bran, pointing to Gruffydd. As Brocmael and Ifor began stripping off the Welsh king's clothing, Bran laid out his plan. "Fly back to town and make for the docks. Find Alan and have him get any ship that's going." Bran began shucking off his boots. "I'll keep them busy while you make good your escape."

The baying of the hounds seemed to fill the forest now, drawing ever nearer.

"What are you going to do?" said Tuck, watching Bran pull off his tunic and trousers.

"Give those to me." He took Gruffydd's tunic and cloak from Ifor. "Get his trousers."

There was shouting from the hunting run; the hunters had found their trail. As the others hefted an unresisting Gruffydd into the saddle, Bran pulled on the Welsh king's trousers and stuffed his feet into his boots.

"I'll stay with you," said Tuck.

"No," said Bran. "Go with them. Take care of Gruffydd. If I don't find you before you reach the town, see you get yourselves on the first ship sailing anywhere. Leave the horses if you have to—just see you get clear of the town with all haste."

"God with you," said Tuck as Bran disappeared into the forest, racing towards the sound of the barking dogs.

"We should stay and help him," Ifor said.

"He can take care of himself," replied the priest, struggling into the saddle. "Believe me, no one knows how to work the greenwood like Rhi Bran."

"I'm staying," Ifor declared, drawing his sword.

"Put that away, lad," Tuck told him. "There's been enough disobedience for one day. We'll do as we're told."

With a grimace of frustration, the young Welshman thrust his blade back into the scabbard and the three took to flight, leading Bran's horse with the wounded king slung sideways across his mount like a bag of grain.

They worked deeper into the wood and heard, briefly, shouts echoing from the direction of the hunting run, and horses thrashing into the close-grown bushes and branches. There was a crash—as if a horse or its rider had fallen into a hedge—and then a cry of alarm, followed by other shouts and the frenzied barking of the hounds sighting their quarry. Then, slowly, the sounds of the chase began to dwindle as the pursuit moved off in another direction.

The riders continued on, eventually working back to the head of the hunting run. By this time Gruffydd was able to sit up in the saddle, so they lashed their horses to speed and made quick work of the remaining distance, keeping out of sight of the castle until they reached the track leading to Caer Cestre. Alan was there on the wharf, waiting where they'd left him. He waved as Tuck and the others came in sight—a quick, furtive flick of his hand. Tuck then saw why Alan was trying to warn them. His heart sank. For between Alan and the dock stood two of the Ffreinc noblemen they had been hunting with the day before, and there was no ship in sight.

CHAPTER 22

Leaping, ducking, dodging through the thick-grown woodland tangle like a wild bird, Bran flew towards the sound of the baying hounds. In a little while, he reached the edge of the hunting run and burst out onto open ground—not more than a few hundred paces from the hunting party: four men on horseback, lances ready. They were standing at the edge of the run, watching the wood and waiting for the dogs and their handler to flush the quarry into the open so they could ride it down.

It was their usual way of hunting. Only, this time, their quarry was Bran.

Without a moment's hesitation, Bran put his head down and ran for the opposite side of the wide grassy corridor. He had made it but halfway across when there arose a shout behind him. *"Arrêt! Arrêt!"*

He ran even faster and reached the far side of the hunting run and flashed into the undergrowth with the riders right behind. There was more shouting behind him and the sound of ringing steel as the four knights began hacking their way into the wood. Bran found a big elm tree and paused to catch his breath. He waited until he heard the hounds again and then darted off once more, this time working his way back through the woods in the direction of the earl's castle.

The chase was breathless and frantic. The hounds were quick on his scent, and as fast as Bran hurtled through the brake, the dogs were faster still. It was only a matter of time before he would be caught and brought to bay. He ran on, trying his best to put some distance between himself and the hunters. He heard the slavering growls as the beasts closed on him. He was searching for a heavy branch to wield as a club when the first hound finally reached him.

The dog bounded over a fallen limb, and Bran turned meet it. The animal—a great, long-legged rangy grey beast—howled once and leaped for him. Bran, standing still in the path, made no move to flee. Instead, he held out his hands. "Here! Come, old friend. Come to Count Rexindo."

The dog, confused now, hesitated. Then, identifying the man who had fed him and befriended him, it gave a yelp of recognition and ran to Bran, put his paws on his chest, and began licking Bran's face. "Good fella," said Bran. "That's right, we're friends. Here, come with me. Let's run."

Bran started off again with the dog loping easily beside him. They were joined by a second dog and, within another dozen running steps, the third hound came alongside. The four of them, dogs and man, flowed through the forest with the ease and grace of creatures born to the greenwood, quickly outdistancing the handler and the hunters still sitting on their horses in the hunting run.

They came onto a path lying roughly parallel to the hunting run; a few flying steps farther and it began sloping down towards a stream which would, Bran guessed, lead to the river and the river to the town. "This way, boys," called Bran, hurtling down towards the water. They splashed into the stream and continued on at a slower pace. After a time, Bran paused to listen.

He heard nothing—no crack and swish of branches, no shouts of hunters keen on the trail, no sounds of pursuit at all. He had outstripped the chase, and without the constant howling of the dogs to lead them, the hunters were floundering far, far behind and likely on a different path altogether.

He paused in the stream, then stooped and cupped water to his mouth and swallowed down a few gulps. Then stood, sunlight splashing down from a gap in the branches overhead, and drew the moist air deep into his lungs. The sky was clear and blue, the day stretching out fine before him. "Come on, lads," said Bran. "Let's go home."

They resumed their long walk, splashing downstream, sometimes in it, more often on the wide, muddy bank. The dogs did not follow so much as accompany him—now running ahead, now lagging behind as they sniffed the air for scent of errant game. Bran kept up a steady pace, pausing to listen every now and then, but heard nothing save the sounds of the forest. Some little time later, the woodland began to thin and he glimpsed cultivated fields through the trees. He stepped out to find himself at the edge of a settlement— a few low houses, a barn, and a scattering of outbuildings with a small pen for pigs. He watched the place for a moment, but saw no one about, so quickly moved on, working his way towards the track he knew he would find eventually—the path that connected the settlement to the town.

Once on the road, he made good time. Reaching Caer Cestre after midday, he hurried down the narrow streets and proceeded directly to the wharf, alert to any threat of discovery. At the lower town, he made for the dockyard and was still a little way off when he saw the mast of a moored ship: a small coast-crawling cog with a single low central mast and broad tiller. Closer, he saw a clump of men standing on the dock, and picked out the plump form of Tuck and, with him, four of Earl Hugh's soldiers. They seemed to be arguing.

He halted, thinking what to do.

There was no sign of the other Welshmen, so Bran resumed his walk down to the dock, picking up his speed as he went until, with a sudden furious rush, he closed on the group of men. He was on them before they knew he was there. Seizing the nearest soldier by the arm, he marched the surprised knight to the edge of the jetty and, with a mighty heave, vaulted him into the river. The body hit with a loud thwack, and the resulting splash showered the dock with water.

Bran dropped lightly down into a small fishing boat moored to the pier below and, seizing an oar from the oarlock, fended off the flailing knight. The soldier's companions stared in slack-jawed astonishment at this audacious attack. One of them dashed to the end of the dock and extended his hand to his comrade. Bran dropped the oar, grabbed the hand, and pulled for all he was worth. The knight gave out a whoop as he toppled over the edge and into the water as well.

The two remaining knights backed away from the edge of the dock and drew their swords. One of them raised the point of his blade to Tuck's throat, while the other waved his weapon impotently at Bran, who remained out of reach in the boat. Both were shouting in French and gesturing for the two Welshmen to surrender. "Tuck!" cried Bran, lofting the other oar. "Catch!"

Up came the oar. The friar snatched it from the air and, gathering his strength behind it, drove the blade into the soldier's chest, propelling him backward and over the edge of the dock to join his two companions in the water. The last knight standing swung towards Tuck, his blade a bright arc in the air.

Tuck was quicker than he knew. Sliding his hands along the shaft of the oar, he deftly spun it up into the man's face. The knight stumbled backwards, retreating step by step. Bran, meanwhile, scrambled back onto the dock. "Now, Tuck!"

Tuck drove forward with the oar, and the knight fell back a step, tripping over Bran's outstretched foot. The knight lurched awkwardly, trying to keep his feet under him. He swung the blade wildly at Tuck, who easily parried the stroke, knocking it wide. Another thrust with the oar sent the soldier sprawling onto his backside, and before he could recover, Bran had grabbed his legs, pulled them up over his head, and pitched the knight heels first off the dock and into the river.

Bran and Tuck paused to look at their handiwork: four soldiers thrashing in the water and crying for help. Owing to the weight of their padded jerkins and mail shirts, they were unable to clamber out of the river; it was all they could do to keep their heads above water. Their cries had begun to draw would-be rescuers to the waterfront.

"Where are Gruffydd and the others?" asked Bran.

"They're hiding across the way," Tuck said, waving vaguely behind him. "I told Alan to keep them out of sight until the ship was ready. It has only just arrived."

Bran glanced around. Two boys stood on deck, laughing at the spectacle played out on the dock. Their shipmates had gone ashore, leaving the youngest crew members to watch the vessel. "Go get them," ordered Bran. "Get everyone aboard the ship and cast off!"

"But the captain and crew are not here," replied Tuck. "They've gone up to the town."

"Just go," Bran urged, picking up the oar. "I'll keep the soldiers busy."

Tuck dashed away, returning as fast as his stubby legs allowed with Alan, Gruffydd, and the two young Welshmen trailing in his wake. They arrived on the dock to find Bran swinging the oar and shouting, keeping the water-logged Ffreinc in the water and the gathering crowd of onlookers at bay. Truth be told, Bran found preventing the rescue far easier than he imagined. Most of the townsfolk seemed to be enjoying the spectacle of the earl's thugs at such an embarrassing disadvantage. Several boys were throwing stones at the knights, who singed the air with curses and obscenities.

"Get aboard!" cried Bran. "Cast off!"

Tuck turned on the others. "You heard him! Get aboard and cast off."

While Ifor and Brocmael untied the mooring ropes, Alan picked up two long poles that were lying on the dock and tossed them onto the deck of the ship. The boat's two young guardians protested, but were powerless to prevent their vessel from being boarded. They stood by helplessly as Tuck and Gruffydd set the plank on the rail and climbed aboard. "Ready!" Tuck called.

"Push away!" shouted Bran, wielding the oar over his sputtering charges.

Using the poles, Alan and Brocmael began easing the cog away from the dock. As the ship floated free, Ifor grabbed the tiller and tried to steer the vessel into deeper water in the centre of the stream. The ship began to move. "Bran!" shouted Tuck. "Now!"

Bran gave a last thrust with the oar and threw it into the water.

Then, with a running jump, he leapt from the dock onto the deck of the ship. He was no sooner aboard than a howling arose from the wharf; he turned to see the three hounds pacing along the edge of the dock and barking.

"Come!" called Bran, slapping the side of the vessel. "Come on, lads! Jump!"

The dogs needed no further encouragement. They put their heads down and ran for the ship, bounded across the widening gap, and fell onto the deck in a tangle of legs and tails. Bran laughed and dived in among them. They licked his hands and face, and he returned their affection, giving them each a chuck around the ears and telling them what good, brave dogs they were.

"You've stolen the earl's hounds," Brocmael said, amazed at Bran's audacity—considering the high price Wolf Hugh set on his prize animals.

"Hounds?" said Ifor. "We've stolen a whole ship entire!"

"The ship will be returned," Bran told them, still patting the nearest dog. "But the hounds we keep—they'll help us to remember our pleasant days hunting with the earl. Anyway, we've left him our horses—a fair enough trade, I reckon."

"Does anyone know how to sail a ship of this size?" wondered Alan.

"Maybe the lads there can help us," Tuck said, regarding the boys—who were thoroughly amazed at what had taken place and were enjoying it in spite of themselves. "Maybe they know how to sail it."

"We don't have to sail it," Bran countered. "We'll let the tideflow carry us downriver as far as the next settlement and try to pick up a pilot there. Until then, Ifor, you and your two young friends will man the tiller and see you keep us in the stream flow and off the bank. Can you do that?"

"I've seen it done," replied the young man.

"Then take us home," said Bran. Ifor called the two young crewmen to him and, with an assortment of signs and gestures, showed them what they were to do. Bran crossed to where Gruffydd was sitting against the side of the ship, knees up and his head resting on his arms.

"Are you well, my lord?" Bran said, squatting down beside him.

"My blasted head hurts," he complained. "Did you have to hit me so hard?"

"Perhaps not," Bran allowed. "But then, you did not give us much choice."

The king offered a grunt of derision and lowered his head once more. "You will feel better soon," Bran told him, rising once more. "And when we cross over into Wales you'll begin to see things in a better light."

Gruffydd made no reply, so Bran left him alone to nurse his aching head. Meanwhile, Tuck and Brocmael had begun searching the hold of the ship to see what it carried by way of provisions. "We have cheese, dried meat, and a little ale."

"We'll pick up more when we stop. Until then, fill the cups, Tuck! I feel a thirst coming on."

PART FOUR

"O cowardly dastard!" Will Scadlocke exclaim'd.
  "Thou faint-hearted, sow-mothered reeve!
If ever my master doth deign thee to meet,
  Thou shalt thy full paiment receive!"

Then Rhiban Hud, setting his horn to his mouth,
  A blast he merrily blows;
His yeomen from bushes and treetops appeared,
  A hundred, with trusty longbows.

And Little John came at the head of them all,
  Cloath'd in a rich mantle, green;
And likewise the others were fancif'ly drest,
  A wonderous sight to be seen.

Forth from the greenwoode about they are come,
  With hearts that are firm and e'er stout,
Pledging them all with the sheriff's yeomen
  To give them a full hearty bout.

And Rhiban the Hud has removéd his cloak,
    And the sheriff has uttered an oath,
And William now smites him on top of his pate
    and swift exit is now made by both.

"Little I thought," quod Scadlocke eft-soon,
    "When I first came to this place,
For to have met with dear Little John,
    Or again see my master's fine face."

CHAPTER 23

"I t is a grand day, my lord Bran," Llewelyn proclaimed, grinning blearily through a haze of brown ale. "A grand and glorious day. Though it shames me to admit it, I never hoped to see our Gruffydd on his throne again. No, I never did. Yet, here he is—all thanks to you. Here he is."

Two days of riotous celebration had followed the rescuers' triumphant return to Aberffraw with their newly freed captive. King Gruffydd's homecoming was heralded as a miracle on the order of Lazarus walking out of his tomb; and Bran, Tuck, Ifor, Brocmael, and Alan were lauded as champions and made to recount their exploits time and again to rapturous listeners until they grew hoarse for speaking. The revel was entering its third day before Bran and Tuck finally found the opportunity to speak to Gruffydd and Llewelyn in private.

"Here are men after my own heart!" declared Gruffydd, closing the door on the celebration to join them in his chamber. Bathed and shaved, his matted, moth-eaten locks shorn to his scalp, arrayed in a new wool cloak and fine red linen shirt, the king of the Northern Cymry finally resembled something worthy of the name. "You should have seen them, Llewelyn," he bellowed. "They were mighty giants doing battle for me. It's true!" Swaying unsteadily, he draped an arm across Bran's shoulders. "I am forever in your debt, my friend. Hear me, Bran ap Brychan, may God blind me if I should ever forget."

"That would be most uncomfortable for you," allowed Bran with a smile, "but, never fear. I have a way to help you."

"Then speak it out, man, and see how quickly it is accomplished," said Gruffydd. Reeling slightly, he looked around for his cup, saw one in Llewelyn's hand, and took it.

Bran hesitated, uncertain whether to take advantage of the king's ale-induced generosity or wait until Gruffydd was sober once more— which might mean a wait of several more days.

"Speak, man, and if it is in my power to grant, you shall have it before the sun has set on another day," boasted Gruffydd. He drained the cup and wiped the foam from his moustache. "What will you have?"

"Your friendship," said Bran.

"That you have in abundance already," replied Gruffydd grandly. He waved his hand airily.

"What else?" prompted Llewelyn, well aware of Bran's true desire.

Bran looked to Tuck, who urged him with a glance to ask for the help he had come north to seek. "As I have aided the return of your king to his lands and people," replied Bran, speaking slowly and deliberately, "I ask the king's pledge to aid me in the return of my lands and people."

A shadow passed over Gruffydd's square face just then. The smile remained firmly fixed, but his eyes narrowed. "Then receive my pledge," Gruffydd said. "How can I help you?"

"With men and weapons," Bran said. "Raise the tribes of Gwynedd and the north and ride with me. Together we can wrest Elfael from the Ffreinc and drive them from our lands."

Gruffydd frowned. He looked into the empty cup as if it had offended him, then thrust it back at Llewelyn. "If that lay within my power," he said, his voice falling, "you would have it this very night. Alas, I cannot grant such a request."

Bran's face tightened. Staring at the king, he said, "You will not help?"

"I cannot," replied Gruffydd, who seemed to have sobered in the matter of a moment. "You must understand," he continued, half turning away, "I have been absent from my realm eight years! For eight years my people have been without a king—"

"They've had Llewelyn," Bran pointed out.

"True enough," granted Gruffydd, "and I am the first to say he has served faithfully and well. But you and I both know that it is not the same thing at all."

"Then you will not help me," Bran said, his voice tight.

"I wish you had asked anything but that," the king replied. "My first duty is to my people and my realm. I cannot resume my reign by running off again as soon as I am home. Much less can I mark my return by forcing my people into a war that does not concern them. If you were in my place, you would see that."

"My friends and I risked all to save you—"

"And for that you have my friendship and gratitude to my dying breath," Lord Gruffydd replied.

"It is not your gratitude I want," Bran said, his tone taking on an edge. "It is your aid in arms."

"That," said Gruffydd carelessly, "is the one thing you cannot have."

Bran made to step closer. Gruffydd held his ground.

"My lord," said Tuck, insinuating his bulk between Gruffydd and an increasingly angry Bran, "if you knew the precarious hold the Ffreinc possessed, you would see our request in a different light."

"How so?" asked Llewelyn, doing what he could to help.

"The Ffreinc forces are few in number," Tuck said, still holding himself between the increasingly angry lords, "and poorly supplied. We have seen to that, have we not? For though we are few in number, living rough in the greenwood on pitiful fare, with families and little 'uns to keep—even so, we have pressed them hard these last two years and more, and they are bent that near to breaking. All it needs is some stout warriors, a few fresh fighters, a last battle or two—a final push over the edge and the thing is done."

"How long would you need the use of the men?" asked Llewelyn.

"A month perhaps," said Bran quickly. "The Ffreinc do not have enough soldiers to make a lengthy campaign. It would be finished in a month—no more. That is little enough, it seems to me."

"Alas," rued Gruffydd, unmoved, "even that little is too much. I wish I could help."

"My lord, I urge you to reconsider," pleaded Llewelyn. "A month, mind you. Surely, it is not beyond our ability to aid them in this—"

His entreaty was cut short by a curt gesture from his king. "I have spoken." Gruffydd turned and stepped towards the door. "My friends," he said, adopting a stiffly formal air even as he clutched the doorpost to steady himself, "you are most welcome to remain with me as long as you like. I am happy for your company. Nevertheless, we will not speak of this again."

With that, the king returned to the celebration.

"Come, Tuck," said Bran, watching Gruffydd through the open

door as the king moved among his kinsmen and friends, embracing some, sharing the cup with others. "We will not remain here a moment longer than it takes to scrape the dung of this miserable place off our feet."

"My lord," said Llewelyn, deeply embarrassed by his king's behaviour, "do not be overhasty. Stay a little longer—a few days only—and we will yet change his mind. I will summon the lords to council with the king, and he will be persuaded. On my word, you will yet have your just reward."

"If only you were king, Llewelyn," replied Bran darkly. Then, remembering himself, he softened his tone and said, "You have shown me honour and respect, and I thank you for that. Nor do I hold Gruffydd's ingratitude against you. But I see now that I was wrong to come here, wrong to ask, wrong to think the fate of Elfael meant anything to my family in the north."

Llewelyn opened his mouth to protest this last assertion, but a warning glance from Tuck prevented him. Instead, he moved quietly to the door, and there he paused and regarded Bran sadly. "I'm sorry," he said, then stepped back into the hall, leaving Tuck and Bran alone.

"And God with you, too, Cousins," muttered Bran to men who were no longer there. "Bring the horses, Tuck," he said after a moment, "and find Alan. We're leaving."

They left the hall and moved out into the yard. It was after midday, and the clouds were low and dark, threatening rain. Tuck thought to argue for staying at least one day longer to allow Gruffydd the chance to change his mind and so they would not have to ride in the rain, but he knew Bran would not hear it. As the cinch belts were being tightened on the saddles, Ifor and Brocmael came into the stables.

"We were looking for you," said Brocmael. "You're leaving?"

"So soon?" said Ifor.

Both young men appeared so crestfallen that Tuck tried to put a better face on it. "We have finished here, and anyway we are needed back home. But, God willing, we'll come back one day," he told them, then added, patting the fresh mount beside him, "Do thank your father for the gift of these fine horses."

"It is the least we could do," said Ifor, "after all you've done for us."

"What about the troops?" wondered Brocmael.

"Your king does not see fit to raise any," Bran told him.

"That's why you're leaving," said Ifor.

"Aye," confessed Bran. "That is why."

"We'll come with you," Ifor offered. He nudged Brocmael, who agreed. "We can fight."

"Your place is here," said Bran. "Your king will not give you leave to go. He has made it very clear he does not think Elfael worth saving." Reaching out a hand, he gave each of their arms a squeeze by way of farewell. "Nevertheless, you have been brave and loyal companions these past days. You have done yourselves and your families proud. No one could have served me better. But here is where it ends."

The two young warriors exchanged an unhappy glance. "What about Earl Hugh's hounds?" asked Brocmael. "Shall I fetch them for you?"

"No, I want you and Ifor to have them," answered Bran. "Consider them a small gesture of thanks for your help."

"We cannot, my lord," protested Ifor. "They are worth a very fortune."

"It is too much," agreed Brocmael. "They are far too valuable."

"No more valuable than the help you gave me when asked," Bran replied. "They are yours, my friends. Make your fortune with them."

Tuck, Alan, and Bran left Aberffraw as soon as the horses were ready. Bran did not speak the rest of the day, but fumed and fretted, working himself into such a dark and threatening gloom that Tuck began to fear for the havoc unleashed when the gathering storm finally broke. He had seen Bran like this before—once in Londein when they had gone to redeem the lands from the crown at the enormous price of six hundred marks, only to have Cardinal Flambard cheat him by raising the price to two thousand. Tuck and Iwan had pulled him off the scoundrel churchman or in all likelihood none of them would have lived out the day. Angharad knew best how to ease Rhi Bran's murderous moods, but she was in faraway Elfael.

"Alan," Tuck had said, "if you know any songs that would put our Bran in a better mood, I pray you sing one now."

"As it happens," replied Alan a'Dale, "I have been thinking of a song he might enjoy. It isn't finished yet—I need a rhyme for Count Rexindo, d'ye ken?"

"Sing it anyway," Tuck told him.

So Alan sang them on their way.

Four days later, he was still singing, as from time to time Bran's dark and dangerous mood threatened to swallow them all. Alan, it seemed, was full of unexpected talents, and ever ready to cheer his lord along with a quip or a joke or a song. Of the latter, most of his ditties were English drinking songs and ballads more appreciated by Friar Tuck than by Bran, who from time to time slipped back into his moody darkness. The French and Welsh songs had lilting melodies—some glad, some mournful to suit their solemn humour—but the best songs were those Alan had made up himself: including the new one that extolled the exploits of Count Rexindo and his merry band, who deceived the wicked earl and won the freedom of the captive king of Gwynedd. Tuck found this highly amusing, but Bran was not so sure he wanted his doings voiced about the countryside like so much scattered seed.

Still, the singing and stories told under the clear, open sky worked their wonders, and by the time the travellers came within sight of the towering green wall of the great forest of Coed Cadw, Bran's temper had cooled to the point where Tuck thought he might risk venturing a thought or two of his own regarding their predicament as it now stood. "Perhaps," he suggested, "it might be well to heed Mérian's advice and go see her father."

Bran considered this only as long as it took to purse his lips and shake his head. "God knows that man is no friend of mine. Even if Cadwgan did not hate me when this began, I will not have risen any higher in his esteem by holding his daughter captive."

"At the first, maybe," granted Tuck. "But she stayed on of her own free will. When given the choice, she stayed."

"Even if he was inclined to help," countered Bran, "he is a vassal of Baron Neufmarché. As it runs against his interests, the baron would never allow it. No," said Bran, shaking his head again, this time with resignation, "we will get no help from Lord Cadwgan."

They skirted Saint Martin's, the abbot's town, and entered the sheltering forest just as the sky of lowering clouds sent rain streaming down the wind. It would be a wet night in the greenwood, but the rain did little to dampen the welcome the travellers received at their homecoming. The Grellon gathered to greet them, and Bran roused himself from his grim melancholy to say that he was glad to be home once more. But as he scanned the faces gathered around, the one looked-for face did not appear.

"Where's Mérian?" Bran asked.

An uneasy hush drew across the forest dwellers, and Iwan stepped forward. "Welcome, my lord," he said, his voice booming in the quiet. "It is good to have you back safely. I trust your journey was successful."

"Your trust is misplaced," snapped Bran. "We failed." Still searching among the Grellon, he said, "Mérian . . . where is she, Iwan?"

The big warrior paused, looking thoughtful. "Mérian is not here," he said at last. "She left and went back to Eiwas."

Before Bran could ask more, the champion gestured to someone in the crowd of onlookers, and Noín stepped forward. "Tell him what happened," Iwan instructed.

Noínina made a small bow of greeting to her king and said, "It is true, my lord. Mérian went home." She folded her hands into the apron at her waist. "It was in her mind to go and ask her father to send men to aid us in the fight against the Ffreinc."

"I see," Bran replied coldly. "When did she leave?"

"Two days after you departed for the north."

"Who went with her?"

"My lord," said Noín, a note of anxiety rising in her voice, "she went alone."

"Alone!" Turning on Iwan, he demanded, "You let her go alone?" When the big man made no reply, Bran glanced around at the others. "Did no one think to go with her?"

"We did not know she was going," Iwan explained. "I would have prevented her, of course. But she told no one of her intentions and left before anyone knew she was gone."

"*Someone* knew, by the rood," Bran observed, indicating the worried Noín before him.

"Forgive me, my lord, but she made me promise not to say anything until after she had gone," Noín said, looking down at her feet. "I did try to persuade her otherwise, but she would not hear it."

"I was halfway down the trail for going after her," said Will Scarlet, pushing forward to stand beside his wife. "Would'a gone, too, but by the time we found out, it was too late. Mérian was already home, and if anything was going to happen to her . . ." He paused. "Well, I reckoned it already did."

Bran took this in, his fists clenching and unclenching at his side. "I leave you in charge, Iwan," he snarled. "And this is how my trust is repaid? I am—"

"Peace!" said Angharad, speaking from a few steps behind him. Pushing through the gathered throng of welcomers, the Wise Banfáith planted herself in front of him. "This is not seemly, my lord. Your people have given you good greeting and the same would receive from their king." She fixed him with a commanding stare until Bran remembered himself and, in a somewhat stilted fashion, thanked his champion and others for keeping Cél Craidd in his absence.

Tuck, drawing near, gave Bran a nudge with his elbow and indicated Alan a'Dale standing a short distance apart from the group, ignored and unremarked. So Bran introduced the Grellon to Alan a'Dale and instructed his flock to make the newcomer feel at home among them. Having satisfied courtesy, Bran retreated to his hut, saying he wished to be left in peace to rest after his journey.

"Rest you will have," said Angharad, following him into the hut.

"But not from you, I see."

"Not from me—and *not* until you learn that berating those who have given good service is beneath one who would account himself a worthy king. Angry with Mérian you may be—"

"She disobeyed me—"

"She must have had good reason, think you?"

"We discussed it and I told her not to go," Bran complained, throwing himself into his hide-and-antler chair. "Yet the moment my back is turned, what does she do?"

"Your Lady Mérian is a woman of great determination and resourcefulness; she is not one to be easily dominated by others." Angharad gazed at him, her eyes alight within their wreath of familiar wrinkles. "It is her own mind she has followed—"

"She has disobeyed me," Bran said.

"This it is that tears at you?" replied the banfáith. "Or is it that she might have been right to go?" Before Bran could answer, she said, "It matters not, for now there is nothing to be done about it."

Bran glared at her but knew that pursuing this argument any further would avail him nothing.

"Too late you show the wisdom of silence," Angharad observed. "So now, if you would put away childish things, tell me what happened in the north."

Bran frowned and passed a hand over his face as if trying to wipe away the memory. He gave a brief account of finding the king of Gwynedd a captive to Earl Hugh and riding into Caer Cestre to free him. "The long and short of it," he continued, "is that we failed to persuade King Gruffydd to rally the tribes to our support. We cannot count on them for any men."

The old woman considered this, nodded, but said nothing.

"Not one," said Bran. "We are worse off than when we began," he concluded gloomily.

Into the fraught and fretted silence of the hut there drifted a soft, lilting melody sung by a clear and steady voice—a sound not unfamiliar in Cél Craidd, but this one was different. Angharad went to the door of the hut, opened it, and stepped outside. Bran followed and felt his anger and disappointment begin to melt away in the refrains of the tune. There, surrounded by the forest-dwellers, his head lifted high and with a voice to set the glade shimmering, Alan was singing his song about Rhi Bran and the Wolf of Cestre.

CHAPTER 24

When Bran learned that Sheriff de Glanville had returned to Saint Martin's with a force of fifty soldiers, he said nothing, but took his bow and went alone into the greenwood. Siarles was all for going after him, but Angharad advised against it, saying, "Think yourself a king to bear a king's burden? His own counsel he must keep, if his own mind he would know." And, to be sure, Rhi Bran returned that evening with a yearling buck and a battle plan.

First, he determined to do what he could to even the odds against him. The fine, dry summer had given way to a blessedly mild autumn, and the harvest in the valleys had been good. Most of the crops would be gathered in now against the lean seasons to follow. The granaries and storehouses would be bulging. Bran decided to help his people and, at the same time, hit the Ffreinc where it would hurt the most. He would attack in the dead heart of the darkest night of the month.

The moon had been on the wane for several days, and tonight

there would be a new one; the darkness would be heavy and would aid his design. Early in the morning, Bran sent spies into the town to see what could be learned of the disposition of the sheriff's troops. Noín and Alan had been chosen—much to Will's displeasure. "I have no objection," Scarlet complained, "so long as I go along."

"They know you too well," Bran reminded him. "I don't want to see you end up in that pit again—or worse. One glimpse is all the sheriff would need to put your head on a spike."

"But you don't mind if my Noín's sweet face ends up decorating that bloody spike," he griped.

"Scarlet!" The sound was sharp as a slap. "You go too far." Angharad shuffled forth, wagging a bony finger. "A proper respect for your king would well become you."

Will glared at her, his jaw set.

"Now, William Scatlocke!"

"Forgive me, Sire," offered Will, striving to sound suitably contrite. "If I have spoken above myself, I do most humbly beg your pardon."

"Pardon granted, Will," Bran told him. "A man would have a heart of stone who did not care for his wife. But the raids I have in mind succeed or fail on what we learn. We need to know how things sit in the town before we go rushing down there."

Will nodded and glanced to Noín, who pressed his hand. "I have gone to market before, you know. That's all it is—just two folk going to market."

"You had best leave now," said Bran. "Stay only as long as it takes to find out what we need and then hurry back. We will wait for you at the ford."

"There and back and no one the wiser, m'lord," Alan volunteered. "Alan a'Dale will see to it." To Scarlet, he said, "They've never seen me before, and I can talk the legs off a donkey if I have to. We'll be back safe and sound before you know it."

Bran commended them to their task, and Angharad spoke a brief blessing of protection over them and the two departed. The rest of the Grellon began preparing for the night's activities: weapons and ropes were readied, and five riders were sent to the holdings and farms in the valley to warn the folk about King Raven's plans and to enlist any aid they could find. In the end, there were so many willing volunteers that they chose only the most hale and hearty to help and told them where to go, and when.

Tuck decided that he would best be served by a new staff, so took himself into the wood to find a sturdy branch of ash which he cut to length and then shaped. As he worked, he found great satisfaction in reciting a few of the Psalms that the young Israelite warrior David composed when seeking deliverance from his many enemies.

By the time the sun began its long, slow plunge into the western sea, all was ready. The raiders, eight in all, departed for the ford to meet the spies. Alan and Noín were already waiting at the forest's edge when they arrived. Will Scarlet was the first to see them and ran to where the two sat beside the stream near the ford. "Is all well?" he asked, and received a brushing kiss by way of answer from his wife.

"No one paid us any heed at all," Alan told them. "Why would they? We were just two humble folk attending the market, ye ken?"

"Well and good," said Bran. "So now, what did you discover?"

"It is true the town is full of Ffreinc," began Alan, "but they trust their numbers a little too much, it seems to me." He went on to explain that the soldiers were everywhere to be seen—at the entrance to the town square, before the abbey gate, clustered around the guardhouse tower—but almost to a man they appeared bored and lax. "You can see those fellas idling here and there, dicin' and drinkin' and what-all. They swagger around like little emperors all, and most of them don't carry weapons—maybe a dagger only."

"No doubt they know where to find a ready blade smart enough when pressed to it," observed Iwan.

"Oh, no doubt," agreed Alan readily. "But I'm just saying what I saw."

"What about the sheriff?" asked Will. "Did you see that rat-faced spoiler?"

"I did not," answered Alan. "Neither hide nor hair. Plenty of soldiers though, as I say."

"You found where they keep the supplies?" asked Bran.

"We did, Lord," answered Alan. Looking to Noín, he nodded. "Noín here did that easy as please and be thanked."

"I went to the church when they rang the bell for the midday mass," Noín reported. "There were but a few townsfolk and a merchant or two, so I knelt in the back and waited for the service to finish. Then I followed the monks to the abbey, pretending that I was hungry and in need of food for myself and my poor starving children three."

"You told them that?" said Scarlet, chagrined at the barest suggestion that he was no fit provider for his family.

"It was only pretence," she said lightly. "But I have been pared near enough to the bone to know how it feels. To their credit the priests took pity on me and let me inside the abbey walls. I was made to wait in the yard while they fetched a few provisions."

"And you saw where these were kept?" said Siarles.

"Oh, aye—made sure of it. There is a granary behind the bishop's house. It looks new to me—wattled and thatched like a barn, but smaller."

"They brought you food from these stores?" asked Tuck. "You saw this?"

"Aye, they did—brought me some grain and a rind of salt pork," Noín told him, "and a handful of dried beans. There was plenty more whence that came, believe me."

"There must be," mused Iwan, "if they are about giving away food to needy Cymry."

"At least," suggested Siarles, "they are not over-worried about running out of provisions anytime soon."

"They will be running out sooner than they know," said Bran. "What else?"

The raiding party listened to all that Alan and Noín had to say about the troops and stores. When they finished, Bran praised their good service and sent them on their way back to Cél Craidd, saying, "Tell the others we're going ahead with the raid. If all goes well, we will return before dawn."

So Alan and Noín continued on their way, and the raiding party settled down to wait, watching a pale blue velvet dusk settle over the Vale of Elfael below. The stars winked on one by one, and the raiders sat and talked, their voices a low murmur barely audible above the liquid splash of the nearby stream.

It is so beautiful, thought Tuck, so peaceful. *"Ach, fy enaid,"* he sighed.

"Second thoughts, Friar?" asked Siarles, sliding down beside him.

"Never that, boyo," replied Tuck. "But it does seem a very shame to violate such tranquillity, does it not?"

"Perhaps, but it will be far more tranquil when the Ffreinc are gone, Friar," answered Siarles. "Think of that."

"I pray that it is so." Tuck sighed again. "It is a beautiful valley, though."

They talked a little while, and then Tuck closed his eyes and drifted off to sleep, to be awakened sometime later by Siarles jostling his shoulder. "Time to be about the devil's business, Friar."

Regaining their saddles, the party rode down into the vale, circling around to the north of the town and the abbey fields. They came to the edge of a bean field which lay just beyond the stone walls of the monastery Abbot Hugo had erected. "If I heard it right, the abbot's storehouse is just the other side of that wall," Iwan pointed out. The wall, like the abbey and town behind it, was an indistinct mass, black against the deeper, featureless blackness of a moonless night.

"Owain and Rhoddi," said Bran, "go and rouse the others. Bring them here—and for the love of God and all the angels, tell everyone to keep quiet." The two warriors turned and rode for the forest's edge north of town. As soon as they had gone, Bran said, "Tuck, you will stay with the horses and keep order outside the walls. Tomas and Scarlet—go with Iwan. Siarles, you come with me. Once over the wall, meet at the storehouse." The old sly smile played on his lips as he said, "Time for Rhi Bran y Hud to fly."

The raiders urged their mounts forward across the leafy field, now black beneath the hooves of their horses. A few paces from the wall, they stopped and dismounted. "God with you," whispered Tuck as they hefted first one man and then the next up onto the top of the abbey wall. When the last raider disappeared, the friar turned to look for Rhoddi and Owain, but could see nothing in the darkness.

He waited, gazing wide-eyed into the darkness and listening for any stray sounds from the other side of the wall, but saw nothing and heard only the sound of the horses breathing and, once in a while, chafing the ground with an idle hoof. After a time, there came a whispered hiss from somewhere above his head. "Ssssst!" Once, and then again. "Ssssst!"

"Here!" whispered Tuck. "This way—to your right."

"Get ready," said the voice. It was Siarles kneeling atop the wall. "We'll send over the grain sacks first. Ready?"

"I'm the only one here," Tuck told him.

"Where is everyone?"

"They're here," came the reply as Rhoddi appeared silent as a ghost out of the darkness. To his unseen companions, he said, "Owain, line 'em up behind me. Keep out of the way, and stay alert."

"How many are with you?" Siarles called down softly.

"Ten," answered Owain "We're ready, so heave away."

A moment later another figure joined Siarles on the wall. There was a dry scraping sound followed by a thick thud as the first sack hit the ground at the base of the wall. Three more followed in quick succession. "Get 'em up," whispered Siarles.

Fumbling in the darkness, the Cymry from the surrounding settlements jostled the bulging sacks of grain onto the shoulders of three of their number, who disappeared into the darkness. "Ready," Rhoddi called quietly.

There followed a pause, and then, without warning, a large, weighty object thudded to the ground. "What was that?" wondered Tuck, mostly to himself. Four more objects were sent over the wall in quick succession, followed by numerous smaller bundles dropped over the wall to form a growing heap on the ground.

"Clear it out," whispered Siarles.

"You heard him, men," said Owain. Again, the waiting Cymry leapt forward and fell upon the bundles, sacks, and casks that had been tossed over the wall. The process was repeated two more times, and each time there were fewer Cymry left to carry the supplies away. Finally, Siarles reappeared atop the wall and said, "There's people stirring in the abbey. I'm coming over." Squatting down, he turned, grabbed an edge, and lowered himself lengthwise down the face of the wall.

"The others are clean away," Tuck told him. "I've got the horses ready."

"We best stir ourselves and get this lot loaded, too," Siarles said. "Bring 'em up, and let's have at it."

The two of them began piling the goods onto the carriers attached to the saddles of the horses. One by one, the remaining raiders joined Tuck and Siarles outside the wall; Bran and Iwan were the last, and all made short work of toting the bundles and casks to the waiting horses. The back-and-forth continued until from somewhere beyond the wall a bell sounded and the raiders halted. The bell tolled three times. "It's *Lauds*," said Tuck. "They'll be going to the chapel for prayer."

"That's it, lads," said Bran. "Time to fly." He glanced away towards the east, where a dull glow could be seen above the dark line of treetops. "Look, now! It's beginning to get light, and all this thieving has made me hungry."

"Luckily, there's ale for our troubles," Scarlet said, picking up a cask and shaking it so it sloshed. "And wine, too, if I'm not mistaken."

The last of the goods were packed and tied into place, and as each horse was ready one of the riders led it away. Bran and Tuck were last to leave, following the others across the broad black expanse of the bean field to the forest edge, where they met with the Cymry who had helped; and a rough division of the spoils was made then and there. "Spread it around to those who need it most," Bran told them. "But mind to keep it well hid in case any of the Ffreinc come sniffing around after it."

The rest of the way back to the forest was a long, slow amble through the night-dark vale and up the rise into the greenwood. They moved with the mist along cool forest pathways and arrived back at Cél Craidd as the sun broke fair on another sparkling, crisp autumn day—but a day that Abbot Hugo would remember as dismal indeed, the day his troubles began in earnest.

CHAPTER 25

King Raven visited the abbey stores again the next night, despite the watch the sheriff and abbot had placed on the gate and storehouse. This time, however, instead of carrying off the supplies, the black-hooded creature destroyed them. Iwan and Tuck rode with him to the edge of the forest and, as they had done the previous night, waited for night to deepen the darkness. The moon would rise late, but it would be only a pale sliver in the sky. In any event, Bran planned to be back in the forest before his trail could be followed.

When he judged the time was right, he donned his feathered cloak and the high-crested beak mask, and climbed into the saddle. "I could go with you," Iwan said.

"There's no need," Bran demurred. "And it will be easier to elude them on my own."

"We'll wait for you here, then," replied the champion. He handed Bran his bow and six black arrows, three of which had been specially prepared.

"Go with God," Tuck said, and passed Bran the chain from which was suspended a small iron canister—a covered dish of coals. "Oh, it's a sorry waste," he sighed as Bran rode away. His dark form was swiftly swallowed by the darkness.

"Aye," agreed Iwan, "but needful. Taking food from the mouth of an enemy is almost as good as eating it yourself."

Tuck considered this for a moment. "No," he decided, "it is not."

The two settled back to watch and wait. They listened to the night sounds of the forest and the easy rustling of the leaves in the upper boughs of the trees as the breeze came up. Tuck was nodding off to sleep when Iwan said, "There he is."

Tuck came awake with a start at the sound. He looked around, but saw nothing. "Where?"

"Just there," said Iwan, stretching out his hand towards the darkness, "low to the ground and a little to your left."

Tuck looked where Iwan indicated and saw a tiny yellow glow moving along the ground. Then, even as he watched, the glow floated up into the air, where it hung for a moment.

"He's on the wall," said Iwan.

The glowing spark seemed to brighten and burst into flame. In the same instant the flame flared and disappeared and all was darkness again.

They waited.

In a moment, the glow fluttered to life once more in midair. It flared to life and disappeared just as quickly.

"That's two," said Iwan. "One more."

They waited.

This time the glow did not reappear at once. When it did, it was some distance farther along the wall. As before, the faint firefly glow brightened, then flared to brilliant life and disappeared in a smear of sparks and fire. Darkness reclaimed the night, and they waited. A long moment passed, then another, and they heard the hoofbeats of a swiftly approaching horse, and at almost the same time a line of light appeared low in the sky. The light grew in intensity until they could see the form of a dark rider galloping toward them. All at once, the light bloomed in the sky, erupting in a shower of orange and red flames.

"To your horses," shouted Bran as he came pounding up. "They'll be wanting our heads for this. I fired the storehouse and granary both."

"Did anyone see you?" wondered Iwan as he swung up into the saddle.

"It's possible," Bran said. "But they'll have their hands full for a little while, at least."

"Tsk," clucked Tuck with mild disapproval. "Such a sad waste."

"But necessary," offered Iwan. "Anything that weakens them, helps us."

"And anything that helps us, helps Elfael and its people," concluded Bran. "It was necessary."

"A holy waste, then," replied Tuck. He raised himself to a fallen limb and squirmed into the saddle. By the time he had the reins in his fist, his companions were already riding along the edge of the field up the long rising slope towards Coed Cadw, a dark mass rising like a wall against a sky alive with stars.

As the news about what had happened spread throughout the Vale of Elfael, everyone who heard about the theft and fire of the previous nights knew what it meant: King Raven's war with the Ffreinc had entered a new, more desperate stage. Burning the abbey's storehouse and granary would provoke Abbot Hugo and the sheriff to a swift and terrible reaction. If an army cannot eat, it cannot fight, and the abbot's army had just lost its supper.

"Sheriff de Glanville won't be dainty about taking what he needs from the poor Cymry round about," Scarlet pointed out after hearing an account of the previous night's raid. "He'll make a right fuss, no mistake."

"I expect he will," Bran agreed. "I'd be disappointed otherwise."

"Will's got a fair point," Siarles affirmed. "De Glanville will steal from the farm folk. It's always them he turns to."

"Yes, and when he does, he'll find King Raven waiting for him," said Bran.

Bran's reply stunned his listeners—not what he said—the words themselves were reasonable enough. It was the way he said them; there was a coldness in his tone that chilled all who heard it. There wasn't a man among them who did not recognize that something had changed in their king since his return from the north. If he had been determined before, he was that much more determined now. But it was more than simple purpose—there was a dark, implacable hardness to it, as if somehow his customary resolve had been chastened and hardened in a forge. There was an edge to it, keen and lethal as stropped steel. Scarlet put it best when he said, "God bless me, Brother Tuck, but talking to Rhi Bran now is like talking to the blade of a spear." He turned wondering eyes on the little priest. "Just what *did* you two get up to in the north that's made him so?"

"It's never the north that's made him this way," replied the friar, "although that maybe tipped the load into the muck. But it's coming back home and seeing how things are here—all this time passing, and the abbot is ruling the roost and the sheriff cutting up rough and all. The Ffreinc are still here and nothing's changed—nothing for the better, at least."

Scarlet nodded in commiseration. "It may be as you say, Friar, but *I* say that little jaunt up north changed him," he insisted. "I'll bet my back teeth on't."

"Perhaps," allowed Tuck. "Oh, you should have seen him, Scarlet. The way he peeled that hard-boiled earl—it was a gladsome sight." The friar went on to describe the elaborate deception he'd witnessed and in which he'd taken part—the clothes, the hunting, Alan's tireless translating, the young Welshmen and their willing and industrious participation, the breathless escape, and all the rest. "We were Count Rexindo and his merry band, as Alan says—albeit, his song makes it sound like a frolic of larks, but it was grim dire, I can tell you. We were tiptoeing in the wolf's den with fresh meat in our hands, but Bran never put a foot wrong. Why, it would have made you proud, it truly would."

"And yet it all came to nothing in the end."

"Saints bear witness, Scarlet, that's the naked bleeding heart of it, is it not? We dared much and risked more to save King Gruffydd's worthless neck," Tuck said, his voice rising with the force of his indignation. "And we succeeded! Beyond all hope of success, we succeeded. But that selfish sot refused to help. After we saved his life, by Peter's beard, that rascal of a king would not lend so much as a single sausage to our aid." He shook his head in weary commiseration. "Poor Bran . . . that his own kinsman would use him so ill—it's a wicked betrayal, that's what it is."

"Raw as a wound from a rusty blade." He considered this for a moment. "So that's the grit in his gizzard—our Bran knows we're on our own now," concluded Scarlet gloomily. "Aye, we're alone in this, and that's shame and pity enough to make man, woman, horse, or dog weep."

"Never say it," Tuck rebuked gently. "We are *not* alone—for the Lord of Hosts is on our side and stretches out His mighty arm against our enemies." The little friar smiled, his round face beaming simple good pleasure at the thought. "If the Almighty stands with us, who can stand against us, aye?" Tuck prodded Scarlet in the chest with a stubby finger. "Just you answer me that, boyo. Who can stand against us?"

The friar had a point, Scarlet confessed, that no one could stand against God—then added, "But there does seem no end o' folk that'll try."

The Grellon resumed the task of accumulating what provisions they could—meat from the hunt, grain and beans from the raid, tending the turnips in the field, making cheese from the milk of their two cows—preserving all they could and storing it up against the days of want that were surely coming.

Bran turned his attention to the other matter weighing on his mind. With everyone else already occupied, he called Scarlet and Tuck to him and announced, "Put on your riding boots. We're going to find Mérian—and while we're at it, we'll see if we can convince King Cadwgan to lend some of his men to aid us."

"This is what Mérian has been arguing all this while," Tuck pointed out.

"Aye, it is," Bran conceded. "I was against it at first, I confess, but our feet are in the flame now and we have no other choice.

Maybe Mérian is right—maybe her family will help where mine would not. Lord Cadwgan holds no kindly feelings towards me, God knows, but she's had a few days with him; I have to know whether she's been able to soften her father's opinion and persuade him. Pray she has, friends—it's our last hope." He spun on his heel and started away at once. "Ready the horses," he called over his shoulder. "We have only this day."

"It seems his disappointment has passed," said Scarlet. "And we're for a ride through lands filled with vengeful Ffreinc."

"Lord have mercy." Tuck sighed. "The last thing I need is to spend more time jouncing around on horseback. Still, if we can convince Cadwgan to help us, it will be worth another saddle sore."

"So now, if the Ffreinc catch us rambling abroad in plain day-light," warned Scarlet, "saddle sores will be least of all your earthly worries, friend friar."

CHAPTER 26

Arriving just after midday, the three riders paused to observe King Cadwgan's stronghold from a distance. All appeared peaceable and quiet on the low hill and surrounding countryside. There were folk working in the fields to the west and south of the fortress, and a few men and dogs moving cattle to another pasture for grazing. "Seems friendly enough from here," remarked Scarlet. "Any Ffreinc around, d'you reckon?"

"Possibly," answered Bran. "You never can tell—Cadwgan is client king to Baron Neufmarché."

"Same as tried to kill you?" wondered Scarlet.

"One and the same. I made the mistake of asking Neufmarché for help, and thought he might behave honourably," replied Bran. "It is not a mistake I shall make a second time."

"A bad business, that," mused Tuck. "It is a very miracle Cadwgan has survived this long under the baron's heavy thumb."

"You know him?" asked Scarlet.

"Aye, I do—we're not the best of friends, mind, but I know him when I see him—for all I've lived in the shadow of Hereford castle for many years."

"That is why I am sending you on ahead," said Bran.

"Me!"

"I dare not show my face within those walls until you have seen how things sit with the king."

"You want me to go in there alone?" Tuck said.

"Who better to spy out the lay of the land?" said Bran. "No one up there has ever seen you," he pointed out. "To the good folk of Caer Rhodl you will simply be who you are—a wandering mendicant priest. You've nothing to fear."

"Then why do I feel like Daniel sent into the lions' lair?"

He made to urge his mount forward, but Bran took hold of the bridle strap and pulled him up. "On foot."

"I have to walk?"

"Wandering mendicant priests do not ride fine horses."

"Fine horses, my fat arse." Tuck rolled his eyes and puffed out his cheeks. "You call these plodders we ride 'fine'?" Complaining, he squirmed down from his mount, landing hard on the path below.

"That grove of beeches," said Bran, pointing a little way down the track the way they had come. "We'll wait for you there."

"What do you want me to tell Cadwgan?" Tuck asked, untying the loop that held his staff alongside the saddle.

"Tell him anything you like," said Bran. "Only find out if it is safe for me to come up there and speak to him. And find out what has become of Mérian."

Tuck beetled off on his bowed legs while Bran and Will rode back to wait in the grove. Upon reaching the foot of the fortress mound, Tuck worked his way along the rising, switchback path towards the entrance. The thought—the fervent hope—of cool dark ale awaiting him in a welcome cup sprang up, bringing the water to his thirsty mouth. By the time he reached the gate atop the long ramp, he was panting with anticipation. A word with the gatekeeper brought the desired result, and he was quickly admitted and directed to the cookhouse.

"Bless you, my son," said Tuck. "May God be good to you."

At the cookhouse, he begged a bite to eat and a cup of something to drink, and found the kitchener most obliging. "Come in, Friar, and be welcome," said the woman who served the king and his household as master cook. "Sit you down, and I'll soon set a dish or two before you."

"And if you have a little ale," suggested Tuck lightly, "I would dearly love to wash the dust of the road from my mouth."

"That you shall have," replied the cook—so amiably that Tuck remembered all over again how well he was so often received in the houses of the great lords. For however high and mighty the lord might be—with his own priests or those nearby to attend him as he pleased—his vassals and servants were usually more than glad to receive a priest of their own class. She busied herself in the next room and returned with a leather cannikin dripping with foam. "Here," she said, passing the vessel to Tuck, "get some of this inside you and slay the nasty dragon o' thirst."

Tuck seized the container with both hands and brought it to his face. He drank deep, savouring the cool, sweet liquid as it filled his mouth and flowed over his tongue and down his chin. "Bless you," he sighed, wiping his mouth with his sleeve. "I was that parched."

TEPHEN R. LAWHEAD

"Now, then," said the master cook, "just enjoy your cup. I won't be a moment."

The cook left the kitchen for the larder, and Tuck sat on his stool, elbows on the board, sipping the good dark ale. In a moment, a young woman came in with a wedge of cheese on a wooden plate. "Cook said to give you this while you wait," said the serving maid.

"Thank you, my child," replied Tuck, taking the plate from her hand.

"If you please, Friar," she said, "I have a sore foot." She looked at him doubtfully. "Would you know of a cure or blessing?"

"Let me see," he said, glancing down at her feet. "Which foot is it?"

She slipped off her shoe—a wooden clog with a leather top—and held the foot up slightly. Tuck saw a red welt at the base of her big toe that looked to him like the beginning of a bunion.

"Ah, yes," he said. "I have seen this before." He gently lifted the young woman's foot and touched the raw, red bulge. "I think you are fortunate to catch this before it has become incurable."

She winced, drawing in her breath sharply. "Can you fix it?"

"I think so. Can you get a little mayweed hereabouts?"

"For a certainty," she replied. "We use it all the time."

"Then you'll know how to make a tisane, do you not?"

The girl nodded.

"Good—make one and drink it down. Then take the wet leaves from the bowl and apply them to the sore. Do this three times a day, every day for five days, and you'll soon feel better. Oh, yes, put off your shoes for a few days."

The girl made a sour face. "My lady does not like us to go barefoot," she said. "Leastwise, not in the house."

"Not to worry," said Tuck. "When you go in the house, just put some willow bark shavings in your shoe. But take off your shoes whenever you can. Oh, yes—find some larger shoes if you can. The ones you are wearing are too small for you, and that, no doubt, is what has caused this ailment." He laid a finger to his lips. "Now, then, I think Saint Birinius is the one to seek on this one," he said. "Bow your head, child."

The young woman did as she was told, and Tuck held his hand over her and sought the blessing of Birinius, whose feet were held in the fire by one of the old Mercian kings as a test of his faith and thus was one who knew the pain associated with various foot ailments. The young lady thanked the friar and left—only to be replaced by another woman bringing a small woollen cloak she had just finished making. "If it is not too much trouble, Friar," she said politely, "I would ask a blessing for this cloak, as I've made it for my sister's baby that's due to come any day now."

"May God be good to you for your thoughtfulness," said Tuck. "It is no trouble at all." And he blessed the soft square of delicate cloth.

When he finished, the cook returned and began placing bowls of minted beans and new greens and a plate of cold duck before him. The woman with the infant's cloak thanked him and said, "My man is outside with a horse he'd like you to see when you've finished your meal."

"Tell him I will attend directly," replied Tuck, reaching for a wooden spoon. He ate and drank and worked out what he wanted to say to Lord Cadwgan. When the cook returned to see how he fared, Tuck asked, "The lord of this place—is he well?"

"Oh, indeed, Friar. Never better."

"Good," replied Tuck. "I am glad to hear it."

"How could it be otherwise? A new-married man and his bride—why, birds in a nest, those two."

This caught Tuck on the hop. "Lord Cadwgan . . . newly married, you say?"

"Lord have mercy, no!" laughed the cook. "It's Garran I'm talking about. He's king now, and lord of this place."

"Oh, is he? But that must mean—"

The cook was already nodding in reply. "The old king died last year, and Garran has taken his father's place on the throne, may God keep him."

"Of course," replied Tuck. He finished his meal wondering whether this revelation made his task easier or more difficult. Knowing little about Cadwgan, and nothing at all about Garran, there was no way to tell, he decided, until he met the young king in the flesh. He finished his meal and thanked the cook for extending the hospitality of her lord to him, then went out into the yard to see the horse. The stablehand was waiting patiently, and Tuck greeted him and asked what he could do. "The mare's with foal," the man told him, "as you can see. I would have a blessing on her that the birth will be easy and the young 'un healthy."

"Consider it done," replied the friar. Placing his hand on the broad forehead of the animal, Tuck said a prayer and blessed the beast, asking for the aid of Saint Eligius for the animal and, for good measure, Saint Monica as well. While he was praying he became aware that there were others looking on. On concluding, he turned to see that he was being watched by a young man who, despite his fair hair, looked that much like Mérian—the same large dark eyes, the same full mouth and high, noble forehead—that

Tuck decided the fellow had to be her brother. "I do beg your pardon, my lord," Tuck said, offering a slight bow, "but mightn't you be Rhi Garran?"

"God be good to you, Friar, I might be and, as it happens, I am," replied the young man with a smile. "And who, so long as we're asking, are you to be blessing my horses?"

"I am as you see me," replied Tuck, "a humble friar. Brother Aethelfrith is my name."

"A Saxon, then."

"I am, and that proud of it."

"Now I know you must be a Christian," replied Garran lightly, "for you speak the language of heaven right well. How is that, if you don't mind my asking? For I've never known a Saxon to bother himself overmuch with learning the Cymry tongue."

"That is easily told," answered Tuck, and explained that as a boy in Lincolnshire he had been captured in a raid and sold into slavery in the copper mines of Powys; when he grew old enough and bold enough, he had made good his escape and was received by the monks of Llandewi, where he lived until taking his vows and, some little time later, becoming a mendicant.

The young king nodded, the same amiable smile playing on his lips the while. "Well, I hope they have fed you in the kitchen, friend friar. You are welcome to stay as long as you like—Nefi, here, will give you a corner of the stable for a bed, and I am certain my people will make you feel at home."

"Your generosity does you credit, Sire," Tuck said, "but it is you I have come to see—on a matter of some urgency."

The young man hesitated. He made a dismissive gesture. "Then I commend you to my seneschal. I am certain he will be best able to help." Again, he turned to go, giving Tuck the impression that he was intruding on the busy life of this young monarch.

"If you please, my lord," said Tuck, starting after him, "it is about a friend of yours and mine—and of your sister Mérian's."

At this last name, the young king halted and turned around again. "You know my sister?"

"I do, my lord, and that right well, do I not?"

"How do you know her?" The king's tone became wary, suspicious.

"I have lately come from the place where she has been living."

Garran tensed and drew himself up. "Then you must be one of those outlaws of the greenwood we have been hearing about." Before Tuck could reply, he said, "You are no longer welcome here. I suggest you leave before I have you whipped and thrown out."

"So that is the way of it," concluded Tuck.

"I have nothing more to say to you." Garran turned on his heel and started away.

"God love you, man," said Tuck, stepping after him. "It can do no harm to talk—"

"Did you not hear me?" snarled Garran, turning on the little friar. "I can have you beaten and cast out like the filth you are. Get you from my sight, or heaven help me, I will whip you myself."

"Then do so," Tuck replied, squaring himself for a fight. "For I will not leave until I have said what I came here to say."

Garran glared at him, but said, "Go on, then. If it will get your repulsive carcase out of my sight the sooner, speak."

"You seem to think that we harmed Mérian in some way," Tuck began. "We did no such thing. Indeed, Mérian was not held against her will. She stayed in the greenwood, *lived* with us in the greenwood, because she believes in the cause that we pursue—the same cause that brings me here to ask your aid."

"What cause?"

"Justice, pure and simple. King William has erred and fomented a great injustice against the rightful lord and people of Elfael, who are most cruelly used and oppressed. A most grievous wrong has been committed, and we seek to put it right. To speak plainly, we mean to drive out the wicked usurpers and reclaim the throne of Elfael. Your sister, Mérian, has been helping us do just that. She has been a most ardent and enthusiastic member of our little band. Let us go ask her," Tuck suggested, "and you can hear this from her own lips."

Garran was already shaking his head. "You're not going anywhere near her," he said. "Mérian is home now—back among her family where she belongs. You will no longer twist her to your treason."

"Twist her?" wondered Tuck. "She has been more than willing. Mérian is a leader among the forest folk. She is—"

"Whatever she *was* to you," sneered Garran, "she is no more. Be gone!"

"Please, you must—"

"Must? Know you, Baron Neufmarché is my liege lord, as William is his. We are loyal to the crown in this house. If you persist in speaking of this, I will report you for treason against the throne of England—as is my sworn duty."

"I beg you, Sire, do not—"

"Daffyd! Awstin!" the king shouted, calling for his men, who appeared on the run from the stables. Thrusting a finger at the friar, he said, "Throw him out and bar the gate behind him. If he does not leave, whip him, and drag him to the border of Eiwas—for I will not suffer him to remain in my sight or on my land another moment."

"I will go, and gladly," Tuck said. "But let me speak to Mérian—"

Garran's face clenched like a fist. "Mention her name again and,

271

priest or no, I will cut out your tongue." He gave a nod to the two stablehands, who stepped forward and roughly took hold of Tuck.

The friar was hauled from the yard and pushed out through the gate. "Sorry, Friar," said one as he closed the gate.

"Bless you, friend," replied Tuck with a sigh, "I do not hold it against you." He took a moment to shake the dust from his feet, and then started the long walk back to where Bran and Scarlet were waiting for a better word than he had to give them.

Nor was Bran any better pleased than Tuck imagined he would be. He listened to all that Tuck had to say about what had taken place up at the caer, and then walked a few paces apart and stood looking at the fortress mound in the near distance. He stood there so long that Scarlet eventually approached him and said, "My lord? What is your pleasure?"

When Bran failed to respond, he said, "If we hurry, we can be back in Cél Craidd before dark."

Without turning, Bran replied, "I am not leaving until I have spoken to Mérian."

"How?" wondered Tuck. "He will hardly allow any of us inside the caer again."

Bran turned and flashed his crooked smile. "Tuck, old friend, I have been in and out of that fortress without anyone the wiser more times than you've et hot soup." He looked around for a soft spot in the shade. "It's going to be a long night; I suggest we rest until it gets dark."

They tethered the horses so that they might graze among the trees, and then settled back to nap and wait for night and the cover of darkness. The day passed quietly, and night came on. When Bran reckoned that all in the fortress would be in bed asleep, he roused the other two. Tuck rose, yawned, shook out his robe, and clambered back into the saddle, thinking that he would be heartily glad when all this to-ing and fro-ing was over and peace reigned in the land once more. They rode in silence around the base of the hill on which the fortress sat, Bran picking his way with practiced assurance along a path none of the others could see in the darkness. They came to a place below the wall where a small ditch or ravine caused the wall to dip slightly. Here, Bran halted and dismounted. "We are behind the kitchen," he explained. "Mérian's chamber used to be just the other side of the wall. Pray it is so now."

"And is this why Lord Cadwgan took such umbrage against you?" wondered Scarlet.

"Now that you mention it," Bran allowed, his grin a white glint in the dark, "that could have had something to do with it—not that any other reason was needed." He started up the steep hillside. "Let's be at it."

Quick and silent as a shadow, Bran was up the slope and over the wall, leaving Scarlet and Tuck to struggle over as best they could. By the time Tuck eased himself over the rough timber palisade and into the yard, Bran was already clinging onto the sill below a small glass window—one of only three in the entire fortress. Bran lightly tapped twice on the small round panes . . . paused, and tapped three more times.

When nothing happened, he repeated the same series of raps.

"D'you think she's there?" asked Scarlet.

Bran hissed him to silence and repeated his signal yet again. This time there was a tap from the other side, and a moment later the window swung inward on its hinges and Mérian's face appeared where the glass had been. "Bran! Saints and angels, it *is* you!"

"Mérian, are you well?"

"I thought you would never get here," she said. "I have been praying you would come—and listening for you each night."

"Are you well, Mérian?"

"I am very well—for all I am made prisoner in my own house," she said tartly. "But I am not mistreated. They think you took me hostage—"

"I did."

"—and held me against my will. They seem to think that if I am given a little time I will come to see how I was tricked into siding with you against the Ffreinc. Until I repent of my folly, I am to remain locked in this room."

"We'll have you out of there soon enough," said Bran. He glanced across to the shuttered window of the kitchen. "Give me a moment and I'll come through there. Is there likely to be anyone awake in the kitchen?"

"Bran, no—wait," said Mérian. "Listen to me—I've been thinking. I should stay here a little longer."

"But, you just said—"

"I know, but I think I can persuade Garran to send men to aid us."

"Tuck tried to ask him already. He asked to see you, too, and Garran refused. He wouldn't hear anything we had to say."

"You talked to him? When?"

"Today. Tuck came up, but Garran had him thrown out of the caer. It's no use; your brother will not go against Baron Neufmarché in any case."

"He has good reason," Mérian said. "He's married to the baron's daughter."

"What?"

"Lady Sybil Neufmarché—they were wed in the spring." She explained about her father's death and funeral, and the match the baron had proposed. "They are living here—Lady Agnes and Sybil, I mean."

Bran dropped lightly to the ground. "They won't let you go. And no matter what you say, you'll never persuade them to join us." He gestured behind him. "Scarlet, Tuck, come here."

"What are you going to do?"

"Free you."

"Please, Bran, not like this. If I stay here I might yet be able to convince them to join us. If I leave now, it will enrage them—and then you will have Garran and his men against you, too. We cannot risk making enemies of those who should be our friends."

"Come with me, Mérian. I need you."

"Bran, I pray you, think what this means."

Bran paused and looked up at her. "I remember once, not so long ago, when I stood where I'm standing now and asked you to come with me," he said. "Do you remember?"

"I remember," she said.

"You refused to come with me then too."

"Oh, Bran." Her voice became plaintive. "This is not like that. I *will* come—as soon as I can. Until then, I will work to bring Garran around to our side. I can do this; you'll see."

Bran started away, fading into the night-shadowed darkness.

"It is for the best," Mérian insisted. "You will see."

"Farewell, Mérian." Bran called over his shoulder. "Come," he said to Scarlet and Tuck, "we are finished. There is nothing for us here."

CHAPTER 27

Saint Martin's

The small steading lay amidst fields of barley in a narrow crook of a finger of the Vale of Elfael north of Saint Martin's—not the largest holding in Elfael, nor the closest to the caer, but one that Gysburne had marked before as a prosperous place and well worth keeping an eye on. Captain Aloin, commander of the knights that had been sent to help the abbot and sheriff maintain order in the cantref, surveyed the quiet farm from the back of his horse.

"Are you certain this is the place?" asked the captain, casting his gaze right and left for any sign of trouble. "It seems peaceful enough."

"The calm can be misleading," replied Marshal Gysburne. "These Welsh are sly devils every one. You must be prepared to fight for your life at any moment."

The sheriff and abbot had determined to begin retaliation for the most recent predations of King Raven and his thieving flock. The sack of the Welsh farms and confiscation of all supplies, stock, and provisions would serve as a warning to the folk of the cantref—especially those who benefited from the thievery. To this end, a large body of knights—fully half of the entire force, accompanied by men-at-arms and four empty hay wains—had been dispatched to the holding with orders to strip it of all possessions and kill anyone bold enough to resist.

"And when we've finished here?" Captain Aloin asked.

"We continue on to the next farm, and the next, until the wagons are full. Or until King Raven and his foul flock appear."

"How do you know he will come?" asked Captain Aloin as he and Gysburne rode out from the caer, each at the head of a company of soldiers.

"He will appear, without a doubt," replied Marshal Guy. "If not today, then tomorrow. Attacking one of his beloved settlements raises his ire—killing a few Cymry is sure to bring him out of hiding."

"If that is so," surmised Aloin. "Then why have you not done this before? Why have you waited so long and put up with his thievery and treasons all this time?"

"Because Count Falkes de Braose—the ruler of Elfael before he was driven into exile—had no stomach for such tactics. He thought it important to gain the trust and goodwill of the people, or some such nonsense. He said he could not rule if all hands were against him at every turn."

"And now?"

Gysburne smiled to himself. "Now things have changed. Abbot Hugo is not so delicate as the count."

"And Sheriff de Glanville?"

"What about him?"

"Where does he stand in this matter? It was de Glanville who begged our services from the king. I would have thought he would ride out with us today."

"But he *has*," replied Gysburne. "He most certainly has—as you shall see." The marshal lifted the reins. "Walk on," he said.

Captain Aloin raised his fist in the air and gave the signal to move out, and the double column of soldiers on horseback continued on. Upon reaching the farmstead, the knights quickly arrayed themselves for battle. While half of the company under the command of Gysburne rode into the yard and took over the holding, Aloin's division fanned out to form a shield wall to prevent any approach to the property and discourage anyone who might be minded to take an interest in the affair.

Sitting on his great warhorse in the centre of the yard, Gysburne gave the command to begin.

Knights and men-at-arms swarmed into the house and dragged out the farmer, his wife and daughter, and three grown sons. There were several others as well, hauled out into the early-morning light to stand in the yard surrounded by enemy soldiers and watch while all their possessions, provisions, and supplies were bundled into wagons. None of the Welshmen made even the slightest attempt to interfere with the sack of their home. The farmer and his sons stood in stiff-legged defiance, glowering with pent rage at all those around them, but said nothing and did not lift a hand to prevent the pillage— which Gysburne put down to their display of overwhelming military might. For once, the superior Ffreinc forces had cowed the indomitable Welsh spirit.

The ransacking of the house and barn and outbuildings was swiftly accomplished. The fact that the soldiers had not had to subdue the hostile natives and the piteous lack of possessions meant that the raid was finished almost as soon as it began. "It is done," reported Sergeant Jeremias as the last grain sacks were tossed into a waiting wagon. "What is your command?"

"Burn it, Sergeant."

"But Sire—Sheriff de Glanville said—"

"Never mind what de Glanville said. Burn it."

"Everything?"

"To the ground."

The sight of torches being lit brought the farmer and his sons out of their belligerent stupor. They began shouting and cursing and shaking their fists at the Ffreinc soldiers. One of the younger boys made as if to rush at one of the knights as he passed with a torch. But the farmer grabbed his son back and held him fast. They all watched as the flames took hold, rising skyward on the soft morning air. The farmwife held her head in her hands, tears streaming down her face. Still, none of the Cymry stirred from where they stood.

When it was certain that the flames could not be extinguished, Marshal Guy gave the order for the knights to be mounted, and the company moved off.

"That went well," observed Aloin when the last of the wagons and soldiers had cleared the yard. "Better than I expected—from what you said about the Welshies' love of fighting."

"Yes," agreed the marshal slowly, "in truth I expected more of a fight. Just see you keep your sword ready. We cannot count on the next one being so peaceful."

But, in fact, the Cymry at the second farm were no more inclined to take arms and resist the pillagers than the first lot. Like those at the previous settlement, the second clan put up no struggle at all, bearing the assault with a grave and baleful silence. If they did not voice their fury outright, their doomful expressions were nevertheless most eloquent. Again, Marshal Guy could not quite credit the odd docility of the natives when faced with the destruction of their homes. But there it was. In spite of this conundrum, he decided to burn the second farm, too—the better to provoke King Raven to show himself.

"What now?" asked Captain Aloin as the smoke rolled skyward. "The wagons are almost full."

"Almost full is not enough," replied Guy. "We go on."

"And if this King of the Ravens does not appear? What then?"

"Then we'll take the wagons back to the caer and raid again tomorrow. We keep at it until he comes."

"You're sure about that, *oui*?"

"Oh, yes, he'll come. He always does."

The third farmstead lay almost within sight of the walls of Caer Cadarn. It was small and, owing to its nearness to the town and stronghold, it had suffered plundering by Ffreinc troops before, and Guy remembered it. The farm was quiet as the soldiers surrounded the property. No one came out to meet the soldiers as they entered the yard, so Gysburne ordered Sergeant Jeremias to go in and bring the farmer and his family out.

The sergeant returned a moment later. "There is no one here, my lord."

"They must have gone into hiding," concluded the marshal.

"They knew we were coming?" asked Captain Aloin. "How so?"

"The Welsh are uncanny this way," explained Gysburne. "I don't know how they know, but word travels on the air in these valleys. They seem to know everything that happens." Turning back to the sergeant, he said, "Ransack the barn and granary. They will not have had time to carry anything away."

Jeremias hurried off. "Strip it!" he called. "Take everything."

The soldiers dismounted and, while the wagons were driven into position, they moved off to the buildings. The first man-at-arms to reach the barn threw open the doors and started in—to be met by the angry wasp-buzz of arrows streaking out of the dark interior. He and two other soldiers dropped dead to the ground; three more staggered back clutching their chests and staring in horror at the oaken shafts that had so suddenly appeared there.

Marshal Guy saw the arrows flash and realized they were under attack. He turned to the soldiers who were just then about to enter the house. "Halt!" he shouted. "Don't go in there!"

But the knight's hand was on the door and he had already pushed it open.

With a sound like that of a whip snapping against naked flesh, the first flight of arrows struck home. Four knights fell as one. An errant arrow glanced off a soldier's helmet and careered off at an angle, striking a horse standing in the yard. The animal reared and began bucking in a forlorn effort to relieve the lethal sting in its side.

Then all was chaos, as everywhere knights and men-at-arms were stumbling back, colliding with one another, fleeing the deadly and unseen assault. With desperate shouts and screams of agony they shrank from the arrows that continued to stream into the yard, seemingly from every direction at once. There was no escaping them. With each flight more soldiers dropped—by twos and threes they fell, pierced by the lethal missiles.

"To arms! To arms!" cried Captain Aloin, trying to rally his troops. "Seal the barn! Seal the barn and burn it!"

In answer to the command, three well-armoured knights leapt to obey. Through the deadly onslaught they ran, their shields high before them as shaft after shaft hammered into the splintering wood. One of the knights reached the right-hand door of the barn and flung it closed. He put his back against it to hold it shut while his two comrades flung the left-hand door closed.

"The torches! Get the torches!" shouted the first knight, still bracing the door shut. He drew breath to shout once more and shrieked in agony instead as, with the sound of a branch breaking in a storm, the steel point of an arrow slammed through the planking and poked through the centre of his chest. He gave out a strangled yelp and slumped down, his body snagged and caught by the strong oaken shaft of the arrow.

His two companions holding the left-hand barn door heard the sharp cracking sound and watched aghast as three more arrows penetrated the stout timber doors to half their length. Had their backs been to the door they would have suffered the same fate as their unfortunate comrade.

Meanwhile, arrows continued to fly from the house—from the door and the two small windows facing the yard, which had become a tumult of plunging horses and frightened men scrambling over the bodies of corpses. The wagon drivers, defenceless in the centre of the yard, threw themselves from their carts and ran for safety beyond range of the whistling shafts. This left the oxen to fend for themselves; confused and terrified by the violent turmoil, the beasts strained at their yokes and tried to break their traces. Unable to escape, they stood in wild-eyed terror and bawled.

When the barn doors burst open once more, a tall slender figure appeared in the gap: a man's form from shoulders to the tips of his tall black boots, but bearing the head of an enormous bird with a weird skull-like black face and a wickedly long, narrow beak. In its hand, the creature clutched a longbow with an arrow nocked to the string. The smooth, expressionless face surveyed the churning turmoil with a quick sweep of its head, picked out Gysburne, and directed an arrow at him. The marshal, who was already wheeling his horse, took the arrow on his shield as three more archers joined the creature and proceeded to loose shaft after shaft at will into the melee.

"Retreat!" cried Gysburne, trying to make himself heard above the commotion. "Retreat!"

Arrows singing around his ears, Guy put his head down and raced from the yard. Those soldiers still in the saddle, and those yet able to walk or run, followed. Five more met their deaths before the last of the knights had cleared the yard.

The Ffreinc raiding party continued to a place beyond arrow's reach and halted to regroup.

"What was *that?*" shouted Captain Aloin as he came galloping in beside the marshal. "What in the holy name *was* that?"

"That was King Raven," replied Guy, pulling an arrow from his shield, and another from the cantle of his saddle. "That was the fiend at his worst."

"By the blood," breathed the captain. "How many were with him?"

"I don't know. It doesn't matter."

"Doesn't matter!" Captain Aloin cried in stunned disbelief. Gazing quickly around him, he counted those who had escaped the massacre. "Are you insane? We've lost more than half our men in a one-sided slaughter and you say it doesn't matter?"

"Six or sixty," muttered Guy. "What does it matter? We were beaten by those God-cursed arrows."

"This is an outrage," growled the captain of the king's men. "Mark me, by heaven, someone will pay for this."

"I daresay they will," agreed Guy, looking away towards the forest, where he imagined he saw the glint of sunlight off a steel blade.

"What are we to do now?" demanded Aloin. "Are we to retreat and let the bastards get away with it?"

"We run, but they won't get away," said Guy. "Sheriff de Glanville will see to that."

CHAPTER 28

"A re they gone?" asked Owain, his fingers tight around the arrow nocked to his bowstring.

"Shhh," said Iwan gently. "Stay sharp. We'll wait just a little and then take a look round." He turned to Siarles, crouched low behind the doorpost of the farmhouse. "See to it, Siarles, but keep an eye out for the wounded. There might be some fight in one or two yet."

Siarles nodded and continued to watch the yard from one of the small windows. Nothing moved outside. The three archers waited a few moments more, alert, arrows on string, listening for any sound of returning horses—but, save for a low, whimpering moan from one of the fallen soldiers, all seemed quiet enough. Siarles rose and stepped lightly through the door, paused and looked around, then disappeared into the yard at a run. He was back a few moments later saying, "They've gone. It's safe to come out."

As they stepped from the house, Bran, Tomas, and Rhoddi emerged from the barn. "To me, men!" Bran called, pulling off the hooded raven mask. When everyone had gathered, he said, "Strip the dead of anything useful. Throw it in the wagons and let's fly home. Scarlet and the others will be tired of waiting."

"Aren't we going to give back all the supplies they've stolen?" asked Owain.

"Aye, lad," replied Iwan, "but not now, not today."

"Your concern does you credit, Owain," Bran told him. "But the enemy will return to the caer and muster the rest of the soldiers to come and retrieve their dead. Unless we hurry, we'll meet them again, and this time we'll not own the advantage."

"Too many Ffreinc around for the few of us," Iwan told him. "We'll return the supplies when it's a mite safer."

"There's eighteen fewer Ffreinc now than there were a while ago," announced Siarles, who had been making a count. "And four more that will likely join 'em before the sun is over the barn."

"Twenty-two!" gasped Rhoddi. "God help us, that must be near half their force—destroyed in one battle."

"There will be hell to pay," muttered Tomas as the realization of the enormity of their success came over him.

"Too right, there will," agreed Bran. "But we must make very sure it is the abbot who pays. Come, men, let's be about our business before the marshal comes back."

So while Siarles kept watch, the other five archers stripped the dead and dying, tossing the various articles into the wagons the soldiers had abandoned in their retreat. Then, leading the oxen from the yard, they departed—not by the road which led away to the fortress and town—but by the field track that led up through the valley towards Coed Cadw, the Guardian Wood.

Owing to the weight of the wagons and the slowness of the

oxen, they could not travel as swiftly as the demands of the situation warranted; even so, they reached the edge of the forest in due course without any sign of pursuing Ffreinc. As they drew in towards the line of trees, however, the leaves of the nearby hawthorn bushes quivered, rattling an alarm.

Bran, in the lead, glanced up in time to see the round gleaming top of a Norman helmet rising from the brush.

The spear was in the air before Bran could shout a warning. He dodged to the side, and the missile caught Owain a few steps behind him. The young man gave out a yelp and fell back. Bran had an arrow in the air before Owain's body came to rest in the grass.

The stone point struck the helmet and shattered, scattering shards into the attacker's eyes. He screamed and sank out of sight. Instantly, another soldier was there in his place, and others were appearing in a ragged rank all along the forest line.

"Ambush!" shouted Bran, loosing an arrow at the nearest head to appear.

"Fall back!" shouted Iwan. Stooping low, he scooped up the wounded Owain, put him over his shoulder as lightly as a sheaf of wheat, and ran to the nearest wagon, ducking behind it as the spears began to fall.

The four archers joined the champion behind the wagon, and all looked to Bran for a way out of their predicament.

"How many are there?" asked Siarles. "Anybody see?"

"Plenty for each of us," Iwan said. "Never you fear."

"Owain?" said Bran. "Owain, look at me. How bad are you?"

"It hurts," groaned the young man through gritted teeth. He held his side above his hip; blood seeped through his fingers. "I'm lying if I say otherwise, but get my feet under me and I can walk."

"We can't stay here," Iwan told them. "They'll charge soon and cut us down in the open like this."

"Right," said Bran. "Everyone nock an arrow and be ready to move. They can't run and throw at the same time, so as soon as they mount the charge, we go for the greenwood."

"Go into them?" said Tomas.

"Aye," replied Iwan. "Headfirst into the charge."

"Smack 'em hard in the teeth," said Siarles, glancing up as a spear head chipped through the side of the wagon above his head. "It'll be the only thing they're not expecting."

"Once we're in the trees we have a chance," Bran said. Reaching over the side of the wagon, he pulled down a Norman shield and handed it to Owain, then took the young man's bag of arrows and passed them around to the others.

"Did anyone see which manjack is leadin' 'em?" asked Siarles as he peered around the back of the wagon towards the tree line.

The question went unanswered, as there came a rising cry from the forest and Ffreinc soldiers rushed up out of the brush towards the wagons. "Ready!" shouted Bran. "Now! Fly!"

Out from behind the wagon he darted. Raising his bow, he drew on the foremost knight just then charging up out of the bush. The bowstring slapped, and the arrow blurred across the distance, lifting the onrushing soldier off his feet and throwing him onto his back. The sudden absence of the soldier created a hole in the line, and Iwan, running hard behind his lord, opened it a little wider by taking out the soldier to the left of the first.

Spears sailed in deadly arcs, slicing through the sun-drenched air, sprouting like leafless saplings in turf. The archers dodged those that sprang up in their path, loosing arrows as they ran. The gap which

Iwan and Bran had opened narrowed as more knights, screaming and cursing, drove in, desperate to close on the fleeing outlaws before they could reach the wood.

Bran loosed the last of his arrows, put his head down, and ran. Two heavily armoured knights lurched into the gap, low behind their spears. The nearest lunged, making a wide swipe with the spear blade, and the second let fly. The throw was low and skidded along the ground. Bran leapt over it easily; but Iwan, coming two steps behind, was not so lucky. The sliding shaft snaked through the grass, gliding between his feet; he tripped and fell onto his left side.

The knight was on him instantly, sword drawn. With a shout of triumph, he swung the blade high and prepared to deliver the killing stroke. Iwan, defenceless on his back, saw the blade flash as it swung up, and threw his hands before him to ward off the blow. But the knight's cry of triumph stuck in his throat, and he seemed to strain against the blade that had become inextricably caught in the air.

The knight, sword still high, crashed to his knees, his eyes wide in shock and disbelief. Iwan had just time enough to roll aside as the knight's body jolted forward with the force of the second arrow, which drove him facedown into the ground.

As Iwan scrambled to his feet, he saw twin shafts protruding from the knight's mail hauberk.

"Here! Iwan!"

The champion looked to the shout and saw Scarlet, bow in hand, waving him forward.

The first knight, still gripping his spear, made a second swipe at Bran, who grabbed hold of the spear shaft with his free hand, pulling the soldier towards him. As the knight fell forward, Bran swung his longbow like a club into the man's face. The knight lowered his head and let his helmet take the blow, then thrust again with the spear. Bran lashed out with his foot, catching the knight on the chin; his jaw snapped shut with a teeth-shattering crack, and his head flew back. Bran swung the body of the longbow down hard, and the mail-clad knight went down. As he sprawled on the ground, Bran, light as a deer in flight, took a running step, planted a foot in the middle of the man's back, and vaulted over him.

He reached the shelter of the trees to find Scarlet waiting for him. "Here, my lord," said the forester, thrusting a handful of arrows at him. "You'll be needing these, I think."

"Thanks, Will," said Bran, breathing hard.

"This way." Scarlet led him along the tree line, and together they loosed arrow after arrow into the Ffreinc from behind until the remaining archers had reached the wood.

Now King Raven and his men occupied the wood, and the Ffreinc were exposed on open ground. As the lethal oaken shafts struck again and again, some of the knights sought shelter behind the wagons. Others crawled back into the wood.

Bran and Scarlet gathered the archers. "How many arrows have you got left?" Bran asked as the men gathered under cover of a bramble thicket. "Two," said Siarles; Tomas and Scarlet each had two as well. None of the others had any.

"Then this fight is over," said Bran.

"Just leave?" objected Siarles. "We can end it now."

"With but six arrows? No, Siarles," Bran told him. "We live to fight another day. It's time to go home."

"Where's Tuck got to?" wondered Iwan.

"He should be nearby," Scarlet replied. "He was right beside me before the charge. Do you want me to go look for him?"

"We can't be leaving him behind for the Ffreinc to capture," said Iwan.

"Scarlet and I will find him," Bran said. "The rest of you start back to Cél Craidd." He held out his hand. "Give us the arrows." He took the remaining arrows and urged them away. "Go. We'll join you on the way."

The others disappeared into the bush. "Where were you when this started?" Bran asked, passing three arrows to Scarlet. "Show me."

"This way," Will told him, starting back along the tree line to the place he and Tuck had been hiding when the attack began.

No sooner had they skirted a large bramble thicket than they heard someone call out. "Scarlet! Here, boyo!"

"I think it came from over there somewhere," said Scarlet. Both men turned and started for the spot. They quickly came to a dense wall of elder and halted. "Tuck! Sing out, Brother. Where are you?"

"Here!" came the voice once more. "This way! Hurry!"

The two pushed through the elder hedge to find the little priest holding a sturdy quarterstaff in one hand and a sword in the other as he stood astraddle an inert figure on the ground. The figure groaned and made to rise, and the friar gave him a sharp rap between the shoulder blades that pushed him back down.

"Thank the Good Lord you're here," breathed Tuck. "I was halfway to wishing I'd never a'caught this one. He's getting to be a handful."

"Here now," said Bran, taking the sword. "Stand aside and let's see who you've got."

Tuck moved away, but kept the staff at the ready.

Bran took hold of the prostrate man's hair and lifted his head from the ground. "Richard de Glanville!" he exclaimed, his surprise genuine. Glancing around to the friar, he said, "Well done, Tuck.

You are a very wonder." He released his handful of hair, and the groggy head thumped back onto the earth. "With a little luck and Providence on our side, we may reclaim the throne of Elfael far sooner than we ever dared hope."

"Truly?"

"Aye," declared Bran, "with the sheriff's valuable assistance, of course. But we must act quickly. We cannot give Gysburne and Hugo time to think."

CHAPTER 29

"Well, here's a prize we never thought to get," remarked Iwan. He put a hand to the sheriff's shoulder and rolled him over onto his back. The sheriff moaned, his eyelids fluttering as he struggled for consciousness, but he made no effort to rise.

Bran had quickly recalled his men, and they gathered once more to receive new instructions. As Bran began to explain what he had in mind, their prisoner regained his senses. *"C'est vous! J'ai pensé qu'il y avait une odeur de merde,"* groaned the sheriff in a voice thick and slurred.

"What did he say?" asked Bran.

"Nothing nice," replied Tuck. He gave the sheriff a kick with the toe of his shoe and warned him to speak respectfully or keep his mouth shut.

"Achevez-moi, et finissez l'affaire."

"He wants us to kill him now and be done with it," offered the friar.

"Kill a valuable prisoner like you?" said Bran. Squatting down, he patted the sheriff's clothes and felt along his belt before with-drawing a dagger, which he took and handed to Scarlet. "I suppose you'd prefer death just now, but you'll have to become accustomed to disappointment." To Tuck, he added, "Tell him what I said."

Tuck relayed Bran's words to de Glanville, who groaned and put his face to the ground once more.

"What is in your mind, my lord?" asked Iwan.

"Bind him," Bran directed, "and get him on his feet. Gysburne and his men will be recovering their courage, and any moment they might take it into their heads to come after us. Siarles, Tomas—see how many arrows you can get from the field, and hurry back."

The two hurried off, returning a short while later with eight shafts collected in fair condition from dead soldiers, which added to the six they already possessed brought the total to fourteen. "I would there were more, but these will have to do," Bran said. "Pray it is enough." He gave arrows to each of the archers, save the wounded Owain and himself. Instead, he shouldered his bow and took the sheriff's sword, and instructed Tuck to ask de Glanville where the Ffreinc had hidden their horses.

Tuck did so, and received a terse reply—to which Tuck responded with another sharp rap of his staff against the sheriff's shins. De Glanville let out a yelp of pain and spat a string of words. "He says they're behind the rocks," reported Tuck, pointing a short distance away to a heap of boulders half covered in ivy and bracken.

While Siarles and Rhoddi collected the horses, Bran turned to Owain. "Do you think you can ride?"

His face was white and he was sweating, but his voice was steady as he replied, "I can ride, my lord."

"Very well." Bran nodded. He turned to Tomas. "I'm sending

you and Owain back to Cél Craidd. Tell Angharad and the others what has happened, and to see to Owain's wound. Then get Alan and bring him. The two of you meet us on the road—the place near the stream where the willows grow."

Tomas nodded. "I know the place."

"Then go. Ride like the devil himself was on your tail." To the others Bran said, "Find us something to drink and be ready to ride as soon as Siarles and Rhoddi return with the horses."

"What about the wagons?" asked Iwan.

"Leave them," said Bran. "If all goes well, we will own not only the wagons but all the rest of Elfael before nightfall."

The graves had been dug outside the abbey walls and the first bodies were being laid to rest under the solemn gaze of Captain Aloin and the chanting of Psalms from some of Saint Martin's monks when one of the gravediggers glanced up and saw, in the crimson light of a fading sunset, a body of men on horseback riding towards them from the direction of the forest. At first thought, he assumed it must be Sheriff de Glanville and his men returning at last from their part in the day's events, so he said nothing. But as the riders came closer, a trickle of doubt began to erode his assumption.

Captain Aloin, bruised and battered by his first encounter with King Raven and the lethal Welsh longbows, had determined to raise the issue of what he considered Marshal Guy's murderous incompetence with both the abbot and the sheriff at first opportunity. Clearly, Gysburne had to go. Aloin was thinking how best to put his case before the abbot and did not hear the monk speaking to him. He felt a touch on his arm and glanced up.

"Mon seigneur, regardez . . . " said the monk.

Aloin shifted his eyes from the corpse being lowered into the grave and looked where the monk was pointing. The approaching horsemen were near enough now to make out their faces, and what he saw was not the sheriff and his men, but strangers riding Ffreinc horses. *"Que diable!"*

"C'est lui . . ."

"Qui?"

"The one they call King Raven," said the monk.

"Blind them! They have Sheriff de Glanville!"

Instantly terrified, the monks and soldiers scattered, running for the safety of the abbey walls. Within moments, the abbey bells were signalling alarm. The few remaining knights who were not seriously wounded scurried to arm themselves and meet the attack. What they met instead were seven outlaws surrounding a red-faced, sullen Sheriff Richard de Glanville bound with his own belt.

The town square had been given over to the wounded from the day's earlier skirmishes; they had been laid on pallets in the open air to have their injuries tended by the monks, who moved among the rows of pallets, bathing and bandaging the injuries and offering what comfort they could to the dying. The outlaws rode to the entrance of the square, and one of them—in good plain French—called aloud for Abbot Hugo. The abbot, heeding the warning of King Raven's approach, had hidden himself in the guard tower to be defended by the eight knights still able to fight. These had arrayed themselves before the tower, weapons levelled, ready for the attack.

When the abbot failed to present himself, the French-speaking outlaw called, "Marshal Guy de Gysburne! Show yourself!"

There was a movement at the foot of the tower. "I am Guy," said the marshal, shoving through the knot of men. "What is this?"

"This," replied Alan, putting out a hand to the sheriff, "is all that is left of the company sent out to plunder the countryside this morning. The battle is over, and we have come to negotiate the terms of surrender."

"Surrender!" scoffed Gysburne. "*Your* surrender, I expect."

"No, my lord," replied Alan a'Dale. "The surrender of Abbot Hugo and yourself, and those of your men still alive. You will bring the abbot now so that we can begin."

A knight moved to take his place beside the marshal. "You must be insane," he charged, "coming here like this." He flung an accusing finger at the outlaw band. "Come down off your horses, you filthy dogs. We will settle this here and now!"

Bran leaned near his interpreter and spoke a few words, which Alan passed on, speaking to Gysburne. "Who is this man? My lord wishes to know."

"I am Captain Aloin, by the blood! Come down here and—"

"Hear me, Marshal Gysburne," interrupted Alan, "you will tell your man to hold his tongue. We have nothing to say to him."

"You arrogant dog!" sneered Guy. He spat on the ground in a show of contempt. "There will be no talk of surrender."

Alan paused to confer with Bran, then nodded and continued, "Rhi Bran urges you to take a good, long look around you, Marshal," he said. "Unless you wish to join your men here in the square—or out in the ground behind the abbey—you will do well to reconsider."

Gysburne and Aloin exchanged a word, and the marshal replied, "We hold this realm by order of King William—"

"You have gone against my lord's longbows twice today and have been beaten both times. Do you truly wish to try again? If so, be assured that you and the sheriff will be the first to die—and then what is left of your men will join you." Alan paused to allow this to sink in among all those listening. Then, in a plaintive tone, he added, "Think, man. There has been enough killing today. Bring the abbot and let him surrender and put an end to the bloodshed."

Bran lifted the sword in his hand and, from their saddles, the archers on either flank bent the bellies of their longbows.

Guy hesitated a moment more, then called out, "Sergeant Jeremias, do as he says. Fetch the abbot."

"Prudence is a virtue," Tuck muttered under his breath as he watched the sergeant dart up the stone steps of the tower, "and wisdom is gained through trials of many kinds."

"Most always too late," added Scarlet.

There followed a tense and uneasy interval in which both sides glared across the square at one another. Captain Aloin, seeing that there were but six Cymry archers, one ragged monk, and an unarmed translator, was for rushing them on the chance that his few healthy knights might overwhelm them. "We can take them," Aloin whispered. "At most they'll only get an arrow or two off before we cut them down."

"Yes, and it's the first arrow that kills you," replied Marshal Guy. "Have you already forgotten what happened at the farm?"

"It is madness to deal with them."

"That is as may be," granted Gysburne. "But do you really want to add another slaughter to your tally today? It is the abbot they want. So, we let him decide."

At last the abbot appeared, and owing to the look of stunned horror on his face he hardly seemed the same man. Clearly, the last thing he expected of this day was to find his enemy standing in the town square delivering demands of capitulation. But that was how things stood.

"Bouchers!" he snarled as he came striding up, trying to rouse his innate defiance. *"Meurtriers!"*

"Silence!" shouted Bran across the yard. "Your life and those of your men is in our hands. Be quiet and listen if you want that life to continue another breath longer."

Alan relayed these words to the abbot, who subsided. "Ask him what he wants—my head on a silver platter, I suppose?"

Bran smiled when he heard this, and replied, "No, Abbot. Your head is worth less than the trouble it would take to carve it from your scabby shoulders. But here is what I want: you are to lay down your arms and leave Elfael—you and all your men, and any of the townsfolk who choose to go with you."

Alan translated Bran's demand, and the abbot's face darkened. "See here!" he protested. "You have no ri—"

"You sent soldiers against me today, and the issue has been decided. I claim the victor's right to the spoils. If you would keep your life, you must leave this place and never return."

"Allow me a moment to confer with my commander," said the abbot when Alan had finished. Without waiting for a reply, he turned to Marshal Gysburne. "Idiot, do something—you just stand there. Attack! Kill them."

"The first man to advance against them is dead where he stands, my lord abbot," replied Guy. "So, please, by all means lead the way."

"But they cannot get away with this—just like that."

"Just like that? They've killed nearly forty of our men today already, priest!" Gysburne's voice was an ugly growl. "Are you blind as well as stupid? Look around you. The soldiers you see on their feet are *all* we have left. How many more must die to satisfy your insane ambitions?"

The abbot gazed around at his sorely beaten troops, as if seeing them for the first time. "This is all we have left?"

"Every last one," replied Gysburne.

"Where are the rest?"

"Either dead or dying—and I'm not joining them. Not like this. Not today."

"The marshal is right, Abbot," conceded Captain Aloin at last. "Make the best bargain you can, and we'll go back to the king and raise a force large enough to vanquish these bandits for once and all. We were beaten today, but the war is not over. We live to fight again."

Bran, having permitted them to speak freely, signalled Alan to bring the discussion to an end. "Enough!" he called. "What is it to be? Lord Bran says you must give your answer now."

Abbot Hugo drew himself up to full height. He lifted his head, some of the old defiance returning. "I agree to nothing," he announced, "until you accept our conditions."

"What conditions?" Bran asked, when Alan informed him of the abbot's reply. "Perhaps you will accept the same conditions you offered those farm families this morning?"

The abbot's lip curled into a silent snarl.

"I thought not," continued Bran, speaking through Alan. "Here are the conditions I offer: you are to depart now, taking nothing with you but the clothes on your back."

This reply occasioned a long and impassioned plea from the abbot.

"What did he say?" Bran asked.

"The coward is afraid you mean to slaughter them all the moment their backs are turned. He wants safe conduct to the border of Elfael."

"Tell him he can have that, and gladly," agreed Bran. "Also, tell him that as long as he abides by the terms of surrender, no one will be killed."

When this was relayed to the abbot, the cleric made another impassioned speech.

"Now what does he want?" said Bran, losing his patience.

"He says he needs time to gather his things—his papers and such," said Alan.

"I wouldn't trust him further than I could spit," muttered Tuck. "Look at him—the old devil. He probably means to empty the treasury before he goes."

"I know I would," added Scarlet.

"Do not let them out of your sight," said Iwan. "There's no telling what he might get up to."

"They have to leave *now*," insisted Siarles. "With nothing but the clothes on their backs."

Bran lifted the reins and urged his mount a few steps closer. "Hear me, Abbot. That you live to draw breath when so many who served you are dead this day is insult to heaven above and God's creatures below. You will go now, taking only what you have hidden in your robes. Your men are to lay down their arms now. When that is done, you will all be escorted from Elfael—never to return on pain of death."

"What about the wounded?" said Gysburne. "They cannot travel."

Bran held a quick consultation with Tuck and Iwan, and Alan relayed the decision. "They will continue to be cared for by the monks of the abbey until they are well enough to leave." He pointed to the sheriff, who sat slumped in the saddle with his head down, miserable in defeat. "When the last is fit to travel, all will be sent along with the monks in the care of the sheriff. To ensure that this agreement is upheld, de Glanville will remain a hostage until that time. His life is forfeit if you fail to honour your part."

"You mean to kill them all anyway as soon as we're gone," said Gysburne.

As Alan relayed the marshal's words, Bran gazed at his adversary with an expression so hard it might have been carved of stone. "Tell him," he replied, "that if I meant to kill them, they would be dead already."

"How do we know you'll keep your word?" demanded Aloin when the translator finished.

"You will all die here and now if the surrender is not agreed," said Alan. "My lord Bran says that if his word is not acceptable, then you are free to take your wounded with you now."

The abbot did not like this last proviso, and made to dispute it, but Bran would not relent. In the end, Gysburne sealed the bargain by turning the sword in his hand and throwing it down in the dirt halfway between himself and Bran.

"God in heaven be praised!" said Tuck. "I do believe they're going to surrender. You've done it, Bran. You beautiful man, you've done it!"

"Steady on, Friar," replied Bran. "This is not finished yet by a long throw. We are dancing on a knife edge here; pray we don't yet slip." He cast his gaze around the square. "I greatly fear a fall now would prove fatal."

"All of you," said Iwan, pointing to the sword on the ground.

One by one, the soldiers added their weapons to the marshal's; Captain Aloin was the last to disarm.

"What now?" said Siarles.

"Gather round, everyone," said Bran, and explained how they were to shepherd the Ffreinc through the forest. "We'll see them to the Vale of Wye and release them at the border of the March. Then, they are on their own."

"It will be dark soon," Tuck pointed out.

"Then we had best get started," Bran replied. "All saints and angels bear witness, on my life they will not spend another night in my realm."

CHAPTER 30

Castle Neufmarché

Four long days on the road brought the weary abbot and his foot-sore company—six soldiers, three monks, and two dejected commanders—to the busy market town of Hereford, the principal seat of Baron Neufmarché. Very possibly, the baron may have been the closest thing to an ally that Abbot Hugo possessed just then. Exhausted, begrimed from his journey, and aching from sleeping in rude beds appropriated from settlements alongside the road, Hugo lifted his sweaty face to the solid stone walls of the castle on the hill above the town and felt what it must be like for weary pilgrims to behold the promised land.

Here, at last, he would be given a welcome worthy of his rank. Moreover, if he sharpened his appeal with hints of clerical patronage—offers of perpetual prayer and special indulgences excusing the baron from certain past sins—Hugo imagined he might enlist the baron's aid to help him recover his abbey and reclaim Elfael from the hands of that blasted King Raven and his troop of outlaws. "Captain

Aloin," he called, climbing down from a swaybacked horse—the only one they had been able to commandeer from the first Norman town they had come to after leaving the March. "You and your men will rest and wait for us in the town. Go to the monastery and get some food and drink—my monks will take you there."

"Where are you going, Abbot?"

"Marshal Guy and I will go to the baron and see if he is of a mood to receive us. If all goes well, I will send for you as soon as suitable arrangements can be made."

The captain, who had risked life and limb in the abbot's service, and whose troops bore the brunt of the failure to roust King Raven from his roost, was not best pleased to be shut out of the proceedings now. But Aloin was too tired to argue, so agreed—if only that he might find a cool place to sit down that much sooner. He waved the marshal and abbot away, ordered his men to go with the monks and fetch food and drink from the abbey and bring some back for him; and then, sitting himself down in the shade of the stone archway leading into the town square, he pulled off his boots and closed his eyes. Before he drifted off to sleep, it occurred to him that this was likely the last he would see of the abbot. This caused him fleeting concern. Yet, close on this first thought was another: if he never saw that grasping, arrogant, conniving churchman again . . . well, all things considered, that was fine too.

Meanwhile, Bernard Neufmarché, Lord of Hereford and Gloucester, was sitting in his private courtyard gazing up at the sky for no other reason than that he thought a shadow had passed over him and he felt a sudden chill. He glanced up to see if an errant cloud had obscured the sun for a moment, but there were no clouds, and the sun shone as brightly as ever. The baron was not a man for

TUCK

omens or portents, but it did seem to him that lately—at least, ever since his lady wife had become smitten with all things Welsh—he often had odd feelings and sudden urges to do things he had never done before, such as sit quietly alone with his thoughts in his pleasant courtyard. Moreover, he often entertained the notion that strange forces were swirling around him, moving him towards destinations and destinies unknown.

He smiled at his own superstitious nature—something else he never did.

When Remey, his red-capped seneschal, appeared in the doorway to tell him that he had visitors, he felt the intrusion like a clammy dampness in the small of his back. Odd, that. "Who is it?" he asked, and before Remey could reply, he added, "Send them away. I do not wish to see anyone today."

"Of course, my lord baron," replied the seneschal smoothly, "but you may wish to reconsider when I tell you that Abbot Hugo de Rainault and Marshal Guy de Gysburne have arrived on foot, alone, and wish to speak to you most urgently."

"Indeed?" wondered the baron, intrigued now. "Very well." He sighed, rising from his warm bench. "Give them something to drink, and I will join them in the hall. I want to speak to Father Gervais first."

"Very wise, my lord." Remey withdrew to find the steward and order some refreshments for the baron's unexpected guests.

When his servant had gone, the baron walked slowly across the courtyard to an opposite doorway which led onto the porch of the little chapel, where he found the family's elderly priest sitting in a pool of light from the courtyard and nodding over a small parchment chapbook in his lap. The baron picked up the book; it was the

309

Gospel of Saint Matthew in Latin. He was able to pick out a few words here and there, and the thought came to him that perhaps it was time he learned to read properly—not like a barnyard chicken pecking seeds willy-nilly.

The old priest awoke with a start. "Oh! Bless me, I must have dozed off. Good day to you, my son, and God's rich blessing."

"Very well, Father," replied the baron, and thanked the priest. "I would not disturb your meditations, but we have visitors—Abbot Hugo de Rainault and his marshal, Guy of some such. I believe you know the abbot?"

"I had dealings with him now and then," replied the priest, "but that was a long time ago. I would not say I knew him."

The baron considered this and turned another page of the book in his hand. "There must be trouble in Elfael," mused the baron idly. "I can think of no other reason de Rainault would turn up at my door."

The priest considered this. "Yes," he agreed slowly, "no doubt you are right about that. Then again, it has been very quiet of late. We would have heard about any trouble, I think."

"Perhaps not," countered the baron. "The outlaws own the King's Road through the forest. Nothing moves in or out of Wales that they do not allow—which is why I expect this visit means trouble."

"You know best, Bernard."

"Well, in any event we'll soon find out," said the baron with a sigh. "I'm going to see them now, but I wanted to ask if you would come with me to greet them. I'd like to have you there, Father."

"Certainly, my son. I'd be delighted."

The baron held out his hand to the elder man and helped him to his feet.

"These old bones get slower every day," said the priest, rising heavily.

"Nonsense, Father," replied Baron Neufmarché. "The years touch you but lightly."

"Bah! *Now* who is speaking nonsense?"

They strolled amiably to the baron's great hall, where, at a table near the wide double door leading to the castle's main yard, a very dusty Gysburne and travel-soiled abbot were finishing their wine and cheese. "My lord baron!" declared Gysburne, standing quickly and brushing crumbs from his tunic. "God be good to you, Sire. My thanks for your inestimable hospitality."

"God with you, Marshal," replied the baron, "and with you, Abbot de Rainault. Greetings and welcome. I hope you are well?"

Abbot Hugo extended his hand to be reverenced. "God with you, Baron. I fear you find me not at all well."

"Oh? I am sorry to hear it." The baron turned to his companion, and they exchanged a knowing glance. "May I present my dear friend, Father Gervais. I think you may know one another."

The abbot glanced at the elderly cleric. "No, I don't think so. I would remember. God with you, Father." He gave the old man a nod and dismissed him with a slighting smile. "It will save us all some bother if I come to the point, my lord."

"I am all for it," replied the baron. "Please, continue."

"There has been a wicked uprising in Elfael. Soldiers under the command of Marshal Guy, here, were slaughtered in an unprovoked attack and the fortress taken. In short, we have been driven from our lands by an uprising of Welsh rebels. I say rebels, and so they style themselves. In truth, they are little more than thieves and outlaws, every last one."

"I see." Baron Bernard frowned thoughtfully. "That is not good news."

"What is more, they have killed a regiment of king's men under the command of one Captain Aloin. The few survivors have been driven into exile with me."

"Hmmm . . ." said the baron, shaking his head.

"These rebels, Lord Abbot," said Father Gervais, "would they be the same that control the King's Road through the forest? We have heard about them."

"The same, since you ask. Yes, the same. Their strength in arms and numbers has grown in these last months, and they have become ever more bold in their raiding and thieving. We had hoped that the arrival of the king's soldiers would have been sufficient to discourage them. Alas, they respect no authority and live only to shed innocent blood."

"How many men did the king lend you?" wondered the baron, summoning a steward with a gesture. "A chair for Father Gervais," he said. "And one for myself. Bring us wine too."

The steward brought the chairs, and another produced a small table for the wine; while the cups were filled, the abbot continued. "How many king's men did I have? Too few, by the rood. If we had received numbers sufficient to the task—and which I specifically requested, mind you—I am certain this disaster could have been averted. It is only through my most stringent endeavours at persuasion that any of us have survived at all."

Marshal Guy stared at the abbot, whose lies he almost believed himself.

"The attack was vicious and unprovoked, as I say," concluded the abbot. "They struck without warning and showed no mercy. Though we mounted a vigorous defence, we were at last overwhelmed. We were fortunate to escape with our lives."

"Yes, no doubt," mused the baron thoughtfully. "You said they were with you, the soldiers who survived the attack—where are they now?"

"In the town," replied Guy. "We've been on the road for four days without horses. We are all of us exhausted."

"Of course," replied the baron.

Guy could not fail to notice that the baron did not offer to send for the troops and bring them to the castle to be fed. In fact, the baron seemed more than content to let the matter rest where it lay. The abbot, however, was not so inclined; he had the spoon in his fist and meant to stir the pot with it.

"My lord baron," said Hugo, offering up his cup to be refilled. "How many men have you under your command?"

The baron waited while the wine was poured. "Not as many as I should like," he answered, raising his cup to his lips, "times being what they are." He drank a sip to give himself a little time to think. "No doubt, King William would be able to raise as many as required." He smiled. "But I am no king."

"No, of course not," replied the abbot. He placed his cup carefully on the table and looked the baron full in the face. "Even so, I would like to ask you to consider lending me some of your soldiers. Now"—he raised his hand as if to forestall an objection he saw coming—"think carefully before you answer. You would be aiding the church in its ongoing affairs, and that would place me in a position to pass along certain indulgences . . . ." He watched the baron for his reaction. "Certain, shall we say, very *valuable* indulgences. The perpetual prayers of an abbey can guarantee salvation on the Day of

Judgement, as we know—which is ordinarily obtained only at great expense."

The baron, still smiling, said nothing.

"You could of course lead your men," continued Hugo. "I would not presume to usurp your place on the field. Indeed, I have no doubt that under your able command Elfael would be rid of the outlaws within two or three days—a week at most."

Baron Neufmarché placed his cup very deliberately on the table and leaned forward. "Your confidence in me is most gratifying, Lord Abbot. And of course, I wish I were in a position to help. Unfortunately, what you suggest is difficult just now—not to say impossible. I am truly sorry."

The abbot's face froze. His white hair wild on his head, his pristine satin robe stained from the toil of his flight, he appeared haggard and old as he gazed at the baron, trying to find a way over the stone wall so deftly thrown into his path. "Ah, well," he said at last, "I find it never hurts to ask."

"You have not because you ask not," declared Father Gervais suddenly. "Saint James . . . I believe."

"Precisely," murmured the abbot, thinking furiously how to rescue his stranded request.

"What plans have you made?" inquired the baron, looking to Gysburne.

"We will go to the king," answered Guy. "His men would return in any case, and we—"

"The king, yes," interrupted the abbot, rousing himself to life again. "It is *his* cantref, after all, and his to defend."

"My thoughts exactly," concurred the baron—as if the point had been under dispute but was now successfully resolved to the satisfaction of all. "It goes without saying that I *would* ask you to stay here and rest a few days, but I can see that the urgency of your journey requires you to reach Londein without delay. I only wish it was possible to lend you horses for the remainder of your journey"—he spread his hands helplessly—"but, alas, such is not the case."

"Your thoughtfulness is commendable," intoned the abbot. He slumped wearily in his chair, looking more and more like an old bone that had been gnawed close and tossed onto the midden heap.

"No, no," countered the baron, "it is nothing. Please, you will stay and eat something before you go. I insist. Then, my commander will escort you to rejoin your men in the town and see you on your way. You've come this far without incident; we don't wish to see anything ill befall you now, do we?"

And that was that.

A cold supper was brought to the chamber, and while the abbot and marshal ate, two mules were loaded with provisions to be led by a driver who would accompany them and bring the animals back upon their arrival in Londein.

As the abbot and marshal were preparing to leave, the baron and several of his men joined them in the yard to bid the visitors farewell. "God speed you, my friends," he said cheerily. "At least you have good weather for your journey."

"At the very least," agreed the abbot sourly.

"Ah," said the baron, as if thinking of it for the first time, "There was a sheriff, I believe, in Elfael. You didn't say what became of him. Killed, I suppose, in the battle?"

"Not at all," answered Gysburne. "Sheriff de Glanville was leading a division of men who were butchered by the rebels. All were murdered, save the sheriff, who was taken prisoner and is being held hostage. They promise to release him once our wounded soldiers are well enough to travel. Although, what is to become of him, I cannot say."

"I see," said Baron Neufmarché gravely. "A bad business all around. Well, I bid you *adieu* and wish you safe travels." He turned and summoned his commander to his side. "See here, Ormand," he said, "my friends are travelling to Londein on an errand of some urgency. I want you to escort them through the town and see them safely to the borders of my realm. Let nothing untoward happen to them while they are with you."

"To be sure, Sire." Ormand, a capable and levelheaded knight who served as the baron's marshal, put out a hand to his new charges. "Shall we proceed, my lords? After you."

The baron, standing at the topmost gate, waved his unwanted guests away; he waited until they were lost to sight in the narrow street leading down from the castle. Then, hurrying to his chambers, he called for a pen and parchment to send a message to the baroness in Wales informing her of the uprising and instructing her to tell King Garran to gather his soldiers and be ready to step in should the revolt show signs of spreading.

"Remey!" he called, waving the small square of parchment in the air to dry the ink. "I need a messenger at once—and see that he has the fastest horse in the stable. I want this delivered to Lady Agnes this time tomorrow and no later."

CHAPTER 31

Londein

Cardinal Flambard pulled up the hem of his robe and stepped over the low rail of the boat and onto the dock. He dipped into his purse for a coin and flipped it to the ferryman, then turned and strolled up the dock, avoiding the gulls fighting over piles of fish guts some unthinking oaf had left to swelter in the sun. He raised his eyes to the Billings Gate and started his climb up the steep bank, stifling an inward sigh. It was his lot ever to run to the king's least whim and answer His Majesty's flimsiest fancy. Like two men sharing a prison cell, they were chained to one another until one of them died. Such was the price of standing so near the throne.

Standing? Ranulf Flambard occupied that gilded seat as often as ever the king sat there—considering that Red William remained in perpetual motion, flitting here and there and everywhere . . . stamping out rebellion, squabbling with his disgruntled brothers, resisting the constant incursions by the Mother Church into what he considered his private affairs. And when the king wasn't doing that, he was hunting. In fact, that was William: always at the sharp end of any conflict going or, failing that, causing one.

And the dutiful Ranulf Flambard, Chief Justiciar of England, was there at his side to pick up the pieces.

It was to William's side that he was summoned now, and he laboured up from the stinking jetty with a scented cloth pressed to his nose. The riverside at the rank end of summer was a very cesspool—when was it not? Proceeding through the narrow streets lining the great city's wharf he allowed himself to think what life might be like as a bishop in a remote, upcountry see. As attractive as the notion seemed at the moment, would all that serenity soon pall? It was not likely he would ever find out. Turning from that, he wondered what fresh debacle awaited him this time.

At the gate to the White Tower he was admitted without delay and personally conducted by the porter to the entrance to the king's private apartment, where his presence was announced by the chamberlain. Following a short interval, he was admitted.

"Oh, Flambard, it's you," said William, glancing up. He was stuffing the voluminous tail of his shirt into his too-tight breeches. Finishing the chore, he started towards the door. "At last."

"I came as soon as I received your summons, Majesty. Forgive me for not anticipating your call."

"Eh? Yes, well . . ." Red William looked at his chief advisor and tried to work out whether Flambard was mocking him. He could not tell, so let it go. "You're here now and there's work to do."

"A pleasure, Sire." He made a tight little bow that, perfected over years of service, had become little more than a slight nod of the head with a barely discernible bend at the waist. "Am I to know what has occasioned this summons, my lord?"

"It is all to do with that business in Elvile," William said, push-ing past the justiciar and bowling down the corridor which led to his audience rooms. "Remember all that ruck?"

"I seem to have a recollection, Sire. There was some trouble with one of the barons—de Braose, if I recall the incident correctly. You banished the baron and took the cantref under your authority—placed it in the care of some abbot or other, and a sheriff somebody."

"You remember, good," decided the king. "Then you can talk to him."

"Talk to whom, Majesty, if I may ask?"

"That blasted abbot—he's here. Been driven off his perch by bandits, apparently. Demanding an audience. Screaming the roof down." The king stopped walking so abruptly that the cardinal almost collided with his squat, solid form. "Give him whatever he wants. No—whatever it takes to make him go away. I'm off to Normandie in a fortnight, and I cannot spare even a moment."

"I understand, Highness," replied the cardinal judiciously. "I will see what can be done."

They continued on to the audience chamber, discussing the king's proposed journey to Normandie, where he planned to meet with King Philip to challenge the French monarch's increasingly flagrant incursions beyond the borders of the Vexin. "Philip is a low, craven ass. His trespasses will not be tolerated, hear?" said William as he pushed open the chamber door. "Ah! There you are." This was spo-ken as if the king had spent the better part of the day in a harried search for the petitioner.

"My lord and majesty," said the abbot, once again resplendent in a simple white satin robe and purple stole. "You honour your servant with your presence."

William waved aside the flattery. "What is it you want? I was told it was a matter of some urgency. Speak, man, let's get it done."

"My lord," said Abbot Hugo, "I fear I bring unhappy tidings. The—"

"Who are you?" asked the king, turning to the young man standing a few steps behind the abbot. "Well? Step up. Let me know you."

"I am Marshal Guy de Gysburne at your service, Sire," replied the knight.

"Gysburne, eh? I think I know your father—up north somewhere, isn't it?"

"Indeed, Majesty."

"Are you the sheriff?"

"Majesty?"

"The sheriff I appointed to Elvile—or whatever the miserable place is called."

"No, Majesty," replied Guy, "I am the abbot's marshal. Sheriff de Glanville is—"

"De Glanville—yes! That's the fellow," said the king as the memory came back to him. "Came to me begging the use of some soldiers. Where is he? Why isn't he here?"

"That is what we've come to speak to you about, Highness," said the abbot, resuming his tale of woe. "It pains me to inform you that the realm of Elfael is in open rebellion against your rule. The rebels have slaughtered most of the men you sent to aid in the protection of your loyal subjects."

Abbot Hugo then proceeded to describe a realm under siege and a population captive to chaos and terror. He spoke passionately and in some detail—so much so that even Gysburne felt himself moved to outrage at the accumulated atrocities, though the abbot's description had parted company with the truth after the first few words. "If that was not enough," concluded Hugo, "the outlaws have seized the throne and taken your sheriff hostage."

"They have, eh? By the rood, I'll have their eyes on my belt! I'll hang the——"

"Your Majesty," interrupted Cardinal Flambard, "perhaps it would be best if I were to sit down with the abbot here and see what can be done?"

"No need, Flambard," retorted the king. "A blind man can see what needs to be done. Rebellion must be snuffed out swiftly and mercilessly, lest it spreads out of hand. These Welsh must be taught a lesson. I've too long been over-lenient with them—too generous, by the blood, and they've used me for a fool."

"Sire," ventured Cardinal Flambard gently, "I do not think this present circumstance is quite as simple as it might seem at first blush. I think I remember this outlaw fellow from Elfael, Sire. Was he not the same who came to you at Rouen with word of Duke Robert's treason? He uncovered the plot against you—that was why Baron de Braose was exiled, if you will recall."

"Yes? What of it?"

"Well, it would seem that the fellow sought restitution of his lands in exchange for his service to your throne."

Abbot Hugo's expression grew grim. He had carefully avoided any mention of the circumstances leading up to the insurrection—lest his own part in the baron's conspiracy against William should inadvertently come to light.

"Ah, yes. Good hunting land, Elvile, I believe."

"The best, Sire," encouraged Hugo.

"What is your point, Flambard? We settled with Duke Robert and his schemers. That is over and done."

"Quite so, Sire," offered Hugo.

"If I may," continued the justiciar, undeterred, "I would suggest that inasmuch as this Welshman did not receive the reward he was looking for at the time, it would seem that he has taken matters into his own hands."

"I am to blame for this?" said William. "Is that what you're suggesting? *I* am to blame for this rebellion?"

"By no means, Sire. Far from it. I merely point out that the two matters are related. Perhaps in light of the present circumstance it would be most expedient simply to allow the Welshman to claim the throne. I believe he offered to swear fealty to you once. If you were to allow him his due this time, I have no doubt he could be persuaded to make good his previous offer."

William the Red stared at his chief counsellor in disbelief. "Give him what he wants—is that what you said?"

"In a word, Majesty, yes."

"By the bloody rood, Flambard, that I *will not* do! If we were to allow these rogues to murder my troops and then take whatever they want with our blessing, the kingdom would soon descend into anarchy! No, sir! Not while I sit on the throne of England. All such insurrections will be crushed. This rogue will be captured and brought to the tower in chains. He will be tried for treason against the crown, and he will be hung before the city gate. That is how we deal with rebels while William sits the throne!"

"Very wise, Your Majesty," intoned the abbot. "It goes without saying that you shall have my entire support—and that of my marshal."

William glanced at the abbot and gave a short blast through his nostrils. "Huff." Turning swiftly on the cardinal, he said, "Summon the barons. I want them to—" He stopped, did a rapid calculation in his head, and then said, "No, send to them and command them to raise their men and attend me at Hereford . . . Who's that?"

"Neufmarché, Highness," volunteered the abbot, with smug satisfaction at the thought that the baron would be forced to help in the end.

"All are to meet me at Hereford Castle with their troops. We will march on Elfael from there and take these rebels. I want sufficient force to quash the rebellion in the egg. It shouldn't take long." He looked to the marshal for agreement.

"A few days, Sire," said Gysburne, speaking up. "There are not so many that they cannot be brought to justice in a day or two of fighting—a week at most."

"There! You see? A week and the thing is done, the rebels brought to heel, and I can go to Normandie."

Cardinal Flambard pursed his lips doubtfully.

"Well?" demanded the king accusingly. "You're sulking, priest. Out with it."

"With all respect, Highness, I still believe an embassy to this nobleman, outlaw as he may be, would achieve the same end with far less cost—and then there is the bloodshed to think about."

"Nonsense," snorted William. "Hang the cost and bloodshed. The rest of Wales will see and understand by this that our sovereign rule will not be violated. Treason will not be tolerated. And *that* will save blood and silver in days to come."

"You can always invade Wales as a last resort, my liege," suggested Cardinal Flambard. "Should the embassy fail, that is, which I doubt . . ."

But William the Red was no longer listening. He had turned his back and was striding for the door. "Send to the barons, Cardinal," he called over his shoulder. "All are to meet me in Hereford ready to fight in six days' time."

PART FIVE

For nine seasons long they lived in the woode
  The sheriff, they vexed, and his men.
The regent's reeve bent but did not yet break,
  and Rhiban was angered with him.

"I must regayne my land and my rights,
  My people needs all must be free.
Let's go with our bows to the true king's keep,
  And there with our points make our plea."

"I rede that not," said Mérian fayre,
  "Belovéd, repent of your haste.
Let's all of us, yeomen and women alike,
  Go with you to argue your case."

So soon they are gone up to greate Lundein Town,
  Wives, maids, and warriors same.
But when city folk 'round there them saw,
  They thought that besiegers there came.

The ploughman he leaves his plough in the fields,
    The smithy has fled from his shop;
And beggars who only a'creeping could go,
    Over their crutches did hop.

The king is informed of the forth-marching host
    And assembles his armies at speed.
He swings-to the gates and he marshals his men,
    Their progress he means to impede.

With Fryer Tuck, Rhiban approaches the king
    Under the true sign of peace.
The king gives him entrance, for he is full wise
    And wishes hostility cease.

"God save the king," quod Rhiban to he,
    "And them that wish him full well;
And he that does his true sovereign deny,
    I wish him with Satan to dwell."

CHAPTER 32

I wan awoke in the hall of the fortress where he had been born, raised, and grown to manhood. As a young warrior, he had become champion to Brychan ap Tewdwr, Bran's father—a hard man, fair but uncompromising, easily angered and stony as flint—and until the arrival of the Ffreinc invaders Caer Cadarn, the Iron Stronghold, had been his home. God willing, it would be again.

He sat up and looked around at the scores of bodies asleep on the floor around him, then rose and quietly made his way to the entrance, pushed open the heavy oaken door, and stepped out into the quiet dawn of a fresh day. He turned his face to the new-risen sun and drew the soft morning air deep into his lungs, exhaling slowly. From somewhere high above a lark poured out its heart in praise of a glorious day. "It should be like this always," he murmured.

Surveying the yard and surrounding buildings, he noted the alterations made to the old fortress during the Ffreinc occupation of the last four years—mostly for the better, he had to admit. The timber

STEPHEN R. LAWHEAD

palisade had been shored up all around, and weak timbers replaced and strengthened; a covered guard station had been erected above the entrance gate; the roof of the hall had been replaced with new thatch and given stout new doors; there were new storehouses, a granary, and the kitchen and cookhouse had both been enlarged. There were other changes he would notice in the days to come, to be sure.

Still, it felt like home to him. The thought brought a rare smile to his lips. He had come home.

What the day held, he could not say, but if it was anything like the last it would be busy. Since the capture of the sheriff and the departure of Hugo and his retinue from Saint Martin's, Cymry had been streaming to the caer bringing provisions and livestock; men and women brought their families for protection and to help defend the caer against the retaliation all knew was surely coming. For now, they were housed mostly in the hall and outbuildings of the fortress— with a few, here and there, sleeping on the ramparts.

He washed his face in the big, iron basin beside the door and then walked across the deserted yard to an empty storehouse behind the stables. Outside the small, square wooden building he found Alan a'Dale sitting slumped against a nearby post, his head on his knees.

"God with you, Alan," said Iwan, nudging the minstrel with his foot.

Alan jolted awake and jumped to his feet. "Oh, Iwan—it's you. Here, I must have nodded off for a few winks just then."

"Never mind," said Iwan. "No harm done. Has our captive made any trouble?"

"Quiet as a lamb," replied Alan. He yawned, rubbing the sleep from his eyes. "Quieter, even. Maybe he has resigned himself to his fate."

"Not likely," replied Iwan. "Open the door, and let's have a look at him."

Alan untied the braided leather rope used to secure the storehouse and pulled open the rough plank door. There, huddled in his cloak on the beaten dirt floor, sat Richard de Glanville, Sheriff of Elfael, chained at the wrists and ankles, red-eyed from lack of sleep, his hair wild on his head as if he had been beating his skull against the walls of his prison. He spat and began cursing as soon as he saw who had come to observe him.

Iwan regarded the enraged prisoner for a moment, then said, "You would think a man so eager for the captivity of others would endure his own with a little more dignity. What is he saying?"

Alan listened to the sheriff's onrushing gush of abuse, then said, "Nothing worth hearing. Suffice it to say that he holds himself ill-used."

"No doubt," Iwan agreed, then addressed the prisoner. "If you think yourself mistreated now, Sheriff, try escaping and whole new realms of woe will open before you." To Alan he added, "Tell him what I said."

Alan did as commanded, which loosed another tirade in snarled French from the captive. *"Tuez-moi maintenant, ou relâchez-moi—je l'exige!"* shouted Sheriff de Glanville. *"Espèces de cochons! Vous m'entendez? Je l'exige!"*

"What did he say?" asked Iwan. "Something about pigs?"

"Aye, swine came into it," replied Alan. "More to the point, he says he wants us to kill him now or set him free."

"If it was left to me," replied the champion, "he would have had his wish long since. But our Lord Bran thinks he may be of some value yet."

"Je suis désolé, Monsieur le Shérif, mais c'est impossible," said Alan to the sheriff, who spat by way of reply.

Iwan said, "I'll send someone to relieve your watch very soon. But before you go, see his water bowl is filled and get him some bread and a little meat if there is any."

"As good as done," replied Alan.

"And tell our hostage that he is going to be with us for a few more days at least, so he must try to endure his captivity with better grace than he has shown till now."

This was passed along to the prisoner, who spat again and turned his face to the wall. Alan retied the rope securing the door, and he and Iwan walked across the yard to the hall. "He is a right rogue, that one," Alan observed. "As black-souled a brute as ever strode the earth on two legs. What if King William will not bargain for his life?"

"Oh, he'll bargain, never fear," Iwan assured him. "For all his faults, de Glanville is a Ffreinc nobleman. And if I've learned any-thing these last years, it is that the noble Ffreinc look out for their own. William may not like de Glanville very much—no blame there, God knows—but he will bargain. All we need do is make sure the ransom is not so high that the king will refuse to pay."

Following the eviction of the Ffreinc from the cantref, Bran had swiftly moved to occupy not only the fortress of Caer Cadarn, but the nearby town as well, reclaiming them for the Cymry. To that end, he had summoned the venerable Bishop Asaph to return and take charge of the abbey at Saint Martin's. Before being forced into exile by Abbot Hugo, the elderly cleric had been the head of Llanelli, the monastery Count Falkes de Braose had pulled down and rebuilt, and around which he had constructed his new town. As soon as Asaph, along with a goodly body of monks, was firmly installed and keeping watch over the town and its inhabitants—both the remaining Ffreinc townsfolk and the wounded knights, all of whom had been left behind by the abbot and his troops—Bran then moved to regain control of the fortress. This was swiftly done, since the Ffreinc had abandoned the stronghold before the last battle; they had never worried that King Raven would attack it in any case, and only ever kept a token occupation in place. Bran gave the defence of the caer and the valley round about to Iwan, with Siarles and Alan to help. He sent Tomas and Rhoddi on fast horses to ride throughout Elfael and to settlements in the nearest cantrefs and spread the news that King Raven had driven out the Ffreinc invaders and taken Caer Cadarn: all who could were to gather weapons and supplies and come occupy the caer—for safety, for defence, and so that Elfael's ancient stronghold would not be abandoned.

With these measures in place, Bran had returned to Cél Craidd; and now, two days after escorting Abbot Hugo and Marshal Gysburne and their few remaining troops to the borders of the March, he planned his defence of his realm. He had spent the day at the caer working with Iwan on the fortifications there, returning at sundown. And now, while the rest of the forest dwellers slept, Bran sat in council with his closest advisors: Angharad, his Wise Banfáith, Friar Tuck, Will Scarlet, and Owain. Mérian's absence was a pang felt by them all.

"Forgive me, Rhi Bran, but I thought—" Owain gave a shrug. "What is the point of driving out the enemy if we still must skulk around in the greenwood like outlaws?"

"We have not seen the last of the Ffreinc," Bran told him. "Iwan and Siarles can direct the defence of the caer, but we need Cél Craidd as well."

"How long, then?" Owain asked.

"Until William the Red recognizes my claim," Bran replied.

"Surely, that cannot be long in coming," Owain said. "The king must recognize your kingship now. We've defeated his lackeys."

"Nothing of the kind, lad," Scarlet told him. "We've bloodied their noses a bit, is all. They'll come back—"

"In force," added Tuck. "You can bet your last ha'penny on that."

Two days of jubilation following the Ffreinc defeat had given way to more sober reflection. It was, Tuck thought, as if the farm dog that chased every passing wagon had, against every sane expectation, finally caught one. Now the forest dwellers were faced with the awful realization that there would be reprisals, and they were woefully outmanned. How could they hope to protect their gains? That was the question in the forefront of their minds, and it leached the joy from their hearts.

"The point is," Bran continued, "we will never be secure in Elfael until we have King William's seal on a treaty of peace and protection. I do not expect Red William to grant that without a fight—which is why we're still skulking around in the greenwood like outlaws." He broke another stick and tossed the ends into the fire, then declared the council at an end.

Scarlet rose and shuffled off to join Noín and Nia in their hut; Owain, whose wound, though still painful, was healing quickly, went to his rest. Tuck and Angharad were left to sit with Bran a little while longer. "You are right to prepare for war, of course," Tuck began.

"Did you think we would gain Elfael without one?"

"But perhaps King William's appetite for this war is no match for your own," the friar ventured, watching the firelight and shadows flicker over Bran's sharp features. "Perhaps even now he is searching for a way to avoid a fight."

"Perhaps," Bran allowed. "What are you suggesting?"

"We might send an emissary to the king with an offer of peace." Bran regarded the little priest thoughtfully.

"Peace, that is," Tuck clarified, "in exchange for fealty."

"If William recognizes my throne, I agree to swear fealty—and the war is over."

"Over before it has begun."

Bran looked to Angharad sitting quietly beside the fire on her three-legged stool. "What do you see?" he asked.

"The friar is right to suggest an offer of peace," observed Angharad. "It is close to God's heart always." She rose stiffly and pulled the edges of her Bird Spirit cloak closed. "But unless God moves in the Red King's heart, peace we will not have."

The old woman made a little stirring motion with her hands in the smoke from the fire, then lifted her palms upward as if raising the fragrance towards the night-dark sky above. Tilting her face heavenward, her small, dark eyes lost in the creases of her wrinkled face, she stood very still for a long moment.

Bran and Tuck found themselves holding their breath in anticipation.

At last, she sighed.

"What do you see, Mother?" asked Bran gently, his voice barely audible above the crackle of the flames.

"I see . . ." she began, drawing a deep breath and letting it out slowly as she searched the tangled pathways of the future. ". . . I see a trail of blood that leads from this place and spreads throughout the land. Where it ends, God knows." She opened her eyes, and her face crinkled in a sad smile. "What we sow here will be reaped not by our children, but by our children's children—or those who after them come. But sow we must; another course we have not."

"Yet, there is hope?" asked the friar.

"There is always hope, Aethelfrith," replied the old woman. "In hope we do abide. As children of the Swift Sure Hand, hope is our true home. You, a priest, must understand this."

Tuck smiled at the gentle rebuke. "I bow to your teaching, Banfáith. And you are right, of course. I used to know a bishop who said much the same thing. Hope is the treasure of our souls, he would say."

"It is an end worth fighting for," mused Bran. "It may be for others to complete what we've begun, but there must be a beginning. And we will carry this fight as far as we can before passing it on to those who come after."

The three of them sat in silence, watching the flames and listening to the crack and hiss of the wood as it burned. From somewhere in the forest an owl called to its mate. It was a sound Tuck had heard countless times since throwing in his lot with the forest folk, but tonight it filled him with an almost unbearable sadness. He rose from his place and bade the other two a good night. "God rest you right well, friends, and grant you His peace."

"Tuck," said Bran as the friar stepped from the hearth, "the Ffreinc are grasping, devious devils—false-hearted as the sea is wide. Even so, I am willing to swear fealty to Red William if it means we can draw a living breath without their foot on our neck. If you can find a way to speak peace to William, I stand ready to do my part. I want you to know that."

That night the friar did not sleep. Though cool and damp, the sky was clear and ablaze with stars; he found a place among the roots of one of the giant oaks and settled down in the dry bracken to pray for Elfael and its people, and all those who would not be able to avoid the war that was coming. He was praying still when the watchers rose, silently saddled their horses, and departed Cél Craidd to take up their posts on the King's Road.

CHAPTER 33

Hereford

S pare me the excuses, Marshal," said King William, cutting off the lengthy beggings of pardon as read out by Guy of Gysburne. Following his eviction from Elfael, his fortunes had risen beyond anything he might have dared to hope. Owing to his intimate knowledge of the Cymry and the lands beyond the March, the young marshal had become an aide-de-camp to William Rufus for the purpose of what the king now referred to as the Harrowing of Wales. "Tell it to me plain—who has come?"

Gysburne allowed his gaze to drop down the parchment roll prepared for him by the court scribes in attendance. "Besides Huntingdon, Buckingham, and Surrey, who marched out with you, there is Bellême of Shrewsbury and de Reviers of Devon. Salisbury arrived a short while ago," he read on. "FitzRobert of Cornwall has sent word ahead and should arrive before nightfall. Earl Hugh of Chester—accompanied by Rhuddlan—will join us tomorrow or the day after. Le Noir of Richmond is on the road; he begs pardon, but the distance is too great and the time too short . . ."

"Yes, yes," interrupted the king irritably. "Go on."

"There is de Mowbray of Northumberland, who also sends regrets and apologies, albeit he is en route and will join you as soon as travel permits." Guy looked up from the roll. "As for the rest, we must presume they are either on their way, or sending petitions of pardon."

The king nodded. "There is one notable absence."

"Sire?"

"Neufmarché, of course. This is his castle, by the bloody rood! He should be here to receive us. Where is he?"

"I have spoken to his seneschal, Sire, who will say only that the baron is away visiting his lands in Wales. The summons was sent on, but it is not at all certain that it reached him, since the messenger has not yet returned."

"I swear upon my father's grave, if Neufmarché does not appear in two days' time, it would be better for him not to appear at all."

"Sire?"

"The baron is a devious, two-faced schemer, Marshal. I snubbed him once to put him in his place—summoned him to attend me and then kept him wearing out the waiting bench for three days . . . and this is how he repays the insult. He should have learned humility."

"So one would think, Majesty."

William began pacing, his short, bowed legs making quick steps from one side of the chamber to the other. "On the martyrs' blood, I will not have it. Mark me, Gysburne, the king will not have it! I will make an example of this vexsome baron for once and all. God help me, I will. If Neufmarché does not appear with his men by the time we leave this place, he is banished and his estates in England fall forfeit to the crown. I vow it."

Gysburne nodded. Clearly, there was some deeper grievance between the two that had caused this rift between the baron and his sovereign lord. Whatever it was, Neufmarché was now in very grave danger of losing everything.

"How far away is Mowbray?" asked William, returning to the business at hand.

Guy glanced once more to the parchment roll in his hand. "The messenger indicated that unless he encounters some difficulty Mowbray will reach the March in three days' time. It will be the same with Richmond, I would expect—three or four days."

"The incursion will be over by then," fumed the king. He spun on his heel and started pacing again. "From what you have said, the Welsh have few horses, no knights, and only a handful of archers."

Gysburne nodded.

"Well then. Two days," decided William. "One day of fighting, and one to sluice down the abattoir floor, as it were. Two days at most."

"That is greatly to be hoped, Sire," answered Gysburne, all the while thinking that it was manifestly imprudent to underestimate the amount of havoc that could be wreaked by a single Welsh bowman. No one knew that better than did Guy himself, but he kept his mouth shut before the king.

"Ha!" said William. "I hope Neufmarché misses the battle entirely. Then I can banish him for good and sell all this." He looked around at the interior of the chamber as if considering how much it might bring in the marketplace. "How many men do we have now?"

"With the arrival of Salisbury's sixty-eight we have three hundred ten knights and five hundred forty men-at-arms at present. All are encamped in the fields outside the town." Anticipating the king's next question, Guy added, "Counting those en route should almost double that number, I believe."

"That, friend marshal, is counting eggs, not chickens," cautioned a voice from the doorway.

Both men turned to see a haggard young man in boots and gauntlets, his green cloak and long dark hair grey with dust. The fellow took one step into the room and went down on one knee. "Forgive my tardiness, Sire," he said, "I was on my way to Londein when I received your summons, but came as soon as I could assemble my men."

"All is forgiven now you're here," said the king, smiling for the first time that day. "Rise, Leicester, and let's have a look at you." The king crossed to the young lord and clapped him in a warm embrace. "Heaven bless you, Robert, I am right glad to see you. It has been too long."

The king called over his shoulder to Marshal Guy, "You can go now, Gysburne. But bring me word if anyone else should arrive this evening." Taking the Earl of Leicester by the arm, he steered the young man to a nearby table and drew out a chair. "What news from your brother?"

"I had word this morning, Sire. Henry is well and has raised two hundred. He hopes to join us tomorrow."

"Two hundred! Splendid! Here, have some wine. You must be parched," said the king. He picked up the jar, but the younger man took it from him.

"Allow me, Majesty," he said, pouring out the wine. He handed the cup to his king. "It would not do for anyone to think that the king served a lowly earl by his own hand."

"Hang what they think," said William recklessly. He took the cup and raised it. "Let us drink to a swift campaign," he said.

"And successful," said the earl.

"Swift and successful!" echoed the king. "This time next week, we shall be on our way to France."

"To be sure," affirmed Leicester lightly. "God willing."

"The Almighty has nothing to do with it," declared William, his nose in his cup. He swallowed down a bolt, then said, "This uprising will be crushed in the egg. We need not invoke heaven's help to apprehend a few scofflaw rogues and rebels."

W hy this *agonie*? I do not see that you have any choice, *mon cher*," said Lady Agnes Neufmarché. "You must go. You must attend the king."

"I know! I know!" snapped the baron. "But this king will be the ruin of us all. He is an idiot. What is more, he is an idiot with a stick and a hornet's nest."

"Perhaps it will not be as bad as you fear," counselled his wife. "And if you were there, *mon cœur*, you could see that our interests were well defended."

Bernard was not listening. "He has no idea of the hell he is about to loose on the land. No idea at all."

"You could warn him," suggested Agnes.

"Too late for that," the baron replied. "I know William. He's just like his father. Once he has his sword drawn, he will not see reason—only blood." The baron shook his head gravely. "There will be plenty of blood . . . on both sides."

"All the more reason to go and see what can be done to prevent it."

Bernard shook his head again and looked at the scrap of parchment on the table. He had received many royal summonses over the years and had always responded—to do anything else invited royal wrath at the very least or, at worst, banishment or hanging. There was no way around it; this summons had come at a most inopportune time: just when the baron was winning over the devotion of his Welsh vassals and preparing to expand his interests in the region, the king declared war. Neufmarché stood to lose years of patient work and hard-won goodwill to the unthinking ire of a flighty king who would tramp around the hills and valleys for a few days and then beetle off back to Londein or Normandie, as the whim took him.

Pretending he had not received the king's summons had bought him enough time to assemble his men and flee Hereford before the king arrived; not the wisest course, he would be the first to agree, but in his mind the only one open to him just now.

"There is something else," Agnes said.

Her tone made him abandon his ruminations on the problems posed by the king's untimely summons. He glanced at his wife to see the pucker of concern between her brows. "And that is?"

"Mérian," she said simply.

"Mérian," he repeated. His heart quickened at the name, but he stifled any sign of recognition. "What of her?"

"She is here," said the baroness.

"Alive—you mean . . ."

"Yes, alive and well—and *here* in this castle. She returned a few weeks ago—escaped from her captors, it seems. Although she does not admit to being held so. She—"

"Mérian . . . here," said the baron, as if trying to understand a complex calculation.

"Oh, yes," said Agnes. "And the curious thing about it is that Garran has locked her in her chamber—for her own safety, of course. Given the chance, there is no doubt she would run straight back to the brigands who took her captive in the first place."

"How extraordinary," mused the baron.

"You should know, husband," continued Agnes, "that she has been saying some very disturbing things about you."

"About *me?*"

"Yes, *mon cher*, about you. It seems that through her ordeal she has come to believe that you tried to kill her. And this is why she fled her home and family for the forest."

"*Mon Dieu*," breathed Bernard. Recalling his bungled attack on Bran that day, his heart beat faster still. "She thinks *I* tried to kill her? Has the poor girl lost all reason then?"

"Oh, no," his wife assured him quickly, "she seems as sane as anyone. But she does cling to this absurd belief—perhaps it was a way for her to keep her sanity while captive. I only tell you about this so that when you see her you will not be taken by surprise at anything she says."

"I see, yes." Bernard nodded thoughtfully, considering the implications of what he had just been told. "I will speak to her, of course, but not just yet, I think. Perhaps when I have decided what to do about the king's summons."

"Well, do see her before you leave," advised the baroness. "If we were able to make her understand just how ridiculous is this notion of hers, then perhaps she might be trusted to obey and we could release her." Lady Agnes smiled. "It is a very cruelty to keep her captive in her own home after the torment she has endured, wouldn't you agree?"

"Oh, indeed," replied the baron, his mind racing to how this meeting might be put off. He was not of a mood to deal with angry, contrary, and likely vengeful women just now, and perhaps not for a very long time. "A very cruelty, as you say."

CHAPTER 34

"They're coming!"

At the shout, Tuck sat up and rubbed his face. He had been trimming the end of his staff and had fallen asleep in the warm sunlight. Now, he rose and, taking up the sturdy length of ashwood, gave it a swing once around his head, offering a grunt of satisfaction at the comforting heft of the simple weapon. He then turned around in time to see the messenger slide down the grassy bank and into the bowl of Cél Craidd. It was Prebyn, the son of one of the farmers whose house and barn had been burned by the Ffreinc when they ransacked their settlement a few days before. "They're coming! The Ffreinc are coming!"

Bran and Tuck hurried to meet the young man. "My lord Rhi Bran! Rhi Bran! They're coming," announced Prebyn, red faced and breathless from his run. "The Ffreinc . . . King William . . . they're on the road . . . they'll be here any moment." He gulped air. "There's thousands of them . . . thousands . . ."

"Steady on, Prebyn," said Bran. "Draw breath." He put his hand on the farmer's broad back. "Calm yourself."

The young man bent over and rested his hands on his knees, blowing air through his mouth. When he was able to speak again, Bran said, "Now, then. Tell me, what did Rhoddi say?"

"My lord Rhi Bran, he said I was to tell you that Red William's soldiers have been sighted on the road at the bottom of the long ridge—where the stream crosses—"

"I know the place," Bran said. "Rhoddi has given us fair warning. We have a little time yet." He sent the youth away with instructions to get something to drink, saddle a horse, and hurry back for new orders. "Well, my friend, we're in it now," he said when the messenger had gone. "I'll send Prebyn to the caer to alert Iwan and Siarles."

"God have mercy," breathed Tuck.

Bran turned and called out across Cél Craidd, "Scarlet! Owain! To me! Tomas—my weapons. To me, lads! The Ffreinc have been sighted."

This call roused the sleepy settlement, and soon the few remaining inhabitants were running here and there to help the warriors on their way. Out from a nearby dwelling, Angharad emerged. Bran hurried to meet her. "It begins," he said.

"So it does." She unfolded a bit of soft leather and handed Bran three coiled bowstrings. "God with you, Rhi Bran," she said. "These I made especially for this day." Her face froze then, and she drew a breath as if to speak, but thought better of it.

"I thank you, Wise Banfáith," he replied, placing the bowstrings in a pouch at his belt. "Was there something else you wanted to say?"

The old woman stared at him, her dark eyes peering as through a mist. Bran could sense her struggling . . . to find the words? To reach him in some way? Finally, she relaxed. Her face softened and she smiled, her wrinkled face smoothing somewhat in simple pleasure. "All that needs saying have I said." Reaching out, she covered his hands with hers and gripped them tight. "Now it is for us to remember."

"Then we will do the work of remembering," replied Bran.

The old woman lifted her hand to his face; then, rising on tiptoes, she brushed his cheek with her dry lips. "I am proud of you, my king. Do remember that."

Prebyn returned then and received orders to tell Iwan and those in the valley fortress that the king's army was on its way. "Come back as soon as you've delivered your message," Bran told him. "There may be Ffreinc outriders around, and you do not want to be caught." Then, turning to the rest of the Grellon, he said, "You all know what to do." There were murmurs of assent all around, and some voices called out encouragements, which the king acknowledged. Then, addressing Angharad one last time, he said, "Pray for us, all of you, and let your prayers strengthen our courage and sharpen our aim."

"I will uphold you in battle with psalms and prayers and songs of power as befits a bard of Britain," Angharad said. Raising her staff, she held it crosswise in her hands and lifted it high. "Kneel before the High King of Heaven," she instructed.

Bran knelt before his Wise Banfáith, to receive her blessing. "Fear nothing, O King," she said, placing one withered hand on his head. "The Almighty and His angelic battlehost go before you. Fight well and behold the glory of the Lord."

Bran thanked his bard and commended his people to her care. Tomas passed him his longbow, and Scarlet handed him a sheaf of arrows which he tied to his belt. "Come, friends. Let's be about the day's business."

Shouldering a thick bundle of arrows each from their sizeable stockpile of begged, bought, and Grellon-made shafts, they climbed the rim of Cél Craidd's encircling rampart and started off along one of the many pathways leading into the forest. Bran had taken but half a dozen steps when he heard a heavy tread on the trail behind him. "What are you doing, Tuck? I thought we agreed you would stay here and help Angharad."

"I seem to recall that we discussed something of the sort, yes," allowed the friar. "But *agreed*? No, I think not."

"Tuck—"

"You leave your flock in safe hands, my lord. Angharad needs no help from me, and I will be more aid to you on the battle line." The priest patted the satchel at his side. "I am bringing cloths and such for wounds. I can serve you better at the sharp end, can I not?"

"Come, then," Bran said, shifting the bundle of arrows on his hip. "It would not do to keep King William waiting."

They marched at a steady pace, moving silently as shadows through the thick-grown trees and heavy undergrowth of bracken and tangled ivy vines and bramble canes, guided by an intimate knowledge of the greenwood's myriad trackways—many of which would be invisible to anyone who had not spent years in the wild woodlands of the March. They changed direction often, abandoning one trail for another, always working south, however, towards the King's Road.

"Do you think William Rufus himself has come?" asked Tuck.

"Perhaps," allowed Scarlet a few paces behind him. "Where you find king's men, you sometimes find a king leading them. Red William is said to like a fight."

"It would be good if he has come," Tuck observed. "Then when we sue for peace he will be ready to hand."

"Sue for peace," said Bran. "I have no intention of suing for peace."

"I was not thinking of *you*, my lord," replied the friar. "I was thinking of the Ffreinc. After a few days, I would not be surprised if we see a flag of truce from William's camp."

"A few days?" wondered Bran. "Tuck, bless you, we have but ten men! If we make it to the end of this day with body and soul knit together, I will count it a triumph."

"Oh, ye of little faith!" the priest scoffed, and on they went.

The land rose steadily beneath to form the long slope of the ridge that was the southern border of Elfael. At the place where the old road crested the ridge—dropping low as it passed between two steep banks of stone like a river flowing through a gorge—Bran had chosen to engage the enemy. They dropped their bundles at the foot of a high rock stack shielding them from view of the road below. While Scarlet and the others took a moment's rest, Tuck and Bran climbed the stack. On a flat rock jutting out above the road, they found Rhoddi lying on his stomach and gazing down the long southern slope towards the foot of the ridge.

"Thank God," said the warrior, squirming upright as Bran crawled up on hands and knees to join him. "Here I was thinking Prebyn had lost his way."

"Where are they?" asked Bran, squatting beside Rhoddi.

"Just there." He pointed down the slope towards a stand of oaks that grew beside the deep-rutted road. "They seem to have stopped. They've been there for a while, but they should come in sight any time now."

Tuck scrambled up at last and, lying on his belly, turned his eyes to the dark stretch of road far down the slope where the intertwining limbs still overhung the deep-sunk path. The Grellon had cleared the trees for a dozen yards on either side of the defile to give themselves a clear and unobstructed view from above.

"How many do you think there are?" asked the friar.

"I don't know," replied Rhoddi. "A fair few, I reckon."

Bran returned to where the others were waiting. "Scarlet, you and Tomas will command the other side. Llwyd and Beli," he said, referring to the two newcomers, both farmers' sons who had been added to their number following the abbot's disastrous raid, "go with Scarlet. He'll show you what to do. You'd better hurry. We don't want the Ffreinc to see you."

The four left on the run, and Bran and Owain took up an armful of bundled arrows and scrambled back up to the lookout post. "I see them!" said Tuck, pointing down the long incline. "That spot of red, there. It's moving."

"It's one of the scouts," Rhoddi told him. "They advance and fall back. They're plenty wary."

"They know we will attack," said Bran. "Trying to tempt us into showing ourselves."

"Brave men," Tuck murmured to himself.

"Brave fools," amended Owain.

"Is this the main body?" asked Bran.

"I made it three divisions," Rhoddi replied, and explained how he had worked his way down to the bottom of the ridge to see what could be learned of the king's army from that vantage. "Most are mounted, but there are a number on foot as well. And those I saw appeared but lightly armed."

"They know they will not be facing knights on horseback," surmised Bran, "so they need not overburden themselves or their animals."

Tuck backed slowly down the rocks and into a little sunny patch nearby; hitching up his robe, he knelt in the long grass and, crossing his hands over his chest, he lifted his face to the clear blue sky above and began to pray, saying, "Commander of the Heavenly Host, You are no stranger to war and fighting. I know You'd rather have peace, and I'd have it, too, if it was left to me. But You know that sometimes that en't possible, and if peace was in William's mind I don't reckon he'd be marching against us now. So, I'm asking You to think back to Your man, Moses, and how You supported him in all his wrangles with the Pharaoh-Who-Knew-Not-Joseph. Great of Might, I'm asking You to support Bran and his men today—and like You did with the Hebrew slaves when Pharaoh chased them out of Egypt, I'm asking You to drown the armies of the enemy in their own bloodlust. Last but not least, I'm asking You to ease the suffering of the wounded and, above all, to treat kindly the souls of those who will be coming to stand before You in a little while. Grant them eternal rest in Your wide kingdom for the sake of Your most Merciful Son, Our Lord Jesus."

Tuck was roused from his prayers by the sound of a trumpet— small but bright as a needle point in the quiet forest. "Amen, so be it," he whispered and, crossing himself, he picked up his staff and hauled himself back up the rocks to where Bran, Owain, and Rhoddi were waiting.

The trumpet sounded again: a single long, unwavering note.

"What is the meaning of that?" wondered Owain. "Vanity?"

"Maybe they think to frighten us," suggested Tuck.

"Take more than a pip on the horn to send a shiver up my spine," said Rhoddi. He nocked an arrow to the string, but Bran put a hand on his arm and pulled it down.

"They're still trying to get us to show ourselves so they can mark our positions," said Bran, "perhaps get some idea how large a force they will face. If they only knew how few . . ." He let the rest of the thought go.

The trumpet called once more, and this time the trumpeter himself rode into view. Behind him came two knights bearing banners: a blue square with three long tails of green and a cross of gold in the centre surrounded by small green crosslets. Behind them could be seen the first ranks of knights; some of these also carried banners of red and blue, some with yellow lions, some with crosses of white and red.

"Owain," said Bran, "find yourself a good position somewhere just there"—he pointed a little farther along the rock wall—"and be ready to loose on my signal." As the young warrior departed, Bran turned to the friar. "Tuck," he said, placing a bundle of arrows upright at his feet, "I want you to see that we do not run out of arrows in this first skirmish. Keep us supplied and let us know how many we have left if supplies run low."

"Good as done," said Tuck. He scuttled back down the rocks and arranged the bundles in stacks of three which he then hauled up to a place just below the archers to keep them within easy reach. By the time he rejoined Rhoddi and Bran, the Ffreinc were much closer. Tuck could make out individual faces beneath the round helmets of the knights. They rode boldly on, scanning the rocks for the first sign of attack. Some were sweating beneath their heavy mail, the water glistening in the sunlight as it dripped down their necks and into their padded leather tunics.

Both Bran and Rhoddi had arrows nocked and ready. "We'll wait until they come directly below us," Bran was saying. "The first to fall will—"

Even as he was speaking there came the whining shriek of an arrow, followed by the hard slap of an iron head striking home. In the same instant, one of the knights was thrown so far back in the saddle he toppled over the rump of his horse.

"No!" muttered Bran between clenched teeth. "Not yet. Who did that?" he demanded, looking around furiously. "Rhoddi, Tuck—did you see? Who did that?"

"There!" said Tuck. "It came from up there."

He pointed to a place where the road crested the ridge and there, four men could be seen kneeling in the middle of the road.

The Ffreinc knights saw them, too, and those in the fore rank lowered their spears, put spurs to their horses, and charged.

"Take them!" cried Bran, and before the words had left his mouth two arrows were streaking towards the attacking knights. The missiles struck sharp and fast, dropping the foemen as they passed beneath the rocky outcrop. Two more knights appeared and joined the first two in the dust of the King's Road.

The archers on the road seemed unconcerned by the commotion their appearance had caused. They calmly loosed arrow after arrow into the body of knights now halted in the road still some distance away from the place Bran had set for the ambush.

"Tuck!" said Bran, furious that his plan had been spoiled—so needlessly and so early. "Get down there and stop them. Hurry!"

While Bran and Rhoddi worked to keep the knights pinned down, Tuck scrambled back into the forest and, tearing through the undergrowth and bracken, made for the top of the ridge where the unknown archers had placed themselves.

"Hold!" he shouted, tumbling into the road. "Put up!"

"Friar Tuck!"

Tuck recognized the voice. "Brocmael! God love you, man, get out of here!"

"We saw some Ffreinc down there and thought to put the fear of God into them, Friar."

"There's a battle on," the friar told him. He glanced at the young man's companions. "Follow me before the whole Ffreinc army falls on your foolish heads."

"Greetings, Bishop Balthus," said the man nearest him.

"Ifor! Bless your unthinking head, that's King William the Red's army you've attacked, and they'll be on us like bees on honeycomb."

By the time the newcomers reached the rocks, Bran and Rhoddi were slinging arrows down into the road as fast as they could draw. Shouts and screams of men and horses crashing and thrashing echoed along the rock walls of the defile. Already, the bodies were thick on the ground. Brocmael and his companions took one look at the chaos below and joined in.

"*Cenau* Brocmael," said Bran as the young man came to stand beside him, "as good as it is to see you, I could have wished you'd held your water a little while longer."

"Forgive me, my lord. I did not know you were lurking hereabouts. Have we spoiled the hunt for you?"

"A little," Bran admitted, sending feathered death into the churning mass of soldiers below. "Would you have taken on the king's army by yourself?"

"I thought it was just a few knights out for a jaunt in the forest." He paused to consider. "Is it really the king's army, then?"

"The king and his many minions, yes," put in Tuck, "along with a right handsome multitude of knights and men-at-arms so they won't be lonely."

"Another sheaf, Tuck!" called Bran, loosing the last arrow from his bag.

Tuck hurried to the pile and, taking a bundle under each arm, climbed up to the archers. He opened one bundle for Bran and placed one nearby for Rhoddi, then took two more to Owain. Across the road, the arrows streaked through the sun-bright air as Scarlet and Tomas and their two farm lads loosed and loosed again in deadly rhythm. Many of the knights had quit their saddles and were trying to scale the rocks. Weighed down by their heavy mail coats, they moved slowly and were not difficult to pick off, but more and more soldiers were streaming up the hill to the fight.

"How many are with you?" Bran asked the young lord, drawing and loosing in the same breath.

"Besides Ifor—only Geronwy and Idris," answered Brocmael, "good bowmen both. I would like to have brought more, but we had to sneak away as it was."

"I expect . . ." Bran began, drawing and loosing again. The arrow sang from his bow into the heaving chaos below. ". . . that your uncle will not be best pleased."

"Then he must accustom himself to displeasure," replied the young nobleman. "It is the right and honourable thing to do."

"And now, gentlemen all," said Rhoddi, picking up his bundle of arrows, "the right and honourable thing for us to do is to leg it into the greenwood."

He started away, and Tuck risked a look down into the chasm. The dust-dry road, where it could be seen, was taking on a ruddy hue and was now made impassable by the corpses of men and horses piled upon one another. The knights and soldiers coming up from the rear were scaling the rocks in a courageous effort to get at the archers above. Even as he looked over the cliff, a spear glanced off a nearby rock, throwing sparks and chips of stone into the air before sliding back down into the road. Duly warned, Tuck scuttled back from the edge.

Bran gave out a loud, shrieking whistle and waved with his bow to Scarlet and the others on the high bank across the road in a signal to abandon the attack. And then they were running for their lives into the deep-shadowed safety of the greenwood.

CHAPTER 35

A mad scramble through the forest brought them to a tiny clearing where Bran and his men paused to regroup. "We had the devils trapped and trussed," Brocmael said, breathing hard from his run. "We could have defeated them."

"There are too many," Rhoddi countered. "We dare not stay in one place very long or they'll surround us and drag us under."

"Like crossing a mud flat," said Tuck, hands on knees, his lungs burning. "The longer you stand . . . the deeper you sink." He shook his head. "Ah, bless me, I am too old and fat for this."

"Will they come in after us, do you think?" wondered Geronwy, leaning on his longbow.

"Oh, aye," answered Rhoddi. "Count on it."

There was a clatter in the wood behind them just then, and Scarlet, followed by Llwyd and Beli, tumbled into the clearing. The two farm lads were looking hollow-eyed and a little green. Clearly, for all their skill with the bow, they had never killed before—at least, thought Tuck, not living men. While Bran and the others exchanged battle reports, Tuck undertook to gentle the skittish newcomers. Putting a hand on each of their shoulders, he said, "Defending your people against the cruel invader is a good and laudable thing, my friends. This is not a war of your making, God knows—does He not?"

The two glanced at one another, and one of them, Llwyd, found his voice. "We never killed before."

"Not like that," added Beli.

"If there is sin in it," Tuck told them, "then there is also grace enough to cover it. You have done well this day. See you remember your countrymen whose lives depend on you and let your souls be at peace."

Overhearing this, Bran turned to address the newest members of his tiny war band. "To me, everyone," he said. "Believe me when I say that I wish no one had to learn this cruel craft within the borders of my realm. But the world is not of our choosing. We have many battles to fight before this war is through, and your lives may be required long since." He spoke softly, but in grim earnest. "You are men now. Warriors. And part of my Grellon. So grasp your courage and bind it to your hearts with bands of steel." His twisted smile flashed with sudden warmth. "And I will pray with every shaft I loose that all will yet be well and you will live to see Elfael at peace."

"My lord," said Llwyd, bending his head.

Beli went one better and bent the knee as well. "Your servant," he said.

Then Bran addressed those who had come with Brocmael. "Greetings, friends, and if you've come to stay, then welcome. But if now that you've had a taste of this fight and find it bitter in your mouth, then I bid you farewell and God go with you."

"We came to help you fight the Ffreinc, my lord," said Brocmael. "As you know me, know my cousins. This is Geronwy." He put out a hand to a slender, sandy-haired youth holding a fine bow of polished red rowan.

"My lord Rhi Bran," said Geronwy, "we have heard how you bested Earl Hugh and would pledge our aid to such a king as could humble that mangy old badger in his den."

The other, not waiting to be presented, spoke up, saying, "I am Idris, and I am glad to lend my bow to your cause, my lord. It seems to me that either we fight the Ffreinc with you here and now—or we will fight them by ourselves later." A stocky lad with a thick, tight-knit frame, he seemed rough-carved of the same yew as the sturdy bow in his hand.

Scarlet, listening to the sounds echoing up from the road and forest behind them, called, "We must fly if we are to stay ahead of the chase. This way!"

"Our horses are back there." Brocmael jerked a thumb in the direction of the road.

"Leave them," Bran said, hurrying after Scarlet. "Horses are a hindrance in the forest. Anyway, it isn't far."

The archers started away again, disappearing into the close-grown trees and bramble and hawthorn undergrowth. It soon became clear that Bran was leading them along a stony trail up the long slope of the ridge where, in no more than a few hundred paces, the path suddenly erupted in outsized stones and boulders big as houses, all tumbled together to form a sizeable cairn—a natural fortress of stone. In the gaps and crevices between the rocks grew holly and briar, into which had been driven stakes of ash whose ends were sharpened to narrow spear points.

"Find a place to hide and wait for my signal," called Bran, disappearing into a holly hedge at the base of the cairn.

"Up we go, lads," called Scarlet. "Get snugged in good. There are arrow sheaves in the hidey-holes. Keep 'em close to hand."

Brocmael glanced at his cousins, gave a shrug, and followed the others up into the storied heap of rocks. They picked their way carefully among the thorns and stakes to find that, in amongst the spaces between rocks, small wooden platforms had been prepared where the archers could stand. The warriors found bundles of arrows tied to the timber supports and stuffed into crevices within easy reach. "I told you Rhi Bran was cunning clever," Brocmael declared to his kinsmen. "And here is the proof."

"Did we ever doubt you?" said Idris.

"Shh!" hissed Scarlet, taking his place on a nearby stand. "Sharp and quiet, lads. They'll likely try to come by stealth, so be ready for the signal."

"What *is* the signal?" wondered Brocmael aloud.

"You'll know it when you hear it," answered Scarlet, "for you've never heard the like in your whole sweet life entire."

"And when you hear it," said Tuck, squirming up onto one of the lower platforms, "be sure you take no fright, for it is only our Bran distracting our foemen from the task at hand."

"If they're about thinking they can run us to ground," added Rhoddi, "they'll soon be thinking twice about chasing blind through the phantom's wood."

"The phantom," said Geronwy. "*Rhi Bran y Hud*—is that who you mean?"

"One and the same," replied Scarlet. "You've heard of him?"

"*Everyone* has heard of him," answered the young warrior. "Are you saying he is real?"

"Brace yourself, boyo," said Tuck, "you're about to see for yourself."

Fitting arrows to strings, the Cymry settled down to wait. The sounds of the chase grew louder as the Ffreinc drew nearer until, with a thrashing of branches and bushes, the first wave of armour-clad foot soldiers reached the base of the rock wall. There they paused to determine which way to go and in that briefest of hesitations were doomed. For as they stood looking at the boulders in their path, there arose a thin, bloodless cry—like that of the wind when it moans in the high tree branches, but no kindly breeze lifted the leaves.

The soldiers glanced around furiously, trying to discover the source of the sound. The cry became a shriek, gathering strength, filling the surrounding woodland with a call at once unnatural and unnerving, full of all the mystery of the greenwood—as if the forest itself had taken voice to shout its outrage at the presence of the Ffreinc.

They were still looking for the source of this fearsome cry when there appeared, near the top of the wall of stones, a strange, dark shape that in the green half-light of the forest seemed far more shadow than substance: a great, bird-shaped creature with the body of a man and the wings of a raven, with a naked, round, skull-like head and a long, wickedly sharp beak. This phantom moved with uncanny grace among the rocks, pausing now and again to utter its scream as a challenge to the wary, half-frightened soldiers on the ground.

One of the knights took up the challenge and, rearing back, loosed his spear, lofting it with a mighty heave up at the strange creature sliding among the rocks. The bravely launched spear struck the smooth face of a boulder, and the iron tip sparked. At the same moment, a black arrow sang out from the dark recess of the stones, struck the knight, and with a sound like the crack of a whip, threw him onto his back, dead before his body came to rest in the bracken.

It took a moment for the rest of the knights to realize what had happened, and by then it was too late. Three more arrows sped to their marks with lethal accuracy, dropping the enemy in their tracks.

The phantom of the greenwood gave out a last, triumphant scream and disappeared once more as the arrows began to fly thick and fast, filling the air with their hateful hiss. The Ffreinc fell back and back again, stumbling over one another, over themselves, over the corpses of the dead to escape the feathered death assailing them from the rocks. Those still coming up from behind choked off the escape, holding their unlucky comrades in place, thus sealing their fate.

And then it was over. The last soldier, an arrow in his thigh, pulled himself into the undergrowth, and all that could be heard was the clatter of the Ffreinc knights in full-tilt retreat . . . and then only the distant croak of gathering crows and the soft, whimpering moans of the dying.

CHAPTER 36

Coed Cadw

The war between Bran ap Brychan and King William for the throne of Elfael continued as it began—with short, sharp skirmishes in which the Grellon unleashed a whirlwind of stinging death before disappearing into the deep-shadowed wood. These small battles were fought down in the leafy trenches of greenwood trails, down amongst roots and boles of close-grown trees and the thick-tangled undergrowth where Ffreinc warhorses could not go and swords were difficult to swing. The Welsh rebels struck fast and silently; sometimes it seemed to the beleaguered knights that the Cymry materialized out of the redolent forest air. The first warning they had was the fizzing whine of an arrow and the crack of the shaft striking leather and breaking bone.

And although there was never any telling when or where the dreaded attack would come, the result was always the same: arrow-pierced dead, and wounded Norman soldiers lurching dazed along the narrow trackways of the greenwood.

After a few disastrous running battles, the Ffreinc knights, whose fighting lives were spent on horseback, quickly lost all interest in facing King Raven and his men in the dense forest and on foot. In this, Coed Cadw lived up to its name—the Guardian Wood—providing the rebels with an immense and all-but impenetrable defensive bulwark against an enemy whose numbers far exceeded their own many times over.

Without the use of their horses, and forced to traverse unknown and difficult terrain, the knights' supreme effectiveness as a weapon of war became nothing more than a blunt and broken stub of a blade. They might thrash and hack along the borders of the wood but could do little real damage, and the elusive King Raven remained beyond their reach.

Still, the king of England was determined to bring this rebel Welsh cantref to heel. He insisted that his commanders pursue the fight wherever they could. Even so, rather than send yet more men to certain death in the forest, they made endless sorties along the road and told themselves that at least they controlled the supply route and enforced the peace for travellers. King Raven was more than happy to grant William the rule of the road, since it allowed his archers time to rest and the Grellon to make more arrows and increase their stockpile.

As it became clear that there would be no easy victory over King Raven in the forest, King William moved to take the Vale of Elfael. The Ffreinc army set up encampment in the valley between the forest and Saint Martin's, laying siege to the Welsh fortress at Caer Cadarn. William invaded the town of Saint Martin's with a force of five hundred knights and men-at arms with himself in the lead. There was no resistance. The invaders, discovering only monks there—most of them French, under the authority of an ageing Bishop Asaph—

and a few wounded soldiers and frightened townsfolk with little enough food to supply those already there, simply declared the town conquered and effectively reclaimed for the king's domains.

Caer Cadarn was not so easily defeated. The occupying Ffreinc troops quickly learned that they could not approach nearer than three hundred paces of the timber walls without suffering a hail of killing arrows. But as the old fortress itself seemed to offer no aid or support to King Raven and the rebels in the wood, William decided to leave it alone, and trust to a rigorous siege to bring the stronghold into submission.

Day gave way to day, and sensing a cold, wet winter on the near horizon, with no advancement in his fortunes and the time for his departure for France looming ever closer, the king decided to force the issue. He called his commanders to him. "Our time grows short. Autumn is at an end, and winter is soon upon us," William announced. Standing in the centre of his round tent with his earls and barons ranged around him, he looked like a bear at a baiting, surrounded by wolves with extravagant appetites. "We must leave for Normandie within the fortnight or forfeit our tribute, and we will have this rebellion crushed before we go."

Hands on hips, he glared at the grim faces of his battle chiefs, daring them to disagree. "Well? We will have your council, my lords, and that quick."

One of the barons stepped forward. "My lord and king," he said, "may I speak boldly?"

"Speak any way you wish, Lord Bellême," replied William. A thick-skinned warhorse himself, he was not squeamish about any criticisms his vassals or subjects might make. "We do solicit your forthright opinion."

"With all respect, Majesty," began Bellême, "it does seem we have allowed these rebels to run roughshod over our troops." The Earl of Shrewsbury could be counted on to point out the obvious. "What is needed here is a show of strength to bring the Welsh to their knees." He made a half turn to appeal to his brother noblemen. "The savage Welshman respects only blunt force."

"And yours would be blunter than most," remarked a voice from the rear of the tent.

"Mock me if you will," sniffed Bellême. "But I speak as one who has some experience with these Welsh brigands. A show of force—*that* will turn the tide in our favour."

"Perhaps," suggested Earl de Reviers of Devon, stepping forward, "you might tell us how this might be accomplished when the enemy will not engage? They strike out of the mists and disappear again just as swiftly. My men half believe the local superstition that the forest is haunted by this King Raven and we fight ghosts."

"Bah!" barked Earl Shrewsbury. "Your men are a bunch of old women to believe such tales."

"And yet," replied Devon, "how is this show of strength to be performed against an enemy who is not there?" He offered the craggy Shrewsbury a thin half smile. "No doubt this is something your vast experience has taught you."

Shrewsbury gave a muttered growl and stepped back.

"The rebels refuse to stand and fight," put in Le Noir of Richmond. "That is a fact. Until we can draw them out into the open we will continue to fail, and our superior numbers will count for nothing."

"To be sure," agreed the king, "and meanwhile our superior numbers are eating through all our supplies. We're already running out of meat and grain. More will have to be brought in, and that takes time. Time we do not have to spare." William's voice had been rising as he began to vent his rage. "My lords, we want this ended now! We want to see that rebel's head on a pike tomorrow!"

"Your Majesty," ventured another of the king's notables, "I would speak."

William recognized his old friend, the Earl of Cestre. "Lord Hugh," he said, "if you see a way out of this dilemma, we welcome your wisdom."

"Hardly wisdom, Sire," answered Hugh. "More an observation. When facing a particularly cunning stag, you must sometimes divide your party in order to come at the beast from unexpected quarters."

"Meaning?" inquired William, who was in no mood for hunting lessons.

"Only this, my lord: that unless these rebels are truly spirits, they cannot be in two places at once. Sending a single large force into the wood is no use—as we have seen. So, send three, four, five or more smaller ones. Come at them from every direction."

"He's right," affirmed Lord Rhuddlan. "They cannot defend all sides at once. We can cut them down before they can escape again."

"We never know where they are," complained another lord. "How can we muster troops on the flanks and rear if we cannot tell where they will attack?"

"We must create a lure to draw them into battle," suggested Earl Hugh, "and when the bastards take the bait, we're ready to sally in from the rear and flanks and slice them up a treat."

There was more discussion then, about how this might be best accomplished, but the plan was generally accepted and agreed: the king's army would adopt a new tactic. They would abandon their normal course of moving into the forest in a single large force, and would instead advance in smaller groups towards a single destination using a body on horseback as a lure to draw the rebels into a fight, whereupon the individual parties would rally to the fight and, sweeping in from the flanks, quickly surround them, cutting off any escape.

The king, satisfied that this plan offered a better way forward, gave his blessing to the scheme and ordered all to be made ready for it to be implemented the following morning. Then, in a far better mood than he had enjoyed since his arrival in Elfael, he ordered a good supper for himself and Earl Hugh and a few others, to celebrate their impending victory.

At dawn the next day, six separate hunting parties rode out with a seventh, larger body of knights and men-at-arms to serve as the lure to draw the rebels into the trap. Upon reaching the forest's edge, they dismounted and proceeded on foot; the six smaller bodies fanned out around the main group and proceeded with all stealth.

It was slow and arduous work, hacking through the vines and branches, searching out pathways and game trails through the dense woodland. But just after midday, their determination was rewarded when the main body of knights encountered the Welsh rebels.

They had been stalking through a rock-lined rill, following the stream, when suddenly the canopy of branches seemed to open and begin raining arrows down upon them. The soldiers took shelter where they could, pressing themselves against the rocks and stones, all the while sounding blast after blast on the trumpets some of them were carrying. The attack continued much as previous assaults, but faltered when there arose a great shout and a second body of Ffreinc knights entered the battle from behind the rebel position. This was quickly followed by the appearance of a third body of knights that drew in from the left flank and mounted a fierce resistance to the killing shafts.

The battle lasted only moments and ended as abruptly as it had begun. There was a rustling in the branches overhead—as if a flock of nesting rooks had just taken flight—and the arrows stopped.

As the king's men reassembled to gather up their wounded and reckon their losses, they found a longbow lying among the rocks in the streambed—one of the rebels' weapons. What is more, it had blood on it. And there was no Ffreinc body in sight.

After the ruinous ventures of the previous encounters, this was deemed a triumph. It shrank in significance, however, when the victorious troops returned to their camp in the Vale of Elfael to learn that the other three search parties had become lost in the forest and unable to join the battle as planned. In their confusion, they had stumbled upon a hidden settlement—a cluster of crude huts and hovels made of sticks and skin around a great oak tree and a stone-lined well, together with a few storehouses and a pitiful field. Caught unawares, the inhabitants scattered. But the knights did manage to kill one of them as they fled—an old woman who seemed to be in some way guarding the place with only a wooden staff.

CHAPTER 37

Tuck half carried, half dragged the wounded Tomas through the wood, pausing now and then to rest and listen for sounds of pursuit. He heard only the nattering of squirrels and birds, and the rapid beating of his own heart. The spear, so far as he could tell, had been hurled in blind desperation up into the branches where the soldier had marked the arrow that killed the man beside him. By chance, the missile had caught Tomas in the soft place below the ribs on his left side. Tuck had been hiding in a crevice behind the tree and saw Tomas fall.

The archer landed hard among the roots of the tree, and Tuck heard the bone-rattling thump. Without a moment's hesitation, Tuck rushed to the warrior's aid and, with a shout to alert the others, hefted Tomas up onto his shoulders and started for home. He paused at the nearest stream to get some water and to assess the injury.

The spearhead had gone in straight and clean and, by the look of it, not too deep. There was plenty of blood, however, and Tuck wet one of the cloths he carried in his satchel and pressed it to Tomas's side. "Can you hold that?" he asked.

Tomas, his face ashen, nodded. "How bad is it?" he asked between clenched teeth.

"Not so bad," Tuck replied, "for all I can see. Angharad will be able to put it right. Is there much pain?"

Tomas shook his head. "I just feel sick."

"Yes, well, that is to be expected, is it not?" replied the friar. He offered the archer another drink. "Get a little more water down you and we'll move along."

Tomas drank what he could, and Tuck hefted him onto his feet once more. Draping the injured man's arm across his own round shoulders so as to bear him up, they continued on. The way was farther than he remembered, but Tuck kept up a ready pace, his short, sturdy legs churning steadily. As he walked, he said the Our Father over and over again, as much for himself as for the comfort of the man he carried.

After two more brief pauses to catch his breath, Tuck approached Cél Craidd. He could see the lightning-blasted oak that formed an archway through the hawthorn hedge which helped to hide the settlement. "Almost there," Tuck said. "A few more steps and we can rest."

There was a rush and rustle behind him. "Tuck! How is he?"

The friar half turned, bent low beneath the warrior whose weight he bore. "Iwan, thank God you're here." He glanced quickly around. "Is anyone else hurt?"

"No," he replied. "Only Tomas here." Tossing aside his bow, he helped ease the weight of the wounded man to the ground. Tomas, now only half-conscious, groaned gently as they stretched him out. "Let's have a look."

"I lost my bow," moaned the injured warrior.

"No matter, Tomas," replied Iwan. "We'll get you another. Lie still while we have a look at you."

Tuck loosened the young man's belt and pulled up his shirt. The wound was a simple gash in the fleshy part of his side, no more than a thumb's length. Blood oozed from the cut, and it ran clean. "Not too bad," Iwan concluded. "You'll be chasing Ffreinc again before you know it." To Tuck, he said, "Let's get him to a hut and have Angharad see to him."

As the two lifted Tomas between them, the rest of the war band appeared. "We're clean away," reported Rhoddi, breathing hard from his run. "No one gave chase."

Scarlet, Owain, and Bran were the last to arrive. Bran glanced around quickly, counting his men. "Was anyone else injured?"

"Only Tomas here," said Iwan, "but he—"

Before the words were out of his mouth there arose a piercing shriek—the voice of a woman—from the settlement beyond the concealing hedge. The cry came again: a high-pitched, desperate wail.

"Noín!" shouted Scarlet, darting forward. He dived through the archway of the riven oak and disappeared down the path leading into Cél Craidd.

The men scrambled after him, flying down into the bowl of a valley that cradled their forest home. At first glance all appeared to be just as they had left it earlier that morning . . . but there were no people, none to greet their return as on all the other days when they had gone out to do battle with the Ffreinc.

"Where are they?" wondered Owain.

The shuddering wail came again.

"This way!" Scarlet raced off along one of the many pathways radiating out into Coed Cadw.

Only a few steps down the path he found his wife standing in the path, bent almost double, her shoulders shaking with the violence of her sobs.

"Noín!" Scarlet rushed to her side. "Noín, are you hurt?"

She turned, her face stricken and crumpled with pain, although she appeared to be unharmed. And then Will looked at the bundle she cradled in her arms. It was little Nia, her arms and legs limp and still. The child appeared to be asleep, eyes closed, her features composed. There was a dark, ugly purple bruise on her throat.

Will Scarlet put his ear to the little one's face. "She's not breathing."

"Oh, Will . . ." sobbed Noín as Scarlet gathered them both in his arms.

"Bran!" shouted Rhoddi. "Over here!"

A few dozen steps farther along the path lay another, larger bundle—a shapeless mass of bloody rags, as if a sack of meat had been rolled and crushed beneath a millstone. Beside what was left of this body lay the banfáith's staff. Bran halted in midstep, staring, his face frozen.

"Angharad!" he cried, rushing swiftly to the body. He sank to his knees beside the pathetic heap of rag and bone and gathered it into his arms. He knelt there, rocking back and forth, cradling the corpse of his beloved teacher and advisor, his confidante, his best and dearest friend.

After a time, Bran collected himself somewhat; he lowered the body to the ground and gently smoothed the hair from the old woman's face and then cupped her wrinkled cheek in his hand. "Farewell,

Mother," he whispered, gazing at the wizened features he had come to know so well. He placed the tips of his fingers to her eyes and drew her eyelids shut, then bent his head in sorrow as his tears flowed freely.

Owain and the others raced off to make a search of the path and surrounding wood. Bran gathered up the broken body of the Wise Banfáith in his strong arms and returned to Cél Craidd; Scarlet and Noín came after, bearing their beloved daughter. Tuck, ministering to Tomas's wound, looked up as Bran and Scarlet returned with the little girl and the old woman. He rose and ran to them as they lay the corpses beneath the spreading boughs of the Council Oak. "Who is it? Who——?" he said and stopped in his tracks. "Lord have mercy," he sighed when he saw who had been killed. "Christ have mercy."

Turning to Noín and Scarlet, he gathered them in a gentle embrace and prayed for them then and there, that the Lord of Life would give them strength to bear their loss. He did the same for Bran and, seeing as there was nothing more to be done just then, he returned to tending the wounded Tomas.

Bran was kneeling by the still body of Angharad when Owain came to him. "We found no one else injured, Rhi Bran. I think—I hope—everyone got away."

He was silent for a moment, watching Bran straighten the old woman's battered limbs. "Do you think they knew it was King Raven's home they attacked?"

"Those knights weren't looking for this place, but they found it anyway."

"But do they know what they found?" asked Owain.

"Perhaps not," allowed Bran. "But if they do come back, they'll come in force, and we will not be able to defend it. We will stay here tonight and abandon Cél Craidd in the morning—and pray we have at least that much time." He folded one of the old woman's wrinkled hands over the other. "Tell everyone to prepare to leave. We'll take only what we can carry easily. Bundle up all the arrows and extra bows—get Brocmael and Ifor to help you secure all the weapons. Tell Siarles to set sentries in the usual places. Go. We must be ready to move at first light tomorrow."

Owain nodded. "Where will we go, my lord?"

"It is a big forest," he said, brushing a wispy strand of hair away from Angharad's face. "We'll find someplace to camp."

It was early evening, and the sun had tinged the sky with a crimson hue when Noín finally brought herself to speak about what had happened, which was that after the war band had departed, the Grellon went about their daily chores. She and Cia had gone to gather blackberries in the wood; she had taken Nia with her, and the three of them had spent the morning picking. When they had filled their bowls, they started back. "Nia was so excited," Noín said, "she'd gathered more and bigger berries than ever before, and she wanted to show Angharad. So she went ahead of us . . . I tried to call her back . . ." Noín paused, choking back the tears. "But she didn't hear me, and anyway she knew the path. I let her go . . ." Her voice faltered. Scarlet, grim with grief, put his arm around her shoulders and pulled her close.

Bran offered her a cup of water. After she had swallowed a little, she continued. "We started back. Cia and I were talking . . . Then we heard shouts and voices . . . scared . . . We met some of the Grellon on the path, running away. Cél Craidd had been discovered, they said; the Ffreinc had found us. Everyone had scattered, and everyone had got away. 'What about Nia? Did anyone see my little girl?'"

Noín shook her head, her lips trembling. "No one had seen her. I started running toward the settlement. But it was all over." She shook her head in bewilderment. "The Ffreinc were gone. There was no one around. I began calling for Nia, but there was no answer. I started looking for her, calling her . . . I thought, I hoped—maybe one of the others picked her up in the confusion, someone had taken her to safety. I searched one path and then another until . . ." She let out a wrenching sob and lowered her face into her hands. "I found her on the path—just before you came. I think she got trampled by a horse . . . one of the hooves struck her head . . ." She turned eyes full of tears to the others. "How could anyone do that to a little child? How could they?"

Bran and Tuck left Noín and Scarlet to their grief then and went to see what could be done for Tomas. The wounded warrior had been laid out on a bed of rushes covered with a cloak.

"He is sleeping," Rhoddi told them. "I did as you said, Friar—I put a clean cloth and some dry moss on the cut. It seems to have stopped bleeding."

"That's a good sign, I think," said Tuck.

Bran nodded. He raised his eyes; the tops of the tallest trees were fading into the twilight. "We must bury Nia and Angharad soon. I will dig the graves."

"Allow me, my lord," said Rhoddi.

Bran nodded. "We'll do it together."

"I want to help," said Tuck.

"Is it wise to leave him alone?" said Rhoddi, with a nod towards Tomas.

Tuck glanced at the sleeping warrior beside him. "We'll hear him if he wakes," he said. So the three went off to begin the bleak task of digging the graves: one pitifully small for Nia, and another for Angharad. Iwan and Scarlet came to help, too, and all took their turn with the shovel. While they were at their work, some of the Grellon who had fled the settlement began coming back—one by one, and then in knots of two or three—and they gave their own account of what had happened.

The settlement had been discovered by a body of Ffreinc knights on horseback—eight or ten, maybe more—who then attacked. The forest-dwellers fled, with the knights in pursuit. They would have been caught, all of them, but Angharad turned and blocked the trail. They had last seen her facing the enemy with her staff raised high, a cry of challenge on her lips; and though it cost her life, the enemy did not follow them into the forest. The returning Grellon were shocked to find their good bard had been killed, and dear little Nia as well. The tears and weeping began all over again.

The women attended Noín, helping her wash and dress little Nia in her best clothes. They combed her hair and plaited flowers in the braids, and laid her on a bed of fresh green rushes. They washed the blood from Angharad's body and dressed her in a clean gown and brought her staff to lay beside her. Bran made a cross for the graves using arrows which he bound together with bowstring. Meanwhile, Tuck moved here and there, comforting his forest flock, giving them such solace as he possessed. He tried to instil some hope in the hearts of the grieving, and show a way to a better day ahead. But his own heart was not in it, and his words sounded hollow even to himself.

When the graves were ready, Scarlet came and, taking Noín by the hand, said, "It is time, my heart." Noín nodded silently. He knelt and gathered up his daughter and carried her to the new-dug grave; Noín walked beside him, her eyes on the bundle in her husband's arms.

Iwan and Owain bent to Angharad, but Bran said, "Wait. Bring her Bird Spirit cloak and put it on her. And her staff. We will bury her as befits the last True Bard of Britain."

Owain fetched the black-feathered cloak and helped Bran wrap it around the old woman, and the two bodies were laid to rest in the soft earth. Iwan brought Angharad's harp to place in the grave, but Bran prevented him. "No," he said, taking the harp. "This I will keep." As he cradled the harp to his shoulder, his mind flashed with the memory of one of their last partings. *"All that needs saying have I said,"* his Wise Banfáith had told him. *"Now it is for us to remember."*

He held the harp, and his mind returned to the time of their first meeting—in the old woman's winter cave hidden deep in the forest. There, she had healed his body with her art, and healed his soul with her songs. "A raven you are, and a raven you shall remain—until the day you fulfil your vow," Bran murmured, remembering the words of the old story. He turned his eyes one last time to the face of his friend—a face he had once considered almost unutterably ugly: the wide, downturned mouth and jutting chin; the bulbous nose; the small, keen eyes burning out from a countenance so wrinkled it seemed to be nothing but creases, lines, and folds. Death had not improved her appearance, but Bran had long ago ceased to regard her looks, seeing instead only the bright-burning radiance of a soul alight with wisdom. "She called me a king."

"My lord?" said Iwan. "Did you say something?"

"She had never done that before, you see? Not until now."

Darkness deepened in the greenwood. The Grellon lit pitch torches at the head of each body and began a service for the dead which Tuck led, praying softly through the Psalms and the special prayers for those recently deceased. It was a service he had performed as many times as christenings and weddings combined, and he knew it by heart.

The mourners held vigil through the night. Bran, Scarlet, and Noín kept watch while others came and went silently, or with a few words of comfort and condolence. Twice in the night, Bran was heard to groan, his shoulders heaving with silent sobs. The tie that had bound him and Angharad together was strong, and it had been cruelly severed, the wound deep and raw.

Then, at sunrise, the Grellon gathered at the graveside. Tuck said another prayer for the dead and for those who must resume life without them. Noín and Will wept as the dirt was replaced and heaped over the mounds. Bran pressed the small wooden crosses he had made into the graves and then knelt, solemn but dry-eyed, and said a last, silent farewell to the woman who had saved his life. Then, while the rest of the forest-dwellers prepared to abandon Cél Craidd, Tuck went to look in on Tomas. Bran joined him a little later to ask after his injured archer. "My lord," said Tuck softly, "I fear we have lost a good warrior."

"No . . ." sighed Bran.

"His wounds were greater than we knew," the friar explained. "I think he must have died in the night. I am sorry." He looked sadly at the still body beside him. "If my skill had been greater, I might have saved him."

"And if there had been no battle and he had not been wounded . . ." Bran shook his head and let the rest go unsaid. He pressed a hand to Tomas's chest and thanked the dead warrior for his good service, and released him to his rest. Then, bidding Tuck to have the body prepared for burial, he rose and went to dig another grave.

CHAPTER 38

Caer Rhodl

W hen were you going to tell me that Friar Tuck had been here?" asked Mérian, her tone deceptively sweet. "Or did you plan to tell me at all, brother mine?"

"I did not think it any of your concern," answered Garran dismissively. He leaned back in his chair and regarded his sister with suspicion. And then the thought struck him. "But how did *you* know they had come here?"

Mérian offered Garran a superior smile. "Bran has been a visitor to these halls more often than you know. Did you really think he would leave without seeing me?"

The king of Eiwas remained unmoved. "You said you wanted to speak to me. I hope it was not merely to berate me. If so, you are wasting your breath."

"I did not come to berate you, but to tell you that there is no need to keep me locked up. I will not try to escape, or leave Caer Rhodl without your permission and blessing."

"Coming to your senses at last, dear sister?" intoned Garran. "May I ask what has brought about this change of heart?"

"I have come to see that there is no point in leaving here without you and your war band to accompany me." Garran opened his mouth to reject that possibility outright, but Mérian did not give him the chance. "Bran and his people are fighting for their lives in Elfael. We must help them. We must ride at once—"

Garran held up his hand. "We have had this discussion before," he said, "and I have not changed my mind. Even if I was so inclined to raise the war band for them, the time for that is past, I fear."

"Past?" inquired Mérian. "Why past?"

"King William has raised his entire army and now occupies Elfael himself. It is said he has more than a thousand knights and men-at-arms encamped in the valley."

"What of Bran and his people? Is there any word?"

"Only that they fight on—foolishly, it seems to me, since no one has come to their aid."

"Then that is all the more reason to raise the war band," Mérian insisted. Clasping her hands before her, she stepped nearer her recalcitrant brother. "You must see that, Garran. We have to help them."

"Ride against King William and his army?" laughed Garran. "There is no force in all Britain that could defeat him now."

There came a knock on the door of the king's chamber, and Luc, the king's seneschal, entered. "Forgive me, Sire, but Baron Neufmarché has come and would see you most urgently. He says—"

Before the servant could finish, Baron Bernard himself pushed past him and stepped into the room. One glance at Mérian brought him up short. He stared at her as if at a ghost, then collected himself. "I see I am intruding," he said. "I am sorry. I will come back in—"

"Pray, do not leave, Baron," said Garran. Mérian noticed her brother's French had become quite fluent—as had her own since returning to Caer Rhodl. "Stay. This concerns you, too, I think. Mérian here is urging us to raise an army and ride to the defence of Elfael. She thinks we should take arms against the king of England's forces for the sake of Bran ap Brychan and his pitiful band of rebels."

The baron raised his eyebrows, but did not condemn the notion. "Does she indeed?" he said, stepping farther into the room. "I would like to hear her reasons." He made a stiffly formal bow to the young woman. "Please, speak freely, my lady. I assure you no harm will come of it."

Garran was quick to protest. "With all respect, Baron, my sister's fancies cannot be seriously entertained."

"Fancies!" snapped Mérian.

"Please," replied Neufmarché. He appealed to Mérian. "If you would kindly explain, I would like to hear your reasons."

Fearing some kind of trap was being laid for her, she replied, "Baron, you have the advantage here. Sending our war band to aid Bran against the king is treason, and if I were to argue such a course before one of the king's noblemen, it would be to my death—if such a thing were to be reported. In any event, aiding Elfael would go against your own interests, and I cannot think you, or anyone else, would willingly choose such a course."

"Exactly!" crowed Garran.

"Do not be so hasty," cautioned the baron. "As it happens, aiding Elfael may sit with my interests very nicely."

Garran stared at his father-in-law and patron, momentarily lost for words.

"Does this surprise you?" wondered the baron. "So long as we are speaking freely, the king is not always right, you know. William Rufus is not the man his father was. He makes mistakes. One of his early mistakes was to cross the Neufmarchés—but that is not at issue here."

He began pacing before the young king's chair, to Mérian's mind the very image of a man wrestling with an intractable problem. She watched him, hardly daring to hope that something good might come from what he was about to say.

"It comes to this—the king has ordered me to attend him and support him in this war against the rebel cantref. To aid the king is to undo all I have worked for in Wales for the last ten years or more. This I will not do—especially since my own grandchildren, when they arrive, will be Welsh. And yet"—he raised a finger—"to fail to respond to a royal summons is considered treason, and my life and lands are forfeit if I do not ride to the aid of the king."

The baron regarded Mérian as he concluded. "The king has left me with a very difficult choice, but a clear one."

Garran did not see it, but Mérian did.

"Which would be?" asked the young king.

"You know it, my lady," said Neufmarché, holding her in his gaze. "I suspect you've known it for some time."

Mérian nodded. "You must march against the king."

"Surely not," complained Garran. "We cannot hope to achieve anything against William and all his men."

"Perhaps not," replied Bernard, "but that is my—that is our— only choice. If we hope to hold onto what we have, we must defeat the king—or at least hold him off until peace can be reached."

"A peace," volunteered Mérian, "that will include justice for Elfael and pardon for all those who have fought for what is right."

"Amnistie royale, oui," replied the baron.

"But we risk everything," Garran pointed out.

"Our only hope of keeping what we have is to risk it all," agreed Neufmarché.

Garran fell silent, contemplating the enormous jolt his life and reign as king had just taken.

"And that, I suspect," continued the baron after a moment, "is why the Welsh noblemen have come."

"Cymry noblemen?" said Mérian. "Here?"

"Mais, oui," Neufmarché assured her, "it is the reason I intruded just now. A number of Welsh noblemen have arrived, and are seeking audience with the king. I asked Luc to bid them wait a little because I wanted to speak with my son-in-law first." He smiled. "So, you see, *c'est fortuit.*"

"Non," corrected Mérian, *"c'est la providence."* She turned to her brother, freshening her appeal in Welsh. "Don't you see, Garran? Riding to the aid of Elfael *is* the only way. And with the baron's help we cannot fail."

The young king was far from convinced, but as client to the baron, he knew he must do whatever his overlord commanded. Still, he sought to put off his consent a little longer. "Perhaps," he suggested, "before going any further, we should see who has come, and hear what they have to say."

"They have been brought to the hall," said Baron Bernard, "and the serving maids instructed to give them refreshment." He held out his arm to Mérian who, after a slight hesitation, took it. Garran went ahead of them, and the baron followed with Mérian on his arm. As soon as Garran had left the room, the baron turned to her and whispered, "Lady Mérian," he said, "hear me—we have not much time.

I do most humbly beg your pardon, for I have not always had your best interest at heart. I pray your forgiveness, my lady, and vow that in the days ahead I will make every effort to find a way to make up for my past mistakes."

"You are forgiven, my lord baron," replied Mérian nicely. "What is more, your determination to aid Bran and Elfael absolves a great many trespasses. I pray now that we are not too late."

"So pray we all," replied the baron.

They followed King Garran and his seneschal into the hall, where they found the benches full of strangers. Some of the king's men had already gathered to host the visitors, and all rose to their feet when the young king appeared.

"My lord king," said one of the visitors, stepping forward at once, "in the name of Our Saviour Jesus Christ, I give you good greeting. I am Lord Llewelyn of Aberffraw at your service." He gave a small bow of deference. "I present to you, my lord, King Gruffydd of Gwynedd"—a tall, lean man stepped forward—"and with him, my lord, King Dafydd ap Owain, lord of Snowdon"—a stern-faced battle chief stepped forward and, putting a hand to the hilt of his sword, gave a nod of his head—"and Iestyn ap Gwrgan, king of Gwent." The last of the great Welsh noblemen stepped forward and made his obeisance to the young king.

"Peace, and welcome to you all," said Garran, deeply impressed that such renowned men should have come to beg audience with him. "You honour me with your presence, my lords. Please, be seated again, and fill the cups. I am eager to hear what has brought you to Eiwas and to my hall."

"Lord Garran, if it please you," said the lanky nobleman called Gruffydd, "I speak for all of us when I say that we are grateful for your friendship and would like nothing more than to sit with you and drink your health and that of your people." His eyes shifted to the baron and he hesitated for a moment, then continued, "Unfortunately, we cannot partake of that estimable luxury. Time presses. Do not think me rude, therefore, if I decline your hospitality. We are passing through your lands on our way to Elfael."

"Elfael," remarked Garran with a glance at his sister, who was quietly translating for Baron Neufmarché. "It does seem to be a busy place of late."

"I will be brief," said Gruffydd. "We go to join forces with Bran ap Brychan to aid him in his fight to reclaim the throne of Elfael from the Ffreinc. As God is my witness, Lord Bran has done me a very great service which I can never hope to repay in full. But I go to do what I can. Moreover, it has been borne upon me with some considerable force"—here he glanced at Lord Llewelyn—"that if any of us would be free in our own land, we must all be free. To that end, I have persuaded these lords to join me." He put out a hand to his august companions and their commanders, who filled the benches at the board. He stepped before Garran to address him more directly. "I would persuade you, too, my lord." He regarded the young king steadily. "Join us, Rhi Garran. Help us right a great wrong and win justice for Elfael, and all who call Cymru home, against the Ffreinc and their overreaching king."

One of the lords stepped near to Gruffydd just then and whispered something in his ear. The king of Gwynedd squared himself, turned, and gazed boldly at the baron. "It seems I have spoken too freely," Gruffydd said. "I am informed that we have a Ffreinc baron among us. Had I known that he was here—"

"Truly," said Garran, "there is no harm done." He turned and beckoned the baron and his sister nearer. "My lords, I present Baron Neufmarché, my liege lord, and with him, my sister Lady Mérian."

"My lord baron," said Gruffydd in stiff acknowledgement of Neufmarché. His hand went to the sword at his side and stayed there.

"As the baron is my overlord," Garran continued, "it is well that he has heard your intentions for himself."

"How so?" said Gruffydd suspiciously.

"For the fact that this was the very course he himself was urging only moments before we joined you here."

"Mes seigneurs et mes rois," said the baron. *"C'est vrai."* Mérian translated for the Welsh kings, and explained that the baron had defied Red William's summons and had come to Eiwas instead, and that he and Garran had just been discussing the need to aid the rebels of Elfael in their struggle against the crown. After a quick consultation with Bernard, she concluded, "Baron Neufmarché wishes you to know that he stands willing to pledge his men to the aid of Elfael, and asks only to be taken at his word."

This provoked a hasty and heated discussion among the Welsh noblemen. Mérian watched as the debate seemed to roll back and forth. It was swiftly over, and the Welsh lords turned to face the baron with their answer. Gruffydd said, "We have argued your offer, Lord Baron, and it is most unexpected, to be sure—but no less welcome for that. We will accept your pledge and thank you for it."

The baron expressed his gratitude to the Welsh kings for placing their trust in him, and then, through Mérian, asked, "How soon can you be ready to march?"

"We are already on the march," replied Gruffydd. "Our men are on their way to Elfael even now."

"Then," replied the baron, when he had received Gruffydd's answer, "we must make haste to overtake them. Among my people, it is counted a very great shame for a commander to lead from the rear."

CHAPTER 39

Rhoddi scrambled through the upper branches of the greenwood canopy, skittering along the hidden path of the sky way, to drop deftly into the little clearing where the Grellon had set up camp after abandoning Cél Craidd the day before. He searched among the sleeping bodies huddled in their cloaks on the ground for the one he sought, and hastened to kneel beside it. "Bran!" he said, leaning close. "Owain says to come at once."

Bran sat up. It was early still, the feeble grey light barely penetrating the heavy foliage of oak and elm round about. Reaching instinctively for his bow, he rose to his feet. "Trouble?"

Rhoddi shook his head. "There's something moving on the King's Road," he said quietly, "something you should see."

"Will," called Bran softly, rousing the forester, "begin waking the others and get everyone ready to move. I'll send word back." To Rhoddi, he said, "Lead the way."

The two climbed up the rope ladder onto the interconnected

arrangement of limbs and boughs, planks and platforms that the Grellon maintained to move easily and quickly to and from the King's Road overlook. A swift and precarious dash brought them to the place where Owain was perched high up among the rocks on the bank of the cliff overlooking the road. "What is it?" asked Bran, climbing up beside him. "More troops?"

"Aye," replied Owain, "it is more troops, Sire. But there is something odd about these ones." He pointed down the road to where a column of knights was just coming into view. "A scouting party passed just a little while ago. I think this is the main body just coming now."

"Ffreinc, yes," said Bran. "I see them. What is so odd about them?"

"The scouts were Cymry," said Owain.

"Cymry!" said Bran. "Are you sure?"

"As sure as I can be. They were Welsh-born, I swear on Job's bones—and all of them carried longbows same as us."

"Not good," muttered Bran. "Our own countrymen going to join King William—not good at all." Before his companion could offer a reply, Bran grabbed his arm. "Look!" He pointed down to the second rank of mounted soldiers riding behind a double row of men-at-arms on foot. "I know that man—I know his standard . . . Saints in heaven!"

"Who is it?"

"Wait . . ." said Bran, straining forward. "Let them come a little closer . . ." He slapped the rock with his hand. "Yes!"

"Do you recognize someone, my lord?"

"It is Baron Neufmarché—or I am the archbishop of Canterbury," said Bran, still squinting down into the road, "and, God help us, that is Mérian beside him."

"Are you sure?"

Bran squirmed around on the rock and called down to Rhoddi waiting below. "Go get Scarlet! Tell him to bring every man who can draw a bow. Tell him I want them to be ready to fight when they get here. We'll have to take them on the fly. Hurry, man! Go!"

In the road below, the soldiers came on, slowing as they neared the place where the road narrowed beneath the overhanging rocks. "Do you think they know we're here?" wondered Owain.

"Perhaps," replied Bran, withdrawing an arrow from the bundle and nocking it to the string. "Come closer, proud baron," he whispered, pressing the belly of the bow forward. "Just a little closer and you're mine."

But when the riders resumed their march, it was not Neufmarché who advanced—it was Mérian, and another, riding beside her. The two advanced together.

"Who is that with her?" said Owain.

Bran stared hard at the mounted warrior beside Mérian.

After a moment, Owain observed, "He doesn't look like a Ffreinc."

"He isn't," concluded Bran. "He is Cymry."

"Do you know him?"

Bran lowered the bow and eased the string. "That is Gruffydd, Lord of Gwynedd. Though what he is doing here in the company of Baron Neufmarché is a very mystery."

"Maybe Neufmarché has taken them captive," suggested Owain.

By way of reply, Bran drew and loosed an arrow into the road. It struck the dirt a few paces ahead of the two oncoming riders. Mérian reined up. She lifted her face to the rock walls rising to either side of the road and then, placing a hand to her mouth, called, "Rhi

Bran! Are you here?" She waited a moment, then said, "Bran if you are here, show yourself. We have come to talk to you."

Owain and Bran exchanged a puzzled glance. Bran moved to rise, but Owain put a hand on his arm. "Don't do it, my lord. It might be a trick."

"From anyone but Mérian," replied Bran. "I will talk to them—keep an arrow on the string just in case."

Bran stood on the rock. He lofted the bow and called down to the riders in the road. "Here I am."

"Bran!" cried Mérian. "Thank God—"

"Are you well, Mérian? Have they hurt you?"

"I am well, Bran," she called, beaming up at him. "I have brought help." She twisted in the saddle and indicated the ordered ranks of troops behind her. "We have come to help you."

"And Neufmarché," said Bran. "What is he doing here?"

"He has joined us," said Gruffydd, speaking up. "Greetings, Rhi Bran."

"Greetings, Gruffydd. I never thought to see you again."

"For that I am full sorry," replied the lord of Gwynedd. "But I beg the chance to make it up to you. I have brought friends—and, yes, Baron Neufmarché is one of them."

"You will forgive me if I am not wholly persuaded," remarked Bran.

"Could you come down, do you think?" asked Gruffydd. "I grow hoarse and stiff-necked shouting up at you like this."

Slinging his bow across his chest, Bran prepared to meet them on the road. "Keep an eye on them," he said to Owain. "When Scarlet and the others get here, position the men on the rocks there and there"—he pointed along the rocky outcropping—"and tell them to be ready to let fly if things are not what they seem."

"God with you, my lord," said Owain, putting an arrow on the string. "We'll wait for your signal."

Bran lowered himself quickly down the rocks, dropping from ledge to ledge and lighting on the edge of the road a hundred paces or so from where Mérian and Gruffydd were waiting. Behind them stood the ranks of the baron's knights and men-at-arms, and Bran was relieved to see that none of them had moved and seemed content merely to stand looking on. Unslinging his bow, he put an arrow on the string and advanced cautiously, keeping an eye on the troops for any sign of movement.

He had walked but a few dozen paces when Mérian spurred her horse forward and galloped to him, throwing herself from the saddle and into his embrace. Her mouth found his, and she kissed him hard and with all the pent-up passion of their weeks apart. "Oh, Bran, I have missed you. I'm sorry I could not come sooner."

"Mérian, I—"

"But, look!" she said, kissing him again. "I've brought an army." She flung out a hand to those behind her. "They've come to help save Elfael."

"Truly," replied Bran, still not entirely trusting this turn of fortune. "How many are with you?"

"I don't know—over five hundred, I think. Baron Neufmarché has come in on our side, and Rhi Gruffydd is here, and Garran and—"

"*Votre dame est très persuasive,*" said Neufmarché, reining up just then. King Garran rode beside him.

"It is true," said Garran. "My sister can be very persuasive. She would not rest until we agreed to come help you."

King Gruffydd rode up and took his place beside the baron. Seeing Gruffydd and Neufmarché side by side seemed so unnatural,

Bran could hardly credit what he saw, and his native suspicion returned full force. Instinctively, he stepped in front of Mérian.

"That is close enough, Baron," said Bran, raising his bow.

"Aros, Rhi Bran," said Gruffydd. "You are among friends—more than you know. The baron has pledged his forces to your aid." Indicating the troops amassed behind him with a wide sweep of his hand, he said, "We have come to confront King William and his army, and would be much obliged if you would lead us to them."

"If you have truly come to fight the Ffreinc," said Bran, "you will not go home disappointed. I can show you all you care to see."

King Gruffydd climbed slowly down from the saddle. He walked to where Bran stood and then, in full sight of everyone there, went down on one knee before him. "My lord and friend," he said, bending his head, "I pledge my life to you and to this cause. My men and I will see you on the throne of Elfael, or gladly embrace our graves. One or the other will prevail before we relinquish the fight. This is my vow." Drawing his sword, he laid it at Bran's feet. "From this day, my sword is yours to command."

"Rise, my lord, I—" began Bran, but his throat closed over the words, and overcome with a sudden, heady swirl of emotions, he found he could not speak. In all that had happened in the last days and weeks, he had never foreseen anything like this: the help he had so long and so desperately needed had come at last, and the realization of what it meant fair whelmed him over.

Gruffydd rose, smiling. "I owe you my life and throne and more. Blind fool that I am, it took me a little time to see that." Taking Bran by the arm, he pulled him away. "But come, Llewelyn is here—he has been most persuasive, too—and I've brought some others who are anxious to meet the renowned Rhi Bran y Hud."

The next thing Bran knew he was surrounded by knights and noblemen—both Cymry and Ffreinc—all of them pledging their swords to him. He greeted all in turn, his thoughts churning, emotion running high as he tried to comprehend the magnitude of the good that had just befallen him. Baron Neufmarché remained a little apart, looking on from his saddle; he motioned Mérian to him and had a brief word. She hurried to Bran and said, "No one is happier than I am for this glad meeting, but the baron wishes me to say that it would not be the wisest course to be caught on the road just now. He asks if you might lead us to your camp, where the commanders can discuss the ordering of the troops and prepare the battle plan."

"The baron is right," allowed Gruffydd. "Is it far, your camp?"

"My settlement was destroyed—"

"Oh, Bran, no," said Mérian. "Was anyone . . . ?"

"I am sorry, Mérian." Bran put a hand to her shoulder to steady her for the blow. "Angharad was killed protecting Cél Craidd, and little Nia by accident. It happened when we were on a raid. Tomas is dead, too—from a Ffreinc spear."

Mérian's face crumpled. Bran slid his arm around her shoulders. "Later, my love," he whispered, his mouth close to her ear, "we will grieve them properly later. I need your strength just now."

Nodding, she lifted her head and rubbed the tears from her eyes. "What would you have me do?"

"Tell the baron there is a place farther on along the road where we can gather." He shook his head. "The troops will have to spread out into the forest and find places to camp of their own. My men can lead them."

Bran raised his bow and loosed a shrill whistle that pierced the forest quiet and resounded among the rocks. From every side appeared his fighting men: Scarlet, Tuck, Rhoddi, Owain, Ifor, Brocmael, Idris, Geronwy, and Beli and Llwyd. They clambered down the rocks to join the company on the road and receive the good news. Moments later, Bran's new army was on the move with Bran himself leading them—through the gorge and beyond it to a place where the land flattened out once more. The forest thinned somewhat around a stand of great oaks and elms, and here Bran gave orders for Rhoddi and Owain to lead the army into the wood round about and let them rest. "Tuck," he said, snatching the friar by the sleeve as he greeted Mérian, "stay with me—and you, too, Scarlet. We are going to hold council to plan the battle."

While men and horses and wagons trundled into a glen in the wood, there to establish a rude camp, the kings and noblemen sat down with Bran to learn the state of affairs in Elfael, and the strength and position of King William's troops. Thus the council began, and it was long before each of the great lords had their say and all points of view had been taken into account. The sun was a dull copper glow low in the west, and the first stars were beginning to light up the sky, when a plan of battle that all agreed upon began to emerge.

Bran was, by turns, impressed with the expertise of his new battle chiefs and irked at the necessity of biding his time while they hammered out details he would have settled long ago. But, all in all, as the last light of day faded, he declared himself pleased with the plan and confident in his commanders. The scouts would go out at dawn and make a final assessment of the enemy position ahead of the battle. Then the rebel forces would take the field against the king's army, led by the Cymry archers, supported and guarded on the flanks by Baron Neufmarché and his knights.

As soon as the council concluded, the lords went to find food and drink with their men. Bran sent Scarlet and Tuck to tell his own war band what had happened, and then sought Mérian. "It is the answer to prayer long in coming," he told her. She stepped easily into his embrace. Feeling the living warmth of her in his arms, he confessed, his voice faltering slightly, "I never hoped to see you again. I thought we had parted for good."

"Shhh," she said. "I will never leave you again." She gave him a lingering kiss and then said, "Tell me all that has happened while I've been away."

They talked then, and the twilight deepened around them. They were still talking when Tuck came upon them. Unwilling to intrude on their intimate moment, he settled himself on the root of a tree to wait, thinking what a strange and wonderful day it had been. And here were Bran and Mérian, such a good match. There would be a wedding soon if he had anything to say about it . . . and, he thought, *if* they were all still alive this time tomorrow.

Leaning back against the rough bole of the old elm, he closed his eyes. From the depths of misery over the recent loss of Angharad, Tomas, and Nia, who could have foreseen that their fortunes would rise to such heights so quickly? Even so, the victory was not yet won—far from it. There were battles to be fought, and the lives of many swung in the balance. Death and destruction would be great indeed. *Oh, Merciful Lord,* he sighed inwardly, *if that could somehow be prevented . . .* "Let this cup pass from us," he prayed softly.

"Ah, Tuck," said Bran, interrupting the friar's meditation, "you're here—good." Still holding Mérian, he turned to the little friar. "I have a job for you."

CHAPTER 40

D awn was still but a whisper in the pale eastern sky when Tuck finally reached Saint Martin's. He paused below the brow of a hill a short distance from the little town and dismounted. He trudged wearily up to the top of the hill and there stood for a time to observe. The moon, bright still, illuminated the hills and filled the valleys with soft shadows. Nothing moved anywhere.

He yawned and rubbed his face with his hands. "This friar is getting too old for these midnight rambles." His empty stomach growled. "Too right," he muttered.

At Bran's behest, Tuck had ridden all night, making a wide, careful circuit of the valley to avoid being seen by any Ffreinc sentries or watchmen posted on the outer perimeter of King William's sprawling encampment, which lay between the forest and Elfael's fortress, Caer Cadarn. Now, coming upon the town from the north, he paused to make certain he could continue to the completion of his mission. Having come this far, it would not do to be caught now.

There did not seem to be any Ffreinc troops around; he could not see anyone moving about the low walls. The town was quiet, asleep. "Well, Tuck, my man, time to beard the lion in his den."

Struggling back into the saddle, he resumed his errand, descending the hill and starting up the gentle slope to the town, keeping his eyes open for any sign of discovery at his approach. But there was no one about, and he entered the town alone and, for all he could tell, unobserved. He dismounted and tethered the horse to an iron ring set in the wall of the guardhouse, then quickly and quietly started across the deserted market square towards the abbey.

The abbey gates were closed, but he rapped gently on the door and eventually managed to rouse the porter. "I have a matter of utmost urgency for the bishop," he announced to the priest who unlatched the door. "Take me to him at once."

The young monk, yawning, shook his head. It was then Tuck recognized him. "Odo! Wake up, boyo. It's me, Tuck. I have to see Bishop Asaph without delay."

"God with you, Friar," said Odo, rubbing his eyes. "The bishop will be asleep."

"There is no time," said Tuck, pressing himself through the gap. "It is life and death, Odo. We'll have to wake him."

Tuck took the young monk's elbow, spun him around, and started walking towards the palatial lodge Abbot Hugo had built for himself. "Never fear, Brother, I would not disturb the good bishop's rest if it was not of highest importance."

"This way, then," said Odo, and led Tuck not to the main entrance, but around the side to a small room where the secnab had lodged. "He prefers a less ostentatious cell," explained the young scribe, knocking on the door.

There came a sleepy voice asking them to wait, and in a moment the door opened. There stood the wizened, elderly priest, barefoot, his haze of white hair a wispy nimbus on his head. One look at Tuck and he said, "How may I serve you, Brother?"

"Bishop Asaph," said Tuck, "it is Brother Aethelfrith—do you remember me?"

The old priest studied his face in the moonlight. Then, recognition flooded into the pale eyes. "Bran's friend! Yes, I remember you. But, tell me, has something happened? Is he well?"

"All is well, Father," replied Tuck. "Or soon will be. I have come—".

Asaph shivered. "Come in, Brother Aethelfrith, and let us sit by the fire." Tuck thanked Odo and stepped inside; the old priest showed him to a stool by a tiny fire in the hearth. "These old bones are hard to keep warm," explained the bishop. "My advice, Brother, do not get old—and if you do, see you keep a little fire going in the corner. It works miracles."

"I'll remember that," replied Tuck.

"Now then," said Asaph, "what has kept you from your bed this night?"

"Bran has sent me with a message," replied the friar, and went on to explain about the miraculous arrival of Gruffydd and the Cymry kings. "And that is not all—far from it!" he remarked. "Baron Neufmarché has joined the rebellion. He is lending the full force of his troops to the cause. It is, I think, the only way he can hope to hold on to his estates."

Bishop Asaph gasped with a sharp intake of breath. "Lord Almighty!" His eyes grew round. "Then it is soon over, praise be to God."

"One way or another, yes," replied Tuck, "and perhaps sooner than you know. The Cymry mean to attack tomorrow. We have not the supplies and such for a prolonged clash. The troops are ready, and the weather is good. We will have the higher ground . . ." He paused. "In short, there is no point in waiting. That is what I came to tell you. The battle attack will come in the morning, when the sun has risen above the trees so that it will be in the eyes of the Ffreinc troops."

"God have mercy." Asaph shook his head. "I will make ready to receive the wounded, of course."

"Yes," agreed Tuck, "and one other thing—we must get word to Iwan and Siarles at the fortress. They must know so they can be ready to strike from the rear if and when the opportunity arises." He paused. "Bran has asked if you will take the message to them."

"Me?" blustered Asaph. "Well, of course, but—"

"Have the king's men made any trouble for you?"

"No, no," replied the bishop quickly. "It has been very quiet. They come here for prayer and confession—and to ensure the wounded are receiving good care. But they leave us alone."

"Well then," concluded Tuck. "Perhaps you might take two or three brothers with you and go to the caer. Take a bell and ring it as you go so the Ffreinc will know you're on holy business."

Asaph nodded slowly. "What if they make bold to stop us?"

"Simply tell them that you are going up to shrive the Cymry in the stronghold, yes? You can do that, too, once you've delivered the message, can you not?"

The old churchman considered this for a moment, then, making up his mind, he said, "If there is to be a battle, soldiers must be shriven. Men facing their eternal destiny have no wish to die with sins unconfessed dragging their souls into perdition. The Ffreinc understand this."

"Thank you, Father," said Tuck. They talked a little more then, and Tuck gave the bishop a lengthy account of all that had taken place in the last days—the running battle with King William's troops in the forest, leading up to the unexpected return of Mérian bringing King Gruffydd and the baron. They talked of the difficulties looming in the days ahead—caring for the injured and wounded in the aftermath of battle, finding food for the survivors, and rebuilding lives and livelihoods destroyed by the war.

Finally, Tuck rose and, with great weariness of body and spirit, made his farewells and moved to the door.

"God with you, Brother Aethelfrith," said Asaph with deepest sincerity.

"And also with you, Father," replied Tuck. "May the Good Lord keep you in the hollow of His hand."

"Amen," said Asaph. "I will leave you to make your own way out. I want to pray for a while before we go up to the caer."

Tuck left the monastery without bothering Odo again. He slipped out of the abbey gate and started across the deserted square of the still-sleeping town. As he was passing the church, he heard the sound of horses approaching and turned just as four or five riders entered the square. Ffreinc soldiers. He was caught like a ferret in a coop.

Instinctively, he dived for the door of the church. It was dark and cool inside, as he knew it would be. A single candle burned on the altar, and the interior was filled with the sweet stale odour of spent incense and beeswax. The baptismal font stood before him, square and solid, the cover locked with an iron hasp. That was vile Hugo—

locking the font lest any poor soul be tempted to steal a drop of holy water.

Gazing quickly around the empty space for a place to hide, he saw—could it be? Yes! In the far corner of the nave stood a strange, curtained booth. Oh, these Normans—chasing every new whim that whispers down the road: a confessional. Tuck had heard of them, but had never seen one. They were, it was said, becoming very fashionable in the new stone churches the Ffreinc built. The notion that a body could confess without looking his priest in the eye all the while seemed faintly ludicrous to Tuck. Nevertheless, he was grateful for this particular whim just now. He crossed quickly to the booth. It was an open stall with a pierced screen down the centre: on one hand was a chair for the priest; on the other a little low bench for the kneeling penitent. A curtain hung between the two, and another hid the priest from view.

Tuck could not help clucking his tongue over such unwonted luxury. Not for the Norman cleric a humble stool; no, nothing would do but that Hugo's priests must have an armchair throne with a down-filled cushion. "Bless 'em," said Tuck. Pulling aside the curtain, he stepped in and closed the curtain again, then settled himself in the chair, thanking the Good Lord for his thoughtful provision.

No sooner had he leaned back in his chair than the door of the church opened and the soldiers entered.

Tuck remained absolutely still, hardly daring to breathe.

The footsteps came nearer.

They were coming towards the confessional. One of the knights was standing directly in front of the booth now, and Tuck braced himself for discovery. The soldier put a hand on the curtain and pulled it aside. The soldier saw Tuck, and Tuck saw the soldier—only it was no ordinary knight. The squat, thick body, the powerful chest and slightly bowed legs from a life on horseback, the shock of flaming red hair: it was none other than King William Rufus in the flesh.

Tuck pressed his eyes closed, expecting the worst.

But the king turned away without the slightest hint of recognition in his pale blue eyes and called over his shoulder to the two with him. *"Le prêtre est ici,"* he said. *"Retire-toi."*

The priest is here, thought Tuck, translating the words in his head. *God help me, he thinks I am the priest to hear his confession.*

King William dropped the curtain and settled himself on the kneeling bench. *"Père, confessez-moi,"* he said wearily.

Knowing he would have to speak now—and that his French was not up to the challenge—he said, *"Mon seigneur et mon roi, en anglais, s'il vous plaît."*

There came a heavy sigh from the other side of the curtain, and then the king of England replied, *"Oui*—of course, I understand. My *anglais* is not so good, forgive *moi*, eh?"

"God hears the heart, my lord," offered Tuck. "It makes no difference to him what language we use. Would you like me to shrive you now?"

"Oui, père, that is why I have come." The king paused, and then said, "Forgive me, Father, a sinner. Today I ride into battle, and I cannot pay for the souls of those who will be slain. The blood-price is heavy, and I am without the silver to pay, eh?"

It took Tuck a moment to work out what William was talking about, and he was glad the king could not see him behind the curtain. "I see," he said, and then it came to him that William Rufus was talking about the peculiar Norman belief that a soldier owed a blood debt for the souls of those he had slain in battle. Since one could never know whether the man he had just killed had been properly shriven, the souls of the combat dead became the survivor's responsibility, so to speak—he was obligated to pray for the remission of their sins so that they might enter heaven and stand blameless before the judgement seat of God.

"Oh, yes," intoned Tuck as understanding broke upon him. The king, like many great lords, was paying priests to pray for the souls of men he had slain in battle, praying them out of purgatory and into heaven.

"By the Virgin, the cost is heavy!" muttered William. "*Intolérable,* eh? It is all I can do to pay my father's debt, and I have not yet begun to pay my own."

"A very great pity, yes," Tuck allowed.

"*Oui, c'est dommage,*" sighed William. "*C'est bien dommage.*"

"Begging your pardon, *mon roi,*" said Tuck. "I am but a lowly priest, but it seems to me that the way out of your predicament is not more money, but fewer souls."

"Eh?" said William, only half paying attention. "Fewer souls?"

"Do not kill any more soldiers."

The king laughed outright. "You know little about warring, priest! *Un innocent!* I like you. Soldiers get killed in battle; that is the whole point."

"So I am told," replied Tuck. "But is there no other way?"

"It could all be settled tomorrow—*sang de Dieu,* today!—if the blasted Welsh would only lay down their weapons. But they have raised rebellion against me, and that I will not have!"

"A great dilemma for you," conceded Tuck. "I see that."

Before he could say more, William continued. "This cantref *infortuné* has already cost me more than it will ever return. And if I do not collect my tribute in Normandie in six days' time, I will lose those too. Philip will see to that."

Tuck seized on this. "All the more reason to make peace with these rebels. If they agreed to lay down their arms and swear fealty to you—"

"*Et payer le tribut royal,*" added William quickly.

"Yes, and pay the royal tribute, to be sure," agreed Tuck. "Your Majesty would not have to feed an army or pay for the souls of the dead. Also you could go to Normandie and collect the tribute that is due—all this would save the royal treasury a very great load of silver, would it not?"

"*Par la Vierge!* Save a great load of silver, yes."

Tuck, hardly daring to believe that he was not in a dream, but unwilling to wake up just yet, decided to press his luck as far as it would go. "Again, forgive me, *mon roi*, but why not ask for terms of peace? This rebel—King Raven, I believe they call him—has said that all he wants is to rule his realm in peace. Even now, I believe he could be convinced to swear fealty to you in exchange for reclaiming his throne."

There was a long and, Tuck imagined, baleful silence on the other side of the curtain. He feared the king was deciding how to slice him up and into how many pieces.

Finally, William said, "I think you are a man of great faith." The wistful longing in that voice cut at Tuck's heart. "If I could believe this . . ."

"Believe it, Sire," said Tuck. "For it is true."

"If I am seen to allow rebellion, every hand will be raised against me."

"Perhaps," granted Tuck. "But if you are seen to practice mercy, it would inspire others to greater loyalty, would it not?" He paused. "The sword is always close to hand."

"Hélas, c'est vrai," granted the king.

"Alas, yes, it is too true."

There was silence again then. Tuck could not tell what was happening beyond the curtain. He prayed William was seriously considering the idea of suing for peace.

When he spoke again, the king said, "Will you yet shrive me?"

"That is why I am here. Bow your head, my son, and we begin," replied Tuck, and proceeded with the ritual. When at last the king rose to depart, he thanked his priest and walked from the church without another word.

Tuck waited until he heard the sound of horses in the square, and then crept to the door. King William and his knights were riding away in the grey dawn of a new day. He waited until they were out of sight and then ran to his own horse and flew to the greenwood as if all the hounds of hell were at his heels.

CHAPTER 41

The sun was well up and climbing towards the tops of the higher trees by the time Tuck reached the safety of the greenwood. The combined armies of Cymry rebels were already amassing at the edge of the forest. Hampered by the trees and undergrowth, Tuck worked his way along the battle line, searching for Bran. By the time he found him, the sun was that much higher and the assault that much nearer.

"Bran!" cried Tuck. "Thank God, I've found you in time." He slid from the saddle and ran to where Bran was waiting with Scarlet, Owain, and his own small war band, engulfed and surrounded by King Gruffydd's troops and those of the northern lords. "I bring word—"

"Be quick about it," Bran told him. "I am just about to give the command—"

"No!" said Tuck, almost frantic. "Forgive me, my lord, but do nothing until you've heard what I have to say."

"Very well," Bran agreed. He called across to Gruffydd and Llewelyn, who were standing a little apart. "Stand ready to march as soon as I have returned." To Tuck, he said, "Come with me."

He led them a little way into the wood, to a place where they would not be overheard. "Well? Is the bishop able to get a message to the caer?"

It took a moment for the priest to recall his original errand. "Oh, that, yes." Tuck licked his lips and swallowed. "I have seen the king."

"The king . . . Red William?"

"The same," replied the friar, and explained what had happened in the town—how he had been surprised by Ffreinc riders and hid himself in the church, how William had mistaken him for one of the abbey priests and asked to be shriven, and their talk about the rebellion.

"Did you shrive him?"

"I did, yes, but—"

"So that means they intend to attack today," concluded Bran. "Well done, Tuck; it confirms us in our plan. We will strike without delay." He started away.

"That is not all," said Tuck. "The king was distraught about the cost of this war. It weighs heavily with him. He stands to lose his tribute money from Normandie."

"Good."

"Above all else he desires a swift end to this conflict," Tuck explained. "I believe he would be moved towards peace."

"That he will not have," declared Bran. "And you are certain Bishop Asaph will warn Iwan and Siarles at the fortress?"

"He will."

"Then all is ready." He commended Tuck for his diligence, and returned to the battle line, where he gave a nod to Gruffydd, Llewelyn, and the others. "God with you today, my lords, and with us all," he called, and raising his warbow, he gave the signal to move out.

The massed armies of Cymry archers and Ffreinc soldiers under the command of Baron Neufmarché slowly moved out from the shelter of Coed Cadw; the knights on horseback and the Cymry on foot, they marched down the slope and into the Vale of Elfael. Their appearance threw William's troops into a chaos of frantic activity as the alarms were sounded through the various camps. The knights, men-at-arms, and footmen were well trained, however, and hastily mustered for battle. As the Cymry drew nearer, the Ffreinc moved to meet them, first one division and then another until the gaps in the line were filled and they had formed a single, dense body of soldiers—the knights in the centre, flanked by the footmen.

Tuck, with his staff, taking his place behind Bran and Scarlet, found himself walking beside Owain. "Whatever happens today," said the young warrior, "I would have you say a prayer for me, Friar."

"And here I have been praying for us all since first light, have I not?"

"Then," said Owain, "I will pray for you, Friar Tuck."

"Do that, boyo," agreed Tuck. "You do that."

The Cymry moved slowly down from the forest, spreading out along the rim of the valley a little north of the King's Road so that when they attacked the sun would be at their backs and in the eyes of the enemy. They came to the steepest part of the slope and stopped so that William's troops would have to toil uphill to engage them, while they could rain arrows down into the ranks of advancing knights as well as those behind.

King William's barons and earls, each in command of his own men, formed the battle line, filling in the gaps between the separate bodies until the knights rode shoulder to shoulder and shield to shield, spears raised and ready to swing down into position when the order was given to charge. The footmen scrambled into ranks behind the knights and prepared to deliver the second assault when the knights broke the enemy line.

Up on the slopes across the valley, the Cymry archers took hand-fuls of arrows and thrust them point-first into the turf before them, ready to hand when the order came to loose havoc on the advancing Ffreinc. Baron Neufmarché, at the head of his troops, drew into position to the northwest—ready to swoop down upon the unpro-tected flanks of William's army the moment the charge faltered under the hail of shafts. If, however, the knights survived the charge and carried the attack forward, he would come in hard to protect the archers' retreat.

"Come on, you ugly frog-faced knaves . . ." muttered Scarlet. He stretched and flexed the stiffness from his injured hand, then plucked a shaft from the ground and nocked it to the string. ". . . a little closer and you're mine."

Other men were speaking now—some in prayer, and others in derision of the enemy, banking courage in themselves and those around them. Bran stood silent, watching the slow, steady advance of the Ffreinc line. He suddenly found himself wishing Angharad were alive to see this day. He missed her and the knowledge that she was upholding him in her mysterious and powerful way. Closing his eyes, he prayed that she was gazing down on him and would intercede with the angels of war on his behalf and sustain him in the battle.

He was still occupied with this thought when he heard Gruffydd say, "Here, now! What's this?"

Bran opened his eyes to see that the Ffreinc had halted just out of easy arrow flight. The early sun glinted off the polished surfaces of their shields and weapons. There was a movement from the centre, and the line broke, parting to the left and right as a small body of knights rode forward. Two of the riders carried banners—one bearing the royal standard of King William: a many-tailed flag with a red cross on a white field and a strip of ermine across the bottom separating the body from the green, blue, and yellow tails. The other knight bore the standard of England: the Cross of Jerusalem in gold surrounded by smaller crosslets of blue; its tails were green, gold and blue, each tail ending in small gold tassels.

These banners preceded a single knight, riding between them. Two more knights followed the lone rider, and all advanced to a point halfway between the two armies, and there they halted.

"Saints and angels," said Gruffydd, "what's the old devil about?"

"I think Bloody William wants to talk," replied Llewelyn.

"I say we give him an arrow in the eye and let that do our talking for us," declared Gruffydd. He nudged Llewelyn beside him. "Your aim is true, Cousin; let fly and we'll see that rascal off right smart."

"No!" said Tuck, pressing forward. "Begging your pardon, my lords, I do believe he wants to beg terms of peace."

"Peace!" scoffed Gruffydd. "Never! The old buzzard wants to sneak us into a trap, more like. I say give him an arrow or two and teach him to keep his head down."

"My lord," pleaded Tuck, "if it is peace he wants, it would be the saving of many lives."

Bran gazed across the distance at the king, sitting on his fine horse, his newly burnished armour glinting in the golden light of a brilliant new day. "If he *does* want to talk," Bran decided at last, "it will cost us nothing to hear what he has to say. We can attack as soon as the discussion is concluded." He turned to Gruffydd. "I will talk to him. You and Llewelyn be ready to lead the assault if things go badly." He motioned to Will Scarlet, saying, "Come with me, Will. And you, too, Tuck—your French is better than mine."

"Baron Neufmarché speaks French better than any of us," Tuck pointed out. "Send for him."

"Maybe later," allowed Bran. "We'll see if there's anything worth talking about first."

Together the three of them walked down the grassy slope to where the king of England had established himself between his billowing standards.

"Perhaps the friar is right," suggested Will Scarlet. "It would not hurt to have Neufmarché with us."

"We will call him if we need him," allowed Bran.

"William speaks English," Tuck told them.

"Does he indeed?" said Bran.

"A little, anyway—more than he'll admit to."

"Then we will insist," Bran decided. "That way we can all be very careful about what we say to one another."

They came to within fifty paces of the knights on horseback. *"Mon roi,"* said Bran, with a glancing nod of respect. *"Parlerez-vous?"*

"Oui," replied King William. *"Je veux vous parler de la paix."*

"He wants to talk to you about making peace," said Tuck.

"Bon," said Bran. To Tuck, he said, "Tell him that we will speak in English and that you will relay my words to him."

Tuck did as he was commanded, and a strange expression passed over the king's face. *"You,"* he said. "Have I seen you before?"

"You've seen us *all* before, you mule-headed varlet," muttered Scarlet in Welsh.

"Steady on, Scarlet," said Bran. "We're here to listen."

"Oh, indeed, yes, Sire," replied Tuck. "We met first in Rouen last year—when my Lord Bran came to warn you of the plot by your brother against your throne."

William nodded. "Somewhere else, I think."

"Yes," said Tuck. "I was at Wintan Cestre when you gave your judgement against Baron de Braose and Count Falkes, and delivered this cantref into the care of Abbot Hugo Rainault and Sheriff de Glanville."

William squinted his eyes and regarded the little friar with a suspicious look—as if trying to decide if the priest was mocking him in some subtle way. "No . . . somewhere else." Realization came to him, and his eyebrows raised. *"Sang de la Vierge!* You were that priest in the church this morning."

"True, Majesty," answered Tuck. "That is a fact I cannot deny."

"Good Lord, Tuck," whispered Scarlet, "you've been a busy fella."

The king frowned, then said, *"C'est la vie*—I am glad you are here." Turning his attention to the task at hand he said to Bran, "Good day for a battle, eh?"

"None better," replied Bran, through Tuck.

"What is this about you, ah . . . *désirer* the throne of this god-forsaken cantref? You have caused me the very devil of trouble, my lord."

"With respect, Sire," answered Bran, "I want only what is rightfully mine—the throne my family has occupied for two hundred years."

"Hmph!" sniffed William, unimpressed. "That is finished. Britain is a Norman country now. I made my decision. Can you not accept it?"

Tuck and Bran conferred, and the friar said, "Again, with respect, Sire, my Lord Bran would remind you that the two of you made a bargain in Rouen—a throne for a throne. That is what you said. Bran helped you save your throne; now he wants the one he was promised."

King William frowned. He took off his helmet and rubbed a gloved hand through his thinning red hair. After a moment, he said, "Your priest here," he jabbed a stubby finger at Tuck, "says you will swear fealty to me. Is that true?"

"*Oui*," said Bran. "Yes."

"If I restore you to the throne," William said, "you will cease this rebellion—is that so?"

Again, Bran and Tuck conferred. "That is what I intended from the first."

"This miserable little cantref has already cost me more than I will ever see out of it," grumbled William. "What you want with it, God knows. But you are welcome to it."

"Your Majesty!" gasped one of the barons attending William. "I fear you are making a grave mistake."

The knight moved up beside the king, and the forest-dwellers recognized him for the first time. "You had your say long ago, Gysburne," Tuck told him. "*Tais-toi.*"

"You cannot just give it back to them," insisted Marshal Gysburne, "not after what they've done."

"Can I not?" growled the king. "Who are you, sir, to tell me what I can do? The priest is right—shut your mouth." Turning to Bran, he said, "It grows hot and I am thirsty. Can we discuss this somewhere out of the sun? I have wine in my tent. Come, let us talk together."

"I would like nothing more," replied Bran when Tuck had told him what the king said. "However, I would like to choose the place of discussion."

"Where, then?"

"The fortress is just there," said Bran, pointing down the slope to the caer on its mound in the near distance. "We will talk there."

"But the stronghold is full of your warriors," the king pointed out.

"Some warriors, yes," allowed Bran. "But farmers and herders, too—the people who have suffered under de Braose, Abbot Hugo, and Sheriff de Glanville these last years."

"Am I to go into this den of wolves alone?" said the king.

"Bring as many of your knights as you wish," Bran told him. "The more who see us swear peace with one another, the better it will be for everyone."

When King William and his knights rode into the fortress yard at midday, Bran and his people were ready to receive them. Bran, with Mérian on one hand and Tuck on the other, was flanked by Iwan and Siarles on the right, and Will Scarlet and Alan a'Dale on the left. Behind him were other members of the Grellon—Noín, Owain, Brocmael, and Ifor, and most of the forest-dwellers. Baron Bernard Neufmarché stood a little apart, with two of his knights holding Sheriff Richard de Glanville, bound at the wrists, between them. Beside the knights stood Bishop Asaph gripping the oaken shaft of his brass-topped crosier, and Odo clutching a big Bible.

The king of England was accompanied by a dozen knights, Marshal Guy of Gysburne amongst them. Around the perimeter of the yard stood the people of Elfael. Outside the walls of the fortress, the army was drawn up and waiting. Beyond them, on the heights above the valley, the Cymry kings and their archers kept watch on the proceedings. If William's army moved to attack, they would move to prevent it.

William Rufus rode to the centre of the yard, where his personal canopy had been set up. He dismounted and was greeted by Bran. Mérian and Baron Neufmarché joined them to make certain that no misunderstandings arose because of a simple lack of language on either side. A small table had been set up beneath the canopy, and two chairs. On the table was a jar and a single bowl.

"Your Majesty," said Bran, "if it please you, sit with me. We will drink together."

"I would like nothing better," said the king. Seeing Neufmarché, he stopped and turned to his wayward vassal. "Baron, do not think that your part in this will be ignored."

The baron inclined his head in acceptance of the king's charge, but replied, "What I have done I did for the greater good."

"Ha!" scoffed the king. "Your own good most of all, I do not doubt. By the Virgin, man, how could you turn against me?"

"It was not so much turning against you, Sire," replied the baron, "but protecting myself. Even so, it is fortunate that we did not have to try one another in battle."

"Fortunate, eh?" said the king. "We will talk of this another time." He moved to take his place beneath the brightly coloured canopy. Bran joined him and sat down, with Mérian on one side and Tuck on the other. The baron stood to one side between the two kings and, acting as steward, poured wine into the bowl. He handed the bowl to Bran, who took it up, drank a draught, and then offered it to William.

Red William accepted the bowl and drank, then returned it to Bran. The back-and-forth continued until the bowl was drained, whereupon Baron Neufmarché refilled it and placed it on the table between them.

"God with you, Your Majesty," said Bran, who between Mérian and the baron was able to make his thoughts known. "And though we might both wish that the occasion was otherwise, I do bid you welcome to Caer Cadarn and Elfael. It is my hope that we rise from this table better friends than when we sat down."

"Let us cut to the bone," replied the king in English. "What are your terms?"

Bran smiled. "I want only what I have always wanted—"

"Your precious throne, yes," answered the king. "You shall have it. What else?"

"Full pardon for myself and my Grellon, and any who have aided me in returning the realm to my rule," said Bran. "And that will include Baron Neufmarché."

The king frowned at this last part when it was explained to him, but gave a grudging nod of assent. "What else?"

"Nothing more," said Bran. "Only your seal on a treaty of peace between our kingdoms."

William gave a bark of disbelief when Neufmarché translated Bran's last remarks. "Nothing else? No reparations? No silver to pay your soldiers?"

"My warriors are mine to repay," said Bran. "We Cymry take care of our own."

"I wish every fiefdom took care of itself, by the blood," replied William. He leaned back in his chair and gave every appearance of beginning to enjoy himself. "If you have nothing else, then hear my terms. I require your oath of fealty and a tribute to be paid each year on . . ." He tapped his chin as he thought, then caught a glimpse of Tuck and said, "You, there, priest—if you *are* a priest—what is the nearest holy day to this one?"

Tuck moved a step forward. "That would be *Gwyl Iwan y Coed*," he replied. "The Feast of Saint John the Baptist, in plain English."

"John le Baptiste, oui," said Neufmarché, passing this along to the king.

"Henceforth, on the Feast of Saint John the Baptist, a tribute of . . ." He looked around at the rude fortress and the mean, common dress of the half-starved inhabitants and the grim determination he saw on their faces and made his decision. "A tribute of one good longbow and a sheaf of arrows to be presented to the Royal Court at Londein and given over to the care of the Chief Justiciar."

Mérian gasped with joy, and Tuck, who caught most of what was said, chuckled and told the others standing round about.

"Oh, Bran," breathed Mérian, giving Bran's shoulder a squeeze. Tuck relayed the terms to the Grellon and all those looking on. "The king has decided to be generous."

Baron Neufmarché and the king exchanged a brief word, and the baron said, "King William will accept the release of his sheriff now." He summoned the knights forward, and de Glanville was marched to the table.

"As a token of the peace we have sworn between us, I release him to your authority," said Bran. He motioned to his champion, standing behind Friar Tuck. "Iwan, cut him loose."

The big warrior stepped forward and, grinning with good pleasure at the astonishing turn events had taken, drew the knife from his belt and began cutting through the bonds at the sheriff's wrists. The rawhide straps fell away, and with a sweep of his hand, Iwan indicated that the prisoner was free to go.

As Iwan replaced the knife and made to step back, de Glanville snatched the dagger from his belt and leaped forward. In the same swift movement, he drew back his hand and prepared to plunge the dagger into Bran's unprotected neck. The naked blade flashed forward and down. Tuck saw the arcing glint hard in the bright sunlight and gave out a yelp of warning. Iwan, startled, put out his hand.

But it was too late.

The knife slashed down a killing stroke.

Then, even as the cruel blade descended to its mark, the sheriff's hand faltered and appeared to seize in its forward sweep. Halted, it hovered in midstroke. The knife point quivered, then fell to the ground.

It happened so fast that almost no one saw what had arrested the knife until Sheriff de Glanville let out a shriek of agony and crumpled to his knees. Only slowly, as if in a dream, did the stunned onlookers discover Will Scarlet standing over the sheriff, his own hand clamped tight over de Glanville's. He gave the captured hand a squeeze, and there was a meaty crunch and pop as the sheriff's fingers gave way.

De Glanville gave out a roar of pain and anger and swung at Scarlet with his free hand. Tuck, snatching the crosier from Bishop Asaph's hand, grasped it like a quarterstaff and swung it once around his head and brought it down with a solid thump on the top of the sheriff's head; de Glanville crumpled to the ground, where he lay on his side, whimpering and cradling his broken fingers.

"Stand him up!" commanded William with an airy wave of his hand. Turning to Bran he spoke with some sincerity. "His Majesty offers heartfelt apologies," Neufmarché translated. "He asks what you would like him to do with the rogue."

"I will leave that to Scarlet," replied Bran, looking to Will for an answer.

"Broken fingers are a long and painful reminder of a man's failure," replied the forester. "As I should know. I am satisfied if he takes that away with him—so long as we never have to see him again."

"That's a far sight more mercy than he deserves," said Bran. "And more than he ever showed you, Will."

"And is my husband not the better man?" said Noín, taking Will's arm.

Bran's decision was delivered to King William, who merely grunted. "This man is no longer one of my sheriffs. Remove him from our sight." Then, rising, he held out his hand to one of his knights. "Your sword," he said.

The knight drew his blade and handed it to the king, who turned to Bran. He spoke and indicated a place on the ground before him.

"His Majesty is saying that he must leave now if he is to reach Normandie in time to collect his tribute," Baron Neufmarché explained. "He says there is but one more thing he must do before he goes."

"Sire?" said Bran.

Again the king spoke and indicated the place on the ground at his feet.

"He says you are to kneel and swear your fealty to him," said Neufmarché.

Bran called Bishop Asaph to him. "Father, will you see that it is done properly?"

"Of course, Rhi Bran," said the old man. "It will be an honour."

As the bishop took his place beside King William, Bran knelt and stretched out his hand to grasp the king's foot. William, holding the sword upright in both hands, directed his newest vassal in the age-old ceremony which bound man to lord, and lord to king. Bishop Asaph lofted his crosier and offered a prayer to seal the vow, and the simple rite was concluded.

William touched the edge of the sword to the back of Bran's neck and told him to rise. "You are now my liegeman, and I am your liege lord," the king told him, and Mérian, standing near, interpreted. "Rule your realm in peace as God gives you strength."

"In the strength of God," replied Bran, "I will." As he said those words, he felt Mérian slip her hand into his, and then he was caught up in the tremendous sea wave of acclamation that rose up from the long-suffering folk of Elfael, whose joy at seeing their king triumphant could not be contained.

King William called for his horse to be brought and his men to depart. "We will meet again, no doubt," he said.

"On the Feast of Saint John the Baptist," replied Bran.

"Rule well and wisely," said the king in English. He searched the crowd for a face, and found it. "And see you keep this man close to your throne," he said, pulling Tuck forward. "He has done you good service. If not for him, there would be no peace to celebrate this day."

"In truth, Your Majesty," said Bran. "I will keep him with me always."

That night Rhi Bran ap Brychan celebrated his return to the

throne with the first of what would become many days of feasting, song, and merriment, and went to sleep in his own bed. And though in the days ahead he would often return to the greenwood to visit Angharad's grave and tell his Wise Banfáith how his kingdom fared, he never spent another night in the forest so long as he lived.

EPILOGUE

Nottingham, 1210

Rumour had it that King John had come north to hunt in the royal forest at Sherwood. His Majesty was lodged with High Sheriff Wendeval in the old castle on the mound overlooking the river. Thomas a'Dale, following the royal progress, had come to Nottingham hoping for a chance to perform for the king and add a royal endorsement to his name—*and* a handsome fee to his slack purse.

As he walked along the dirt track, humming to himself, he recalled the last time he had been here; it was with his father, when he was a boy learning the family trade. As he remembered, he had juggled while his father played the psaltery and sang the songs that made his family a fair living. Thomas remembered Nottingham as a good-sized city with a lively market and plenty of people from whom to draw the crowds a minstrel required. Passing quickly through the town now, he saw that the market was just opening and merchants beginning to set out their wares, including a pie man who carried his steaming gold treasures on a long plank from the bakery oven to his stall. The aroma brought the water to Thomas's mouth, and he felt the pinch in his empty stomach.

Still, hungry as he was, he did not dally. He marched straight-away to the castle and presented himself at the gate. "God bless you right well, sir," he addressed the gateman. "Is the lord of the manor at home?"

"He is," replied the grizzled veteran controlling the castle entrance, a man with one eye and one hand: both lost in some nameless battle or other. "Not that it is any business of your'n."

"Oh," replied Thomas lightly, "that is where you mistake me, sir. I am a minstrel, Thomas a'Dale by name. I've performed before the crowned heads of many a land, and now I've come to entertain the lord high sheriff and the king."

"What makes you think the king is here?" queried the gateman, sizing up the wanderer with a long, one-eyed appraisal.

"That is all the talk of the countryside," answered Thomas. "You can hear it anywhere."

"Do you believe ever'thing you hear?"

"And do *you* believe everything you see?" countered Thomas. Producing a silver penny from his purse he held it up between thumb and finger for a moment before placing it on his eye. Squinting to hold the coin in place, he showed both hands empty, palms out. Then with a shout, he clapped his hands and the coin vanished.

The gateman gave a snort of mild amusement and said, "Where's it gone, then?"

By way of reply, Thomas opened his mouth and showed the sil-ver penny on his tongue.

"That's a good'un, that," the old man chuckled. "You have more o' those japes, sim'lar?"

"As many as you like," said Thomas. "And more of *these*, too," he added, offering the man the penny, "for a fella who speaks a good word of me to his lordship's steward tonight."

"I reckon I'm that fella," answered the porter, plucking the penny from the young man's fingers. "You come back at e'ensong bell, and you'll find a welcome."

"Good man. Until then," replied Thomas. "God be good to you, sir."

Having secured his employment, he returned to the town square and found a place to sit while he watched the market folk. When the first rush of activity was over—the wives and maids of wealthier house-holds, first in line to buy the best on offer—the market assumed a more placid, easygoing air. People took time to exchange news and gossip, to quench their thirst at the tavern keeper's ale vat, and to more casually examine the contents of the various booths and stalls lining the square.

Thomas pulled his psaltery from its bag on his back and began tuning the strings, humming to himself to get his voice limbered and ready. Then, slinging the strap around his neck, he strolled among the market-goers, plucking the strings and singing snatches of the most fashionable tunes. One by one, folk stopped to listen, and when he had gathered enough of an audience, he cried, "Who would like to hear 'The Tale of Wizard Merlyn and the Dragon King'?"

A clamour went up from the throng. "I sing all the better with the sweet clink of silver in my ear."

He placed his hat on the ground before him and strummed the psaltery. In a moment, the chink of coins did ring out as people pitched bits of pennies and even whole coins into the minstrel's hat. When he reckoned he had got all there was to get, he began the song: a spirited and very broad tale with many humorous and unflattering allusions to the present reign thinly disguised as the antics of King Arthur's court.

When he finished, he thanked his patrons, scooped up his hat, and made his way to a quiet place to count his takings. He had managed three pence—enough for a pie or two, which he bought; leaving the market, he strolled down to the river to find a shady spot to eat and rest. He took from his bag an apple he had found in the ditch, and ate that along with his pork pie. Having slept badly in the hedge beside the road the night before, he napped through the warm afternoon, waiting for the long summer day to fade.

At the appointed time, Thomas roused himself, washed in the river, gave his clothes a good brushing, combed his hair, and proceeded up the track to the castle once more, where he was admitted and led to the great hall. The meal was already in progress, but it would be a while yet before the crowd was ready to be entertained. He found a quiet corner and settled back to wait, snatching bits of bread and cheese, meat and sweets from the platters that went past him. He ate and tried to get the measure of his audience.

In the centre of the high table, resplendent in blue silk, sat King John, called Lackland by his subjects—not well liked, but then, truth be told, few monarchs ever were while still alive. John's chief misfortune seemed to be that he was not his brother, Richard, called Coeur de Lion. The lionhearted king was better regarded—perhaps because he had hardly ever set foot in England during his entire reign. And where Richard was remembered as tall and robust, John was a squat, thick-necked man with heavy shoulders and a spreading paunch beneath his tight-stretched silks. His best years were behind him, to be sure; there was silver showing among the long dark locks that his shapeless hat could not hide.

The High Sheriff, Lord William Wendeval, was a bluff old champion who was said to rule his patch with an authority even the king himself could not claim. He was a tall, rangy fellow with long limbs and a narrow, horsy face, and short grey curls beneath his hat of soft green velvet. The king and his sheriff had been drinking some time, it would seem, for both men wore the rosy blush of the vine across cheeks and nose. And both laughed louder and longer than any of the revellers around them.

Slowly, the meal progressed. As the many dishes and platters circulated around the tables, musicians trooped into the hall and sent a fine commotion coursing among the throng at table. This Thomas considered a good sign, as players always gave an evening's roister a more festive air. When men enjoyed themselves, the money flowed more easily, and never more easily than when they were in a celebratory mood.

He watched and waited, listening to the happy clatter around him and idly tuning the strings of his instrument; and when he judged the time to be right, he rose and walked to the high table.

"My lords and ladies all!" he cried aloud to make himself heard above the raucous revel. "A songster! A songster!"

"Hear!" shouted the high sheriff, rising from his chair and pounding on the board with the pommel of his knife. "Hear him! Hear him! We have a minstrel in our midst!"

When the hall had sufficiently quieted, Thomas faced the high table and, with a wide sweep of his hat, bowed low, his nose almost touching his knee. "My lord high sheriff, my best regards," he said. He bowed again, lower still, and said, "Your Majesty, I beg the honour of your attention on this splendid festal evening." Turning to the rest of the company, he waved his arm. "My lords and ladies, gentlefolk all, it is my good pleasure to sing for your amusement."

"What will you sing?" called the sheriff, resuming his seat.

"Tonight, I have prepared a special surprise right worthy of this splendid occasion—but more of that anon. I will begin with a tune that is sure to please Your Majesty." He began strumming, and soon the hall was ringing to the strains of a song called "The Knight and the Elf Queen's Daughter." It was an old song, and most minstrels knew it. Though not the most taxing on a songster's abilities, it had a soothing effect on a restive audience and made a good prelude to better things.

The song concluded, and the last strains were still lingering in the air when Thomas began the lay known as "The Wooing of Ygrain"—also a firm favourite among the nobility, what with its themes of flirtation and forbidden love.

He sang two more short songs, and then, pausing to retune his psaltery, he announced, "Majesty, Lord Sheriff, distinguished lords and ladies, hearken to me now! Tonight in your hearing for the first time anywhere, I give you a song of my own composing—a stirring epic of adventure and intrigue, of kingdoms lost and won, and love most fair and wondrous. I give you 'The Ballad of Brave Rhiban Hud'!"

In fact it was not, strictly speaking, the first time he had sung this song. He had laboured over its verses, true, but in the main it remained much as it had been composed by his grandfather and sung by his father. Indeed, the song had earned his family's reputation and never failed to find favour with an audience so long as the singer took care to adapt it to his listeners: dropping in names of the local worthies, the places nearby that local folk knew, any particular features of the countryside and its people—it all helped to create a sense of instant recognition for those he entertained, and flattered his patrons.

Thomas strummed the opening notes of the song and then, lifting his head, sang:

Come listen a while, you gentlefolk alle,
That stand here this bower within,
A tale of brave Rhiban the Hud,
I purpose now to begin!

The song began well and proceeded through its measured course, pulling the audience into the tale. Very soon the listeners were deep in the singer's thrall, the various lines drawing, by turns, cheers and cries of outrage as events unfolded.

Thomas, knowing full well that he had captured them, proceeded to bind his audience with the strong cadences of the song. For tonight's performance, the tale was set in Nottingham and the forest was Sherwood. William Rufus and the Welsh March and Richard de Glanville never received a mention. Tonight, the king of the tale was John, and the sheriff none other than Sheriff Wendeval himself. It was a risky change of cast—noble hosts had been known to take umbrage at a minstrel's liberties—but Thomas perceived the mood was light, and everyone thrilled to the daring of it.

"God save the king," quod Rhiban to he,
"And them that wish him full well;
And he that does his true sovereign deny,
I wish him with Satan to dwell."

Quod the king: "Thine own tongue hast curséd thyself,
For I know what thou verily art.

Thou brigand and thief, by those treasonous words,
    I swear that thou lyest in heart."

"No ill have I done thee," quod Rhiban to king,
    "In thought or in word or in deed,
Better I've served than the abbot's foule men,
    Who robbéd from them in sore need.

"And never I yet have any man hurt
    That honest is and true;
Only those that their honour give up
    To live on another man's due.

"I never harmed the husbandman,
    That works to till the ground;
Nor robbed from those that range the wood
    And hunt with hawk or hound.

"But the folk you appointed to rule my stead,
    The clergymen, shire reeves, and knights,
Have stolen our homes and impoverish'd our kin
    And deny'd us what's ours by full rights."

The good king withdrew to consider the case
    And did with his counsellors sit,
In very short time they had come to agree
    On a ruling all saw justlie fit:

"King Bran, thenceforward, full pardon shall have,
    By order of royal decree.

And the lands that his fathers and grandsires kept,
    Have no other ruler than he."

Quod Rhiban: "Praise Christ! This suits me full goode,
    And well it becomes of us both.
For kings must be e'er protecting their folk
    So hereby we swear you our troth.

"And vow we this day, to the end of the earth,
    shall grief ne'er come 'tween us twain."
And the glory of Rhiban Hud, eke his king,
    i'this worldsrealm always shall reign.

Thomas led the crowd a merry chase through the greenwood and the exploits of the noble rogue Rhiban and his struggle to regain his birthright. Justice denied and at last redeemed was a theme that always swayed an English crowd, and it seemed now as if he played upon the very heartstrings of his audience as blithely as he plucked the psaltery. Both king and sheriff listened with rapt expressions; there were occasional sighs from the ladies, and grunts of approval from the men. Deeper and deeper did the spell become, recounting those days long ago—times all but forgotten now, but kept alive in his song. Inevitably, stanza gave way to stanza and the song moved to its end, and Thomas, singing for his king as he had rarely sung before, delivered the final lines:

The seasons pass quickly in the realm of King Bran—
    As seasons of joye always do.
John and Will Scadlocke many children now owne
    And each have another past due.

Strong sons and fayre daughters to them and their wyves
    The Good Lord upon them has blest.
But the fairest and strongest and smartest who is,
    None of them e'er has guess'd.

And Rhiban the Hud now feasts in his hall,
    For marriéd now has he beene.
And summer has settled in clear, peaceful lands,
    For Mérian reigns as his queene.

But we see not the fryer who wedded them two,
    What has become him his luck?
Lo, newly installed in the bishopric there,
    Is one: Bishop Fryer Tuck.

Good gentlefolk all, we have finished our laye—
    A song of brave Rhi Bran the Hud;
Taking only from others what never was theirs,
    He restoréd his land to the good.

But one final ride has our Rhiban to make,
    Before his and our paths shall part.
See, he has outlived his queene and his friends
    And bears he within a sadde heart.

He rides on his steede with a bow by his side,
    Much as he has done of olde.
His long hair is white and his eyesight is weak
    But he calls in a voice strong and bold:

"Once again, O, my fine merrye men,
    We shall in the greenwood meet,
And there we'll make our bowstrings twang—
    A music for us, very sweet."

AUTHOR'S NOTE

The High Cost of Heaven

And so . . . the legend grew, extending its reach far beyond the place and time of its birth. Not only did it travel, it changed in the telling as poets, singers, and wandering storytellers the likes of Alan a'Dale and grandson Thomas charmed their audiences by adjusting their tales to more closely conform to current local tastes. Rhi Bran y Hud the British freedom fighter may have faded in the process—transformed at last into Robin Hood the loveable outlaw—but the legend endured, and still delights.

Some readers may bridle at the central premise of this series: that a scant handful of homegrown volunteer warriors could successfully stand against the combined might of an entire army of heavily fortified professional soldiers.

As unlikely as it seems, this exact scenario was repeated time and again in British history. One of the best examples took place in 1415 in what has become famous as the Battle of Agincourt. Not only did a vastly inferior British force confront the best and boldest knights of France on a muddy farm field a stone's throw away from the little northern town, but the beleaguered British dealt them a blow never to be forgotten.

Henry's ragged no-hope army was largely made up of volunteers and vassals, most of them sick with dysentery and exhausted from a summer-long campaign in miserable weather. Harried and hopelessly outnumbered, they prepared to face the flower of French nobility a few miles from Agincourt. The French army, under King Charles VI's commander, Constable D'Albert, numbered in excess of twenty thousand men, mostly knights. Opposing them, King Henry V commanded around six thousand ragged and starving men—*but*, of those, five thousand were archers, and most of them Welsh.

On that bright Saint Crispin's day in October, the great French army was massacred. Accounts of the battle read like a "What *Not* To Do" handbook of combat. The French produced blunder after blunder in bewildering array, so many as to be almost literally incredible. Even so, it would have taken a military miracle for French horse-mounted knights to succeed when, by some estimates, upwards of seventy-two thousand arrows were loosed in the first fateful *minute* of the conflict. Of this devastating power, historian Philip Warner writes, "Fear of the longbow swept through France. Its deadly long-range destruction made it seem an almost supernatural weapon." Prayers against it were offered in churches at the time; this was a last resort, for nothing else came close to stopping it.

Britain's losses that day in the fields of Agincourt numbered around one hundred—and many of those were noncombatants: unarmed, defenceless baggage boys and chaplains who were slaughtered out of extreme frustration by the already-beaten French who attacked the supply wagons encamped a mile or so from the battlefield. On the other side of the equation, the French lost around two thousand counts, barons, and dukes; well over three thousand knights and men-at-arms; and more than one thousand common soldiers for a tally in excess of six thousand dead. These numbers are conservative: some accounts of the time estimate that as many as twelve thousand were killed or captured that day.

In any event, it was a defeat so devastating that it would be a generation or more before France could regain its military confidence against the British. As military historian Sir Charles Oman put it: "That unarmoured men should prevail against men cased with mail and plate on plain, open ground was reckoned one of the marvels of the age."

Decisive as it may have been, Agincourt was not by a very long shot the first battle to be decided by the longbow, nor would it be the last. But it was, perhaps, the most powerful demonstration of a now little-remembered law of medieval combat—namely, that when two opposing forces met, those with the most archers would invariably win. A sort of corollary stated that when both sides boasted roughly the same number of archers, the side with the most *Welsh* archers would win. Such was the highly recognized talent of the Cymry with the longbow, and their renowned fighting spirit.

As we are once again reminded by the British chronicle of the Saxon kings, the *Brenhinedd y Saesson*: "The men of Brycheiniog and the men of Gwent and the men of Gwynllwg rebelled against the oppression of the Ffreinc. And then the Ffreinc moved their host into Gwent; and they gained no profit thereby, but many were slain in the place called Celli Garnant. Thereupon, soon after that, they went with their host into Brycheiniog, and they gained no profit thereby, but they were slain by the sons of Idnerth ap Cadwgan, namely, Gruffydd and Ifor . . ."

This rebellion provoked a reaction: "In that year King William Rufus mustered a host past number against the Cymry. But the Cymry trusted in God with their prayers and fastings and alms and penances and placed their hope in God. And they harassed their foes so that the Ffreinc dared not go into the woods or the wild places, but traversed the open lands sorely fatigued, and thence returned home empty-handed. And thus the Cymry defended their land with joy."

It was precisely this fierce and tenacious spirit that the Normans faced in their ill-advised invasion of Wales. The unrivalled talent with the longbow—though born in the forests and valleys of Wales—was honed to lethal perfection in the white heat of contention following William II's decision to extend the dubious benefits of his reign beyond the March. It was a decision which sparked a conflict that was to sputter and flare for the next two hundred years or more, and provided the fertile ground from which sprang the legends featuring that shrewd archer, Robin Hood.

Wily Welsh archers were not the only plague in William's life, however; he also suffered from that acute affliction of his time: fear of purgatory.

Like a great many prominent men, William Rufus found himself in continual debt to the church, paying out huge sums of money for prayers to be said for the departed under his purview. All throughout the Middle Ages, abbeys and monasteries large and small did a roaring trade in penitential prayer, employing their priests on a perpetual, round-the-clock basis. The holy brothers prayed for their patrons and their patrons' families, of course, and also for the souls of those unfortunates their patrons might have killed. For the right fee, the local abbot could guarantee that the requisite time in purgatory would be shortened, or even excused altogether, and no one would have to suffer eternal damnation.

Quaint as it might seem today, buying and selling prayers for cash was a business conducted in dead earnest at the time. For it would be difficult to overestimate the fear of hell and its attendant horrors for the medieval mind. As tangible proof of this deep-seated and widespread phobia, the abbeys rose stone by ornately carved stone to dominate the medieval landscape of Europe. These beautifully wrought works of art can still be visited a thousand years later: belief made physically manifest.

Though greatly reduced in every way now, all through the Middle Ages the monasteries amassed enormous wealth on the exchange of prayer for silver, becoming ever more powerful, extending their influence into all areas of medieval life and commerce. It was to be their downfall in the end. For when the wealth and power grew so massive as to exceed that of the monarchy, the threatened kings fought back.

For William II, bucking the trend was not an option. He was caught in the stifling embrace of a system he could neither control nor ignore. He was not the last monarch to discover that the need for money to pay his debt to the church would intrude on, if not dictate, his political agenda. Decisions of polity often bowed before the expediency of keeping the clergy cheerful—even in weightier matters such as war and peace. The medieval king might not like it, but more often than not he swallowed his resentment and did what was necessary to pay up. Whoever said heaven would come cheap?

Stephen R. Lawhead is the author of many acclaimed historical fantasy novels, including the Pendragon Cycle and the Celtic Crusades. He lives in Oxford, England. Visit his website at www.stephenlawhead.com

Find out more about Stephen and other Atom authors at www.atombooks.co.uk

THE WARLOCK LORD

by

Terry Brooks

Living in the remote hamlet of Shady Vale, the young half-elf Shea Ohmsford knows little of the outside world. And yet, in the desolate, ruined lands of the far north, a dark-hearted sorcerer is plotting his death.

The ancient warlock has dispatched a band of deadly Skull Bearers to track Shea down and murder him. For Shea is the last descendant of an ancient Elvin king, and the only person living who can wield the fabled Sword of Shannara – a weapon with the power to thwart the Warlock Lord's terrifying plans.

Only the druid Allanon knows where the sword is hidden and even now he rides to Shady Vale to offer his aid. But the Skull Bearers are swift and ruthless, and Shea Ohmsford's destiny may be over before it has begun!

And so begins the incredible legend of The Sword of Shannara – a classic story of magic, adventure and epic conflict, from one of the world's greatest living storytellers.

www.atombooks.co.uk

THE MAGICIANS' GUILD

by

Trudi Canavan

Each year the magicians of Imardin gather to purge the city streets of beggars, urchins and miscreants. Masters of the disciplines of magic, they know that no one can oppose them. But their protective shield is not as impenetrable as they believe.

As the mob is herded from the city, Sonea, a young street girl, furious at the authorities' treatment of her family and friends, hurls a stone at the shield, putting all of her rage behind it. To the amazement of all who watch, there is a flash of blue light and the stone passes straight through the barrier and cracks a magician on the temple, rendering him unconscious.

After five hundred years of order, the guild's worst fear has been realised — an untrained magician is loose on the streets. She must be found, and quickly, before her uncontrolled powers unleash forces that will destroy both her, and the city that is her home.

www.atombooks.co.uk

THE HUNDRED-TOWERED CITY

by

Garry Kilworth

What awaits Jack, Annie and Davey when they are transported back in time to the gothic city of Prague, to search for their missing parents? Trying to avoid capture by the secret police, they find themselves running through dark and dangerous cobbled streets and meet some very shady characters.

Where are their parents and who has stolen the key to the time machine?

Alchemists, mythical creatures and a man with a hook for a hand hold the answers they're looking for.

Will our young heroes be in time to save their parents from eerie Karlstein Castle? And even if they do, how will they return to the present day without the key?

www.atombooks.co.uk